To get rid of him she blurted, "Well, it was nice to meet you." Fumbling with her keys in preparation to activate the remote locking system, she gave him an impersonal smile.

"I'll see you into your car, just to make sure you're okay. I wouldn't want anything to happen to you."

His quiet words sent a spurt of adrenaline through her veins, those disturbingly bleak eyes sliding over her body, making her feel exposed. Shivering in the balmy May evening, she tried to ignore the inner voice whispering warnings in her head.

As fast as she could, she lugged the gear over to her truck and loaded it in back. When she finished he was still standing there, expressionless but for the weird glow in his eyes. Was he planning on trying anything? Her pulse jolted. Maybe she should have kept a hold on one of those bats, just in case. She almost dove for the driver's side, scrambled into the cab.

When she looked up he was standing next to her door. Christa barely stifled the gasp that rose in her throat.

"It was nice to meet you, finally," he said, watching her with that eerily intent gaze. "I'll see you next game."

Great. Either he wasn't getting her signals of disinterest, or worse, he chose to ignore them.

"Drive carefully," he added, stepping back from the truck. His mercurial eyes seemed to glitter at her in the darkness. "Most accidents happen at night when you're close to home."

Her heart leapt. Was he threatening her?

Swallowing the lump of fear trying to lodge in her throat, she pretended she hadn't heard him over the rumble of the engine and sped off. Turning out of the parking lot, she took a last glance in her side mirror and found him standing there, perfectly still, watching her drive away.

Out Of Her League

by

Kaylea Cross

FEB 11, 2009:

FOR JACKIE!

THANKS FOR BEING MY CHAPTER
BUDDY. I EXPECT TO READ YOUR BOOK
IN PRINT SOON. IF I CAN DO IT, SO CAN
YOU!

LOVE, KARI XO :)

(AKA Kaylea Cross)

Out Of Her League

Contact Information: info@thewildrosepress.com

Cover Art by *Kim Mendoza*

The Wild Rose Press
PO Box 708
Adams Basin, NY 14410-0706
Visit us at www.thewildrosepress.com

Publishing History
First Crimson Rose Edition, 2008
Print ISBN 1-60154-310-7

Published in the United States of America

Dedication

To Todd, Brett and Cole: Love you to infinity.
And to Jacquie, for showing me the ropes.

CHAPTER 1

In the middle of the sixth inning, the back of Christa's neck prickled. The subtle, subconscious warning raised the fine hairs on her nape, tightened her muscles. He was out there again, watching her. His eyes followed her even here, in the safety of the dugout, tracking her every move like some predatory animal.

"Hey, Chris—looks like your number one fan is back."

She glanced up from strapping on her shin guards and looked toward the bleachers. Sure enough, there he was, clean-cut with short, dark-blond hair, of medium build and average height, around thirty or so. He sat in his usual spot right behind home plate, making this his eighth consecutive appearance at her games. At first, she'd thought he might be a scout, but now he just unnerved her. He was always there, focused on her, calling out comments to her. And if her teammates had noticed it too, she wasn't being paranoid.

"I wish he'd take up another hobby," she muttered, grabbing her mask from the bench.

"Yeah," said her first baseman, giving a shudder. "That guy's starting to bug the hell out of me."

"Me too." Christa headed onto the field, careful not to let her eyes stray toward him. Maybe if she ignored him long enough he would go away. Besides, she had more important things to worry about if she wanted to make the Olympic team. She couldn't afford to let herself be distracted by an obsessed spectator, no matter how uncomfortable he made her. With only one last cut standing between her and her dream, no one was going to take it away from her, least of all him.

She exhaled and cleared her mind, concentrating on the field in front of her until she'd blocked out the buzz of the crowd in the stands.

Focus.

Tugging on her mask, she crouched behind home plate, took the starting pitcher's warm-up pitches and hurled the ball down to second base.

"Looking good, nineteen," her fan called out, addressing her by her uniform number. She tuned him out and went down into her crouch as the batter set up in the box. It was her job to act as quarterback and call the pitches and the plays. She had to take charge and be the leader, and with national team scouts scrutinizing her performance, every play counted.

Her team retired the side, and in the bottom of the same inning, Christa was the first batter up. She went through the rituals of adjusting her kneepads and batting gloves, settled her helmet firmly on her head and stepped into the box. She focused intently at the release point near the pitcher's hip. Everything else faded into the background as she stood there, planted and ready to face the first pitch.

"You're the best, Christa."

Him again. Somehow his voice had cut through all her efforts to shut him out. Damn it, she had to—

"Show them, Christa. Show them why you're the best."

Teeth gritted, she tried to push that voice out of her head and regain her concentration, but it was no good. "Time," she said to the umpire, holding up one hand.

"Time." The umpire suspended play. Christa stepped out of the box, jaw still clenched, and took a breath. *Get your head in the game, you idiot. Just shut him out and hit the damn ball.* Once she regrouped, she went into her stance and watched the first pitch come in.

"Strike!" the umpire yelled.

Unperturbed, she took a big cut at the next pitch, narrowly missing it. Now she had only one strike left to play with. She stared out at the pitcher's right hip, expecting either a waste pitch or a changeup. *All right, sweetheart. Hit me with your best shot.*

But the next pitch came in low, too close to the strike zone for her to leave it.

"You're the best."

His shout came just as she began her swing,

throwing off her timing and making her miss the ball entirely.

"Strike three!" the umpire called.

She froze in disbelief, then whirled around and stalked back to her dugout, disgusted with herself. Before heading inside, she glanced back at the bleachers with a dark look and found the guy staring right at her, not even trying to be discreet. Worse, he had the gall to wink at her. Oh yeah, the jerk knew exactly what he was doing. What was he—a jealous relative of some player on the cut list, bent on sabotaging her career? Or was he doing it for kicks?

Irritation surged. God, why couldn't she just *ignore* him? There was no excuse for letting him get to her.

Despite her poor plate appearance and the idiot in the stands, Christa and her teammates won the game. After the post-game meeting, they gathered up the equipment and headed off the brightly lit diamond, a half-moon hovering in the midnight blue sky. Past the last set of bleachers in the outfield, she realized she'd left her batting gloves in the dugout and hurried back to grab them, as fast as she could while carrying her catcher's gear and her own equipment bag, plus the team bats. She juggled them to try and find a comfortable position, but it was a heavy load.

"I can take some of that for you," a male voice said from behind her.

She stiffened, warning bells clanging in her head. He'd never physically approached her before.

"Here," he offered with a pleasant enough smile. "Let me take something. I'm heading to the parking lot myself." Up close his eyes were a pale gray, and the bleakness in them made her uneasy. They had a strange, silver gleam to them, like a timber wolf's.

Striving for friendly politeness despite the choice words she had in mind, Christa turned away and shook her head. A glance toward the parking lot showed the last of her teammates already getting into their vehicles. Her black truck was parked against the line of forest on the far side, and she wanted nothing more than to climb into it, lock the doors and get the hell out of there. But he was blocking her way and no one was around to come to her rescue.

She straightened her spine and circled him, evading eye contact. "Oh, thanks anyway, but this'll help keep my shoulders strong."

"Are you sure?" he persisted. "It's no problem, really. Let me take one bag."

"No way, then you'll unbalance me." Despite the urgency tugging at her she hoped her attempt at humor would take any sting out of the rejection. The last thing she wanted was to make him angry. "And besides," she continued, "it wouldn't be right to make our fans haul our stuff around."

He shrugged. "I wouldn't mind. I'm Seth, by the way." He held out his hand, the picture of charm. "I already know your name's Christa," he added with another smile. It should have been pleasant, but it reminded her of a predator baring its teeth. A chill shivered up her spine.

She couldn't ignore his offered hand without risking insult, so she gripped it for a moment, then snatched hers back to get a better hold on the bags. They were finally nearing the gate to the parking lot, thank God.

To get rid of him she blurted, "Well, it was nice to meet you." Fumbling with her keys in preparation to activate the remote locking system, she gave him an impersonal smile.

"I'll see you into your car, just to make sure you're okay. I wouldn't want anything to happen to you."

His quiet words sent a spurt of adrenaline through her veins, those disturbingly bleak eyes sliding over her body, making her feel exposed. Shivering in the balmy May evening, she tried to ignore the inner voice whispering warnings in her head. Until now she'd never noticed how poorly lit the parking lot was, but tonight the ribbon of forest that edged the ballpark transformed into a sinister place of swaying branches and deep shadows where danger might lurk, where a rapist or killer might drag their prey.

Get a grip, Bailey. Stop letting your imagination run away with you.

As fast as she could, she lugged the gear over to her truck and loaded it in back. When she finished he was still standing there, expressionless but for the weird glow in his eyes. Was he planning on trying anything? Her pulse jolted. Maybe she should have kept a hold on one of those bats, just in case. She almost dove for the driver's side, scrambled into the cab.

When she looked up he was standing next to her door. Christa barely stifled the gasp that rose in her throat. She hadn't even seen him move. Breath freezing in her lungs, she had to force herself not to cringe from him. *Don't let him sense your fear. He'll feed off it.*

Pasting on a friendly smile, she started the ignition, trying to seem unaffected by his nearness. What did she have to do to make him leave her alone? She didn't want to be rude in case it made him angry. There was no telling what he'd do if he were mad, and besides, it wasn't in her to be impolite. *Firm but kind*, she decided, willing herself to stay calm. *I'm not interested, so leave me alone. Just go away.*

"It was nice to meet you, finally," he said, watching her with that eerily intent gaze. "I'll see you next game."

Great. Either he wasn't getting her signals of disinterest, or worse, he chose to ignore them.

"Drive carefully," he added, stepping back from the truck. His mercurial eyes seemed to glitter at her in the darkness. "Most accidents happen at night when you're close to home."

Her heart leapt. Was he threatening her? Swallowing the lump of fear trying to lodge in her throat, she pretended she hadn't heard him over the rumble of the engine and sped off. Turning out of the parking lot, she took a last glance in her side mirror and found him standing there, perfectly still, watching her drive away.

No way could she go home to her empty house right now, not after that encounter. So she drove to her best friend's place instead. She pulled her truck into the driveway in the neatly kept subdivision and used her spare key to enter the side door.

"Hello? Anyone home?"

When Teryl's curvy figure appeared around the corner, Christa felt better already. "Hey! To what do we owe this honor?" Her long blonde hair was pulled back into a loose ponytail and she was wearing sweats—a sure sign she'd just hopped out of the bath.

"I thought I'd stop in and say hello," Christa said evasively. "Hope I didn't interrupt anything."

"Of course not, don't be silly. Come on in. Drew and Hutch were just going over the plans for our new deck."

Christa halted in mid-stride, her heart tripping at the second name. "Rayne's here?" Rayne Hutchinson, the cop with the gorgeous face and rock-hard body, star of her romantic fantasies. God, maybe this visit wasn't such a good idea.

Teryl eyed her in amusement, leading the way through the kitchen toward the family room. "Yeah. His car's in the shop so Drew picked him up at the station after work. Why? That a problem for you?"

"No." A swarm of butterflies fluttered around in her belly. On a drool scale of one to ten Rayne was easily a twelve, and here she was straight from the ballpark in her uniform and tracksuit. She felt like the high school geek pining over the star quarterback. And apparently she wasn't even all that bright a geek either, because his being out of reach hadn't stopped her from having an agonizing crush on him ever since she had first met him through Teryl and Drew a couple years ago.

She glanced down at herself, dismayed. Somehow, whenever she saw him she was always covered in dirt from her work as a landscaper or from softball. He probably expected it by now.

"C'mon," Teryl coaxed, holding out a hand and pulling Christa after her into the family room.

Rayne's dark head was bent over the coffee table next to Teryl's husband Drew, his strong hands cradling a beer bottle as they pored over some sketches. She mentally cringed at her grubbiness.

"Hey, look who I found," Teryl announced.

The two men glanced up at her, the impact of Rayne's hazel gaze slamming into her like a sixty-mile-an-hour fastball. The air seemed to hum with his masculine energy, and that intimidated the hell out of her. On the ball diamond she could stare down any pitcher without a qualm, block any throw or pitch you could shell out and throw harder than a lot of men she knew. She could cook pretty much anything, turn a patch of weeds into a gorgeous flowerbed, fix a leaky pipe and rewire her light fixtures—but put an attractive man in front of her and she was all jittery nerves and tongue-tied awkwardness. She had her last relationship to thank for that.

"Hi guys. Big plans?" *You moron. He'll think you're retarded, using monosyllabic words like that.* She couldn't help lifting a hand to restrain a lock of hair that had escaped her long chestnut braid.

Drew waved her over. "Hey, sweet stuff. It won't be anything as fancy as your porch, but it'll have to do."

"The deck I showed you in that magazine layout," Teryl put in. "The boys are finally going to build it for me."

Rayne settled back against the sofa, the smooth fabric of his shirt stretched taut by the muscles underneath. "So, who won the game?" he asked, his eyes raking over her disheveled form.

"We did." She fought the urge to fidget under his scrutiny. At least his gaze didn't scare her like her disturbing fan's did.

"She's going to make the national team this season," Teryl announced proudly, beaming at her. "They're already down to their last few cuts, and she's a shoe in."

Hardly. And if she allowed that voice behind home plate to keep distracting her, she wouldn't make the squad at all. "Not that you're biased or anything."

"Tough game, was it?" Rayne asked.

Oh, boy. She *did* look awful. "Um, yeah, tonight was a real workout."

Teryl motioned upstairs. "Why don't you grab a quick shower?"

"That'd be great." At least then she'd feel more confident about being in the same room with Rayne.

But in the guest bath, Teryl shut the door behind them and pinned her with narrowed eyes. "All right," she demanded, hands on hips. "How come you came over tonight?"

Christa sighed. "Is it that obvious?"

"Honey, I'm your best friend. After twenty-two years, you don't think I can tell when something's wrong? So come on, spill it."

"That guy was there again tonight," she said simply.

"The Stalker?" The name she and Teryl had laughingly given the guy didn't seem so funny anymore.

"Yeah, only this time he followed me out to my truck to introduce himself. His name's Seth." As she spoke, Teryl's brows drew together. "Then he stood there staring at me while I loaded my stuff, and told me to be careful because 'most accidents happen at night when you're close to home'."

"That's creepy, Chris. Have you told the coaches about him?"

"Not yet, but I will. And from now on I'll never leave the park on my own."

Teryl made a huffing noise. "Is that why you came over? Were you afraid he was going to follow you home or something?"

"He didn't. I checked to make sure I wasn't being followed on my way here." Christa moved her hands apart in a helpless gesture. "I'm probably being paranoid, I know, but something about him scares me. Almost like I can sense...I don't know, evil in him." She smiled ruefully. "See what having an overactive imagination does for you?"

"Rayne would tell you that's not always a bad thing." She reached into a cupboard and pulled out some towels. "Want me to say something to him?"

"No, thanks. I don't want to make a big deal out of it. I just wish the guy would leave me alone."

"Well, be careful then, okay? The guy sounds like he's a few bricks short of a load." She offered a friendly pat on the back. "Go ahead and clean up and we'll see you downstairs."

When she had gone, Christa confronted her image in the mirror above the sink and winced. No wonder Rayne had looked like he was trying not to smile when he'd first seen her. Dirt had streaked all over her face, the catcher's mask trapping it in sweat lines along her jaw. Her braid was barely intact, and during the game she had somehow developed wings that stuck straight out from her temples, apparently eager to assist in an emergency landing. She glanced at the back of her head to see if maybe a rudder flap had appeared too. Nope—just a couple of sweaty, tangled ringlets at the nape of her neck. She showered and toweled off, then dressed in the clothes Teryl had left outside the door. She had no make-up with her but pulled her hair into a ponytail before heading down to the family room.

The sight of Rayne's tall, broad-shouldered frame sitting there on the couch caused her heart to skip a beat, and she chided herself. Even if he were interested in dating her, she had a list of specific reasons why she didn't want a man in her life. One: she was too busy with work and her softball career. Two: Rayne had a reputation that would make Casanova seem like a choirboy. Three: no way did she ever want her heart broken again. She couldn't survive that kind of pain a second time.

Keeping this firmly in mind, she chose a seat on the other side of the coffee table and tried to pretend his smile didn't make her insides do somersaults. She glanced down at the deck plans spread across the table. "So, when will you guys start?"

"Next week, if I can get all the stuff together," Drew said. She loved Drew dearly and was so glad Teryl had married him. He was funny, supportive, and most importantly, not afraid to stand up to Teryl's infamous temper. "Just think of all the flowers you can put in the planter boxes."

"Now you're talking. So long as you promise not to kill them, Teryl."

Teryl narrowed her eyes. "Maybe you should plant artificial ones, then."

"They've been telling me about the gardens at your place," Rayne interjected, the lamplight highlighting the green and gold in his darkly lashed eyes. "I'd love to see the house sometime."

"Anytime," she told him, intending friendly politeness rather than eagerness. "It might even remind you a little bit of Charleston," she pronounced it "Chahlston", "so you'll feel right at home."

He raised an eyebrow. "Are you making fun of my accent?"

"Not at all. You know I love your accent. It reminds me of when I used to answer the phone in my stepfather's office. Michael's an American history professor, remember? He teaches mostly about the Civil War."

"You mean the war of northern aggression," he corrected softly, lips curving.

"Ah...okay."

"It's a very important distinction," he assured her.

She held up a hand in acknowledgement. "Duly noted."

Drew pushed to his feet and stretched. "Well, this has been a fascinating history lesson, but you said you're on early shift so I'd better take you home, Hutch."

"Sure." Rayne rose from the couch.

"I can take you home," Christa blurted. The others gawked at her. "I'm heading home anyway, so I can drop you off on my way. If you're okay with it," she added, hoping her face wasn't flaming.

"That'd be great," Rayne said.

She faced Drew. "There's no sense in you going out when I can easily drive right past there."

"Hey, you don't have to talk me into it." He regarded Rayne with an arched brow. "We can trust you to behave yourself with Christa, right?"

Rayne winked at her, sending her pulse skyrocketing. "Maybe."

"Ha-ha," Teryl said, sending him an arctic glare. "He wouldn't dare try anything because he knows I'd rip his legs off."

Christa laughed. "I love it when you get all protective of me. Makes me feel all warm and fuzzy inside."

"Damn right I'm protective of you." Teryl had a habit of referring to Christa's ex as 'The Shithead', which was true enough, but what would happen if she ever found another boyfriend? Teryl would scare him away before he'd had a chance.

"You should never dare me, darlin'," Rayne murmured, eyes full of mischief.

Christa's eyebrows shot upward. The idea of Rayne coming on to her was ludicrous. She was no more his type than he was hers. So macho and good-looking, a known ladies' man—not exactly what she was looking for. Men like that were trouble, and getting involved with one would guarantee heartbreak. She would be worse than stupid to pursue anything, even if by some miracle he did show an interest in her.

"Well, *I* would never dare you," she assured him, and gathered up the bag holding her dirty uniform. "You ready to leave?"

"Sure."

At the door Teryl leaned up and kissed Rayne's cheek, then rubbed away the lipstick mark. "Okay, go off and save the world for us tomorrow. But don't shoot anyone unless you have to."

"I'll try and restrain myself," he said, and let Christa precede him outside. The cool night air was damp and smelled of freshly cut grass, stars twinkling overhead. He followed her to her truck and opened her door for her.

"Oh, thanks," she said and scrambled up into the cab.

"You're welcome." He even closed her door before rounding the hood and climbing in himself, the truck suddenly seeming small with him in it. Well over six feet tall, broad through the chest and shoulders with no fat on him, he made her feel petite and fragile, and with a five-eight medium build, that was saying something.

He dominated whatever space he occupied, his air of confidence so absolute she'd once mistaken it for arrogance. Now she understood it was merely part of his personality. He was a natural leader, an alpha male loaded with charisma and sex appeal. As the notches on his bedpost no doubt proved.

She started the ignition and pulled out of the driveway. "You live down by the beach, right?" No sense tipping him off that she'd committed every detail she knew about him to memory. Kind of obsessed, like her stalker, but way less scary. And more pathetic.

As she thought of her fan her eyes scanned the street, but nothing suspicious caught her attention.

"Just down from the pier, on Marine Drive."

"You must have an incredible view."

"It's pretty tough to take, all right." He swiveled his head to study her, and as she bore his scrutiny her fingers tightened on the steering wheel. "Where's your place? We've known each other a while, so how come you've never invited me over?"

"Huh?" She shot him a glance. That had come so far

out of left field she wasn't sure she'd heard him correctly. "I didn't know you *wanted* to be invited over."

"Well, all I ever hear is Drew and Teryl raving about your cooking, your yard and your house, and you've never once asked me over with them."

She didn't know quite how to respond to that. "Well, it wasn't on purpose, I swear. I promise, next time I'll invite you too. Deal?"

"Deal."

As he settled back into the seat with a creak of his leather jacket, she caught the tangy scent of his citrusy cologne. It was cruel for a man to be so beautiful and smell that good. She had to fight the urge to lean over and breathe him in. Instead, she checked the rearview mirror to make sure no one was following her. As awesome a distraction as Rayne was, she couldn't forget about that weird encounter at the park.

Through the open window, the salt of the ocean teased her nostrils, the lone cry of a seagull blending with the background music of the radio. In the distance the shadowy forms of the San Juan and Gulf Islands rose out of the Strait of Georgia, the lights of Semiahmoo Resort winking across the water. Moonlight shimmered silver across the bay, silhouetting the gentle contours of the shore and isolating tidal pools on the exposed sand, their crescents glimmering like a scalloped lace hem stretching the length of the beach. On Marine Drive they headed east, past the people strolling along the promenade and the illuminated pier jutting into the dark tide, past the gift shops, restaurants and ice cream parlors, the trees lit year-round by delicate strands of lights.

Maybe she was too wound up about this whole stalker thing, she thought as she checked the mirror again. If he hadn't followed her to Teryl's, and he wasn't following her now, then chances were—

"Something wrong?"

She cast a startled glance at Rayne, then focused back on the road. "No, why?"

"You seem distracted, and you keep looking in your mirror like you expect to find someone behind us."

His bang-on observation left her speechless. Maybe she should tell him. He *was* a cop. But what if Seth was harmless and she was just overreacting? Last thing she wanted was for Rayne to think she was a head case. "Sorry. It's nothing."

"Okay." He let it go. "My building's on the left at the next corner." He indicated a condo complex in sleek lines of stucco and glass.

"There you are," she announced, pulling to the curb. "Service with a smile."

He tipped his head. "And a beautiful one at that. Thanks for the lift." His grin had her heart tripping.

Flattered, but not allowing herself to dwell on it, she shrugged. "Anytime." He climbed out of the truck, thigh muscles stretching the fabric of his jeans, and she had to will her heart to slow down.

"Don't forget to call me," he reminded her.

"I won't." She was more likely to forget to breathe.

"I'll give you my cell number. That's the best way to reach me." He searched in his pocket for a piece of paper, then leaned on the truck to write. "No excuse now."

"Thanks." Now that she'd given her word, what choice did she have but to follow through? Her schedule was so crazy, though, between work and ball—"Wait … how about tomorrow night? For dinner," she clarified when he stood there frowning. Hard to tell which one of them was more surprised, and she felt like an idiot for blurting out the invitation. She swallowed, a difficult task when her foot felt like it was stuffed halfway in her mouth. "I know it's short notice, but I don't know when else I'd—"

"I work until seven. Seven-thirty okay?"

Relief flooded through her. She'd make it work, even if it had to be breakfast at five a.m. "Sure. I was planning to invite Teryl and Drew anyway." There. Now she'd covered her bases and made it plain it was definitely not a date.

"Okay. Give me your address."

She recited it, said goodnight and rolled up the passenger window, then pressed a hand to her galloping heart.

Pulling out her cell phone, she begged her oldest friend to be there tomorrow night and Teryl agreed with a good deal of suspicion. Christa pulled away feeling almost giddy, wiping her damp palms on her thighs and glancing in her rearview mirror, but Rayne had already disappeared inside.

Well, of course he had, she told herself. Only the weirdoes watched until you were out of sight.

****

The following afternoon Christa loaded her border collie cross, Jake, into the Chevy Avalanche for a trip to the local plant nursery, where she'd filled a cart to overflowing with pots of deep blue delphiniums, bright yellow marigolds and cheerful purple pansies with gold faces. Now, sitting back on the heels of her gardening shoes, she wiped the sweat off her forehead with her arm and paused to survey her hard work.

The May sun had climbed steadily, bringing a humid heat that promised to become sweltering. The reflection from the windows on the south side of her house made the pale yellow exterior glow—an excellent backdrop for the plants she'd tucked in along the front walk, if she did say so herself. Gazing up at the Victorian gabled and turreted roof, Christa felt a swelling of pride.

Her house was a source of joy, a haven of warmth and coziness that wrapped around her like a hug. The first summer she'd moved in she'd added gingerbread trim around the wraparound porch and in the gables, and had installed dark green shutters. Last fall she and Michael had completed the landscaping, then made the stained glass panels in the transom window above the kitchen sink, and when the sun hit them just right, shards of cobalt, ruby and gold dappled the gleaming hardwood floors she'd re-finished. The glow of satisfaction curling inside her made every penny she'd put into the place worthwhile. So what if she still had a sizeable mortgage, even after spending her grandparents' trust money? It was her dream, her perfect little nest to do whatever she pleased with. No chemically imbalanced stalkers to worry about here—just a retreat from her busy life.

Giving Jake a scratch behind his ears, she picked up her tools and replaced them in the shed, painted to match the house, before settling into her favorite deck chair under the pink dogwood canopy. She had stained the chair cobalt to match the drifts of delphiniums shooting their spikes into the air in the perennial beds. Basking in the peace of a job well done, she surveyed the carefully placed arbors and obelisks draped with twining wisteria and clematis, the stone fairies peeking out from behind a leafy hosta or clump of merlot and saffron-colored pansies. She had just swallowed an icy mouthful of tea and leaned her head against the backrest when the cordless phone rang.

"Hello?"

"Hi hon, it's me." Teryl's cheery voice greeted her.

"Hey! You checking in to find out what's on the menu for tonight?"

"Uh, actually, no...I've been called to a crisis at the office. My client's gearing up for a hostile takeover tomorrow morning, so we've got to get everything prepped today. Sorry, hon."

"Oh, but Rayne's coming too, and the meat's already in the oven. Are you sure you won't be finished in time for dinner? You could come later and I'll save a plate for you." *Please don't leave me alone with Rayne.*

"Sorry, sweetie, but I'll be at the office all evening. I'll make it up to you, though. Steaks on me sometime next week, okay?"

Well, crap. What should she do? Dinner alone with Rayne felt too much like a date, and she didn't want him getting the wrong idea. "Sure," she agreed, striving to keep the nervousness out of her voice. "That sounds great. Thanks for letting me know." When she hung up, she pondered her options. Talk about awkward. What was she going to tell him? She kicked off her gardening shoes and went into the kitchen in search of the piece of paper with his cell number on it, then came back outside and dialed.

He answered on the second ring. "Hutch here."

"Hi Rayne, it's Christa."

"Hey, darlin'. What's up?"

She fumbled with the strap of her overall, befuddled by that deep drawl, the easy way he said the endearment. Like hot fudge dripping over melting ice cream. "About tonight..."

"What about it?"

"Teryl just called to say they can't make it. So I was

wondering if you wanted to have dinner some other time instead."

A pause met her words. "Are you uninviting me?" His voice held notes of both suspicion and amusement, but still managed to make her tummy flutter.

"Of course not. I didn't want you to be uncomfortable with only me here, that's all." Who was she kidding? *She* was the one who'd feel uncomfortable. What did she really know about him, after all? In the two years since she'd met him, she'd discovered he had grown up in Charleston and had done a stint in the Marines, stationed in Hawaii of all places—which would account for some of his reputation as a ladies' man—then moved to Vancouver and become an Emergency Response Team officer. Although she was drawn to his combination of looks and easygoing personality, they'd never spent any time alone together except for when she'd driven him home last night.

His warm laugh cut into her analysis. "Why would I be uncomfortable? I can't remember the last home-cooked meal I ate, and I'd love to find out if you're as good in the kitchen as everyone says you are."

She didn't want to make him feel unwelcome. And how could she turn down an opportunity to show off her cooking skills? "Okay, then. If you're sure."

"Can I bring anything?"

"No, thanks. I'm all set. So I'll see you at seven-thirty then?"

"You can count on it, sugar."

When the dial tone buzzed in her ear, she sank into her chair, nerves jumping in her stomach. What the hell was she doing? Begging for trouble, that's what. Rayne was everything that terrified her in a man. Gorgeous and confident with a great sense of humor, and enough sex appeal to make women faint in a trail behind him.

Charisma oozed from his skin, his stride, his smile, his voice. A rumor was going around that he'd actually had an escort pay *him* for an evening, though even Drew couldn't say for sure it was true. He had 'dated' (and therefore presumably slept with) countless beautiful women, many of them models. She'd met plenty of them over the past two years.

Until her stalker had appeared in her life she'd led a fairly boring existence, which was exactly the way she preferred it. She rarely dated anymore. According to her ex-boyfriend she was nothing special in bed, and if any of the stories she'd heard about Rayne were true, he'd find her a dismal disappointment. Getting involved with him would be like committing emotional suicide.

Maybe she should call her ex, Cameron, to remind herself what heartbreak felt like. That ought to cure her of any romantic fantasies about Rayne.

She checked her watch to see how much time she had. T minus three hours and twenty-one minutes.

Way to go, Bailey. You've done it now.

CHAPTER 2

At seven twenty-seven, Rayne parked in front of the yellow Victorian-style house. He didn't usually pay much attention to houses but this place really was something to look at, like one of those fancy bed-and-breakfasts people paid a fortune to stay at. When he walked to the back gate, he stepped into a genuine fairyland decked out with strands of white lights trailing along the lattice fence, over an arbor and tangled amongst the trees. Lanterns hung from various shrubs, and tall candles flickered invitingly on the patio table.

Wow. Martha Stewart had nothing on Christa Bailey. If she could cook half as well as she kept her home, he was going to be in heaven.

A black and white dog came barreling out, skidding to a stop at his feet, dancing around him. Rayne held out his hand to let the dog smell him and saw from his collar that he had just met Jake. He gave his ears a ruffle. "Hey, fella. You're a pretty friendly guy, aren't you? Do you always let strangers into the yard when your mistress is alone?" The dog leaned into his touch, which Rayne guessed meant Christa's dog approved of him. That had to count for something.

"Hello?" he called out, heading toward the French doors off the patio.

"In here," Christa answered from the kitchen, pulling something that smelled spicy and garlicky out of one of the two wall ovens. An island topped with pale granite graced the center of the room, surrounded by acres of granite counters and walls of white cabinets. A white apron front sink sat under the window overlooking the backyard, a butcher block stuffed full of professional quality knives next to it. On the far wall was an intimidating stainless steel gas range that looked like it had come straight out of a gourmet restaurant. The place was clean and bright, cozy without being too feminine. He liked it.

"Hi," she said, smiling as she swept back a stray lock of hair the color of espresso, the overhead lights making it gleam with chestnut highlights. She looked fresh and pretty in a pale yellow blouse and worn jeans that clung in all the right places, making her legs seem a mile long. He'd always been a sucker for long, shapely legs.

"Hello yourself," he answered, glad he'd accepted the invitation. When she'd called out from the truck he'd had the impression she hadn't meant the words to come out, and then when she'd phoned him earlier he'd been sure she was going to cancel on him. Funny, how she seemed so at ease with everyone else yet tended to clam up around him.

For some reason he'd always wanted to get to know her. From the moment they'd met he'd enjoyed being around her, but then, everyone liked Christa. She was intelligent, kind, thoughtful and sweet. Need help moving? Call Christa. She'd even lend you her truck. Need your bathroom painted? Christa would be happy to help. Got the flu and no one to look after you? She'd be right over with some home-made chicken soup and a bottle of Nyquil. The quintessential girl-next-door, the kind of woman you'd take home to mom—the exact opposite of every woman he'd been with, but even that didn't squelch the growing attraction.

He decided to stop thinking and focus on his hostess' legs instead. "Whatever you're doing in here, it smells amazing." Her cheeks were flushed a rosy pink from the heat of the oven, and her incredible robin's-egg blue eyes danced as she shot a grin at him over her shoulder. He loved that she was so quick to smile.

"Braised spare ribs with Yorkshire pudding and roasted potatoes," she told him in that slightly husky voice that made his insides tighten every time he heard it. "I heard you were a meat and potatoes guy."

"You heard right, lady." He sniffed appreciatively, picking up the scent of chocolate. She stood on tiptoe to gather some plates from a cupboard, revealing a few inches of taut, smooth midriff as her shirt rode up. An image of him nuzzling that satiny strip entered his brain before he could stop it. He nearly groaned. "What's in there?" He gestured to the other oven.

"Homemade pudding cake."

Oh man, he was already drooling. He leaned over the island counter, propped his chin in one hand and gazed at her. "Run away with me," he said earnestly, and earned a laugh.

"Flatterer. You'd die of boredom within a week."

Don't bet on it, sweetheart. "Was that your way of trying to let me down easy?"

She gave him another playful grin and went back to prepping their dinner, his lips tugging upward when he read her apron: "Kiss the cook." Maybe he'd kiss her after dessert, once she'd relaxed a little, and see how she reacted.

Interesting how she made a habit of laughing off his attempts at flirting with her. She'd been doing that since the day they'd met, probably to keep him at a comfortable distance. Or was it that she didn't take him seriously? Scary thing was, he didn't flirt with her just to get a reaction anymore.

She deftly covered the meat with tinfoil and gave the herbed potatoes a final toss. "Okay with you if we eat outside?"

"Sure." He took a dish of vegetables from her and headed onto the patio, set it on the table. "Did you do all this yourself?" He indicated the riot of blooms filling her garden.

"I have a landscaping business, remember? Until I scrape enough together to start my own landscaping design company."

Oh, he remembered. A landscaper, a great cook, a hell of an athlete, and a sweetheart to boot. He couldn't understand why men weren't crawling all over her, except that the air of maternal serenity he had come to associate with her suggested she'd be the marriage-and-kids type. He nearly broke out in a rash at the prospect of taking wedding vows, convinced that a long-term, committed relationship would put a monkey wrench in his lifestyle. Like shoving a stick through the spokes of a speeding bicycle. All his previous relationships had been short, fun and physical, just the way he wanted them. Christa didn't seem like the kind of woman who would be into that sort of arrangement, so why didn't that dull his interest in her?

While Ella Fitzgerald crooned in the background they sat down to enjoy the meal, a half-moon beaming like a yellow lantern and the chirp of crickets in the air.

"So, I've always wanted to ask you—how come a guy from the southern States is working in Canada?" she asked as she dished up the ribs and potatoes.

He eyed the plate appreciatively, waited until she'd served herself before digging in. The food tasted even better than it looked, the beef tender, the potatoes aromatic with garlic and rosemary. Man, he could get used to this. "I was raised in Charleston, but born in Montreal."

"So how come you ended up in Vancouver?"

With his attention riveted on her fork as it slipped between her lips, he lost the thread of conversation. God, she had a sexy mouth. Realizing she was staring at him expectantly, he struggled to remember what she'd asked him and cleared his throat. "Right after I left the Marines I moved here to live with Nate and his family. He's kind of like my surrogate father, heads up the serious crimes unit for the force."

She glanced up from her plate. "And you knew him because…?"

Rayne leaned back in his chair, smiling at her curiosity. She seemed genuinely interested. "Nate did a tour in Beirut and became best pals with my dad. While I was a teenager, I used to come out here to spend the summers with Nate's family. They've got a beach house down on the Oregon Coast they still let me use. And since I'm a dual citizen it was easy enough to move to Vancouver when my enlistment was up." He savored another bite of meat. "This is amazing, by the way."

"Thanks." Her smile made her eyes shine like aquamarines. "So your dad was a soldier?"

Rayne shook his head, swallowed the mouthful. "A Navy SEAL."

Her eyes widened. "Really?"

"Yep. He's a real-life professional ass-kicker." In spite of all the bad history between them, he couldn't keep the pride out of his voice.

"That must have been some tough act to follow. Is that why you joined the Marines?"

He had to laugh. "No. Dad didn't want me in the service at all, but the summer I turned eighteen I was kind of a handful and piled my mom's car into a bus stop after I'd been out drinking with some friends, and I knew there was gonna to be hell to pay. My parents split up when I was eight, so when I woke up the next morning and saw my dad standing in the doorway, I knew I was in deep shit. He'd flown in from Louisiana that morning to kick my ass. He took one look at me and said, 'Downstairs. Ten minutes.' Don't think I'd ever moved so fast." Now, he could chuckle at the memory. "He handed me a packed duffel bag, made me apologize to my mom and then told me to get in the car. Drove me straight to Parris Island without another word."

Christa stared at him, her fork frozen halfway to her mouth. "That's pretty harsh, Rayne." Her head tilted as she considered him. "And you stayed there? No arguments?"

He nearly laughed at the idea of taking on his father, verbally or otherwise. "Oh, I stayed all right. Nobody argues with my dad, Chris, not even me when I was dumb and eighteen. I've got three inches and twenty pounds on him, but believe me I still wouldn't mess with him." He reached across the table and helped himself to another Yorkshire and gravy. "In the end I guess he figured a stint in the Corps would straighten me out. He never imagined I'd end up following in Nate's footsteps, become a tactical officer once I was out."

Her pale eyes gleamed in the flickering candlelight. "He must be proud of you."

"I couldn't say." Honestly, he didn't care one way or the other. "He came to my Marine Corps graduation, though, and when I marched onto the parade ground there he was, decked out in his dress whites with about six pounds of medals decorating his chest. I went up and saluted him in my uniform, feeling all macho, and after he saluted back the son of a bitch actually handed me his Trident—that's the pin the SEALs wear. God, I had goose bumps about an inch high all over me." He'd never admit it to his old man, but he always carried it in his fatigues when he went on an operation. Like a talisman or something.

Christa set down her fork and propped her chin in one hand. "Sounds like you admire him a lot."

Man, she had no clue how beautiful she was. "I did, once."

"Oh. You don't anymore?"

He shifted in his seat. Nothing like some light conversation to set the mood. "He kind of fell head first off the pedestal I'd put him on when he dumped my mom and me. Upped and left, just like that." He snapped his fingers.

She lowered her lashes. "Oh. I'm sorry."

"That's okay." He patted her shoulder, savoring the firm muscles beneath the warm, smooth skin. The combination of strength and vulnerability fascinated him. "When I came home from school one day, he was gone and my mom was hysterical." He traced the condensation beading on his water glass. She made him feel like he could tell her anything. "The strangest goddamn part of it is that they're still in love with each other. He still wears this chain she gave him— a Saint Christopher medallion engraved with some message of protection. He's never taken it off in all the years they've been apart. My mom would have him back so fast his head would spin, but my daddy's too stubborn. He's got his reasons I guess, but I sure as hell don't pretend to understand it all. Anyway, we don't see much of each other." He glanced at her, hoping his expression wouldn't reveal all the buried bitterness. "What about your parents?"

She wiped her mouth with her napkin before answering. "My step-dad, Michael, married my mom when I was six, and then they divorced when I was nine. He's the love of my life, hands down." Her mouth curved upward, making his muscles tighten.

"And your mom?"

She hesitated, and when her gaze clouded over he felt bad for asking. "My mother isn't the easiest person to love," she confided, and he leaned toward her, giving her his complete attention. "She's very…involved in her work. We've never been close, even before Michael. She's one of those women who should never have had children."

Without thinking, he took her hand and wrapped his fingers around hers. She smiled a little, left her hand in his. He liked the feel of those slim, cool fingers against his palm.

"When I left for university in Arizona we agreed to see each other only at Christmas, and only if it was convenient. I think she was relieved." Despite the sadness in her voice she shrugged as if it didn't matter. "I have my life, and she has hers."

Her loss, he thought. He was still holding her hand; he should probably let it go, in case she took it as a come on and got the jitters. He *was* coming on to her, wasn't he? He never questioned his instincts when it came to a woman—if there was one thing he knew, it was women—but sitting across from Christa tonight he felt like a teenager on his first date, fumbling along on a quest to get to first base. Unbelievable.

Probably because this woman was so unlike any of the others and had never given any indication of welcoming anything but friendship from him. She was so easy to be with, but whenever he'd tried pushing things further her body language gave off clear 'stay away' signals. They were both single, and he was pretty sure he wasn't mistaking their mutual attraction.

Had something—or someone—made her so skittish? She hadn't removed her hand though, and he again toyed with the prospect of kissing the cook, gauging her reaction. When he stroked his thumb across her knuckles she slid her hand away and started arranging the dessert dishes. *Back off, dumb-ass, before she slams up that invisible wall.* He'd seen her use it more than once when an interested guy came too close. "So I've been wondering—how did you get so involved in softball?"

She served the pudding cake, her shoulders more relaxed. "Teryl and I started playing when we were six but she quit a few years ago because it took too much time from her career. It's too bad, because we were great together."

His mouth watered at the heady aroma of chocolate, and at the scoop of ice cream she added. "Somehow I have trouble imagining you on the ball diamond."

She arched a brow at him. "That's because you've never seen me with my game face on. I'm told I'm rather intimidating."

"I'm a cop—I know all about game faces. I just can't picture you being scary, that's all. You're too sweet."

"Well, you'll have to see me in action then, won't you?" She brandished her spoon at him. "Teryl told me I turn into a kick-ass bitch when I step onto the field and believe me, I'm all business."

"I'll believe that when I see it."

"Well." Her eyes held a hint of challenge. "I've got a game tomorrow at two, if you can make it."

"I'll see what I can do. Who are you playing against?"

"A select team from Seattle. They're coming up for the week."

He'd never even watched women's fastpitch before, but he was intrigued enough that he wanted to see her in action. "I'm on call tomorrow, but I'll be there if I can," he told her, already looking forward to it.

Her cheeks colored. "I hope I don't strike out while you're watching. I'm not sure if I'll be catching or playing third base, but you'll see me. And if you can't, just check out my number-one fan in the stands. He's the crazy one who shows up to every game and sits right behind home plate as my personal cheering section. When he's not trying to throw me off, that is."

Though she tried to make light of it, the rigid set of her spine suggested an undercurrent of anxiety. The thought of anyone frightening her made his hackles go up. "Yeah? How long has he been doing this?"

Another shrug. "Since the first week of the season, I guess, but it's nothing. He's just creepy, that's all."

He folded his arms across his chest. "Does he ever single you out? Leave you notes? Anything like that?"

A frown formed. "Well, after my game last night he followed me out to my truck. So now I'm going to make sure I never leave without one of my teammates. And I've never initiated a conversation with him."

"But you've talked to him?"

"Only to be polite. Though he did say something weird to me the other night."

He fastened his eyes on her, waiting for her to

elaborate.

"He told me to be careful because most accidents happen close to home." She pushed a melting lump of ice cream around her dish with her spoon. "I'm not sure if he was warning or threatening me, but that's pretty much why I stopped by Teryl's place yesterday. I was afraid he might try and follow me home or something."

"So that's why you kept checking your rearview last night." God, why hadn't she just told him? At least he could have followed her home to make sure she got there okay. "You should have told me. Told someone, anyhow."

She swallowed a spoonful of dessert and stared at him with her big blue eyes. "I told Teryl. The Stalker's just a nickname we've given him. And then last night I *thought* he might be threatening me but I wasn't sure, so I didn't want to make a big deal out of it."

All his cop instincts were jangling. "If he's at your game tomorrow, I'll let you know if I think he might be a problem. But if I were you I'd steer clear of him."

"I will," she promised. "I don't really want to believe he might be a threat, but if you're concerned, I'll be more careful." She gave him a grimace, glanced away. "Now I've told you and Teryl about him, he probably won't even show up tomorrow and I'll look stupid for worrying about it."

"Hey." He took hold of her wrist and her gaze jerked back to his as he'd intended. "Worrying about something like that isn't stupid."

When he released her she pushed her plate away and let out a sigh, leaving half her cake untouched. "Well, that certainly spoiled the ambiance, didn't it?"

With his point made, Rayne wanted her to relax and enjoy herself, so he let the matter drop. "What do you mean? I was getting ready to ask for more dessert."

A smile spread, smoothing the worry lines across her forehead. "The way to a man's heart is through his stomach, right?" Embarrassment flitted across her face. "That came out wrong," she blurted. "Pretend I never said it."

He ventured a wink, his pulse quickening at her denial that she might be hitting on him. "Trust me, darlin', I'm not offended. As it happens, home cooking *is* one of the ways to my heart, so pass the cake, will you?"

She let out a breath. "Let me fill 'er up, then." She served another heaping portion of the gooey chocolate dessert and ice cream.

"And just for the record," he paused long enough to lock his gaze with hers, "you can hit on me anytime you want." Her nonplussed expression was priceless.

As he ate the first warm bite he let out a throaty purr, trying not to smile as her gaze flicked up to him, then down to her plate. Wary was good, he decided. The fact he'd gotten under her skin meant she wasn't as disinterested as she wanted him to believe.

CHAPTER 3

"Now batting for White Rock," the announcer informed the crowd, "number six, Dani Miller." A cheer erupted from the home fans. Dani was a favorite, and their team was trailing by two runs in the fifth inning. Christa was on deck with her long braid hanging down her back, in full battle gear: lower legs covered with socks and stirrups, knees cushioned by pads and thighs concealed with sliding shorts. Two national team coaches were watching her tonight.

Not only were the people holding the keys to her dream in the crowd, but her stalker was once again behind home plate, forcing her to blank out his frequent comments and leers. On top of all that, Rayne had shown up a few minutes after the game had started, so her brain kept bombarding her with the awareness that he was sitting in the third base bleachers next to Teryl. Between innings she'd permitted herself a single glance and wave at them, then put her game face back on and tried to tune out everything else.

The crowd murmured as Dani grounded out to shortstop.

"Next up for White Rock, number nineteen, Christa Bailey." The announcement brought another round of cheering as she made her way to the plate from the on-deck circle.

"Come on, Christa," a girl in a little league uniform shouted. "You can do it." Her friends joined in with encouragement, clapping excitedly, a dozen grade schoolers all sporting inside-out hats backwards like rally caps.

Christa settled herself into the right-hand batters box, holding up one hand toward the umpire until she was ready. The pitch smacked into the catcher's glove, outside and low. "Strike!" yelled the umpire.

She returned to the box, awaited the next offering from the opposing pitcher, who shook off two signals before agreeing on a pitch. It zoomed in high and tight, causing her to jerk back to avoid being hit in the head. The crowd booed.

"Go get her, Christa!" her number one fan shouted.

Coolly she climbed back into the box, set comfortably into her stance and took a big cut at the next pitch, smoking it over the shortstop's head, and zoomed off in a dead sprint. The crowd went crazy as the throw home came too late and the runner on third scored. Christa went into overdrive, heading for second base.

The catcher wound up and hurled the ball down to the second baseman, who whipped her glove down in a sweep tag. Christa executed a hook slide and managed to grab the edge of the bag on the way by.

"Safe," called the base umpire, and the crowd roared as Christa called time and dusted herself off.

The next batter struck out, leaving Christa stranded at second base. The teams cleared the field and White Rock assumed their defensive positions, a back-up catcher taking the first few warm-up pitches while Christa hurried to get her gear on. She jogged onto the field and crouched behind the plate, taking the last pitch and launching it down to second.

"Be a leader out there, Christa! You're the best they've got."

The stalker's voice. She gritted her teeth. If her head had been locked into the game properly, she would never have heard him. She honed her focus as the inning started.

With two out, a runner was at second when the hitter pounded a line drive between the right and center fielders. The runner's base coach waved her on, and she rounded third in a spurt for home. Christa had thrown off her helmet and was standing at the plate, directing the first baseman into position for a possible cut-off play. The center fielder hurled the ball into the infield, but it was offline.

"Cut home," Christa yelled above the crowd, bracing herself over home plate as her first baseman caught the ball and whirled to throw it home, the runner only a few strides away and not slowing.

She caught the ball and dropped to her knees to block the plate, bracing herself for the inevitable impact. *Oh, man, this is going to hurt.*

The runner attempted a late slide and barreled into her, sending her flying. Her head slammed into the ground, blinding lights exploding before her eyes. She lay flat on her back, gasping to breathe. The ball...Had she managed to hold onto the ball? Voices murmured and blurry faces stared down at her before fading into swirling blackness.

****

Rayne shot to his feet. Christa lay unmoving in the dirt, curled on her side, while the umpire gestured for the coach and first-aid attendants. The base runner wobbled to her feet and with the help of a teammate limped off toward her dugout, favoring her right leg.

"Oh, God, Chris..." Teryl had also jumped up, one hand over her mouth as the trainer rushed onto the field and bent to speak to Christa, then shook his head at the coach. Rayne's heart thudded in his chest. How badly had she been hurt? The trainer was checking her neck and spine, and when they turned her onto her back, her lips moved. He let out a relieved breath.

"She's conscious," he told Teryl, holding her arm.

"Oh, thank God."

"What the fuck was that?" The guy who'd been yelling comments at Christa throughout the game—presumably her stalker—pounded on the chain link fence. "What was that bitch trying to do, kill her?" A chorus of voices added to his tirade. "Yeah, you'd better hide in your dugout, lady. You're dead meat, do you hear me?" His face was a mottled red as he screamed at the shaken base runner, huddled amidst her teammates with an ice pack on her ankle.

"Sir, that's enough." The umpire approached on the other side of the backstop. "We have everything under control."

"Bullshit! She deliberately ran her down, we all saw it. What are you going to do about it?"

"I've called the runner out and the inning is over, that's what I've done about it. Any more outbursts like

30

that and you'll be asked to leave this park."

"She should be charged with assault for that stunt. Maybe she needs a taste of her own medicine, huh? Maybe I should show her how it feels to be knocked out." The crowd gasped.

"That's it, you're out of here." The umpire's face was crimson as he pointed to the outfield.

Rayne was about to offer assistance in removing the crazed fan when a couple of security guards made their way into the stands and escorted him away. He continued to shout all the way out of the park, everyone staring at him.

"You were great, Christa, do you hear me? She won't get away with this."

Rayne was definitely worried now. The guy had serious issues.

In the wake of the outburst the park seemed quiet, every eye riveted to the inert form lying on the diamond. Finally, after an agonizing wait, Christa struggled to her knees amidst the roar of applause, wiping a smear of blood from her mouth. With a wave of reassurance to the crowd, she allowed her coaches to carry her from the field.

"Thank God," Teryl breathed again and pulled out of Rayne's grasp. He followed her to the third base dugout, wondering if Christa would be taken to hospital. He hung back as Teryl made her way to the trainer and then to Christa's side. She waved him over so he hurried through the dugout, past her milling teammates, and hunkered down beside her and Teryl.

She stared up at him with dazed blue eyes. "Hey," she said.

"Hey yourself. You okay?" He studied her face as the trainer ran his hands over her ribs and stomach, glad she didn't give any indication of pain.

"Yeah. She rang my bell pretty good, though," she admitted shakily.

"She lost consciousness for a few seconds," the trainer told him, "but since she refused to have an ambulance called, she should go to the hospital for an exam."

"I'm fine," she protested, her speech slurred from her swollen, bleeding lip. She smiled sheepishly up at Rayne.

"At least she was out. It always hurts less if they're out."

"Oh, shut up," Teryl snapped, helping to undo Christa's shin pads and cleats. "Only you would talk like that when you're lying there all smashed to hell."

Christa winced. "She just knocked the wind out of me."

"Whatever," Teryl huffed, then regarded him. "I think we should take her to the hospital, just in case."

"Sure." He looked Christa in the eye, fighting that tug of awareness in his belly. "You okay for me to carry you?"

"I can walk—"

"You can't," Teryl interrupted and shot him a glower. "Hutch, this is vintage Christa you're witnessing. 'No no, just because I got knocked unconscious, don't worry about me. I'll just crawl off somewhere by myself to pass out so I don't bother anyone.'" She angled a fulminating glare at her best friend and stuffed the last of her gear into her bag. "C'mon, tough girl, let's go."

"I'm fine, really," Christa insisted.

Rayne reached to scoop her up in his arms and felt her stiffen. He tightened his hold, a primitive part of him thrilling at the curl of her warm body against him.

She wrapped her arms around his neck and hung there, rigid. "I'm not exactly a light weight," she mumbled.

He smiled down at her dirt-streaked face, started for the parking lot. "To me you are," he said simply.

He moved quickly, Teryl dogging his steps and peppering questions at Christa: "Are you sure you didn't break anything? Are you seeing double? Are you nauseated?"

"No, but you aren't helping my headache."

Teryl narrowed her eyes at her but fell silent until they rounded the outer fence. "Oh, and the hits just keep on coming," she remarked as they came face to face with Christa's obsessed fan. He catalogued the facial features. Medium height and build, dark blond hair, clean cut. A regular enough kind of guy on the surface, but those were often the ones you had to be wary of.

He caught sight of them, his eyes all for Christa, but when he saw Rayne carrying her he went still. His face crumpled and he seemed to take a moment to collect himself. "Are you all right, Christa?" he asked, trailing after them.

She tensed and pressed tighter to Rayne, and he gathered her closer against his chest. "I'm fine, thank you," she called out, keeping her eyes downcast. Why couldn't the guy take a hint? Rayne wondered. She wasn't interested. End of story.

But the stalker stood there as they loaded Christa into her truck. "Is she going to the hospital? Because I can come up there and—" He took a step back when Rayne closed her door and leveled his gaze right at him. He made sure it was a possessive look, one that warned him to back off and leave her the hell alone.

Rayne stared the guy down, hoping he wouldn't have to get physical to get his point across. "She's fine," was all he said, and rounded the cab to slide into the driver's seat. He started the engine and pulled out of the parking space without looking back.

****

A few minutes before midnight they pulled into her driveway with Christa slumped in the passenger seat. She would have driven herself home if the dizziness hadn't made it impossible.

Rayne surveyed her. "I'll come in while you get settled, okay? I could even stay and wake you every hour like they said at the hospital."

"No way," she cried, dread flaring. God, imagine her waking up to see Rayne beside her bed all night. "You've already gone to too much trouble as it is. I'll just ice my leg, then go to bed."

"You wouldn't let Teryl stay with you either, but I'd feel much better if I knew you weren't alone."

Her heart stuttered. "Why, do you think something might happen?" She'd let him drive her home instead of Teryl because after the stalker's persistence at the ballpark, she felt safer with Rayne.

He reached out and tucked a stray lock of hair behind her ear, the contact giving her goose bumps. "I would just feel better if I was there in case you needed anything."

His non-answer didn't reassure her. "Because you're

my friend, or because you're a cop?"

He lifted his shoulders. "Both. And let's not forget you've got a mild concussion."

She chewed her tender lip. She *was* pretty banged up. And if Rayne seemed concerned about the potential for overnight encounters with her crazed fan, maybe that was reason enough to have a cop in the house. But what was she thinking? He'd had dinner with her last night for the first time, and now she was debating letting him stay over?

"You could help me inside, if you don't mind," she finally relented, and let herself out of the truck. Her head pounded like someone was playing a kettle drum in her skull and her neck was so sore she couldn't turn it without wincing. When she let them into the house they were greeted by an ecstatic Jake, who seemed thrilled his mistress had brought company home. He wagged his tail and gazed up at Rayne with adoring brown eyes.

"You're a suck," he told him, but reached down to stroke his velvety ears anyway.

"I need a quick shower," she said from the bottom of the staircase. "If you insist on babysitting me, you might as well make yourself at home."

"Okay, but call me if you get dizzy or anything, all right?"

"Sure." And then he'd come charging in to the bathroom while she was naked in the shower, and she'd have heart failure for sure. Those big hands sliding over her wet skin...

Stop that.

The hot shower helped relax her battered muscles, and she threw on a top and shorts under her robe before heading back downstairs. Rayne was on the couch watching the sports highlights. She liked that he seemed so comfortable in her house. After finding a bag of frozen corn from the freezer she wrapped it in a dampened tea towel and joined him, propping her feet on the coffee table and placing her makeshift ice pack on her swollen, discolored thigh.

"Feel any better?" he asked.

"By better do you mean has my head stopped feeling like it's about to explode? Or have I stopped seeing double?"

"Both."

"Then yes. Thank you." She pushed aside the nerves that skittered through her stomach at his presence in her house, his nearness. He had seen her inside and made sure everything was secure, so now she should ask him to leave. But the prospect of spending the night alone tied her stomach in knots.

"Do you want something to drink?" she asked instead. What in the world was she doing? She must have hit her head harder than she realized.

"I'm fine, thanks."

She settled deeper into the couch, making sure she kept some distance between them. "So, while I was conscious, did you think I was intimidating out there?"

He stretched his long, muscular legs out in front of him. "I have to admit, I was impressed. You've got one hell of an arm. And you were like a general, leading from the front. Sort of scary to watch, actually. I'd never have believed it if I hadn't seen it."

She laughed, adjusting her ice pack. "After people see me on the field for the first time, I'm suddenly Jekyll and Hyde."

"That's probably because the rest of the time you don't seem capable of throwing your weight around like that."

"Adds to my mystique."

"Too bad you won't be able to play for a while."

A hot spurt of alarm hit her. The final cuts to the national team were about to be made, and she needed to be out where the scouts could see her. "Oh, man. Why did this have to happen now?"

When she met his intense gaze, she stilled. Whatever he was thinking about, it was even more serious. "What?"

"Never mind your ball career. You've got a way bigger problem, kiddo," he told her without preamble.

Dread formed a tight ball inside her. "You mean my stalker?"

"I don't think he's playing with a full deck, if you know what I mean."

Oh yeah, she knew what he meant. The guy was obsessive, persistent. What would he do to her if he caught her alone again?

"If he keeps following you around, I think you should consider getting a restraining order against him."

Her eyes widened. "You think it's that serious?"

"I think it could get real serious. You didn't see him when you got hit, but he completely freaked out. He threatened the runner who hit you, threatened the umpire, and security had to drag him out of the park."

No, she hadn't seen any of that because of all the spots swimming before her eyes. "And then he was waiting for me outside the gate."

"And then he was waiting for you outside the gate," he repeated, frowning. "I've seen this kind of behavior too many times, and I only want you to be careful. You need to put a stop to this before it escalates, because it most likely will. Never leave the park on your own, always be aware of your surroundings, check your truck before you get into it. Always alarm your house when you're alone."

Some basic precautions made sense, she supposed, but the scenario as he painted it made her skin prickle. "Do you think he knows where I live?" The idea made her heart lurch. All at once she realized how vulnerable she was, a woman alone on an acre property in a rural area. Would anyone hear her if she screamed for help? Her eyes darted out the window, as if he might be out there right now, hiding in the darkness.

"Want me to stay after all?"

Yes! her brain screamed. She wouldn't sleep a wink now, waiting up all night with her bat beside her in case her stalker tried to break in. Right now she felt too sore to swing it, but surely adrenaline would kick in if she needed it. "Thanks," she heard herself say, "but I'll be okay." *I hope.*

Rayne studied her. "My mother raised me to always help a lady in distress, and I am a cop, after all."

Precisely. And maybe he was only doing his duty, but was he playing on that? Had he just scared the heck out of her, warning her about her stalker, in the hope it would persuade her into letting him stay with her? Her instincts were telling her his intentions were honorable, his concern for her welfare genuine. After all, he was a long-time friend of Teryl and Drew's, which had to count for something. But how did you know who to trust?

Man, she hated feeling so vulnerable, so helpless. Growing up feeling like a burden to her mother, she'd learned early on to take care of herself and not bother anyone, then had moved out as soon as her university scholarship came through. Having been independent for so long it was hard for her to lean on anyone, but she had to admit she would feel a lot safer with him in the house. "So you'd sort of be like my knight in shining armor?"

"Kind of, yeah. I even carry Kevlar around with me in the trunk."

Her head began throbbing again, as if to remind her the concussion was reason enough for him to stay over. What if she lost consciousness again? It wasn't likely, but...

That clinched it. Smarter to have him stay the night rather than send him home because she was worried he might get the wrong idea. "Well, okay then. But you'll have to sleep in my guest room," she warned, a teasing glint in her eyes. "And I should warn you, it's pretty girly. There are flowers on the sheets."

He smoothed a hand over her hair. "I'll live."

The brief contact sent her senses spinning, and she had to give herself a mental shake to clear her head. "Okay, follow me," she said, leading the way up to the second floor with her thigh protesting every step. She would have one hell of a bruise there come morning.

In the guest room she turned back his bedding, gathered some towels in the en suite and set a new toothbrush on the counter for him. "I would never have asked you to stay, you know." Had she done the right thing? Her nerves jittered at the prospect of the two of them spending the whole night in her house together, but that had to be better than being totally alone, at the mercy of her stalker. Didn't it?

"I know. I figured you wouldn't want to put me out, right?"

"Something like that. But anyhow, I really appreciate this. I was going to sleep with my lucky bat under my pillow after you left."

He chuckled and sat on the edge of the bed. "Well, that should make anybody think twice about coming after you. You've got one hell of a swing."

She stood in the doorway watching him, startlingly powerful and masculine amidst all the feminine decoration. Her stomach flip-flopped. "I was hoping to impress you at your first game, but instead I ended up as road kill."

He gave a snort of laughter. "Bad-ass road kill, though. You gave her a wicked limp."

"Yeah, well, she gave me a limp *and* a concussion."

He winced in sympathy. "Did you take your anti-inflammatory?"

"Yes doctor, I did, and I beg you, please don't wake me up every hour."

"That's what the hospital ordered, darlin', and it's only because I'm worried about you."

Her heart squeezed at his concern. And because he called her darlin', even though he didn't mean anything by it. "All right. Sleep well."

"You too."

Yeah, right. If she managed to nod off between his hourly checks on her. She'd probably lie awake all night imagining that muscular body in bed on the other side of the hall. Wasn't that ironic? A gorgeous hunk was sleeping in her guest room, and the only man who seemed interested in her was a stalker who might be out there hiding in her azaleas.

CHAPTER 4

He followed their progress through the house with every light she turned off, the bitterness of her betrayal gnawing with each passing second. Bad enough his Christa had let that other guy take care of her after she was injured, but now she was letting him stay the night with her? *No one can take care of you like I can,* he fumed, a hot stab of jealousy spiking through him. How *dare* she reject him like that. The idea of her sleeping with that stranger while he was standing outside helpless to prevent it nearly choked him.

He didn't want to believe the truth, even when it was staring him in the face. His angel, his paragon of womanhood was a whore after all, just like all the others had been. Like his drunk of a mother had been. The disappointment swamping him was almost suffocating.

Calm down, calm down, he commanded himself, setting aside his binoculars and trying to understand. All his life he'd battled to keep the rage at bay. His breath came in quick, sharp pants as he fought to regain control. *Breathe. Slow...slow...*

She had just been in a terrible collision and wasn't herself. She was in pain, probably still shaken up, and he couldn't expect her to behave normally. Maybe the man was only staying the night to take care of her. How he hated to see her hurting, especially when that bitch who'd hit her had gotten away with a sprained ankle. She was testing his loyalty, that was all. When she discovered how devoted he was to her, she would see they were meant to be together. She'd *know*.

Christa Bailey was nothing like the others. From the first day he'd seen her, carrying pots of flowers into a condo at the beach, he'd accepted that fate had intervened. When she'd emerged onto the deck and tucked the plants into their containers, he'd been struck by how fresh and feminine she was. All his research showed her to be an independent, hardworking single woman, and a quality human being. Those attributes alone made her precious, but with her added beauty and kindness...she was perfect. He had to be careful not to let his admiration of her interfere with his plans. They had a connection, Christa and him. He was her destiny.

He made his way back to the screen of trees surrounding the property, careful to erase any footprints from the spongy ground. He didn't want to be caught now, when he was so close to achieving his goal. He'd become an expert at being seen only when and by whom he wanted to be seen. He rather enjoyed the game, pushing the limit each time to see how close he could let them get without being caught. Stupid cops. He hated them all.

Back at the car he changed into the fresh shirt, jeans and shoes he'd brought with him, placing the soiled items into a plastic bag. He couldn't abide being dirty. Christa was clean, pure. Wasn't she? He should do something to get her attention. Something special. His lips curved as the plan came together in his head, imagined her expression when she learned what he'd done. She always appeared to sense when he was around, and though he obviously made her nervous, she never seemed sure if she should be afraid of him or not. His smile widened as he drove down the darkened road.

People should trust their instincts; they were usually right.

****

Curled up in her antique brass bed, she dreamed Rayne was whispering her name. She sighed and shifted onto her side, flinching when her swollen leg touched the mattress.

"Christa?"

She rolled over, saw his silhouette outlined in her doorway. He really was standing there, had come to check on her. Thankfully he hadn't removed his jeans and t-shirt. Had he been bare-chested she might have hyperventilated. "I'm awake. What time is it?"

"A little after four." He came toward the bed.

Breath clogging in her throat, she stayed very still as

he sat next to her atop the pink and green patchwork quilt, the mattress dipping under his weight. He placed one hand on the back of her head, where the lump was throbbing as if it had a heartbeat of its own.

"How do you feel?" he asked, voice husky with concern. His long fingers probed her skull.

She swallowed, the warmth of his touch spearing through her. "I'm okay. Just a bit spacey. Those meds sure knocked me out."

His fingertips traced her sensitized scalp. "Not dizzy?"

"No." Not from the concussion, at least. It was his nearness that overwhelmed her and shortened her breath. She had to fight the desire to crawl into his lap and press against all those finely tuned muscles. "Bit sore, though."

He held out his other hand to her, offering her a glass of water. "Here," he said, pressing it into her palm. "You should take another dose."

Obedient as a child, she accepted the tablet and swallowed it. He took the glass back from her, the warmth of his fingers making her hand tingle. The scent of fabric softener from his shirt teased her nostrils. Downy had never smelled so good.

"You must've been sleeping okay, 'cause you didn't move at all the other times I looked in on you."

"Like a rock," she assured him, oddly warmed at the idea of him watching over her while she slept and glad he was there, soothing her anxieties about a nocturnal visit from her stalker. "You?"

"I was a little worried the flowered sheets would keep me up, but it turned out not to be a problem."

He was such a sweetheart. Why couldn't she find someone who was into long-term relationships? Although to be honest, right now a fling didn't look so bad.

"I'll be gone by the time you wake up," he told her, getting to his feet. "I've got an early morning warrant to serve to an unsuspecting drug dealer." Enjoyment edged his tone. "One of the perks of my job."

"I'm sure." She didn't pretend to understand him, but she admired him all the same. "Personally, I'd rather stare down an Olympic-caliber pitcher."

He chuckled and stroked her cheek. "See? Now that would scare the hell out of me," he confessed. "Sleep well, and call me if you need anything, okay?"

She could barely think, with her cheek tingling like it was. The man was a hazard to her nervous system. "I will. Thanks for everything, Rayne. I really do feel better knowing you're here."

She thought he smiled at her in the semi-darkness. "Anytime, kiddo."

Watching him pull the door closed behind him, she let out a deep sigh and settled back under the covers, staring up at the shadows on her ceiling. Never mind her stalker, her heart was putting her in greater danger.

****

As expected, Rayne was gone by the time she came into the kitchen the next morning. He'd left a note on the table reminding her to keep everything locked and to call him and let him know how she was doing. Pushing any fears about her stalker from her mind she smiled her way through breakfast, then phoned her coach to let him know she was going to live.

"I guess you're kinda sore today," were among Matt's first words.

He sure had a knack for understatement. She felt as if she'd been in a car accident. "So, did we make a comeback?"

"Nah. Went from bad to ugly. We came the closest I've seen to a bench-clearing brawl."

Her fingers tightened on the phone. "Really? What happened?"

"The girls didn't take too kindly to their favorite teammate being taken out like that. We hit the first batter up between the shoulder blades...kinda hard to argue it was an accident."

"No kidding." She was oddly touched by her pitcher's efforts.

"Anyway, it all went downhill after that, and I barely managed to avoid disaster by charging out and physically restraining their coach from going after her. Too bad you missed it."

Christa laughed, though it hurt her head to do it. "Did anyone get thrown out?"

"Yeah, Patty and Lindsay."

That would be the backup catcher and the first baseman. Both big girls, too. "Well, I'm sorry I missed it all."

"It was something, I'll grant you that." He cleared his throat, and Christa knew something else was coming.

"Thing is, Chris, I got a call from their coach this morning."

"Is he still mad at you?"

Matt sighed. "It wasn't that. He..." Silence filled the next few seconds. "I guess the girl that took you out, well...she got hurt in the parking lot of their hotel. A hit and run, her teammates said."

Christa's stomach plummeted.

"A big SUV came flying around the corner, must not have seen her until it was too late. No one else was hurt, but the driver kept going and it was too fast for anyone to get the license plate. We got two witnesses, though, who say they saw the guy."

Christa swallowed. "Is she all right?"

"She's in the hospital with a broken thigh and some fractured ribs. Whole lot of road rash, too."

She winced. The girl must have already been banged up enough after their collision, which would have made it even harder for her to get out of the way in time. "That's awful. Should I go see her?"

"I guess she'd like that. Meantime you take it easy, get better soon. Don't want our star player out of action for too long, do we?"

"Don't remind me." She'd spent much of the night brooding about her enforced absence, the opportunities she'd miss. To be so close to selection and then have to sit out was tying her into knots of frustration.

"I've already spoken with the national team head coach, so she's aware of your injuries and I don't think missing a few games and practices will hurt your chances. So don't worry about it. I'll come by and see you, maybe tomorrow after practice. Okay?"

"Sure. See you then." She hung up, staring across the room, something nagging at her. Was she being paranoid?

It didn't matter, the awful suspicion had already formed. She'd been so sore last night, so exhausted, that she'd almost forgotten what Rayne had told her about her stalker threatening the umpire and the runner before getting thrown out of the park. Was it so crazy to wonder if the left fielder's accident hadn't been an accident at all?

Hoping she was wrong, she got up and located Rayne's cell number. He'd told her to call if something came up, hadn't he? She dialed and waited, expecting his voicemail to pick up.

"Hutch here."

"Hi Rayne, it's Christa," she began.

"Hey, kiddo. How are you feeling? Did you sleep okay?"

"I'm fine, thanks. Listen, I don't want to bother you, but—"

"You're never a bother, darlin'. What's up?"

She dropped into her favorite chair in the family room, drew a blanket over her chilled skin. "I just talked to my coach, and he told me the girl who slid into me last night has been hospitalized by a hit and run in their hotel parking lot."

A telltale pause met her words. "Was the driver arrested?"

"It all happened too fast for anyone to get a plate number, but witnesses said it was a man driving an SUV." She lifted a hand to her mouth and absently chewed on a fingernail. She'd love to be way off base about this.

"I'll make some calls, see what I can find out."

The concern in his voice confirmed he was every bit as suspicious. She took a steadying breath and put her fear into words, if only to make it real. "So is it just me, or do you think it might not have been an accident?"

"Well, it's kind of coincidental, after the player who took you out was publicly threatened, wouldn't you say?"

"Yeah." She fought down the nervous energy in her stomach. "I was going to go to the hospital and see the girl today."

"I don't think that's such a good idea, kiddo."

The words made her swallow. "Oh." Surely he wasn't suggesting she shouldn't leave her house?

"I'll have a friend of mine check into a few things, but in the meantime keep your head up, okay? Pay attention to what's happening around you. Tonight after work I'll come over and give you a crash course on self-defense and counter-surveillance. Never hurts to take precautions, right?"

Oh God, next she'd have to play cloak-and-dagger games, wear camouflage gear. Maybe she'd carry her lucky bat with her after all. "Okay, thanks," she answered mechanically, brain struggling to keep up. "Have a good day at work."

"Thanks darlin'." She detected a hint of a smile in his voice. "See you later."

So now she was imprisoned in her own home. Wasn't *that* lovely.

Forcing her stiff body out of the chair, she headed upstairs, senses on high alert. She was halfway to the bathroom when the doorbell rang, sending her heart into a desperate gallop. Clutching a hand to her chest, she snuck a peek out the window and saw someone set something on the porch. The footsteps retreated, then an engine purred and she glimpsed a white delivery van speeding down her driveway. Did florists deliver on Sunday?

Calling Jake to her, hoping he would go for the throat if anyone was waiting out there to hurt her, she cracked open the front door and glanced at the mat. A dozen long-stemmed red roses lay at her feet. Hands clammy, she slowly reached down and plucked the white card from the bouquet.

Everything has been taken care of. Get well soon.

The note bore the number nineteen—her uniform number—on the front. It fell from her nerveless fingers and fluttered to the ground. With the hairs on the back of her neck standing on end, Christa fled inside the house and slammed the door shut, locking out the threat with one measly deadbolt. She sank to the floor, her breathing choppy.

Well, now she had no doubt—he definitely knew where she lived.

CHAPTER 5

As promised, Rayne showed up at her door that evening, looking altogether edible in faded jeans and a t-shirt that emphasized his pecs and flat stomach. She had practically every light in the house burning and her lucky bat was always in the room with her. Those flowers had been the last straw, and she'd immediately called the police station to file a report, then updated Rayne. Within an hour a uniformed officer had arrived to take her statement and the note, cautioning her to monitor the situation carefully and call 911 right away if she suspected she was being followed. They could do nothing more at this stage, the young cop had told her apologetically, since they only had Seth's first name and description, but if she found out his last name and address she could file a no contact order.

Gee. She felt ever so much better now. If things escalated, she could always stop and ask him his last name and address before he went after her. Yep, she was gonna sleep like a baby tonight.

At Rayne's knock, she hurried over to let him in. "Hi," she said, almost weak with relief at having someone else there with her. Constantly staying alert took a lot of energy.

"Hey." He assessed her with one long look. "How are you holding up?"

"I feel like I'm in one of those cheesy teen suspense movies."

He laughed. "But in those movies, the characters never had an ERT officer with a double black belt to train them in self-defense."

"There is that. Plus you look like you could bench-press a small car."

"What, you mean like a Mini Cooper?"

"Oh, at least. And speaking of cars—any word on the

SUV that hit the left fielder?"

"Yeah." His grim expression and tone made her heart sink. "Stolen, and witnesses described the driver as a male, either blond or light brown hair. Add the note, and it's pretty hard to deny our theory." He studied her.

"The way my luck's been going lately?" she scoffed.

"Oh, please." She took a deep breath and raised her chin. "Okay, let's get this over with. Do your worst."

He tilted his head. "You sure you're feeling up to this? Your head isn't hurting you?"

"Just don't beat me up any more than I already am, okay? A girl can only take so much."

He shrugged out of his jacket, never breaking eye contact. "You'd be surprised how gentle I can be."

Would she? Try her. She fought not to smile, shook her head in exasperation. He flirted like that with all the ladies, so she knew he meant nothing by it. "You're *bad*. Stop trying to distract me." Now, if only her insides would stop melting at the idea of wrestling with him in mock combat, she was good to go.

He went around the room, moving furniture out of the way. Christa's eyebrows hiked up toward her hairline. "You planning on throwing me around?"

"Scared?" he taunted, a wicked gleam in his hazel eyes.

She snorted at him towering above her five-foot-eight frame. "Why should I be? You're only what, two-fifty and nine feet tall?"

"Two-thirty and six-three, you mean." He lifted onto his toes and stretched his arms. "C'mon, this won't hurt, I promise."

No easy way to back out now and besides, she was no quitter. Lifting her chin, she strode toward him. At least she'd thought to put on perfume, so she smelled nice.

"Tell me what you know about self-defense," he prompted, bringing her to stand in front of him.

"Nothing, except that if I have to end up fighting, I don't want to fight like a girl."

His eyes twinkled. "The first thing I want to stress is you're not trying to beat up the guy, you're only trying to stun him long enough so you can run away and yell for help."

She could do that. "I'm a good yeller, and I'm fast."

"Okay, come here." He took hold of her fingers and moved so that he was behind her.

His arms slid around her waist and the faint lemony scent of him made every one of her muscles rigid. She hoped nothing would jiggle at an inopportune moment.

First he showed her how to make a proper fist, shifting her thumb safely out of the way. "This is what you do if someone grabs you from behind. Use either your fist or your elbow if you can, and smash it into his face or throat. If he grabs your arms, then use the back of your head or jam your heel down against the top of his foot." He moved her arm for her, showing her the motion. His build made her feel delicate, as if he could snap her like a dry twig. Until now she'd never been aware of how vulnerable she was to a man's strength.

"What about the groin? Shouldn't I try to knee him in the groin at some point?"

"If you can get a shot in, go ahead, but that's the first place men automatically block. Do whatever you can to disable him long enough to get away." He went through the moves again, coming at her from the front, the side and from behind, showing her how to direct the various blows, making her repeat them over and over. At first she was acutely aware of his muscles pressing against her, but soon she started trusting him not to hurt her, and to defend himself against anything she might manage to dish out. The next hour went by in a blur as he showed her how to break holds, how to use her legs, which were much stronger than her upper body, and more about the vulnerable points of the human frame than she'd ever wanted to know.

"This is a strike point only to be used as a last resort, because it can kill someone," he told her, placing her fingers at the outside corner of his eye. "The edge of the temporal bone is here. It's thin, especially at the temple. Jab here hard enough and you can cause internal hemorrhaging. Even with light pressure it can make someone toss their cookies."

She widened her stare. "Right there?"

"Yup."

He made her grapple with him and to get loose she

had to use so much force that it was just shy of hurting her. By the time they were done the bruises on her leg were killing her, she had damp spots between her breasts and under her arms, but he was barely breathing hard. She stumbled back from him, wiping her sleeve across her face.

"Had enough?" He stood there before her, all hard muscle and sex appeal.

"How much more is there?" She'd been certain they'd covered everything except how to rip out someone's kidney with your bare hand.

He tweaked her nose. "I've still got a few tricks to share. But if you're feeling more secure about defending yourself, that's all that matters."

"I am, thanks. But remind me never to jump you in a dark alley."

His eyes lit up. "You can jump me any time you want, darlin'."

She'd walked right into that one. "I'm sure." Taking charge before her nerves started to show, she limped into the kitchen to pour them each a glass of iced tea.

"Your leg okay?" he asked, as if he'd only now remembered her injuries.

"I'll put some ice on it in a bit." She replaced the pitcher in the fridge, glanced over her shoulder. "I made a lasagna, if you're hungry." Plus she'd made cookies, and a cake, and a batch of homemade soup. That's what happened when she was holed up inside by herself all day. To keep from being bored out of her skull she cooked everything in sight, and wound up with enough food for five people.

"I'd love some." He seated himself on a stool at the island as she removed a casserole dish from the oven and set a generous portion in front of him. He took a mouthful, murmured his enjoyment and dug in. "You gonna be okay here by yourself?"

She climbed onto the neighboring stool. "Between what you've shown me tonight and my lucky bat, no one in their right mind would come after me." She hoped.

"I know that note scared the hell out of you, Christa. You're welcome to stay with me for a while if you want. Or I can stay here until we get to the bottom of this."

Her heart tripped at his consideration, at the prospect of staying at his place. "I appreciate the offer. But don't you think he'll back off now since I've gone to the police? The officer who came earlier said I should call 911 if he bothers me again, and then maybe I could get a no contact order."

"You mean assuming they can verify his name really is Seth something-or-other, track him down and serve him the papers before he does anything more?"

Oh, right. Those *were* important little details. "Good point."

"Hey, he probably won't do anything. I just don't like you being out here all alone in this big house."

"Don't forget, I've got Jake."

Hearing his name, Jake came loping up to them and put his furry chin on her lap.

Rayne scratched the dog's ears. "He's pretty scary all right."

"He might not be intimidating, but he's really smart. Aren't you, boy?" Jake gazed up at her with intelligent brown eyes. "See?"

"I'd better stay over."

Was he joking, or did he mean it? The *Hallelujah Chorus* blared in her head. Did she dare call his bluff? "Suit yourself."

"And I think I'll take you over to meet Nate, get his two cents on all this."

She swallowed her dinner past the constriction in her throat. "Sure, if you think he can help." As much faith as Rayne seemed to put in the man he'd described as his surrogate father, it didn't thrill her to consult the head of the serious crimes unit regarding her personal dilemma. All it did was remind her she might be in serious danger.

Rayne stood to take the dishes to the sink, rinsed them and loaded them into the dishwasher. He seemed so comfortable in her home, as if he belonged there. "In fact, let's go see Nate right now."

She'd rather he came over and kiss her senseless, but hey, as far as distractions went, she'd take whatever she could get. And spending the whole evening with Rayne would do nicely.

****

50

Rayne knew Nate took a shine to her immediately by the way he teased her, and he guessed the same applied to Christa because she dished it right back. She was a curious mixture of independence and vulnerability, and it drew him to her like a magnet.

Nate regarded him with knowing eyes. "So is this a social call, or for something specific?"

Leave it to Nate to get down to business. "Actually, Christa's been having a problem with this guy who keeps following her around at her softball games. Yesterday she got injured and he lost it right there in front of everyone. Now the girl who slid into her is in the hospital after a hit and run."

Nate's chocolate-brown gaze darkened. "Was it him?"

"No evidence confirming that yet. But she had some roses delivered this morning, along with a note telling her everything was 'taken care of'."

"You should get a no contact order," Nate told her.

"I tried to, but I don't know his last name."

He drummed his fingers. "I don't like the feel of this at all. Seems to me he's escalating things every time. If he comes near you again, call 911. No reason to risk him getting close. Over ninety percent of rapes are committed by someone the victim knows, and it wouldn't surprise me if he'd already fixated on you sexually."

Rayne saw her shiver and spare a nervous glance at him. "You think he's planning to *attack* me?" Her eyes were enormous.

Nate leaned back in his chair. "I think he's at least fantasized about it. That's what most stalkers are after. You need to be aware of the danger, because this guy is a potentially serious threat."

Rayne slipped his hand onto her shoulder to rub the tension away.

"If, God forbid, he does come after you," Nate continued, "do not under any circumstance go with him into a vehicle or secluded place. Even if he has a weapon, chances are he won't use it because it would draw attention to him, and if he did, the odds are he would only wound you."

Rayne cringed. "Nate, maybe this is a little too much information—"

"No, Rayne. She needs to know what to do. If it scares you, Christa, I apologize, but I see this kind of thing every day in my job, and I don't want it to happen to you if I can help it."

"Okay," she said in a small voice. "What else?"

"If you do somehow end up in a vehicle with him, you might have to crash it in order to get away. If he pulls a knife, you—"

"Jesus, Nate." He reached down to wrap his fingers around hers, finding them ice cold. "Can't we just reinforce that she should steer clear of the guy, keep her eyes open, and leave it at that?"

Nate sent him a weighted stare. "You so afraid of scaring her that you're willing to risk her life?"

"Trust me, you've already scared her."

Nate's eyes softened. "If that's true, I'm sorry, but you do need to be aware of the risks involved with a stalker. Stay away from him and if you ever see him again, call the cops right away."

She forced a smile. "Wow. Looks like I'll be toting my lucky bat around with me everywhere now. And maybe an air horn."

They made an attempt at small talk after that, but soon Rayne ushered her out to his car. As he drove, he glanced over at her every so often. She stared out the window at the darkened street, chewing her lip.

"Nate's a great guy, but he's kind of a pessimist sometimes. Comes with his job description, I guess. Don't let what he said upset you, kiddo. You know to look out for yourself, and you'll be fine."

"You know, I was thinking," she mused, "about what I would do if I had to leave home for a while." Her gaze remained on the road ahead of them. "I'd hate it, you know. Leaving. I love my home more than anything, it's like my safe haven. I'll only give it up if I have no other choice."

"I understand." No one could set foot in the place without feeling Christa in every square inch.

"During various counseling sessions after my last breakup," she explained in a dry tone, "I learned I have a deep need for security and peace in my life. My house gives me those things, and I won't let him take it from me."

Her breakup had sent her to a counselor? He filed that information away and reached over to squeeze her hand. "Let's not worry about that unless we have to, okay?"

Her words solidified everything he already knew about her, since her need for security matched the calm, steady persona she projected to the world. It was the other more secret side of her, the soft, sweetly vulnerable and insecure part that brought his protective male instincts to blazing life. He'd never met anyone like her. She kept up her place by herself, gardens and all, and ran her own small landscaping business. He'd seen her happily and adeptly at work in her kitchen, watched her acting as tough as his ex-drill sergeant on the ball field, putting her body on the line to stop a run from scoring.

According to Teryl and Drew she was a devoted and loyal friend who would do anything for those she cared about. And, she was *real*. With Christa, what you saw was what you got, without any pretense. No manipulation, no head games. Wrap that up in an attractive feminine package and he couldn't help but be interested in her, couldn't understand why she put up that force field instead of making the most of the male attention. A piece must be missing from the puzzle, because it didn't add up. Hey, look at him, the confirmed bachelor—he had no trouble picturing her running a house full of kids, driving back and forth to their soccer games in a minivan, and he wasn't running in the opposite direction. What the hell did that mean, anyway?

It meant he was losing his freaking mind, that's what.

He turned down her driveway and when he cut the engine, she sat there gazing up at the turreted outline of her house.

"It'll be okay, darlin'."

"Yeah." Trying to smile, she let herself out of the car, unlocked the back door and he followed her inside. "Were you serious about staying over again tonight?"

"Dead serious." Please just let her buckle under and agree.

She tilted her head at him. "I can look after myself,

you know. I'm used to it, and my head's feeling much better now. If I need to, I guess I could stay with Teryl for a few days."

"You could," he agreed, "but you just said you didn't want to let him force you to leave. If you go, in a sense he's won. He'd know he's gotten to you."

"True," she hedged. "I'd much rather stay here..."

He hated seeing her so torn. All he wanted to do was protect her from that maniac. "Look, I don't want to force my presence on you but I know you're worried about the situation. Who wouldn't be?" He ran a hand through his hair. How could he persuade her? "After that note he left this morning, and our visit with Nate—which in hindsight I kind of regret putting you through—can you honestly tell me you'd feel safe all alone?" She didn't react. No sigh of resignation, no flicker of relief on her face. What, did she need him to beg?

But then she flashed him that sweet smile, her big blue eyes gazing up at him with complete trust, and every protective instinct he had roared to life. Another few seconds of her staring at him that way and he'd start sprouting fur on the backs of his hands, then drag her away and lock her up someplace where no one could touch her. Like some caveman.

"I hate to lean on you so much. It's not in my nature."

"That's not leaning, it's being smart. And it's in *my* nature to protect people. Especially you."

"I guess I would feel better if you stuck around."

"Good." He hung his jacket on the antique coat rack and pulled off his boots. "So, do you want to stay up and watch a movie or something? Take your mind off everything?"

She stifled a yawn. "Thanks but I'm beat. Will I see you in the morning?"

Evasion tactics? Disappointment filled him. "Not unless you're up by oh-five-hundred."

She grimaced. "Oh. No, then."

She shifted on the bottom stair, sent a skittish glance around the house. "Come here, kiddo." He held out his arms to her.

She stared at him for a moment before moving forward and he gathered her against him, despite her tension. She felt so small and fragile in his embrace, he practically surrounded her. He hugged her close, running his hands over the thick, shiny hair spilling down her back until she relaxed. He'd always wanted to find out if her hair was as soft as it looked. It was, and it smelled like green apples. "Don't be scared," he said quietly against the crown of her head. She swallowed and stayed where she was, her cheek pressed against his shoulder.

"I'm not." She didn't sound convincing.

"I won't let anything happen to you." His hands kept up their soothing motion until she was completely resting against him, then he kissed the top of her head and leaned away to gaze down at her. "Sleep well."

"I will, with you here." She put on a bright smile, and he figured his innocent kiss was responsible for the color in her cheeks. Fighting the temptation to kiss her properly, he let her go. On the third tread, she paused. "Rayne?"

"Yeah?"

"Just so you know, I'm a lot tougher than I look."

He nodded. "I know you are, kiddo." She had a backbone of steel to go with that tender heart, and it made him want her even more.

His eyes followed her all the way up the stairs.

CHAPTER 6

Someone was moving around on the front porch.

Christa lay frozen in her bed peering into the inky darkness. Another faint shuffling broke the silence.

Heart pounding, she threw back the covers and ran to find Rayne. His car was parked out front, so whoever was sneaking about had to know she wasn't alone. Would her stalker be crazy enough to break in while she had company?

"Rayne?" She whispered as loudly as she dared, moving down the dim hallway to the landing, her clammy bare feet sticking to the hardwood. The guest room door was open, revealing darkness, so presumably he was still watching TV in the family room. She started down the stairs, her bare footsteps muffled by the carpet runner, and nearly leapt out of her skin when he appeared holding Jake by the collar.

He cut off her exclamation with an upraised hand, then held his finger to his lips. When he pushed Jake toward her she grabbed hold of him, his entire furry body quivering.

"Stay there," Rayne commanded in a whisper, turning his head toward the front door, listening, primed for action.

She stood rooted on the third step as he sank into a crouch and crept to one of the windows flanking the door. Weak light from the streetlamps at the end of the driveway filtered through the glass, casting a dim glow. Without disturbing the sheer curtains he peered out at the porch, careful to stay in the shadows below the window ledge.

Jake let out a whine, straining to get free.

"Jake, no," she hissed, tugging his collar. He trembled against her, staring at the front entrance with the single-minded intensity only a border collie could display.

A muffled thump hit the floor and she struggled to hold Jake still as Rayne ducked lower. Head swiveling to face her, he jabbed a finger upwards, ordering her back upstairs. For a second she lingered, reluctant to leave either him or herself alone, but then the adrenaline kicked in and she dragged her struggling dog to her room, grabbing the cordless phone from the nightstand. Breath coming in shallow pants, she edged back to the landing, peering down into the dark hallway. Rayne had moved to the other window in the foyer, still hunkered down and poised.

The grandfather clock chimed quarter to the hour, echoing in the awful stillness. She swallowed, the reflex almost impossible past the lump in her throat. Should she call 911? Rayne hadn't indicated she should, and he had his own cell phone with him so maybe he'd already called it in. Her finger hovered over the first number on the touchpad, ready to dial at the slightest hint of trouble. Her skin prickled, moisture damp on her palms.

Jake growled low in his throat, and she yanked him close and wrapped her hand around his muzzle before it could become a full-fledged snarl. "Shhh," she warned, eyes glued to the man who stood between her and whoever was on her verandah. More shuffling sounded outside, then stilled. She held her breath. What if the stalker had a weapon? Her blood ran cold.

"Shit," Rayne muttered, stood and flipped on the light, then threw open the door and yelled, "Get!"

Christa jumped. Her heart thundered in her ears.

Letting out a rush of breath, he shut the door and threw the deadbolt, then looked up at her with a rueful expression. "Raccoon," he said in disgust. "Sorry about that."

She stared at him, speechless under the numbing effect of the adrenaline crash. Jake tore free from her limp fingers and flew down the stairs to the window, jumping up to rest his front paws on the sill and barking hysterically, his black and white tail wagging hard enough to make the sheers billow. Rayne ushered him to the back door and the dog raced out, his frantic barks fading into the distance.

Not a weapon-toting, would-be rapist stalker at all, but a raccoon, for God's sake.

If her legs would have held her up, she would have chased down the stupid animal herself. But since her knees had taken on the consistency of unset Jell-O, her only option was to stand there and gape at Rayne, who was having a hard time not laughing.

Well, pardon her for not being amused. Hand pressed over her chest, she closed her eyes and leaned against the banister while her heart began its journey south from her tonsils.

"Hey." His warm fingers brushed her cheek before he sat both of them on the top stair, the pressure of his hip comforting. She didn't dare open her eyes in case he saw the tears she was fighting. "You okay?"

Lips pressed together until she could get a grip on herself, she could only nod.

He slung an arm around her shoulders. "Sorry about that." His fingertips grazed the lace strap of her nightgown, making her already jangled nerves shriek. She wasn't wearing anything under the jersey gown. She wrapped her arms around herself to shield her body and swallowed.

"Jake started growling," he continued, "and then I heard something outside, so I wanted to check it out just to be sure."

She lifted her head from the balustrade. "I heard it too. I was coming to find you." She hadn't bothered to open her eyes, but at least her voice was steady. "I'm going to kill that goddamn raccoon."

A chuckle vibrated through his chest. "If he's smart, he's halfway up a tall tree by now. I think Jake's got the situation under control anyway."

"He hates raccoons. Has since he was a puppy." She leaned against him, letting his body heat chase away the lingering chill.

"You gonna go back to bed now?" His hand stroked her hair from the crown of her head to her shoulder blades.

She pulled back and gawked at him. "You think I can sleep after that?"

His eyes softened. "Still worried?"

"Well, of course I am. Even you thought it might have been you-know-who out there."

"Yeah, I did," he conceded. "But it wasn't."

This time. The words hung between them as clearly as if he'd spoken them out loud.

She dropped her head into her hands. "God, this *sucks.*" The clock chimed midnight. Monday, May nineteenth. "Hell of a way to start your birthday," she murmured.

His hand stopped its soothing motion in the middle of her back. "It's your birthday? You didn't say anything about that."

"Gee, it must have slipped my mind somewhere between finding out about the hit-and-run and Nate telling me what to do if the stalker pulls a knife on me."

He made a strangled sound, as if he was struggling not to laugh—*laugh*, for crying out loud. "Happy birthday, darlin'."

"Thanks." Still single at twenty-nine years old and here she was, cuddled up to Rayne in her sheer nightgown, clammy with perspiration. She tightened her arms over her chest. "I think I'll go take a bath." Maybe the warm water would soothe her enough to sleep.

He hesitated before releasing her. "Want me to wait up? I could tuck you in afterward." His boyish grin melted her tripping heart.

She blinked up at him. It was getting harder and harder to tell whether he was teasing. She assumed he was, but that glint in his amber-and-green eyes had her thinking otherwise. "I'm sorry, I'm too tired and rattled to joke with you right now."

"Who's joking?"

"You are."

"Am I?"

Wasn't he? She stared into those eyes, mesmerized by the unexpected hunger swirling in their hazel depths. Unable to pull her gaze away, she watched him glance down at her mouth, mere inches away, and bend his head a fraction. *He's going to kiss me.* Mouth dry, pulse hammering, she scrambled to her feet. "I'll just go, um, take that bath now."

His expression unreadable, he nodded.

"Thanks for checking things out." Did he mistake her sudden retreat for disinterest? It would serve her right if he did. Well, no way to fix it gracefully now.

Thank God she'd agreed to let him stay, though. Thank God he'd offered, been so insistent. No other guy she'd known would have put his own life on hold to take care of her this way. But then, no one else had ever had to. She'd never had to let them.

"No problem. Sleep tight, kiddo."

Coward, her conscience sneered as she fled up the stairs to the bathroom.

****

She couldn't stay away from Softball City. The place, the game, were like a drug and she needed a fix. In broad daylight she felt safe around her teammates, so when one of them had called and offered her a ride to watch the practice, she'd agreed. Rayne had gone to work so she was alone in the house anyway. Besides, it was her birthday. Going to the park would be her present to herself.

When she showed up Matt shook his head at her in exasperation, but since her stalker hadn't been seen around the ballpark since he'd been thrown out for freaking over her injury, Matt let her stay. She sat through the workout while her teammates sweated it out, hating the frustration eating away at her.

Coming here was a risk now that her stalker knew where she lived, but as she and Dani had driven over here she'd made sure they weren't being followed. Rayne wouldn't be happy, but she couldn't stand having her life stripped away because of some whacko. Besides, she needed a distraction after last night's almost-kiss. She'd been awake a long time afterward, kicking herself for not going through with it. And kicking herself just as hard for wanting him to. What if she'd missed her only shot at him? When she'd gotten to sleep she'd dreamed about him pressing her down into the sheets with that strong, lean body—

"Chris." She came out of her reverie to find Matt holding out a pen and clipboard. "Mind charting a few of our hitters for me?"

Grateful to have something useful to do, she spent the rest of the practice making up charts and joking with her teammates. They all wanted to know who the hunk was who had carried her from the park after she'd been injured, so keeping her mind off Rayne wasn't an option.

She was waiting for Dani so they could leave when her cell phone rang. She checked the number and didn't recognize it, but the phone was her work line so she assumed it was a client. "Green With Envy Landscaping, Christa speaking."

Silence.

"Hello?" she asked, plugging her other ear with a finger. Nothing. She lowered the phone to check the signal strength: full.

She was about to disconnect when a voice spoke.

"Happy birthday. How come you're not out there with the rest of the team? Still got a headache?"

She stilled. A male voice. Something familiar about it nagged at her.

"That color pink looks good on you."

The breath left her lungs in a rush, her eyes swinging up from her pink t-shirt to scan the park. *Him.* He was watching her right now. "Where are you?" she demanded.

He gave a chuckle.

All right. No more. Her thumb slid to cut the call.

"I assume you got my flowers."

Breathing fast, she held off disconnecting, half hoping he would give her a clue to help the police catch him. "Leave me alone and don't call me again."

Silence tautened across the line.

Her throat tightened. "Don't call me again," she repeated, voice hoarse, and hung up. At least she'd sent the message that she would not be cowed by him, but a shiver ripped through her as she stared toward the outfield fence. Was he there, out of sight, watching her right now? Her skin crawled, instincts shrieking at her to flee, and she went to tell Matt about the call. He promised to alert the staff to any sightings of the stalker and stood over her while she called the police.

Safely home, she opened the back door into the kitchen, flipping on the overhead light. A ripple of apprehension slid down her spine. Where was Jake? He always met her at the back door, without fail.

"Jake?" She glanced around the great room, surprised he wasn't already underfoot clamoring for attention. She stuck her head out the doorway, calling his name again. Nothing. No answering distant bark, no jingle of his collar. Only silence. "Jake?"

A buzz of alarm sounded in her brain. Something was wrong, she could feel it. Had the stalker done something to her dog? Dread curled in the pit of her stomach, her heart tripping.

She called his name again, louder this time, and headed for the staircase, panic rampaging. A whisper of movement came from behind her, and she stopped. Frozen like prey scenting danger, she listened.

A creak, somewhere to the left, like someone stepping on a loose floorboard. Fear gripped her chest. Stupid! She never should have come inside alone, should have let Dani accompany her. Heart pounding, she whirled around to head back into the kitchen, ready to make a run for the back door.

"Surprise!"

Christa jumped, her heart almost stopping altogether. A dozen or more of her friends emerged from their hiding spots, Teryl rushing toward her with a bottle of her favorite wine and Jake in tow.

"Happy birthday, sweetie!" She beamed.

Christa stood there with a hand pressed over her poor shocked heart and smacked Teryl on the shoulder.

"Ow!" she yelped. "What's that for?"

"You scared me to death, you idiot," Christa laughed, willing her heart back down her esophagus. She bent to gather Jake into a bear hug and let out a sigh, weakened by fading adrenaline. Rayne materialized out of the crowd, making her dizzy with relief, and she threw her arms around him.

"Whoa," he chuckled as he hugged her back, pressing a kiss to her cheek, his warm lips on her skin making her tingle all over. She had no business tingling when it came to Rayne. "Miss me that much already? Happy birthday, darlin'."

She clung to his shoulder, reveling in the sense of security he exuded.

"Hey. Something spook you?" He frowned down at

her and jerked a thumb at Teryl. "Blame your pal. It was her idea to hide and jump out at you."

"It's not that," she whispered into his ear. "Something happened at the ballpark. He...he called me."

Anger burned in his eyes. "Did you call it in right away?"

"'Course I did. They're checking my cell phone records."

"Good. I'll call the detachment myself, make sure they're onto it."

"Thanks. I feel better with you here, anyway."

"Off you go then, and play hostess." He gave her butt a playful tap.

She greeted the rest of her guests then fled up the stairs to make herself more presentable. When she came back down everyone was at the island helping themselves to platters of food. Teryl sauntered over.

"Here," she said, thrusting a glass of wine at her. "I'm already three glasses ahead of you, so hurry and catch up."

"Yes ma'am." Amid cheers she drained the glass. Drew came over and hugged her tight.

"You don't look a day over twenty-nine," he told her, grinning.

"That's good to know. And thanks for throwing the party."

Teryl waved a hand. "It was no trouble and besides, you deserve a little fun after recent events, right?"

"You're not kidding. But you guys nearly gave me a heart attack."

Drew gave her a boyish smile. "Teryl got a little carried away. She's drunk, by the way."

Their conversation was interrupted by a group of her teammates arriving. She waved them over to the makeshift bar at the kitchen counter where Rayne was playing bartender. Once they all had something to drink, she went around visiting with everyone, making introductions and small talk.

"C'mon, hostess," Teryl chided. "No working tonight. This is your birf—birthday, I mean," she corrected herself, swaying a bit on her four-inch heels.

"You sure you've only had three glasses?" Christa

teased.

Teryl gave her a tipsy smile and tossed her blonde hair over one shoulder. "I never said I'd only had three. I said three more than you." She whipped around. "Where's my studly hubby gone?" she asked, wobbling on those precarious heels, reaching out to grab onto Christa's shoulder to steady herself. "Hey, Drew! Get over here."

Christa smothered a laugh into her wineglass as Drew started toward them.

"Isn't he the sexiest thing you've ever laid eyes on?" Teryl gushed.

"The sexiest by far," she agreed, but she was staring at Rayne. As though he sensed it, he looked up and met her gaze, held it. Gave a slow wink that sent her pulse skittering.

Drew peeled his wife off Christa, hugging her into his side to keep her steady. "You're so cute when you're smashed.

"I know," she sighed, melting against him. "And I'm also really horny—"

Oh, God. Christa winced and with one look into Drew's laughing eyes, made her escape. She went to stand with Rayne and introduced him to her teammates, their eyes bright with curiosity. The moment he went back to serving drinks they pounced on her, pressing for details.

"Sadly," she informed them, "there are no details." But for the rest of the evening they shot her sidelong looks and waggled their eyebrows.

"So, tell me," Rayne interrupted, leaning on his elbows to survey the room. "Any of your friends here, you know...'bat for both teams'?"

She gave him a disbelieving glare. "Are you serious?"

"Isn't it true—"

"That we stay up all night on road trips massaging each other with hot oil and have pillow fights in our underwear? Yeah, it's true."

He laughed out loud, then rubbed a hand over his face. "Oh, man, you sure know how to hit a guy where it hurts. I'll be up all night thinking about that now."

"Poor baby." It was a good thing she felt so comfortable and safe with him, or she'd never be able to flirt like this. Teryl was making her way toward them, her lipstick smeared from doing who knew what with Drew, a crooked smile on her face. "Teryl, tell Rayne about the time in California when—"

"When we almost got thrown out of the hotel for skinny dipping?" Her eyes danced.

Rayne groaned, and Teryl gave a wicked smile. "The whole team was buck naked out in the pool when this elderly couple came out to have a hot tub. The old guy stands there gawking at us as if his fondest wish had come true. He turns to his horrified wife and says, 'Estelle, I can finally die a happy man now.'"

"You were out there too?" he asked Christa, as if having trouble imagining her being that brave.

Teryl winked at him. "Yeah, it's her one claim to fame—her one and only bad girl deed, and she only did it because we were all giving her such a hard time."

"Well, I did it, didn't I?"

"You sure did, sweetie, and I'm glad. God knows she needs to loosen up from time to time," she confided to Rayne. "That's my birthday wish for you, Chris. I want some hunk to come along and blow your mind with wild, unattached monkey sex."

"Thanks." She gave Teryl a quelling look, didn't dare glance at Rayne.

Teryl leaned closer to him, crooking a finger until he bent his head so she could stage-whisper in his ear. "Did you know she hasn't gotten laid in almost *five years*?" She made it sound like a century. "We have Cameron the Shithead to thank for that."

"*Teryl!*"

"It's all right, sweetie, it's just between us friends." She patted her shoulder. "And now I've got to take Drew home and have some wild monkey sex of my own. If you'll excuse me," she drawled. She moved two steps away, then turned back to Rayne and give him an upheld hand, fingers spread wide. *Five years*, she mouthed, eyes widening, then shrugged as if to say she'd never understand how someone could be celibate that long, and went on the prowl after her husband.

"Oh my God." Christa had her hand pressed to her mouth. "Someone please kill me now." Or at least let the floor open up and swallow her whole.

Rayne laughed and pulled her hand from her lips, giving it a squeeze. "Don't sweat it, darlin', that was her wine talking."

She peeked up at him, her face burning. The sexiest, most notorious bachelor she'd ever come across knew she'd been living like a nun. "So what are you saying, that she should live after humiliating me like that?"

He grinned, took her wineglass and refilled it. "Has it really been five years?"

She glared up at him, knowing he was teasing, but she still felt like a pathetic loser. She took a fortifying gulp of wine, careful not to snap the stem of the wineglass with her clenched fingers. "I've had lots of dates." Six or seven actually, but he was only on a need-to-know basis. "It's just that I've been busy," she added, face burning, aware of how ridiculous it sounded. "I haven't had time for...that kind of...thing." She swallowed the rest of the wine in one shot, prayed it would stay in her churning stomach. Maybe if she got drunk enough, none of this would be embarrassing anymore. Maybe it would even be funny.

"So who's Cameron the Shithead?"

She huffed out a breath, sent another withering glare after Teryl. Great. Let's air out all her dirty laundry in front of the man she fantasized about. "He's my ex," she explained, careful to keep emotion out of her voice. Cameron was so far in the past he didn't deserve any emotion. After living with him for two years, she'd discovered that while she'd been daydreaming about their wedding, he'd been dreaming about how many women he could nail while she was away on road trips. "He cheated on me, so I dumped him." There. It sounded so neat and tidy that way, revealing none of the crushing pain she'd felt, the gaping wound he'd left where her naïve heart had once been.

"So you broke up five years ago and there's been no one since?"

If her face got any hotter she might spontaneously combust. "No one important." The crux of the problem? She wanted someone to take care of her, someone to one day have a family with, but she was way too scared of being burned again. The classic fear of abandonment. No wonder, after growing up feeling unwanted by her mother and Cameron's infidelity. According to her counselor her need for a stable, committed relationship reflected her desire to heal that pain, blah, blah. Understanding its source was an important step, but it didn't make it any easier to risk opening herself again to that kind of emotional agony.

Rayne came around the counter and set an arm around her shoulders. "I can't understand it, but c'mon. Let's go start on your presents."

"Yes, presents," she agreed, latching onto the idea, and let him lead her to the gift table. Everyone gathered to watch as she unwrapped a silver photo frame from Rayne and a yellow raincoat and hat for Jake from her adorable Irish neighbor, Patrick. They all laughed when the dog paraded in his new outfit, ever the showoff.

Teryl snapped photos with her digital camera, stopping in front of her and Rayne. She relished the warm, hard muscles of his forearm across her shoulder as he pulled her into him, her frantic heartbeat reminding her of their almost-kiss on the staircase. She soaked up his easy affection like a thirsty plant.

He gave her a squeeze and released her to open the rest of her gifts. Teryl, bless her thoughtful heart, had given her what appeared to be a lifetime supply of condoms and a card that read "Go get some, girlfriend!"

Rayne fished out one that glowed in the dark and let out a low whistle. "Wow. Who's the lucky guy?"

Her face burned as she glared at him. "Teryl. *Dies*," she muttered under her breath. Murder in her eyes as she swept a glance around the room, Christa couldn't find Teryl anywhere.

Someone was getting some all right, maybe at this very moment, but it sure as hell wasn't her.

****

He's going to kill me.

Sitting in the dugout at South Hill Park in Vancouver, Christa couldn't get the words out of her head. The officer who'd checked her cell phone records had traced yesterday's call from her stalker to a prepaid calling card. Another dead end.

Rayne had cautioned her not to return to the

67

ballpark until the guy was caught, but she wanted the coaches to know she was serious about making the national team, even if her injuries were keeping her temporarily sidelined. Besides, she was perfectly safe with her teammates, wasn't she? It wasn't like he could come and kidnap her in sight of everyone, even if he was crazy enough to try.

She still had a life to live, even if someone mentally unstable was obsessed with her. In the reassuring light of day, she even wondered if they might not be blowing this whole stalker thing out of proportion. Look how terrified she'd been the other night, when she'd thought he was prowling around her house preparing to make his move, and it turned out to be a raccoon.

One of her teammates hit the ball into the gap and ran to second for a stand-up double. Frustration ratcheted up another notch, the pressure in her chest increasing painfully. She wanted to be out there. To be given the chance to score the winning run, to make the critical plays.

Being selected for the national team would be the culmination of a lifetime of hard work, of countless hours in the gym hitting the weights to keep in shape during the winters, working through the off-season with the pitchers to stay in good condition, remaining late after every practice to improve. She thrived on the challenge, on pushing herself. Her skill was the product of years of discipline, of playing through all sorts of adversity—tyrannical coaches, heat exhaustion, bruises, sprains, strains and broken fingers. Making the final cut would prove she'd done something important with her life, something she could look on with pride. Now it was within reach, just beyond her straining fingertips...

Her spine tingled.

Eyes were boring into her back. She whipped her head around, froze. There he was, in the stands behind home plate. His cold gray eyes stared back at her, and then he winked, licked his lips.

She tore her gaze away, not wanting to give him the satisfaction of rattling her, and tried to stem the flow of adrenaline flooding through her. She couldn't believe his audacity. How long had he been sitting there? She'd been so stupid, blithely dismissing the danger. Why hadn't she listened to Rayne and stayed home? He couldn't come with her to tonight's game because of a briefing, but maybe he'd answer his cell phone.

She dug in her bag for her phone and dialed his number, moving to the end of the dugout to keep a low profile. She closed her eyes in relief when he answered.

"It's me," she whispered, casting a sidelong look to the bleachers. "I'm at—" He was going to blast her when he found out, but, "—at a game downtown—"

"What? You'd better frigging *not* be."

She winced. "I know, but—"

"What the hell's wrong with—"

"He's here."

Tension crackled across the line. "He's at the park?"

"Yes, right behind the plate. He's watching me."

She could hear his chair scrape back as he spoke to her, his voice anxious. "I'm going to call this in and get you help. Where are you right now? Are you safe?"

"I'm in the dugout with the team. Nobody knows what's going on."

"Stay right there, Chris. Promise me you won't move until help gets there."

His worried tone left her cold all over. She shivered. "I won't move."

"I'll come out to meet you as soon as I can get out of here."

"Okay. Thanks."

"Chris."

"Yeah?"

"Be careful."

She swallowed. "I will." Hanging up, she regretted her rash behavior more than ever.

Every cell in her body screamed at her to do something. She took one last glance into the stands but the seat behind home plate was empty. Her heart rate doubled. She scanned the crowd but he was gone. That scared her more than him sitting there staring at her. At least then she'd known where he was. Now, he could be anywhere.

The police arrived within minutes, and Christa gave the two officers the stalker's description and relayed the events of the past week or so. They completed a thorough check of the park and reported that someone matching his description had driven off in a dark blue pickup. By now it was almost eight-thirty; Rayne should be off duty any time. Should she leave right away, or wait until she could get hold of Rayne? The idea of staying here sent prickles up her spine, as if every pair of eyes in the crowd belonged to *him*. No, she'd rather get out of here now in case he came back. She left Rayne a voice-mail asking him to drive out to meet her as soon as he could. Man, she hated being so scared, but she had no choice. The stalker had given her no choice.

Minutes after leaving the park, she noticed a dark blue pickup in her rearview mirror. Her skin erupted into gooseflesh. Was it him?

The vehicle advanced to a few car lengths behind her, changing lanes when she did, passing when she did, always remaining the same distance away. Every detail came into sharp relief.

Don't panic. Stay focused on the road and lose him any way you can. Of course, she might be totally paranoid about her tail, so she made several turnoffs to determine if she really *was* being followed. Her every move was closely mirrored. When she slowed to make the pickup pass her, it slowed almost to a halt. Now she was ninety-eight percent sure it was him. The last thing she could do was go home...why had she taken a chance and not waited for Rayne?

She forced herself to think. Rayne would call her as soon as he checked his messages. She couldn't drive around for hours to avoid her pursuer, and what if he got desperate and tried to ram her or something? Who knew how nuts he was? What she needed was a safe place to go before things got any worse. Maybe she'd pass a police cruiser and could flag it down.

None of this was much help. She needed to do something now. Her hand tightened around the cell phone in her lap and she punched in 911, explained her near-certainty that the guy the cops had reported leaving the ballpark in a dark blue pickup was following her. The dispatcher gave her directions to the nearest police station and advised her to drive there immediately. She made the first turn, checking her mirrors. Sure enough, there was the blue pickup a few cars behind her.

She stepped on the gas, racing through a yellow light. Her shadow ran the red light, swerving to miss the oncoming traffic, racing to catch her. When he pulled in behind her, she memorized the license plate and the few identification details she could see in the glare of headlights. She clutched the steering wheel with shaky, clammy hands, heart slamming in her chest, and hit the accelerator, dodging slower traffic left and right. She couldn't make it to the police station—she needed help now. When the pickup was still with her at the next light she cut into a gas station, took a deep breath and jumped out, making a run for it inside. He wouldn't be insane enough to chase after her in front of everyone, would he?

The attendant eyed her suspiciously when she asked him if he could see a blue pickup. "Yeah, right there out front."

"Can you see the driver?" Her voice shook.

"Sort of."

She swallowed. "Can you tell me if it's a man or a woman and what color hair they have?"

He squinted out the window. "A man, with light-colored hair, I think."

She called 911 again and told them where she was. Then she called Rayne, praying he would pick up this time. He answered after two rings.

"Hey kiddo, I just got your message—"

"He's following me."

"What? Where the hell are you?"

"At a gas station. I've called the cops. He tailed me from the park."

"You left the park on your own, after he was there? Jesus, Christa, I told you not to—"

"I know!" she snapped, nerves stretched to the breaking point. "I thought I'd be safe enough until you could meet up with me, but I guess your briefing took longer than expected." If she sounded shaky and a little accusatory, well, she couldn't help it.

"I'm coming to get you," he said, his voice taut. "Just stay there. Can he see you?"

"Yes."

"Does he know you're onto him?"

She gnawed on her lower lip. "Probably, by now. But I didn't actually see *him*. The gas station attendant said it was a man with light-colored hair." It didn't make any sense, now that she thought about it. Wouldn't he have dyed his hair, grown a beard, developed a sudden myopia that required corrective lenses to disguise his appearance?

She forced herself to turn around and the second her eyes lit on the pickup, it peeled out of the forecourt. "He took off," she said, hand pressed over her pounding heart.

"Did you get a license plate?" She gave him the details she had noted, and her location. "Good girl. I'll be right there."

She waited anxiously inside until the cops arrived and felt like an idiot when she had to admit that her stalker had vanished, although the attendant was able to confirm seeing a dark blue pickup entering the gas station immediately after her. No sooner had the police left than Rayne pulled up and she ran outside to meet him.

His concerned gaze raked over her. "You okay?"

"Yeah, I think so. Shook me up a bit though."

His jaw tightened. "Well, it's good to know something can." He gathered her to him, held her tight against his chest. A strong finger tilted her chin so she had to look at him. "You scared me," he told her. "I thought you'd be at home, cuddled up on the couch, but no, you went by yourself to a game downtown. And not only did Seth whatever-his-name is show up, but he followed you afterward." He cupped her face in his hands, stared into her eyes. "Do you realize how lucky you were? You could be in the hospital right now, if you'd been in an accident because you ran one too many lights, or rolled your truck trying to lose him. Don't you understand? Making that team is not worth putting your life at risk, Chris. Who the hell knows what this guy is after, so until he's caught you're putting your life in danger every time you go out alone. Do you get that? Promise me you won't do anything so stupid again."

Tears of frustration welled. He could never understand what the team meant to her, how hard she'd worked to get this far. But it wasn't just that. She wanted her freedom, wanted to live her life like any other person. It wasn't her fault some deranged maniac had fixated on her. She would have defended herself to him but the worry on his face took the fight out of her. "I'm sorry," she said. "I didn't mean to scare you. I'll be more careful from now on." Seeing how much he cared about her formed an even bigger lump in her throat.

He let out a deep breath and pulled away. "I called the boys and they checked out the license plate. The pickup's stolen, and they're looking for it right now."

"I guess I can't go home then?"

"Not on your life, darlin'." Absolute steel rang in his voice.

She forced down the spurt of panic at the prospect of being banned from her home. Her life was being stripped away from her; first softball, now her house. What would be next? She hated Seth whatever-his-name-was for it. "Okay," She dug way down to stay calm. No point blasting Rayne for her predicament. It wasn't his fault, and it wouldn't solve anything. "So what now?"

"You could stay at my place."

Oh yeah, like she would move in with him and make it that much harder to keep her feelings to herself. She arched a brow at him.

"Oh, come on," he snapped. "I'm not expecting anything from you in return, so don't look at me like that."

"Like what?" she demanded. She'd be an idiot to put herself through that kind of torture. Live in his space, seeing him day in and day out and be nothing more than friends.

He pinched the bridge of his nose like he had a killer headache, then glared at her. "That's it. If you don't have the sense to go somewhere safe, I'll damn well drag you there over my shoulder."

"Maybe I could go and stay with Michael, but I'd rather not leave town entirely. Besides, this creep could follow me anywhere, so how does it matter where I am?"

"At least if you're not alone, he can't hurt you, can he?" His voice rose. "If you won't stay with me, pack your stuff and get over to Drew and Teryl's. This is not something you can handle on your own anymore, Chris, do you understand me?"

She did, and she didn't like it one bit. She hated the fact that some creep could turn her life upside down and scare her to the point where she actually had to leave her own home to find some security. "I don't know if staying with them is such a good idea. I'd feel awful if I put them at risk."

"And is that as important as keeping you from ending up in the hospital? God, are you even listening to yourself? If Teryl could hear you right now she'd kick your ass."

Yikes, he was really mad. Even his drawl had disappeared. This was no laid-back Southern boy. His eyes were like twin lasers burning holes through her. "Okay, fine. I'll call and see if I can move in with them for a while." She could practice her invisibility skills.

"You do that. I want this stopped before it starts, Chris. We have body armor and guns. You don't."

"Yes, but I've got—"

"Jake and your lucky bat, yes I know."

"Well, thanks for the cheery pep talk."

"Hey, I'm just trying to keep you safe." He was still ticked at her, but at least he wasn't yelling anymore. "I'm worried about you."

Under different circumstances his words might have made her feel all warm and fuzzy. "I'll need to go home to pack some things and pick up Jake."

"We can stop by there right now. I'll follow you."

She didn't dare argue, and felt much safer seeing his license plate in her rearview mirror all the way home.

On the way into her house she gathered up her mail, leafing through it as they followed Jake into the kitchen. Between her bills and the newspaper was a small envelope, her uniform number on the front. Her stomach dropped.

"Rayne…"

"What?" He came over immediately.

Immobilized, her brain refusing to acknowledge her fears, she pushed aside the dread and opened it.

Do you like nursery rhymes? This one's my favorite: Run, run, as fast as you can Do you remember how it ends, sweet Christa?

Her vision blurred, icy panic skidding through her. Oh, she knew how it ended.

You can't catch me, I'm the gingerbread man.

CHAPTER 7

A cop. Her boyfriend was a fucking *cop*.

The irony of it ate at his gut like acid. Yesterday he'd hacked into the Motor Vehicles database and looked up the boyfriend's license plate. More background checking revealed that the man Christa had chosen worked on some kind of SWAT team.

How could he despise her and worship her at the same time?

Earlier today he'd visited his esthetician. He'd admired the sway of her hips as she sauntered ahead of him in her little black sandals. Around twenty, with curly blonde hair and almond-shaped brown eyes, she had an innocent air about her, but he knew better than to believe it was anything more than an act. Eyeing her from behind his dark glasses in the dimly lit treatment room, he pulled off first his shirt, then his pants, his pulse rate increasing.

"So we're doing your chest, arms and legs today?"

He climbed onto the table and lay face down. Part of the planning was making sure you had good explanations ready. "Yes. I'm a competitive swimmer, and I've got an important meet this weekend."

She made a murmur and wiped down his legs, sprinkled talcum powder and applied the first sweeps of hot wax over his skin. He sighed at the warmth of it, anticipated her pressing the adhesive strip down, yanking it upward.

He embraced the stinging. It centered him.

Rip...rip...rip...

He was no stranger to pain, had learned how to control the rage it triggered. He'd made a point to learn from his mistakes, studying the system from within, learning early never to trust cops. Of course he'd already learned that lesson at home.

He exhaled deeply as the hatred rose in a red haze, threatening to choke him. Whenever the memories surfaced he locked them in a vault in the back of his mind. His temper was harder to tame, despite his efforts to curb it. It was all his mother's fault. Her pathetic excuses, always turning a blind eye when he stumbled downstairs covered in bloody welts, seeking protection and comfort from the woman who should have rearranged the universe to keep him safe. At eleven, Seth had been no match for Henry's meaty fists.

When he'd run away and gone to the police for help, they'd done nothing. None of Henry's DUI charges seemed to make it to court, and his mother's allegations of domestic abuse by her second husband were never investigated. The cops had closed rank around their fellow officer, leaving Seth and his mother to suffer their private hell. The abused adolescent boy he'd been had learned that women were spineless, deceitful creatures and the so-called upholders of the law were deserving of nothing but his contempt.

"Okay, sir, you can turn over now."

Seth rolled onto his back, considered the pretty young woman applying warm wax over his thighs. Her eyes darted away from his growing erection, porcelain cheeks pinking. Charming, that she would blush over something as simple as basic physiology. He pondered his options. She didn't fit with his others, so nothing could link her with the rest. The idea interested him. He still had some time before Christa.

Christa. The thought of her regenerated his bad mood.

Tomorrow he had one more delivery to make. Afterward he'd go home and shave his head and remaining body hair, minimizing the risk of leaving DNA evidence. His fingerprints were on file somewhere from when he'd been hauled in for questioning a couple years ago, and unless the cops were totally incompetent they had to have at least one other set of his prints by now. But even if they put all the clues together, they still had to catch him. He was continually surprised they hadn't figured it out yet, but it wouldn't do to make it too easy for them. So close to his goal, he wouldn't let anything jeopardize his success.

Christa would pay for her betrayal.

****

The morning after moving into Teryl and Drew's, Christa was knee deep in a hole she'd dug in their garden. Since Rayne had said she wasn't allowed to go anywhere on her own, not even to work if she could avoid it, she had delegated the most important jobs to her two part-time employees and prayed the cops would pull her stalker in soon. She couldn't afford to turn away any landscaping contracts and besides, she was bored. She figured the least she could do was be helpful while she was staying at her friend's place.

Except that being helpful was going to herniate a disc in her lower back, she feared, wrenching at a stubborn stump. It was only little as far as stumps went, but it had taken her nearly all morning to dig around the base.

"All right you little bugger," she muttered, and positioned herself for another go. Planting her scarred boots squarely beside the hole, she gave the whole works a mighty heave backward, straining every muscle in her back and shoulders until the last taproot gave with a pop, sending her sprawling flat on her back.

She lay there a moment, taking inventory of each sore muscle and ligament, then loaded the stump into her wheelbarrow and finished smoothing the new topsoil. At least her job kept her in great shape, sparing her from working out at a gym except during the winter. It allowed her the flexibility to shuffle her jobs around her softball schedule. And it gave her contacts for once her landscape design business was up and running, something she could do from home while raising a family. She frowned. Assuming she could find a husband, that is.

Inside she hopped into a cool shower, letting the water soothe her aches and wash the dirt from her hair and face. She toweled off and drew her hair into a ponytail, pulling on a breezy top and shorts before heading down to the kitchen for a cold drink. Teryl was sitting on the couch in the family room.

"I just finished hauling out that stump for you, so Rayne and Drew can start on the new deck."

Teryl barely turned her head. "Yeah, thanks."

Christa frowned. "What's up?"

"Nothing. I'm fine." Her voice was about as animated as a stick man.

Oookay, Miss Moody Pants. Maybe something to eat would cheer her up. Christa went to the fridge and dug out some veggies, chopped them and served them with dip. "I've never seen you like this before. Not like you at all."

Teryl chewed on a carrot. "Yeah, well, I've felt better."

Actually, she didn't look so good. She'd lost weight, and the shadows under her eyes made her seem even paler under the dusting of freckles scattered across her nose and cheeks. "You'll get sick if you don't start taking better care of yourself."

"Too late. I've been puking my guts out all day yesterday and most of this morning."

Christa placed a hand on her forehead. Cool and clammy. "You should have said something. I could have brought you some ginger ale or something."

Teryl gazed up at her with bloodshot eyes. "Want to make it up to me by bundling me up and fussing over me?"

Fussing was Christa's specialty. "Sure, honey. You get comfy and I'll bring you some tea. Do you have peppermint tea? It'll help settle your stomach. And I'll try and find you some crackers." She bustled around the kitchen while Teryl ensconced herself deeper into the sofa. "Okay, princess. Start with these crackers, and if they stay down I'll make you some Jell-o."

"It won't stay down."

"Oh, come on. Just one bite." She waved a cracker in front of Teryl's nose. "Open up the tunnel," she sang, as if feeding a fussy toddler.

Teryl's face crumpled and she burst into noisy tears.

"Whoa, hon—I'm sorry. Forget the cracker." She patted her friend's shoulder.

"I'm p-pregnant," Teryl wailed, burying her face in her hands.

"What? Are you sure?"

Teryl nodded, tears dripping off her chin and onto

the throw she'd bundled around her curled up legs. "I peed on the stick yesterday. It turned blue."

"But honey, that's amazing!" Christa threw her arms in the air. "You're going to have a baby!"

Teryl gave her a watery smile, wiped her face. "I am."

"How far along are you?"

"About six weeks, I think. So it can't be the night of your birthday party. That's the only other time we've...done it."

She pulled away, mopped up some of Teryl's tears with her sleeve. "Does Drew know?"

Teryl fished a wad of Kleenex from the arm of her sweatshirt and wiped her nose. "Yeah. I told him last night."

"And?"

"He...he said he was happy."

Christa raised her eyebrows. "So help me out here. You're pregnant and your husband is happy about it, but you're crying."

Teryl shrugged, as if she didn't understand it herself. "I know. I should be happy, but I feel so sad." She cried some more into her handful of tissues. "What's wrong with m-me?"

Christa had to bite the inside of her lip to keep from smiling. Her friend had always been more emotional than most, but this was over the top, even for her. "Sweetie, I bet it's your hormones."

"Hormones," she repeated, as if testing the word. "You mean, you th-think this is normal?"

"Of course. You just found out you're going to be a mother, and you're not feeling well, and you're a little scared, maybe a little fragile, and you miss your mom, right?" Teryl's mother had passed away from cancer a couple years back, and the fact that she wouldn't be around to meet her grandchild had to be weighing on her friend's mind.

Teryl's pretty face scrunched up as fresh tears began. "Yeah, I wish my mom knew."

"She knows, honey, I know she does." Christa put an arm around her quaking shoulders. "And you know what else? You'll be an amazing mother, and this is the luckiest baby in the whole world."

"Really?"

"Of course. You guys are going to be awesome parents. I think you're exhausted and you need a nice long nap."

"Yeah. You're right." She allowed Christa to help her up and settle her in the master bedroom.

"Congratulations, mommy," she whispered, bringing a smile of wonder to her friend's face. "Now get some sleep."

"Okay." Teryl smoothed her hand over her flat abdomen in an instinctively maternal gesture. "Sorry I had a meltdown back there."

"It'll be like when we used to travel for ball: What happens on the road stays on the road. Drew won't ever know."

"Thanks, babe. Love you."

Christa winked. "Love you too." She shut the door behind her.

So Teryl was going to be a mother. Who would have guessed Teryl would have been first to have a baby? Christa shoved the pang of envy away. She wasn't anywhere near ready to start a family. Having kids required finding a man to have them with, and for her that meant marriage. Since she wasn't even dating anyone, that was sometime off in the misty future. Plus, her ball career only had a few good years left. She'd have plenty of time afterward to settle down and have children. She couldn't wait to read them bedtime stories and bake cookies with them, covered in flour trying to help mix the batter. She allowed herself a wistful sigh to ease the ache in her chest, and headed back to the kitchen.

In the middle of cleaning up Rayne called her cell phone.

"Hi kiddo. We're kinda busy here but I wanted to let you know they found the blue pickup parked at an apartment complex downtown."

Hope spurted inside her. "Did they get him?"

"Nope. Pickup was stripped clean. The good news is one of the forensics guys thinks he might have a partial print. I've asked Nate to rush putting it through the database. He'll let us know if anything shows up."

She withheld a strangled sound of frustration. Yet

again her mystery fan had managed to stay one step ahead of the police. "So what's next? Do they have a clue if his name really is Seth, or where he lives?"

"They're still working on it, and once Nate checks it out we'll know more. Even with me pulling in favors these things can take time, so you still need to be careful."

She rubbed her hand across her forehead. Not only could she not go home, but her softball career was on ice for a while longer. Nice timing, considering the final cuts would take place any time now.

"Have you called the cops about that note you found last night?" he asked.

"First thing this morning. I spoke to the officer in charge of my file just like you told me to."

"Good. I gotta fly now but I'll keep you posted if anything new develops."

She thanked him and hung up, wishing he could be there. The way she saw it she had two choices, either scream in frustration or have a private pity party.

Since it required the consumption of chocolate, the pity party won. What the hell. What was a pound or two of chocolate going to hurt at this point? She didn't have anyone to impress with her body anyhow. No man, not even the national team coaching staff. With a sigh, she went to the pantry and fished out a half-empty bag of chocolate chips, then sat down to polish it off.

****

He sat on a bench along Marine Drive in White Rock, enjoying the warm weather and the young women flitting in and out of the boutiques. Couples lunched on restaurant patios in the sunshine while mothers pushed toddlers in strollers, the older ones toting bags filled with shovels and pails for building sandcastles on the beach beyond the railroad tracks. The air smelled of deep-fried fish and chips and pungent malt vinegar. Bursts of petunias, pansies and nasturtiums spilled from window boxes and pots in riots of orange, purple and yellow. Christa would love them. He was as familiar with her routine as she was, and knew she'd be by later that afternoon to bring the old lady her groceries. She'd unpack them for her, then tend her balcony garden before sitting in the wicker chairs for tea and cookies.

Such a charming picture they made, he mused, touched by Christa's loyalty. At first he'd assumed she was visiting her grandmother, but when he'd checked he'd learned she had no surviving grandparents. It wasn't often you came across someone as caring as she was to the old lady. Yet another quality he admired in her.

He hummed a tune to himself, twirling the long-stemmed red rose between his fingers, waiting for the old lady to return from her aqua class at the local pool. She always stepped off the Handy Dart bus at exactly the same time.

On the bench beside him a mother handed her little daughter an ice cream cone, instructing her not to move until she came back, then left her there. So like something his own mother would have done, and he fought his rising anger. Didn't she realize there were perverts out there who would love nothing better than to get their hands on that sweet little girl?

When she licked her ice cream the scoop toppled to the ground and she bit her lip, fighting back tears, searching for her absent mother. Unable to find her, the girl hurried to the ice cream counter to grab some paper napkins, then cleaned up the mess. She tossed it into the garbage can and sat back down on the bench to await her mother's return, pink Crocs-clad feet swinging back and forth, her adorable face a study in misery. He couldn't stand it. He went and bought her another one.

"Thank you," she said, smiling tremulously up at him with big brown eyes. Such pretty manners. Her mother didn't deserve such a precious child.

He mussed her hair and returned to his seat, keeping a careful eye on her until her neglectful mother came back to herd her away. The girl waved at him, shyly, and he waved back.

He began whistling, pondering the card in his pocket, relishing his own wit, the irony. He prided himself on his skills. Being organized not only made him feel centered, it was the only way to keep a step ahead of the cops. Control was equally important to him, but it was hard won.

Clinically, his personality had obsessive-compulsive tendencies, and he was borderline schizophrenic. He understood the ramifications of the diagnoses, knew the risks they posed. Despite these limitations, he was smart. His IQ was close to genius level. That, and his belief in fate, had to be why he was still free.

How could they not know about him yet? Stupid cops were always a step or two behind him. A step or two was all he needed in this game. Strange, how things seemed to fall into place for him.

The bus pulled up at the old lady's building and she hobbled down the steps with the help of her cane. The poor dear looked especially stiff today. Anticipation bubbled through his veins.

He waited until she was halfway to the front door, then approached her, his sunglasses shielding his eyes. "Good afternoon," he said in a friendly voice, and she turned.

"Good afternoon," she replied with a regal nod.

"I was hoping you could do me a small favor," he said. She cocked an eyebrow and he poured on the charm. "I was walking past recently and happened to see you sitting on your deck with a young lady, and—" he placed a hand over his heart, "since then I haven't been able to get her out of my head."

Her white eyebrows climbed higher. "Is that a fact?"

"So I wondered if you might be willing to give her this for me the next time you see her." He held out the rose and the card.

The ancient face beamed. "How charming. I'll make sure she gets it."

"Thank you so much." He winked at her, and she shuffled past him to the door. "Let me get that for you. It's the least I can do."

She chuckled as she entered the building. "I think my young friend is in big trouble if she ever meets you."

Lady, you have no idea.

****

When Christa arrived around four Margaret Boone was leaning over her balcony railing, smiling down at her. She was glad she hadn't canceled their get-together, even though she'd had to ask one of her employees to drive her into town and wait until she was inside. Besides, plenty of people were enjoying an early supper in the restaurants fringing the beach, so she figured she was safe enough.

"Hi, Mrs. Boone," she called up, hefting two armfuls of grocery bags and some gardening tools. "How are you?"

"Fine dear, just fine. Beautiful day, isn't it?"

"I'll be right up, okay? I got you some local strawberries, they looked really good."

"That's wonderful, we can have some with our cookies."

As she entered the apartment complex she waved to her employee, signaling she was okay. He'd come back to pick her up her when she called him. At the third-floor condo Margaret was waiting in the open doorway and Christa bent to peck a kiss on her friend's papery cheek. Doing some light chores and having tea with the lady who'd given her a ridiculous steal on her dream home didn't seem like much of a burden. She'd insisted on repaying her any way she could, knowing the few things she helped out with could never compensate for the money she'd refused to take when she'd sold Christa her beloved house.

She set the bags on the kitchen counter and started putting everything away while Margaret boiled the kettle. While the tea brewed Christa went outside to prune the wisteria tendrils winding their way onto the rooftop, deadheaded some pansies and gave the roses a spray with fungicide, noting with satisfaction all the buds about to burst open. Their cream and strawberry and peach petals would bloom throughout the summer, their spicy-sweet fragrance carrying on the breeze blown in off the water. Along with the sweet alyssum and cherry-pie scented heliotrope stuffed into the planters, it would smell like heaven up here for the next couple of months.

"Here we are," Margaret announced, placing the china teapot and cups onto the wicker table.

Christa tucked her gardening gloves into her pocket and sank into one of the chairs, admiring the view of the bay. With the tide out almost to the end of the pier, children were busy digging in the sand and splashing through the sun-warmed tidal pools. The sky glowed sapphire blue, puffy white clouds drifting across it. A cool breeze wafted off the water, bringing the saltiness of drying seaweed to mingle with the perfumed flowers. "I always look forward to this," she told her hostess, sipping on her tea, savoring the comforting notes of bergamot. They always drank Earl Grey. "It makes my whole week."

"Lovely of you to say so." She set her own cup into its saucer with a delicate clink and leaned forward. "I have some news for you," she said, eyes sparkling.

"Oh?" Maggie always had juicy gossip to share.

"A handsome young man stopped me on the street today—"

"You got hit on by a younger man?" she teased, mouth open and eyes wide. "Way to go, Maggie!"

Margaret snorted and slapped her leg. "Don't be fresh. Anyway, he said he'd seen us up here one day and had been thinking about you ever since."

Really? Someone thought she was unforgettable? Maybe her luck with men was finally going to change for the better. Or maybe...

"He asked me to give you this." From beneath the table Margaret retrieved a rose and a small envelope.

Christa stared at the piece of paper with the number nineteen on it, at the blood-red flower. Just like the dozen that had been delivered to her house a few days ago. *Not again.* The tea turned bitter and acidic in her stomach. Heart careening in her chest, she scanned the streets, the parking lots, the esplanade, the beach. He was nowhere to be seen, but that didn't mean he wasn't watching her right that second. "What did he look like?"

Margaret pursed her lips. "Well, he was a little taller than you, light brown hair I think, though he was wearing a ball cap. Why?"

Christa set the rose on the table, feeling cold all over. Then in a burst she picked it up, tore off the bloom and tossed the pieces over the balcony. Hopefully he saw her do it, the deranged bastard.

She stared at the note, wishing she didn't have to open it but she had to know what kind of cryptic message he'd left her this time, then report it to the police. Her eyes skipped over the spidery handwriting.

She recognized the song lyrics from *Every Breath You Take,* and the words chilled her blood. Wherever she went, whatever she did, he'd be watching her.

CHAPTER 8

You've got to be freaking kidding me, she thought for the hundredth time as she slid out of her employee's truck at Drew and Teryl's place. What was she supposed to do now? Not go anywhere at all, become a hermit? She should have known better than to think she could get away with visiting a friend in town like any normal person. All the way home she'd been peering over her shoulder, searching for his face, a vehicle sticking too close. This was driving her nuts.

She went into the kitchen where Teryl was tossing a salad for their barbecue dinner while the guys worked on the deck. Beside her stood Rayne, looking like he'd come straight out of a Levi's commercial, naked from the waist up with all those beautiful, rippling muscles exposed, his jeans hugging powerful thighs, a tool belt strapped around his lean hips. Any other time the sight would have made her mind go blank, and as it was the breath caught in her lungs. With effort she wrenched her gaze up to his face.

"Hi, kiddo." His smile was full of relief. "I guess I should give you a lecture for sneaking out while Teryl was sleeping, but since you're back safe—"

"He left me another rose. And a note."

"What?"

She tried not to wince at the anger in his voice. "He gave them to Maggie earlier, made it out to be some kind of romantic gesture."

Teryl made a sympathetic sound and moved to wrap her arms around Christa, who fought tears at the gesture of comfort.

"I just want him to leave me alone." She let her head drop onto Teryl's shoulder. "I want my goddamn *life* back."

"Where are they then?" Rayne asked. "The rose and

the note?"

"I threw the rose away and took the note to the police station."

"Let's hope he left some good prints on it. What did it say?"

She told him and his face darkened. "Great. A song by The Police now. Son of a bitch sure gets off on messing with your head."

She turned to Teryl. "Sorry, but it looks like you'll have to put up with me for—"

"Don't you dare apologize or I'll have to smack you. We love having you here, and at least we know you're safe while you're with us. Now, I want you to go outside and sit down with a glass of wine." She gave her a nudge toward the patio.

Christa dropped into a lounge chair. How long was this going to go on? She'd been positive the guy would have lost interest in her by now. When Rayne came and sat beside her she looked up at him in bewilderment.

"Why is it so hard to catch him? If he can track me down all over the place, why can't the police find him?"

"He's been real lucky lately, sweetheart, that's all. They'll collar him."

He sounded so sure, which helped ease her anxiety. "I keep remembering all the things Nate said to me."

"Don't," he said, reaching out to touch her arm. "You'll make yourself crazy that way. Just be more careful and don't let him get to you."

Don't let him get to her? That was a double entendre, and while she was certainly doing her best to steer clear of him, his ominous notes were not something she was capable of ignoring. "While I was at the police station they had me work with a sketch artist."

"Good. To be honest, I'm surprised they didn't do that sooner."

"Why me?" she demanded. She worked hard, paid her bills and taxes on time, donated to charity every Christmas. She was kind to animals, got along with everyone. How could this be happening? "I'm a good person, Rayne. Why would someone want to scare me like this?"

"I don't have a clue, except you're single and you're

hot. Maybe you intimidate him and he figures he couldn't get your attention any other way."

She glared at him. "I'm not hot." If she was, why had she been single the past five years?

"Yeah darlin', you are."

Her cheeks heated. "And why would he be intimidated by me? I haven't been out with a guy in so long it..." She shook her head. "I mean how pathetic is that? The one guy who wants me turns out to be a sicko."

His eyes glowed at her. "Maybe you're too busy to notice the ones that aren't sickos."

She reached for her wine glass. This was way too embarrassing, sitting here discussing her non-existent love life with the most gorgeous man she'd ever met. Could he tell how she felt about him? It was so hard for her to keep it hidden. Maybe it was obvious from her expression whenever he was around. Lord knew he had had enough experience with women to know when one was attracted to him. Other than their almost-kiss that night on her staircase, he'd never tried to make a move on her so she assumed he wasn't interested in her that way, which made it even more important to keep her wishful thinking to herself.

"You okay, babe?" Teryl asked when she came to set the table.

Christa forced a smile. "Yeah, I'm fine. Rayne's taking care of me, as usual. How about you? Feeling any better?"

"Much. Thanks to you."

"So let's put this whole mess away for a while and have a nice dinner."

She was filling the last water glass when Rayne came up behind her and wrapped his arms around her waist. She nearly dropped the pitcher but he tightened his hold until her back pressed against his chest. Did he have his shirt on? Please, God, let him have his shirt on. If he didn't she'd pass out right here on the patio. "You're a sweetheart, you know that?" he said against her temple, raising goose bumps. He must have guessed she'd shoved everything aside for Teryl's benefit.

Christa gazed up at him, her heart knocking against her ribs, acutely aware of every inch of contact between them, even though he was indeed wearing his t-shirt. "Thanks," she said, patting one of his iron-hard forearms locked around her clenched midriff, applauding herself for seeming unaffected by the feel of him. "You are, too."

"So you've finally noticed that, huh?"

"What, that you're a sweetheart? I've known that for a long time, but don't worry, I won't tell anyone. I'd hate to ruin your macho reputation." She returned to filling the glass, pretending she didn't want to turn and fling her arms around him. "You've been really good to me, and I appreciate it."

"My pleasure, kiddo." The honeyed drawl made her belly flip.

"So, you hungry? Let me go get those steaks on the barbecue." She needed some space between them, before she did something stupid like grab hold of him and never let go.

"That's a grill, not a barbecue. Barbecue's what us Southerners do back home—wood chips, dry rubs, cooking long and slow. See the difference?" Humor glinted in his hazel eyes. "Just so you know."

"I'll never confuse the two again," she promised.

He squeezed her once more before letting her go. "You sit tight. I'll do them."

Grateful for the distance he'd given her, she drew her first deep breath since he'd wrapped his arms around her.

When Drew arrived home they sat out on the sunny deck amidst Teryl's flowers, feasting on salad and roasted potatoes and tender steak. "So, how's the dinner settling, Mommy?" Christa asked as they neared the end of the first course.

"Mommy?" Rayne glanced from Teryl to Drew and back again.

"Yep." Teryl's face lit up in a smile as she clapped her husband on the back. "He's a potent guy. Did it in one shot."

Drew's cheeks went ruddy. "What can I say? I'm good."

"Congrats, y'all," Rayne got to his feet and shook hands with his buddy before giving Teryl a hug. "So when's Junior supposed to arrive?"

"Mid-January, give or take," Teryl gushed. She

popped another bite of steak into her mouth. "If I live through this pregnancy, that is. I've got morning sickness, which is the most ridiculous term I've ever heard since I puke all day and all night. Some male doctor must have come up with that one. I can't wait to find out what other euphemisms the medical community has..." Her eyes fastened on something in the distance. "Uh-oh. Chris, you'd better get Jake."

Christa glanced beyond the unfinished deck where a fat raccoon sat on the lawn, scoping the remains of their dinner with his beady black eyes. "Oh crap," she breathed and hurried to intercept her dog before the hunt could begin. She found him frozen behind the French doors, staring out at the newcomer with a 'go-ahead-make-my-day' expression. She grabbed him by the collar and hauled him away to the garage. "Sorry boy," she said, appeasing him with a scratch beneath the chin but he turned his head away. "I'll let you out after dinner, okay?" He snorted and went to lie in the corner, his brown eyes accusing.

"I gotta go," Rayne announced when she returned to the table. "We've got a sting planned for oh-four-hundred."

"Why didn't you tell us?" Teryl demanded as he pushed back and stood. "You should have gone home hours ago to get some sleep."

"Nah. The company was too good." He winked at Christa, said his goodbyes to the others. "Will you come lock the door behind me?" he asked her.

"Sure." Grabbing his jacket from one of the deck chairs, she followed him through the house to the foyer where he bent to put on his shoes. "I hope you won't be too tired in the morning." It worried her he might be groggy enough to dull his reflexes.

Moonlight filtering through the door's side panels illuminated his face as he straightened. "Don't worry about me, darlin'. I'm going straight home to sleep so I can spend every possible second dreaming about you." He shrugged into his jacket.

A smothered giggle escaped her. The guy was unbelievable. "You just can't help yourself, can you?"

Something flickered in his eyes. "Nope. Not where

you're concerned."

The silly smile on her face disappeared. Her mouth went dry as tension crackled in the air between them. Before she could say anything, Rayne slid his hands around her back and brought her close, staring down into her wide eyes as her hands flattened against his shoulders. She swallowed, heart slamming against her ribs.

This didn't feel like 'just friends' anymore.

Long fingers came up to brush the hair away from her hot cheek, trailed down to the curve of her jaw, leaving trails of fire in their wake. She swallowed again, waiting breathlessly to find out what he would do next.

His gaze locked with hers, then dropped to her mouth. He bent his head and she held her breath, eyes drifting closed as she tilted her face up, her heart knocking against her sternum.

"Christa, you there?" Teryl's voice floated around the corner.

Christa leapt back guiltily. "Yeah?" she blurted.

Teryl's head appeared around the corner. "You're dessert's ready. Better come eat it before it melts." She looked from her to Rayne with a tight smile. "See you later, Hutch."

Christa darted a glance at him. Had Teryl just dismissed him? Too flustered to say anything, she stood there staring at him in mortified silence. Compounding her uncertainty, he dropped a kiss on her forehead and stepped back. She almost whimpered in protest. A rueful smile curved his lips. "Night," he said. "Don't forget to lock up behind me."

When the door shut behind him, Teryl patted her arm. "Come on. Ice cream's melting."

Ice cream? Christa stared after her. What the hell did she care about ice cream? She'd just been cheated out of the kiss she'd been fantasizing about for two whole years. Standing there in the empty foyer, Christa wanted to scream with frustration.

It took a few minutes before she felt steady enough to go back to the patio to join the others. Teryl didn't say a word to her about the incident, giving a big-eyed "what?" look when she caught Christa's glare. The innocent expression didn't fool her for a second. No way had Teryl interrupted them by accident.

Man, her day couldn't get much worse, could it?

Without Rayne there to distract her, that nagging sense of unease came back, lingered all through dessert and the clean up. She felt the loss of his presence as a physical ache. Teryl and Drew were both in the house with her, so she was perfectly safe. Still, she couldn't get the ominous lyrics from the note out of her head.

Did he know she was staying here? Probably, which put Drew, Teryl and the baby in danger. Maybe she should leave. Heart pounding, she peered out the guestroom window, straining to see anything in the shifting light as tattered clouds obscured the moon. The cul-de-sac was empty, trees swaying their leafy branches, casting patterns of shadow and light on the lawn. *You're fine.* She forced her thoughts back to Rayne, the security of his arms around her. *We'll all be fine.*

****

Nate let himself into his office and flipped on the lights. Rayne had asked him to run the partial print taken off the pickup through the system himself, to speed the process. Laughable, considering that this was the first opportunity he'd had all day. He swallowed the last dregs of coffee in his cold mug and grimaced at the bitterness before logging on to his computer and entering the password that accessed the main database, fighting back a yawn. He'd put in over forty hours this week, and the clock was still ticking. He closed his eyes while the machine whirred, fantasizing about a nice thick, medium rare steak. Maybe he'd take his wife out for dinner tomorrow.

He glanced down at the identity sketch in his hand, hating the guy on principle, whoever the hell he was. Probably a certified whack job who got his kicks terrorizing vulnerable women. He sighed and rolled his head from side to side to ease the tension from his neck and shoulders.

A couple of minutes later the computer let out a beep and his eyes snapped open. He leaned forward and pulled up the sorted file, dread seeping through him as a mug shot stared back at him from the computer screen. He scanned the information, heart picking up speed, and sucked in his breath.

"Oh, Christ," he breathed, and shot out a hand to snatch the phone from its cradle.

****

Christa was folding the last of her laundry when Jake started barking outside, as if he'd cornered something. The raccoon again? "Oh, for the love of—" She stilled, hoping he would quiet down. Teryl and Drew had already gone to bed and given how lousy Teryl had been feeling, she didn't want anything to disturb them.

Jake kept on barking. She'd have to go and deal with the dog before he woke the entire neighborhood, so she grabbed a broom from the utility closet and hurried to the patio doors.

Way to go, Jake, make everyone mad so you'll have to stay in a kennel.

She unlocked the doors and stepped out onto the deck, triggering the security lights and scanning the yard. Jake was poised below a cedar tree at the rear fence, staring into the darkness beyond.

"Jake!" she whispered. "Come here." She should have known better than to expect a border collie to obey that command when he was concentrating on something else. "Jake, shhhh! You'll wake the whole neighborhood." Resigned, she set off toward him with a sigh, broom in hand.

Outside the reassuring circle of light cast by the motion sensors, Jake froze into place. What if it wasn't the raccoon? Maybe she should go get Drew, just in case.

No. She refused to disturb him and Teryl. She was probably being paranoid. She crept closer to Jake.

His hackles went up, a growl coming from his throat. Her fingers tightened around the broomstick, lifted high, but she saw no sign of the raccoon.

In the shadows something moved. The branches in the wind? No, something else. Something big. She stepped back, bumping into a tree. A roaring filled her ears, the metallic tang of fear filling her mouth.

Run.

Her mind screamed it, her flesh prickling and

94

crawling, her legs paralyzed.

Run!

The shadow moved again, materializing into a man's silhouette.

He'd shaved his head completely.

The scream clawed its way up her throat as she pivoted to flee, the kitchen light a beacon of safety. A hand clamped over her mouth after only a thread of sound could escape, snapping her head back, his body bearing her down to the dew-wet grass. Jake yelped and lunged at her attacker, who caught him in the stomach with a kick. The dog gave a shriek and disappeared under a bush.

She fought with every ounce of strength, swinging her elbow at his face. Before she could do any damage he caught her wrist and twisted it halfway up her back, his other hand stifling her screams. She flailed underneath him, trying to land a blow with her knee, her foot, but he was too fast. And strong. Too strong. His breath sawed in and out as he flipped her face down, tugging her arms behind her.

He slapped something wide and sticky over her mouth, and she wrenched her head back and forth trying and dislodge it. Duct tape. She could hardly breathe, sucking in gulps of air through her nose. Panic gave way to hysteria, making the world tilt as her vision blurred. Her voice was hoarse from the bloodcurdling cries tearing out of her, only to be muffled by her gag. After the rip of more tape being peeled off, her limbs were immobilized. Trussed and helpless, she struggled against her bonds as he dragged her through the yard and the open gate into the alley, muscling her toward a vehicle.

Don't let him get me in the car, she prayed, twisting and thrashing, rolling her eyes back toward the house. No one had heard her scream. No one would be coming to help.

Please God, don't let him get me into that car.

Nate's words swam through her terror-numbed brain. If he got her into that vehicle, she was as good as dead. *Do whatever you can to disable him long enough to get away*. Rayne's words.

With all her strength she threw her head back, and he grunted as her skull smashed into his chin. His grip loosened and even as she fell she rolled away. Cruel fingers wrenched her backward, digging with bruising force into her skin.

"Bitch," he snarled, jerking the car door wide and yanking her upright before throwing her straining body onto the floor beneath the back seat. He pinned her to the stale carpet with his weight and tied her with a rope to the front seat, then locked the rear doors.

Choking on her fear, she struggled to lift her legs high enough to kick at the windows with her bound feet, hoping someone would hear or see her.

"Go ahead and kick," he taunted, gunning the engine. The gag distorted her gurgle into a muffled moan. *I don't want to die...I don't want to die...*

Streetlights cast alternating light and shadow over the car's interior as he drove. Where were they going? Would he stab her? Strangle her? Rape her? Tears streamed down her face, the sobs making it even harder to breathe.

"You threw away my rose."

The chill in his voice sent another shockwave through her. *Oh, God.* She'd wanted him to see her ripping his flower apart and tossing it over the balcony, but she'd never dreamed she would provoke him to this extent.

"I know you've been talking to the cops," he continued, cocking his head as they sped onward. "Don't you think that was a little over the top? I was only being friendly. I'm your biggest fan. Not that it matters now." He stopped at a traffic light.

She raised her chin and met his gray stare in the rearview mirror. Her breath was coming in rasps and her body wouldn't stop shaking. Her heart slammed so hard against her ribs she was sure he could hear it. Where was he taking her? The minutes ticked by before he slowed and made another turn before stopping and killing the engine.

"Here we are. Home sweet home."

Her house? He would carry out whatever he had planned inside her own home, where no one would hear her scream.

Unless she could trigger her security system. A spurt

of hope surged within her.

She jerked away from his hands hauling her from the vehicle, straining from his touch as he manhandled her through the back gate, closing it behind them, and dropped her by the door. Lying on her side, she lifted her head as he jimmied the locks, reached up and punched in her alarm code. How had he known her password?

"You really should invest in a better security system. This one isn't very safe."

He yanked her to her feet and shoved her ahead of him, then secured the door behind them. She yelped when he ripped the tape off her mouth, wincing at the sting. He shoved her facedown on the floor and fumbled with the tape on her wrists and ankles. Why bother? Was he playing with her? Making her think she had a chance at escaping? Icy panic crept up her spine.

"Scream all you like," he whispered. "There's no one to hear you."

Nausea roiled in her stomach. She craned her neck around for a weapon, trying to come up with a plan. The cordless phone was ten feet away, sitting on the kitchen counter. Maybe she could bash him in the head with it and race out the back door, then use it to call the cops.

As soon as he freed her feet she leapt up, tearing herself from his grasp. Throat clogging, she bolted for the phone. His arms wrenched her backward, and she landed a blow to his face using her elbow, producing a satisfying crunch. He howled and released her, and she grabbed her chance to make a run for the door. She was quick and agile, and if she could only get outside she could sprint to her neighbor's house.

Two steps away from freedom, he managed to snag the end of her braid, snapping back her head like a flower on a broken stem. Reeling, she hit the floor, the breath whooshing out of her as his weight crushed her into the hardwood. His hands flipped her over and she stared up at him, into those frigid gray eyes, trying with all her might to shove him off, to wrench her hands free to jab at the corners of his eyes with her fingers. As Rayne had taught her.

"I warned you." His face was white with rage, a trickle of blood leaking from one nostril.

"G-get *off* me," she mumbled.

He smiled. An evil, cruel smile she had come to know too well. "I always hoped it would come to this." He wrenched her arms above her, ignoring her cries, her crazed strength.

The blow came from nowhere, her head cracking to one side with the impact of his fist. Gasping, she lay there, trembling all over.

"I'm going to leave you with something to remember me by."

When she dared open her eyes, he was holding another length of rope. The ball of ice congealed in her stomach.

He tied the loops around her wrists, her resistance futile against his strength. Then he hauled her up by her braid, one hand manacling her as he heaved her up the stairs, panting at the effort it took him to subdue her. She managed to reach up and claw him across the face but he merely jerked on her braid and kept moving.

From the landing he pulled her writhing form into her bedroom and shoved her face down on her antique quilt. He climbed on top of her, jamming a knee into the small of her back and securing her left wrist to the brass headboard. Afraid she might pass out with terror, she fought as hard as she could to keep her other hand free. A raw, half-mad growling noise issued from deep in her throat, a primitive sound of rage and denial. He seized her right arm, squeezing the wrist and lashing it to the bedstead. She stifled a sob.

She tried to twist away, but even in her adrenaline-fuelled state, her body was weakening. He kept his knee pressed hard into her spine and leaned back to tie her kicking legs at the ankles, spreading her thighs apart.

Bile rose and she gagged, shaking so hard the bed trembled as he reached past her to set something on the nightstand. A picture of her and Rayne.

"Now your boyfriend can have a front-row seat to watch the main event."

Christa was so numb she couldn't even shake her head. "He's not—not my boyfriend."

"Don't lie to me." He wrapped his hands around her throat and squeezed, choking her until black spots swirled. "Don't you *dare* lie to me." When she went dead still he finally let go and she heaved in a breath, coughing as her airway reopened.

He moved off her so she could see him, poised there beside her. "I brought something to show you," he said, and her eyes focused on the gleaming silver of a knife. The iron taste of fear returned, filling her mouth, burning her throat as she fought against the ropes scraping and gouging her wrists. He laughed and leaned closer, his gray eyes as cruel and bright as the blade he moved toward her shrinking flesh.

Her screams echoed through the empty house.

CHAPTER 9

Patrick Flannery loved and cherished all God's creatures, to the point of transferring lost spiders out of his house into the yard where they would be safe from his wife and the spider-sucking attachment of her vacuum. He fancied he might have been St. Francis of Assisi in a former life, if it weren't for his distaste of chickens. He stared hard at the chicken coop, as a man who was facing a mortal enemy might, held his breath and went in.

He swore loudly, flapping his arms about his head as the smelly beasts stirred up a cloud of dust and foul feathers thick enough to choke him. Lord Jesus, but what did a man have to do to gather his eggs? With the one lungful of air he grabbed as many as he could and retreated into the moonlight. In his basket he saw nine dirty little eggs. Well now. Nine was plenty, wasn't it, though? Tomorrow morning he'd fry himself an omelet and make one for the missus.

"Patrick Flannery, did you find us some vittles or not?" his wife yelled out their bedroom window. She looked a picture this fine evening, standing there with her hair up in curlers and the blue robe he'd given her for Christmas wrapped around her.

Patrick brandished the basket. "'Course I did, me darlin'. Nine of the little beggars."

Her mouth formed an 'O'. "Your lungs must be gettin' bigger, don't you think so?"

"Aye, I do. Will you be wantin' an omelet with me in the mornin', then?"

She flapped a hand. "Not likely. They've too much cholesterol and fat for a woman my age. Why don't you go and see if Christa will take some?" She shut the window and disappeared from view.

Well, wouldn't you know it? Hadn't he built the damn chicken coop because she'd insisted they needed their own, fresher-than-fresh free-run eggs from happy grain-fed hens? Women! He'd almost lost his hands to those pecking, bloodthirsty creatures and for what, might he ask?

He sighed and scratched his head. He was forced to follow every fad diet that came along, even if she found it in the pages of the *Enquirer* or the *Star*. One week they could eat nothing but green things, the next only fruit. Damn woman was going to kill him someday, just see if she didn't. For an instant he thought of keeping the eggs, in case it might be that next week they were to eat nothing *but* eggs. Was it too late to go over to Christa's and give her the rest of them? Maybe *she'd* make him an omelet, right this minute.

But now that he thought about it, he hadn't seen his pretty neighbor all day. Usually he'd spot her loading up her truck with plants and spades, or hauling around a bagful of sporting gear. And this was the second night he'd not seen a light in the house. Had she maybe gone off to one of those ball tournaments she never missed? Except when she did, she usually asked him to look after Jake...now there was something. He'd not seen nor heard Jake either.

Just then headlight beams cut along her driveway, and he chided himself. Here she was after all, heading home. But no, that wasn't her vehicle. In fact, he'd never seen that car before. He hovered, fretful. If he went interfering and she thought he was a daft old coot for worrying about her, well, so be it. She'd have a fit if anything happened to her house. She was a woman living alone and he liked to look out for her.

Still grouching to himself he made his way through the hedges, getting a face full of spider web as he did so. Well, that was gratitude for you. It probably housed one of the spiders he'd rescued from the vacuum cleaner.

Pushing on, he strolled across the fresh cut lawn, saw nothing out of the ordinary. He pushed open the back gate in the picket fence, wandered through the garden and checked the rest of the property. If some dumb teenager fancied to break into the house, they'd have him to deal with. If only Jake were here, Patrick would have known for sure whether something was wrong. He had seen a program on the telly a couple nights before about animals doing things like sensing fires.

He tried the doorknob, but the back door was locked so he fished in his pocket for the spare key Christa had given him for when he came to check on things while she was away. Inside, all was dark. In the empty kitchen he set the eggs on the counter just as a faint sound came from upstairs. A squeak.

A squeak like a mattress moving. Patrick's cheeks heated and he whirled on his heel. What had he gone and walked in on? She must've found herself a new boyfriend, that was all. Not that he'd ever known her to have one, but...Lord, he'd never be able to look her in the eye again.

He was almost out the door when he heard something else. Muffled noises, like growling—he strained to hear—then a sob.

"Christa?" he called. "Are you there?"

As he moved toward the staircase someone coughed. "Hello?" Surely he wasn't hearing things?

A thud. And screams. Lots of them, fearful enough to curdle the eggs for his omelet. Heart thumping, he grabbed a knife from the butcher block and darted up the stairs, sure he was going to have a coronary. "Christa? 'Tis Patrick. What's wrong?"

He was nearly at the top when a figure shot out of her bedroom and pushed past him, sending him tumbling down the stairs, caught in a tangle of legs. In the weak moonlight filtering into the stairwell, a bald head gleamed. Sure now that he must be hallucinating, Patrick picked himself up and without bothering to check if anything was broken, dashed up to the landing.

He was about to grab her bedroom door handle when she squealed. "N-no! Don't don't come in. J-just call...the police...please."

What was he to do? Didn't he have to find out if she was all right? Without thinking better of it, he threw the door open. "Christ Jesus!" She wasn't wearing a stitch, tied facedown on her bed, blood on her face and the sheets about her body.

"Nooo!" she wailed, squirming as she tried to cover herself, but she couldn't move.

"Who the hell did this to you?" Keeping his eyes

averted he rushed to untie the cruel bonds, revulsion and helplessness almost knobbling his arthritic knees.

"Please, P-Pat. Call them."

He ran to dial 911.

****

Rayne's cell phone shrilled from the nightstand, awakening him with a start. "Hello."

"Hutch. Where are you?" Nate's voice was unusually grim.

"In bed, trying to get some sleep. Why?" His heart leapt to his throat.

Nate sighed, which was never a good sign. "Something happened—"

"Goddamn it Nate, you're freaking me out here. Just tell me already."

"It's Christa."

His whole body went rigid, as if tensing for a physical blow. "Is she all right?"

"No, she's not."

He swallowed, hard. "What—"

"Her stalker made his move, worked her over. The ambulance is transporting her to Memorial."

Oh my God. Oh, Christa, sweet God, no... "Is she— was she—" Christ, he couldn't even speak.

"She's pretty spooked, and there was some blood, but she'll pull through." He cleared his throat. "She asked for you."

She'd asked for him, and he hadn't been there. Waves of nausea rolled inside him; he focused on breathing in and out. *There was some blood...* "Did they at least catch the bastard?" His hands were actually shaking.

A moment of awful silence lingered. "Negative. Not yet. I found his prints in the system, confirmed they belonged to a Thomas Sutherland, a suspect in a homicide two years ago. He's got a sealed juvie record as well. I called to warn her, but it was too late. I'd barely hung up when I got called to the crime scene. We've issued the APB and notified the border crossings. He won't be out there for long."

"Christ, when did this happen?"

"Not long ago. I called you as soon as I got a chance.

Her neighbor came by to check on her house or something and found her. Scared the bastard off."

"So he didn't...?" A sharp pain sliced his chest. He couldn't breathe. It took a minute before he could get a grip on himself. "For Chrissakes Nate, did the bastard rape her?"

"We don't know yet. They'll check it out."

Please, not that. "You heading to the hospital?" He tugged on a pair of jeans.

"Yup. We need to get a statement from her and...well, you know the drill. But not until I'm sure she's all right."

"Okay. See you there." He cut the connection, threw on a shirt and drove like a madman, praying he'd be strong enough to hold it together when he saw her.

"Rayne!"

The raw anguish in her cry ripped through him like a lightning bolt, nearly sending him to his knees. He steadied himself before answering. "I'm here, kiddo." He put on his best game face, blotting out the sight of her lying on the examination table in a hospital gown, reeling as though someone had punched him in the gut.

Her face was black and blue, three butterfly bandages closing deep cuts around her mouth, and her left eye was swelling shut. She lifted a shaking hand toward him, bandages wrapped around both wrists. Bastard must have tied her and she'd cut herself up struggling to get loose. He wrapped his fingers around hers and bent to gather her close. "I'm here," he repeated, not knowing what else to say. He felt privileged to be able to hold her, to know she wanted him there. He pressed a kiss to the top of her head, then rested his cheek against her silky hair.

"Keep holding my hand, sweetheart," he murmured, wiping the tears from her face. "I'm not going anywhere, so squeeze my hand if you need to, all right?" He made sure he kept eye contact, sensing she needed him to focus her away from the pain. The fear and shock in her eyes tore him up inside and he had no way of lessening it.

The doctor cleared her throat. "Okay, Christa, I've got to check you inside now."

She shook her head, paling. "But I t-told you, I don't

need—"

"I'm sorry, but it's necessary in a case like this."

"Can't you at least give me a few m-minutes? Haven't I been thr-through enough?" Her voice was shrill, rising with growing hysteria.

The doctor looked up at him. "Maybe you should leave while I do the internal."

"Want me to go, kiddo?" he asked her. "I'll come back in a few minutes."

"N-no. No." Her face was chalky white. "Stay, please."

"Sure, honey." He moved closer and turned to face her fully, giving her as much privacy as possible.

The doctor gathered her equipment. "Try to relax. I'll be as gentle and as quick as I can."

She saw the speculum coming and went rigid, squeezing her eyes shut and turning her head away. Rayne's own body tensed as he stroked the hair from her face, leaning partly over her to shield her from the glare of the lighting. She sucked in a breath and he felt her struggle to hold it there.

Just when he thought he'd kill the doctor, Christa sagged and shuddered.

"Are you finished?" she asked hoarsely.

"Almost." The doc tossed the speculum in the steel basin beside her with a clang.

"Is it over?" she breathed, resting her cheek in his palm.

She sank onto the table, trembling. The doctor and nurses fussed with her some more, but she barely noticed them, she was so lost in her own shock. They gave her an injection in her hip, and her eyelids drooped. "Rayne," she cried, fighting the sedative. "Please don't go."

He cradled her head against his chest. "I won't leave you, Christa. You need to rest now, okay? Don't fight it, just let go and sleep. I'm not going anywhere."

****

Teryl perched beside her friend's bed, tracking the slow rise and fall of her chest, the hushed, even whisper of her breath. Christa looked so damned fragile lying there, all cut and bruised, torn emotionally. She glanced over at Rayne, seated at the foot of the hospital bed. His eyes were haunted, one hand buried in his dark hair. It galled her a little that Christa had wanted him there when she'd first been admitted. She could be setting herself up for a big fall. Could she survive a relationship with Rayne, especially after this?

To his credit he'd been here all night, with Christa every second, holding her hand and stroking her hair, revealing a tender side of him Teryl had never seen before. Her heart softened toward him. "You look tired. Maybe you should go home."

"I'm fine."

He didn't look fine. He looked exhausted, with heavy shadows under his eyes. "At least she's peaceful right now."

"Yeah."

"Should I take her home with me when she's discharged?" She stared at Christa's beaten face. "I'd hoped it was as safe a place as any, but he still got to her. We both assumed Jake was barking at that raccoon, and by the time Drew went down to check it out..." Her voice was fraught with guilt. Had she been awake she would never have let Christa go outside alone. "As soon as we realized she was gone I called the police and Drew went to find Jake. Said the dog had crawled halfway down the alley, trying to go after her." She wiped her damp cheeks with her hand. "The vet said he'll be okay, so if she wakes up and I'm not here make sure you tell her, because I know she'll be worried. And tell her I talked to Michael. She should probably call him herself when she wakes up, before he hops a red-eye flight."

Rayne came over and gave her a hug and she leaned into him with a sigh. She already felt miserable enough, the guilt and fatigue fueling her nausea. She'd thrown up twice since arriving at the hospital.

"It wasn't your fault. You and Drew did all you could to help keep her safe. Problem is, she's probably not safe anywhere right now. But we need to figure something out, because the doc told me she can leave here later today."

"What about your sting operation?" Teryl remembered.

"I've called in and they're handling it without me."

"So why don't you go home and get some sleep? I'll

stay as long as she needs me."

Rayne shook his head. "I told her I'd be here."

"I'm pretty sure she'll sleep awhile yet." She'd barely twitched for hours.

He grunted.

"She'll be fine with it. I'll tell her I kicked you out. She wouldn't doubt it for a second."

After a moment's hesitation, he nodded. "Okay, but call me if you need anything, and tell her I'll be back later." He moved toward the door.

"Hutch."

He stopped, glanced over his shoulder. "Yeah?"

Her lips thinned. There was so much she wanted to say to him, and she was too upset to mince words. "Please promise me you'll be careful with her."

He frowned. "Of course I will."

"That's not what—" She gave him a narrowed look. "I mean, be careful with her heart. Don't break it, okay?"

He towered over her, arms folded across his chest. "What's that supposed to mean?"

Her chin jutted outward. If he thought his size intimidated her...she was exhausted, worried, pregnant and puking, not to be messed with. "You weren't there after she broke up with Cameron the Shithead, so you wouldn't understand. It wasn't pretty, and it took her about a year to smile again. So let me ask you this, Hutch—" She fixed him with a hard look. "How does it feel to be the most important person in the universe?"

His brows rose, betraying his otherwise guarded expression. "Did she tell you that?"

"She didn't have to tell me because I can read her like a book. I'm her best friend and I'm begging you, be careful with her."

"I see. And you assume I'll hurt her because that's the kind of guy I am?"

"Come on, Hutch. You know I adore you, and I know you wouldn't hurt her on purpose. It's you hurting her by accident that scares the hell out of me." That's why she'd gone looking for Christa the night before, and she'd gotten there just in time, too. The way she saw it, preventing that kiss had staved off disaster. Well, for the moment at least.

107

Had she said too much? Christa would be horrified, but Teryl felt it was her duty to protect her when she was clearly unable to protect herself. And no matter if Christa thought she was ready for a relationship, she was way out of her depth with a man like Rayne Hutchinson.

He stared down at Christa's inert form for a moment before meeting her gaze. "I would never do anything to hurt her," he said, his voice husky.

The heat and tenderness in his eyes left her speechless, which was saying something. When he walked out, she stared at the closed door through eyes blurred with tears.

****

All that had stopped the scathing comeback on his tongue was the strain on Teryl's face. How could she think he would hurt Christa? It had been hard enough to leave her in that hospital bed, for Chrissake. As it was, he battled with his conscience all the way out of the hospital to the parking lot.

By the time he got home his hands were shaking on the steering wheel. Imagining what that bastard had done to her made fury pour through him in a crimson haze. Blood pounding in his head, he tore up to the workout room, wrapped tape around his knuckles and slammed his fist into the heavy boxing bag so hard the impact jarred all the way up to his shoulder. Then he threw himself at it as if it were Christa's attacker, swinging mindlessly, holding nothing back, and exorcising his rage with every bit of power he could muster.

Over and over his fists exploded into it until his knuckles split and bled, until he was blinded by his own sweat, until he gasped for breath. Only then did he stop, staggering back as weariness took over in the wake of the tumult that had drained out of him. Chest heaving, he bent forward at the waist and unwrapped his hands, inspecting the damage he'd inflicted. They were starting to hurt like a sonofabitch. Swearing, he headed to his condo for a shower.

A couple hours later, he parked next to Nate's vehicle in front of Christa's house, steeling himself for what he was about to see. He hadn't been able to sleep after all, despite his exhaustion. He needed to see the crime scene for himself, find out what the forensic team had uncovered. After tossing restlessly he'd called Nate, who'd told him to meet him at Christa's.

In a daze he pushed through the crowd on the porch and entered the house, feeling as if he was watching a movie. He passed through the homey kitchen and family room, the cozy décor at odds with the heinous crime carried out within the walls. At the top of the stairs he moved toward Christa's bedroom, following the murmuring voices and the click of a camera's shutter, the flashes illuminating the hallway. Nate stood at the door, waiting for him.

"You all right?"

Rayne merely nodded, forcing back the dread gathering inside.

"Forensics are almost done," Nate continued, gauging his emotional state. "No semen or pubic hair, but she did have some of his skin under her fingernails. Some of the bloodstains don't match her blood type, so we're testing for a match with his."

Well, at least she'd managed to claw the bastard. Good for her. "Are you going to let me in or not?" Enough with the bullshit already. Nate held his stare, then stepped aside.

Bracing himself, Rayne took a deep breath and entered the room, bile rising up his throat. His eyes riveted to the bed, to the four pieces of rope tied to the brass frame, coated with blood. Her blood.

He forced air into his lungs, willed his heart to slow down. He looked up at Nate with tortured eyes. "What the hell did he do to her?"

Nate gazed down at him. "You know I can't tell you that," he said sympathetically. "If you want to know what happened, you'll have to ask her."

A member of the forensics team walked past carrying a plastic evidence bag. He sucked in a sharp breath. "A knife?" he demanded, grabbing Nate. "He used a fucking *knife* on her?"

Nate pried the clenched fists from his shirt. "Rayne, calm down."

"Don't tell me to calm down—*did he use a knife on*

her?" He was ready to explode, recognized it in some distant part of his brain that was still miraculously functioning.

"She said he used it to strip her, but didn't actually cut her with it," Nate answered carefully.

Rage swamped him until he thought he'd lose his mind. "I need some air," he muttered, and hurried downstairs to the porch, sucking in oxygen, sinking onto the top step. He couldn't bear to imagine what she'd gone through.

After a while Nate's footsteps sounded behind him. "You okay?"

"Yeah." The anger and shock were wearing away, replaced by an awful helplessness that felt a whole lot worse. "I can't believe anyone would hurt her like that." He looked up at him. "Honest to God, Nate, she's a sweetheart. The nicest girl I've ever known. How in hell could someone do that to her?"

"I wish I knew." He came and sat next to him. "I need to ask you about something." He held out a framed picture. "Does this mean anything to you? It was sitting on the nightstand, right next to the bed."

Rayne took it from him, stared at it. Him and Christa at her surprise party a few days ago. He had his arm around her shoulders, and they were gazing at each other, laughing. Teryl had taken it. He'd bought her the frame for her birthday gift. And her neighbor had given her a yellow raincoat for Jake. That's what they were laughing at in the photo. She'd put it in the frame he'd given her and set it next to her bed. The implications squeezed his heart, reminding him of Teryl's warning about not hurting her.

He shrugged. "Never seen it before."

"Might be nothing. Seemed odd that it was displayed like that, though. Everything else around the bed was trashed."

Rayne clenched his fists. Bad enough that she had been attacked in her own bed, in the house she loved more than anything. A hundred times worse to know that she may have looked at that photo picture and seen him, to imagine how helpless she'd been while she stared into his eyes in the picture. His skin crawled.

"Have them get rid of that mattress. I'll buy a new one for her. New sheets, all of that." He wanted it all gone before she came home. If she ever came home. He wouldn't blame her for never setting foot here again.

"Sure thing. Tell her we're doing everything we can, okay?"

Whatever they were doing, it would never be enough. For him, or for her. On rubbery legs he headed for his car, was halfway down her driveway when an elderly man flagged him down. Patrick, Christa's neighbor. They'd met at her birthday party.

"Will she be all right, lad?"

"I think so. I saw her at the hospital, but—"

"When they catch the bastard, I hope he never sees the light of day again." His voice caught. "Who would do such a thing to her? She's such a lovely lass, never has a harsh word for anybody. The kindest person we've ever known, the wife and me."

The hot, quick rage swept through him again and he fought it down, had to get control. She needed him to be her rock.

"You'll watch over her for us, won't you? Let us know how she is."

"Sure will. And thanks for...for what you did."

He couldn't think about what might have happened had Patrick not shown up. Right now all he wanted was to see Christa again. What should he say to her? What *could* he say to her? His imagination kept conjuring up all sorts of images. He had to get a grip on himself so he could be there to soothe her, comfort her. The memory of her big blue eyes formed in his head, haunted eyes filled with pain. He wanted to kill that goddamned animal with his bare hands.

CHAPTER 10

Christa awoke stiff and sore. Where was she? In the hospital? It hit her like a Mack truck, each detail flashing through her brain like a movie. Shock held her immobile. Had it really happened to her?

She curled into a fetal position, wincing at the throbbing from the rope burns on her wrists and ankles, the sting on her cheek where he'd hit her. Between her legs was only a tender, bruised feeling. It made her feel sick when she thought of it.

The TV was tuned to a local newscast, the newscaster reporting an aggravated assault, asking the public for information that might lead to the whereabouts of a dangerous sexual predator, possibly armed, described as medium build, gray-eyed and bald. Watching it felt surreal, as if it had happened to someone else.

Well, at least they were trying hard to find him. She huddled deeper under the blankets. Cold, she was so cold.

A knock sounded and Rayne opened the door.

"Hi," she said, sitting up straighter as he came toward her.

"Hey kiddo." He bent down to hug her gently.

"You didn't have to come back," she breathed, pressing close to him. The instant their bodies had touched she'd felt safer. *He* would never hurt her.

"Of course I did. I'm only sorry I couldn't get here sooner." He lifted a hand to touch her face but she recoiled, hiding it from his view. "Let me see, sweetheart," he coaxed, his eyes full of concern as he tilted her chin and studied her. She felt so self-conscious, hated that he could see the ugly bruises forming on her cheeks and jaw. He pressed a kiss to her temple and tightened his arms around her with a heavy sigh. "I can't stand it that the sick bastard did this to you."

She tensed, trying to absorb the security of his arms, the warmth from his body that seeped into her, his scent. He was familiar, trustworthy—the only person she welcomed such close physical contact with. She laid her head on his wide chest and breathed him in, savoring his strength. All too soon he pulled away.

"Can I get you anything?"

"No thanks." She made room for him beside her on the bed and tugged at her sleeves, trying to hide the bandages circling her wrists.

"So, is there anything new to report?"

"Not yet. Nate's working your case, so he'll be right on it. A description's been issued throughout Canada and the western U.S." Her eyelids flinched. "Sweetheart, we don't have to talk about it if you don't want to."

She stared down at her hands. "I shouldn't have even gone outside, but I thought...well, I guess I wasn't really thinking at all, was I?"

He took her hand in his. "This was *not* your fault, Christa. None of it was." He rubbed her arm in silent sympathy. "I wish there was something I could do."

"Rayne?" She fought the wave of shyness, tentatively meeting the concern in his eyes. The words did not come easily for her, and she doubted they ever would again. "Would you hold me?" When his brows rose, her confidence faltered. "Just for a little while."

But Rayne was already moving. He scooped her up, blankets and all, went dead still when she gasped and stiffened. "Sorry. I'm fine." As if she was made of porcelain, he lifted her out of the little nest she'd created in her hospital bed and set her on his lap. Giving the impression he needed the comfort of holding her as much as she did, he enveloped her, cradling her against him.

Christa sighed in relief at the sense of instant security, even though it was only a temporary illusion. Rayne was so warm, her mythological knight in shining armor. She snuggled closer, reveling in the way his muscles moved as he shifted to hold her more tightly, surrounding her body with his. She couldn't remember being held so wonderfully before. Her head rested in the hollow of his shoulder, the rhythm of his heartbeat steady under her cheek. It soothed her. Her eyes closed in reverence. "I tried to fight him," she whispered, battling the shame crawling over her. Rayne's muscles went rigid under her cheek.

She should have fought harder. She should have tried something else. "I did some of the things you taught me, but he was...he was too strong." She swallowed as she thought about it. Only a little taller than her, and he'd overpowered her with laughable ease. "And then I was too scared to fight anymore. I thought maybe I was making it better for him by struggling, so I stopped. Tried to play dead." But then he'd—

Rayne's troubled sigh cut off the terrible memory. He hugged her tighter. "You couldn't have done anything to stop it, sweetheart. Don't blame yourself." Gentle fingers caressed the curve of her cheekbone. "When you're discharged I'm taking you home with me," he informed her. "It's the safest place for you right now. But nowhere around here is safe enough, so if you're up to it we could drive down to the beach house in Lincoln City in the morning."

"Nate's place, in Oregon?"

"You got it. I think taking you away for a while's the best thing. Just for a few days, until they catch him."

Just for a few days, he says, as if it's nothing. Only the two of them. Alone. She swallowed. "I called Michael this morning. He wants me to fly back east and stay with him."

"Up to you. That's an option."

But even though she loved Michael to pieces, she'd prefer he didn't see her like this. She'd rather be with Rayne, although she had no idea how she was supposed to be alone with him and pretend she only wanted to be his friend. "I thought Nate has to take my statement and all that."

"He said he'll come and do it at my place when you're ready."

What else was there to say? She refused to put Teryl and Drew in danger again by returning to their place, and no way could she go home, even if she wanted to. She wouldn't be in control of her life anytime soon, so she'd better get used to it. "I guess ... Lincoln City sounds okay to me."

He tightened his arms and drew her head back down, as if willing her to draw comfort from his strength. She sighed and burrowed into his chest like a lost kitten in need of affection. Curling as close as she could, she found the courage to ask the question that frightened her the most. "Do you think they'll catch him?" The fear she tried to conceal in her voice made it unsteady.

"Oh, yeah. They'll catch him, sweetheart, and soon."

His assurance left a hollow feeling in her stomach. If

he was prepared to drive her all the way down to Oregon in an attempt to keep her safe, he must consider her stalker a major threat. Which meant he was putting himself at risk for her sake, and she would never forgive herself if something happened to Rayne because of her. Battling nerves and fatigue, she made herself take a calming breath and focus on the man holding her, trusting him to keep vigil, and let herself drift off to sleep.

****

Rayne had never felt so protective of anyone as he gazed down at her battered face, cradling her as tightly as he dared. He knew he eventually had to let her go, but hated like hell to do it. He'd feel like he was deserting her.

What had she gone through? The devastation in her bedroom had chilled his soul. At least the doc had confirmed that she hadn't been raped, so he wouldn't have to think of her being violated that way.

In her quiet manner she was strong, probably stronger than anyone else he knew. How did that saying go? 'Still waters run deep.' He didn't question whether or not she'd recover from her ordeal. Christa was a survivor. From what she'd confided to him so far, she'd lived through an emotionally traumatic childhood and a devastating breakup, and despite everything had triumphed. She would overcome this as well. It would be tough as hell but they'd take it day by day, and he'd be right there with her.

When he was sure she wouldn't wake up, he eased her back onto the bed and covered her carefully with the blankets, wondering if his words had comforted her at all. He'd tried to reassure her without giving her unrealistic promises. He could only hope they would catch her attacker before he got to her again. Because sure as hell, he was going to try. Stalkers always did.

****

He'd made the news. Seated on the sofa in his immaculate living room pressing an ice pack to his face, Seth watched transfixed as the pretty newscaster gave vague details of the attack while his name and picture filled the screen. She described him as a dangerous sexual predator. The slow-witted cops were finally on to him. The rush hit him like a heroin fix.

No wonder people became infatuated with their own fame, obsessed with replicating their crimes, striving for unattainable perfection. But fame was addictive, a drug that would lead to his capture if he let it. He debated risking upping the stakes and drawing more attention to himself.

Maybe he wouldn't need to. They must have finally found a smidgen of a fingerprint and run it through their fossil of a computer system. Carelessness on his part, but it had taken them long enough. How much more did they know? Did they have DNA evidence on him, despite all his precautions? She'd clawed him across the cheek, so maybe they'd found a sample under her fingernails. And when her elbow had smashed into his face his nose had bled enough to leave a good sample, so maybe they'd already made a match. Were they finally putting the pieces together?

No matter. He loved taunting them. They'd come closer than they knew to catching him two years ago, and here he was, still a free man. Fucking idiots, all of them.

He needed to lie low now—that was the smart thing to do. But his fantasy had been interrupted. He didn't take the failure lightly.

Christa was still out there. Did she savor each sweet breath she took, knowing how precious life was? Did the sky look bluer and the air feel fresher now that she'd had a glimpse of her fate? It wasn't over. He couldn't abide leaving loose threads. They had a way of tripping you up.

****

"This is all yours?" Christa glanced around Rayne's penthouse suite.

"Yep." He took her jacket and laid it over a chair in the black granite and stainless steel kitchen. She peeked into the family room and found the requisite big-screen TV in the corner, surrounded by black leather couches and a matching La-Z-Boy chair. A glass-topped coffee table with stainless steel legs stood in the middle of the carpet. *See?* her brain chimed in. *Yet another reason why we're completely incompatible.* She did her best to repress a shudder at the décor. What was it with men and black leather furniture, anyway?

"You hungry?"

More than anything she was dead tired and wanted to go to sleep, but Nate was coming over to take her statement. With nerves jumping in her stomach, she doubted if anything would sit well. "No, thanks."

"Let's get you settled then, and we'll watch a ballgame until Nate gets here."

"Okay." She followed him down the cream Berber-carpeted hallway to what must have been the spare room. He placed her bag next to the queen-sized bed covered in an emerald duvet, smiling at her in the mirrored closet on the far wall.

"This all right?"

"Great."

"Bathroom's across the hall, and I'm right next door."

Yeah, like she needed to be reminded of that. Despite everything that had happened in the last twenty-four hours, she still would have loved to snuggle up in bed beside him, purely for the physical reassurance of being protected. Not that she could get much safer than she was now, in a secure condominium with a cop to protect her.

"You seem like you've got something on your mind."

She opened her mouth, closed it. "I was just..." Thinking about things she ought not to be thinking about. "I'm still a little dazed, I guess. Sorry."

He waved her words away. "Don't apologize." He came over and settled an arm around her, his forearm warming her shoulders, making her long to burrow into his shirt.

No clinging, Christa. Clinging is the surest way to make a man run in the opposite direction.

She didn't resist when he stepped back and took her hand to lead her out of the room. "Come on. Let's watch the game for a while." He settled her on the couch. "I think all I've got in the fridge is water and beer."

"Water would be great."

He came back with a chilled bottle and flipped on the TV, scanning to the Mariners' game. Three innings later the phone rang.

"Hello...Hey Nate. Come on up."

Her stomach clenched.

After Rayne had let him in Nate strode over to her.

"Hi, Christa. This big guy been taking care of you?"

"He's spoiling me, for sure."

"Good." He regarded Rayne, poised in the entryway, then back at her. "Tell me how you want to do this, honey." His deep brown eyes were kind. "You want Rayne to stay, or would you be most comfortable with just me in the room?"

She weighed the pros and cons. She really didn't want Rayne to hear it all yet, but if she asked him to go, would it make him feel she didn't trust him? She cast him a glance.

"Don't worry about me," he told her, as if reading her mind. "I'll stay if you want me to, but I totally understand if you'd rather I didn't."

She felt shaken. Part of her was terrified at facing this without him, and the other part of her was too ashamed to let him hear her statement. "I think I'll talk to Nate by myself, if you don't mind." Her voice came out uneven.

"Not at all, darlin'." He must have seen how close she was to losing it, because he crouched in front of her and set his warm hands over hers as she rubbed her damp palms on her jeans. "I'm right down the hall if you change your mind," he told her, those hazel eyes boring directly into hers, lending her strength.

"Thanks," she whispered. He squeezed her hands and left her with Nate, who chose the La-Z-Boy.

"How are you holding up?" he asked, leaning forward with his elbows propped on his knees.

"As well as can be expected, I guess." She was holding it together so far, wasn't she?

He pulled a tape recorder and a pad of paper out of his briefcase. "It's standard to record the victim's statement for future reference," he told her, starting the machine. First he announced the date, her name and file number.

She answered all his questions with as much detail as she could, outlining Jake's barking in the yard, the moment she'd realized it was Seth advancing from the shadows, the struggle to get away before he forced her into the car and drove to her house. She told him about the alarm, that Seth had known the code, and the instant of freedom in the kitchen before he'd caught her again.

"I think I might have broken his nose, because it made a real crunching noise when I hit him, and he was bleeding. It didn't slow him down much, though, because he grabbed me by my hair and wrestled me down." She had to swallow twice before continuing. "Then he dragged me up to my room and...and tied me to the bed."

"Face up or face down?"

His matter-of-fact tone jarred her, and she had to remind herself he wasn't being callous, only doing his job as an investigator. "Face down."

Nate nodded, made some notes on his pad, peered across at her. "And when did he produce the knife?"

Her throat clamped shut at the memory of him holding the glinting blade above her, making her think she was about to be stabbed. "First he put a picture of Rayne and me on the nightstand..." She explained that Seth thought Rayne was her boyfriend, described how infuriated he'd become when she'd denied it, had tried to choke her. "Then he used the knife to cut off my clothes." The tears threatened then, she blinked hard to hold them back.

"Take your time," Nate murmured, watching her with sympathetic eyes.

She shook her head, closed her lids. "I'm okay." She would not fall apart. If she allowed herself to let go, she might never be able to put herself back together.

"And after he cut your clothes? What happened then?"

She wrapped her arms around herself. "He tried to rape me, but he couldn't, um..." Humiliation burned like acid.

"Couldn't maintain an erection?" Nate supplied.

"Yes." Which was why she'd been so upset with the doctor about the need for an internal so soon after the ordeal. He hadn't been able to penetrate her.

"And when he couldn't perform sexually, what then?"

Her jaw trembled along with the rest of her body. Her teeth chattered. "H-he bit me, on m-my shoulder." She was cold, so cold, the wound throbbing. She heard again her own scream, relived the bright haze of pain that sliced through her, and the warm stickiness of her own blood trickling over her skin. The nauseating tang of it.

"Did anything else happen before you heard your neighbor Patrick Flannery calling you?"

"No. That was about it." Thank God for Patrick. He'd saved her life, she was sure of it.

Nate finished his last questions swiftly, then shut off the tape recorder and sat next to her on the couch. "All over now, Christa," he soothed. "Want me to call Hutch back in?"

She shook her head. She didn't want him to see her until she was back in control.

"Okay, I'll give you a few minutes." He settled a blanket over her, and she flinched when his hand touched her back. "You did real well, honey. Your information will be a big help to finally put this guy away forever, so he won't be able to hurt another woman."

She hoped so. God, she hoped so. No one should have to go through this agony.

After a few minutes the trembling eased and she was able to breathe normally again. A heavy, almost drugged feeling of fatigue dragged at her, making her lean into the cushions.

Nate studied her a moment longer, then stood. "Okay, Hutch," he called, "we're through here."

Rayne appeared, his gaze locking with hers. "You all right kiddo?"

"Just glad it's over," she answered. "No offense, Nate."

His lips quirked. "None taken, honey. I'll keep you informed of any developments, and feel free to call me anytime day or night, as a cop or a friend. In the meantime I'll have Victims' Services contact you."

"She'll be gone for a few days, Nate," Rayne told him.

"Gone? Gone where?"

"If it's all right with you I'm taking her to the beach house for a while."

Nate stared at him. "Oh."

An undercurrent simmered between the two men, though she didn't know why. Rayne's expression was inscrutable.

"You okay here for a minute while I see Nate out?"

A-ha. They wanted a private conversation. She

waved him away. "Sure, go ahead." The door closed behind them, leaving her to wonder what was so terrible it couldn't be said in front of her.

****

Nate eyed him levelly. "What the hell are you doing? I don't mind you using the beach house, but have you considered the implications? I mean, there's always protective custody—"

"You want to scare her even more? She's already freaking about this guy. Besides, she'll be in protective custody. Mine."

Nate spread his hands. "I hear ya. I've known you almost your entire life. You're like a son to me. I know I can trust you to take care of her."

"So what's the problem?" Rayne leaned back with his arms folded across his chest.

"I know, I know," Nate placated him, "you don't want to hear it. But I'm going to say it anyway. First of all, whatever has happened between you and Christa is—"

"Nothing's happened, Nate."

"—is none of my business," he finished. "But it's obvious you care about her a lot."

"That's right."

"I can see it." He cleared his throat. "And I can't help feeling you might be getting in over your head here."

"I appreciate your concern, but I won't change my mind."

His fingers drummed on his briefcase. "I'm concerned about her too. Hell, she's a sweet girl, and didn't deserve any of this. But even when we catch the bastard, she may still be...well, she might...you know as well as I do that she has a long, tough recovery ahead of her. She's totally vulnerable and not up to dealing with any more *stress* right now."

What the hell? Rayne stood straighter, leaning forward on the balls of his feet. "So, what are you saying?"

"I'm saying that you'd better tread real carefully here."

His hands squeezed into fists. "You mean I can't just take her to bed like every other woman I've been with, right? Like I have no control over my sexual urges or something."

"You know exactly what I mean. Your lifestyle isn't exactly a big secret."

Rayne's teeth clenched. Jesus Christ, did everyone think he was a hormone with feet? He had always treated the women he'd dated well.

"All I'm saying is that you'd better think long and hard before you put the moves on Christa Bailey."

"So you *do* mean sex." His brow hiked closer to his hairline.

"Partly. Take it easy, for her sake. She's not ready for that kind of thing. She may never be ready again."

He had heard enough. It was one thing to be offered fatherly advice, but quite another to have your lifelong idol insult your morals. Who the hell did Nate think he was to talk, anyway? His reputation had been even worse than his, for God's sake. "Just so there's no confusion about it," he said with dignity, "I'm taking Christa with me to Lincoln City. And if I happen to go to bed with her, rest assured I will not have *sex* with her. You of all people should understand I won't rush her."

Nate gave an ear-to-ear smile and burst out laughing. "Well I'll be damned."

****

Christa picked at the pizza Rayne had placed on a tray for her. She wasn't hungry but she needed to eat, so she suffered a few bites of ham and pineapple, usually her favorite.

She knew the interview with Nate had been necessary, though she'd dreaded having to relive everything, all the awful details. Partly because she could hardly bear to think about them herself, let alone expose them to strangers. That would come later, in the inevitable psychiatric appointments.

And that's when it happened. The full impact of what had happened crashed down on her, a suffocating weight. Her heart raced, sweat popped out on her forehead, her skin tingling as if covered with a million skittering bugs.

She was unclean, violated. She could smell the faint scent of him that lingered on her skin.

She shoved the tray off her lap and leapt up. Her body was contaminated, and she needed to wash the filth off, *now*.

"I need a shower," she blurted, heading for the bathroom. The walls closed in on her, her vision blurring as the world tipped onto its side. She stumbled, but Rayne was right behind her, helping her to her feet.

"Chris, you're scaring me."

"I just need a shower," she gasped, desperate to get under the spray of water. She ripped off her clothes, throwing them into a heap before yanking at the faucet.

"Chris?"

She slammed the glass door behind her and stood under the blistering hot spray, the urgent, panicked sensation remaining. She scrubbed her body, violently cleansing every patch of flesh she could reach, continuing even when her skin shone red and raw.

Rayne opened the door and yanked the washcloth from her before killing the spray.

Christa blinked at him. Had he been there in the bathroom with her all along? She covered herself with her arms, trembling, her shoulder stinging. As if she were coming out of a fog, she stared down with detached curiosity at the pink rivulets dripping from her fingertips. Blood stained the water. Her blood.

"Oh, God." Rayne's eyes were glued to her bleeding shoulder. He grabbed a towel from the cupboard and wrapped her in it, applying firm pressure to stop the bleeding. "You're okay," he told her, maintaining eye contact. "You're okay now."

Still she watched the blood drip, shivering. Then her knees gave out and she slid bonelessly to the floor. "D-don't," she mumbled when he reached for her. She was naked, for God's sake! She didn't want anyone—least of all him—seeing her right now, lying in a heap with only a towel covering her, her skin raw because she'd morphed into a mad woman.

He hunkered in front of her outside the shower stall, stemming the flow of blood while trying to preserve what was left of her dignity. Then he carried her to his bed, shoving pillows under her ankles to elevate her feet above her head.

"It's okay, Chris. Everything's fine now. You need to lie still for a bit." He deftly rolled her to get a better look at her wound. "When the bleeding slows I'll apply a pressure dressing."

She shut her eyes as the room spun around her, buzzing filling her head. She was too tired to care about what anyone else was thinking, so she let herself drift, aware only of Rayne's hand rubbing her arm.

"Should I call someone?" he asked eventually. "Teryl?"

"A shrink. No, an exorcist. An evil spirit has taken over my body."

"Everything hit you at once and it overloaded your brain."

"I shorted out." Maybe she had smoke coming out of her ears.

"Exactly."

"Promise me you won't tell anyone about this," she demanded.

"Of course not."

"I'm so embarrassed." The understatement of the year. He'd seen her naked while she was freaking out; not exactly the scenario she'd fantasized about.

"Nothing to be embarrassed about, kiddo." He tipped her chin and met her eyes. "I was too distracted by the blood dripping down your arm to notice anything else."

He might be lying, but it was sweet of him to try to put her at ease. Some of the mortification faded.

He left briefly and returned with a first-aid kit, unwound a strip of gauze with practiced ease and applied the dressing, then gave her one of the sleeping pills the doctor at the hospital had prescribed. She swallowed it, willing it to kick in and sent her into sweet oblivion. She welcomed Rayne's presence, the sense of security he gave her. She wanted to crawl into his pocket and stay there. Why oh why did she have to fall for someone so far out of her league?

CHAPTER 11

As planned, they left the following morning as the sun started to peek over the tops of the coastal mountains in the distance, entering the States at the Peace Arch border crossing and soon picking up the I5 for Portland. Even though they were in a rented car and leaving the country, she couldn't help sneaking glances into the side mirror to make sure they weren't being followed. After her third peek, Rayne reached over and squeezed her shoulder, kneading the tight muscles.

"Our tail is clear, darlin', so you can relax," he assured her with a note of amusement. "You'll get a kink in your neck that way."

Her face went beet red. She should have known he was taking precautions. "Sorry. I didn't think I was being that obvious."

He didn't seem offended. "The chances of him crossing the border are pretty much nil, unless he's a master of disguise with a fake passport—"

She cast him a worried look.

"—which isn't likely, so I'd say we've got a better chance of being hit by lightning than running into him."

Now *that* was more along the lines of what she wanted to hear. Her muscles eased and she let out a breath of relief before turning her attention to the gorgeous man whisking her away to a beachfront cottage. There was something indefinably masculine about the way he drove, so confident, shifting so smoothly she could barely feel the transition. The confidence and charisma he exuded was a definite female magnet. He could be driving a tricycle with a rubber horn on it and women would still find him sexy. She must be insane for going ahead with this whole plan, not that she'd had much choice. And why the hell did she have to analyze everything all the time?

Jake came up behind her to rest his furry muzzle on

her shoulder and she reached back to scratch under his chin. The vet had confirmed that his injuries had been superficial and okayed him to come along on the trip. Her rush of joy and relief had been tempered by a surge of loathing for the lowlife who had hurt him, the stalker who was shattering her life. Spending a few days away suddenly didn't seem so insane.

At Portland they exited the I5 and headed toward the coast, passing rolling farmland, vineyards and forest before the sign appeared welcoming them to Lincoln City. Rayne cruised past the shops and motels lining the main drag until the ocean came into view, taking her breath away. Sparkles of sunlight crested the waves breaking against an endless expanse of sand. They turned toward the water and pulled into the driveway of a white clapboard bungalow with a cherry red door and shutters, its front steps adorned with scarlet geraniums spilling from matching cobalt pots.

"Here it is," he told her with a smile, and got out to unload their luggage.

Christa let Jake out of the car and followed Rayne up to the red front door. "It's pretty," she said, liking it already.

"Wait 'til you see the view from the living room." He unlocked the door and pushed it open, stepping into the cream-tiled hallway. The house smelled a little musty, but it looked clean enough. In the second room on the left he set her bag down and she peered past him to the double bed covered with a green and blue pieced quilt. "I'm next door and the bathroom's right across the hall." He dropped his own bag into his room and led her through a yellow and white kitchen into the front room, painted a crisp white and lined with bookshelves. A bowl of seashells sat on the white crackled coffee tabletop. "I saved the best part for last."

The rush of the ocean greeted her as she stepped toward the bank of picture windows overlooking the green-gray waves. "Wow. I could stare at this all day."

"Be my guest. I could never get tired of that view."

She believed it, listening to the hypnotic rhythm. "Jake's going to love walking along there."

"We can go out after we eat, if you want. We might

bump into Bryn. She lives down the beach, and I've spent practically every summer with her since I started coming down here with Nate's family." Affection warmed his voice.

Oh, great. She would wind up staying here all by herself while Rayne went off and did whatever it was he did with Bryn. Only his presence was keeping her from reliving the nightmare. "You could take me to pick up groceries and stop by to see her. I'll come back here and make us some dinner."

He slipped his arms around her, making her wonder if he even realized what he was doing. "No way. I'm taking you out for seafood and then we'll go for a stroll. All that fresh, salty air will have us both sleeping like babies tonight."

She doubted that, but kept it to herself.

After stocking up with groceries they drove to a seafood joint perched on the end of a pier and dined on halibut and steamed veggies, admiring the blue-green rollers thundering against the craggy black cliff jutting into the ocean like an outstretched finger. They crashed against the tumbled rocks at the bottom and spewed up geysers of white foam tinted by the sun's golden-orange rays. When she turned her head, she noticed people staring at her bruised face and she couldn't look any of them in the eye, hoping no one thought Rayne was responsible. She stayed close to him, his eyes alert.

Safely back at the cottage, he built a bonfire on the beach, gathering roasting sticks for their marshmallows. Christa sat across the red-hot coals from him, her head resting on a driftwood log. Enjoying the warmth of the flames on her face, she absorbed the sky's transformation from tangerine to crimson and purple, hypnotized by the muted thunder of the ocean. Smoke mingled with the smell of the sea, taking her back to happy childhood memories of seaside hikes with Michael.

"Pretty nice, huh." Rayne raised his beer bottle in salute. "Nate first invited me down here with his family the year I turned fourteen. I got to be too much for my mom to handle so she was happy enough to send me here with Nate until I moved in with him. And I've managed to come back every year since. I love it."

"I can see why." The beating waves could lull her to sleep.

Tearing her gaze from a couple holding hands and sharing secretive smiles as they strolled along the foaming surf, she noticed a lone figure materializing out of the mist, heading toward them. The trim curves of the silhouette left no doubt it was a woman.

Rayne followed her gaze and jumped up from the campfire with a grin. "Hey!" he called, heading toward her, leaving Christa behind.

Something squeezed in her chest as he wrapped the newcomer in his arms, lifting her off the ground and swinging her around in an exuberant circle. Then he draped a possessive arm around her and they started back toward the fire.

"Chris, look who found me. Bryn."

Bryn's clear, dusky skin was made for firelight, as was the cloud of ebony hair streaming down her back and her obsidian eyes. "Hi." Christa held out her hand.

Bryn shook it firmly. "Good to meet you." She made herself comfortable, helping herself to a beer and leaning against Rayne. As they reminisced, Christa couldn't help envying their mutual affection and the easy camaraderie between them. And, to be truthful, they looked *good* together, like a beautiful couple you'd see on the cover of a magazine. For lack of something better to do, she skewered another marshmallow and toasted it, consumed it and several others, just to keep her hands busy. Despite Rayne's efforts to include her in their conversation, she had no shared past with them and waited until the next pause in their conversation before getting to her feet.

"I'm beat, and I ate too many marshmallows." She made a sickly expression. "Nice to meet you, Bryn."

Rayne jumped up, caught her arm. "You okay? You want me to walk you back?"

"No need, it's only a few yards.

He frowned. "Okay, kiddo. I won't be long."

She waved away his concern. "I'm fine, take your time."

She headed to the cottage alone, feeling colder with each step, and not just because she'd left the heat of the fire behind.

****

He watched her retreating figure until she was safely inside, her shapely silhouette moving down the hallway.

"Your friend's pretty shy," Bryn remarked. "Been seeing her long?"

"Christa? We're not seeing each other." Not technically, anyway.

"So what's she doing here, then?"

He took a sip of beer, wondering if he should go and make sure she was safe. Boy, she'd taken off in a hurry. "She needed a vacation."

"With you?"

"Yes."

Bryn drained her beer and reached for a marshmallow. "Was she in a car accident or something? Either that or somebody's been using her as a punching bag."

His eyes snapped to hers. "Something like that, yeah."

"Ah. So she's not your latest fling?"

"No," he said emphatically, jaw tensing. Did everyone think he used women like that?

"What happened to her?"

His hands fidgeted with the bottle. "She was beaten and nearly raped by a stalker who hasn't been caught yet."

"Jesus. She okay?"

"No." And it damn near killed him to feel so helpless about it.

"Oh." She put her arm around him in silent comfort.

"I want to kill that son-of-a-bitch, Bryn. I want to kill him slowly, with my bare hands." She rubbed his back and he welcomed the contact. "She's the sweetest, kindest, bravest person I've ever known."

"Wow. That's saying a lot, coming from you."

"And she's so vulnerable, and too trusting for her own goddamn good. It pisses me off that some asshole could do this to her."

"So you've got to help her."

"I only wish I could."

She rested her forehead against his, so that their noses were almost touching. "You will," she said simply. "I have yet to see Rayne Hutchinson fail at anything he sets his mind to, especially when it comes to a woman."

Together they watched the fire shimmer and crackle against the night sky.

****

Face down on her bed, she steeled herself against him, writhing to free her hands, the rope burning, chafing the insides of her wrists and ankles. His chilling gray eyes gleamed down at her, evil and hungry. And always his voice haunted her, husky, rasping in her ear, making her quake.

He lifted the knife to the side of her throat. "No one's coming to save you this time."

The blade glinted in the moonlight streaming through the window. She shrank from it, whimpering, the dull side scraping against her cringing flesh as he slashed through her nightgown. She flailed, screamed, begged for mercy, but he had none.

"I can hurt you in so many ways," he breathed, "and your boyfriend's even bigger than me. Imagine the damage a guy his size could do."

She cried out. Rayne would never hurt her, never demoralize or terrorize her.

"You wouldn't have a chance against him."

He tried to force himself inside her. At the realization of his impotence he started screaming obscenities, pounding her head, her back. She tried to buck him off, eliciting a guttural snarl. His fang-like teeth punctured the skin of her shoulder, making her scream.

She jerked awake covered in sweat, heart thudding, breath sawing in and out of her starved lungs. She sat up and flipped on the bedside lamp with trembling fingers, gulping in air.

You're in Oregon with Rayne. You're safe.

She sat there numbly until Jake came and propped his chin on her legs in silent comfort. She went and peered out the bedroom window, scanning the yard for movement, but saw nothing, heard nothing except her own ragged breathing and the muted roar of the ocean.

Rayne was right next door, on the other side of the wall. Maybe she should just go to him.

No. She didn't want him to see how bad things had

gotten. Time to suck it up, just like she had always done. Her lungs pulled in a deep, shuddering breath, let it out slowly.

You're an adult, not a frightened little girl. Deal with it.

The sharp words slapped some calm into her.

When she finally felt safe enough to crawl between the sheets and pull the covers up to her chin, she stared at the lamp beside her, somewhat reassured by its warm glow chasing the shadows into the corners and holding them there, keeping evil at bay. For the first time in years, she went to sleep with the light on.

Sliding into a fitful slumber, she heard Seth's voice whispering in her ear, saw him raise that wicked, gleaming blade. She woke with a scream trapped in her throat.

****

He was on his freaking vacation and he couldn't get one decent night's sleep. Rayne thumped his pillow, sick of tossing restlessly. He couldn't seem to shut his brain off. He imagined Christa stretched out on the bed in the next room, wearing nothing but a tank top and shorts, her hair spread across her pillow, how she would curl into him if he slipped in beside her. The images filtered through his head, torturing him. It made him sick with rage to think of anyone hurting anything so beautiful. And she *was* beautiful, inside and out.

He lay there staring at the ceiling when a sound came from her room. A glance at the clock told him she should have been sleeping soundly for hours now. He got up and was standing in his open doorway listening, debating whether he should go in and make sure she was okay when she padded into the hallway.

"Hey, kiddo."

She jumped.

He leaned against the doorframe, arms folded across his chest. "You all right?"

Her hand was pressed over her heart. "Sorry, I didn't mean to wake you."

"You didn't. I couldn't sleep either."

She sighed, touching her fingertips to her temples. "I need some aspirin."

Her eyes were swollen from crying, reddened and underlined by dark circles. He went to take her by the shoulders and her gaze dropped to her bare feet.

"Do you want to talk? It might help."

She hesitated. "I dreamt part of it over again. Twice." She shuddered. "I can't talk about it yet. Sorry."

He led her into the kitchen, found some Tylenol and poured her a glass of juice. Her hands fidgeted with the glass, the scraping on the countertop the only sound. "This might sound crazy to you," she said slowly, "but I can't seem to feel clean anymore. Even with all the scalding hot showers and anti-bacterial soap."

"I wish I knew how to make it go away." He felt even more helpless when her head dropped into her hands. "At least I can help get rid of that headache. Come with me."

In the living room he perched on the edge of the couch and motioned for her to sit on the floor in front of him. Then he swept her hair over one shoulder, running his fingers through the silky mass.

"Here," he murmured, "lean against me." He eased her shoulders toward him. "Now close your eyes."

She stiffened at the intimate contact, but didn't pull away. His legs bracketed her body, her head resting against his stomach. She sighed when his strong fingers began to soothe the tension in her neck, careful to avoid the bandage near her shoulder blade. He wanted to lull her, turn off that busy brain of hers for a while.

The movement of his hands grew languorous, and she let her head loll against him, absorbing the comfort of his nearness. He relished the swish of her dark hair, the softness of her skin. She always smelled so good. That she trusted him so implicitly after all she had been through amazed and humbled him. His little Christa was a survivor, and her inner strength made him proud of her.

Since when did he consider her to be 'his little Christa'?

When he'd first met her he hadn't wanted a serious relationship with any of the women he'd dated. He'd had lots of one-night stands because it was less complicated that way, had been in lust lots of times, had even cared about some of them a lot, but had never been in love with any of them. The sex was safe, hot and plentiful, but when he got restless, he broke it off. He'd never given it much thought, but until he knew he'd found 'the One' he refused to make promises he might not be able to keep. In case he had even one shred of his father in him.

It was different with Christa. She'd awoken something in him he hadn't known was there. The problem was how to go about convincing her he cared. She was well aware of his checkered past and would no doubt take any move he made toward her as purely physical. Silvery words and calculated touches would only scare her away, especially after the ordeal she'd just suffered. So he'd decided to try a tactic previously foreign to him—patience.

If that would help his little Christa heal her scars, he was willing to give it a go. For weeks now his daydreams had been filled with images of him making sweet love to her. A quiet moan, his whispered name, her eyes closed, her face caught with the strain of ecstasy. *It might never happen now, after what that bastard has done to her.* Rayne swallowed, her hair caressing his wrists as he massaged her neck.

If she had any idea what he was thinking right now she would probably leap up and run from the room. That was the dilemma. Between what Teryl had said and the way Christa looked at him he knew she was attracted to him and that she cared about him. But thanks to her asshole ex-boyfriend the very idea of intimacy scared the hell out of her, even before she'd been attacked. And so far, she seemed oblivious to his feelings for her. Normally he would just lay it all out, but he was sure she'd bolt. He'd never felt so unsure of himself and he hated the weakness, the loss of control.

She stifled a yawn. She must be exhausted, poor thing. He pulled her onto the couch and patted his lap. Again, the hesitation.

In the end she stretched out beside him, letting him cradle her head, and closed her eyes, snuggling closer. The small victory was heartening.

She drifted off, turned her face into his abdomen and nuzzled him with her cheek. Rayne thought he might stop breathing. Her fatigue had lowered the protective shield around her. Without her mind dictating every move, she was responding more naturally to his nearness. He knew she had no idea what she was doing to him. His body was rigid with longing but thankfully she was too sleepy to notice. He had to put her in her own bed, now.

She jerked awake as he lifted her and peered at him with startled eyes. "What are you doing?"

"It's okay, sweetheart. I'm putting you to bed." She relaxed slowly, her sleepy brain processing the words. Raising her arms around his neck, she sighed and pressed her face against his throat. He fought a groan and hurried to her bedroom, where he turned back the covers and set her down, helping her into the sheets. She stretched, her supple body arching against the mattress like a cat. He blinked at the innocent display. She was driving him crazy.

Moving fast, he tucked her in and smoothed the hair from her face. "Sweet dreams."

She'd made him ache inside. God knew he'd never get to sleep now.

CHAPTER 12

The next morning, Christa curled up on the sofa on the screened-in porch, her journal in her hands. Writing down bad experiences was supposed to be good therapy, according to the social worker who'd visited her in the hospital. She flipped the page, absently reached to scratch Jake's ears as he sat warming her feet. Maybe if she vented her trauma onto the paper her nightmares would stop and she could sleep without waking up in the middle of a panic attack. Maybe she could sit here without her spine tingling, as if someone were lurking outside, tracking her.

The door banged open and she jumped, the book flying to the floor. Post-traumatic stress disorder, they called it. P.T.S.D. It made her feel like a head case, especially when people stared at her like she was some skittish, trapped animal, like Rayne was doing now.

"Sorry, didn't mean to startle you." He bent and retrieved the journal, and she fought the urge to snatch it from him before he handed it to her.

"No problem," she said, feeling stupid. He'd been so good to her last night, massaging her pain away and comforting her until she dozed in his lap, then putting her to bed like the frightened child she now was. She tried to stop the nervous movement of smoothing the bent pages, keeping her head downcast to disguise the purple smudges of exhaustion under her eyes.

"What's that you're working on?"

"Just a journal I'm keeping." She sighed. "I'm supposed to write down some things before I go to my first counseling appointment." She let out a relieved breath when he didn't question her further.

"I wanted to tell you Bryn's coming for dinner tonight."

Her gaze flew up to meet his. "Oh. That's nice." Was

he trying to tell her politely to get lost? "Do you want...I mean, should I go?"

His brows drew together. "You're not going anywhere, darlin'. Don't you want to have dinner with us?"

"Sure I do. I only thought maybe you'd want a quiet evening to...catch up."

"We already did that."

Yeah, she could just imagine. "Do you need some help with dinner?"

"Nah, I'll pick something up." He edged Jake aside to sit next to her, stroked a thumb over her cheekbone, making her skin tingle. "You okay? You look tired."

"I am, I guess." That was the most pathetic understatement in the history of humankind.

"You should go take a nap then, sweetheart. This is supposed to be recuperation for you. If you want to spend all day in your pajamas and sleep every two hours, then go for it."

What she really wanted was to sleep through the night like any normal person. She was so sick of dreading going to bed, afraid of falling asleep when she knew perfectly well she'd wake up with a scream lodged in her throat and her heart freaking out. Maybe if she could exhaust herself during the day with long runs her brain would be too tired to create more nightmares.

"Some vacation you're having, thanks to me, huh?"

"Oh, I don't know. I'm spending some time off in my favorite beach cottage with a beautiful woman who can cook so good it brings a tear to my eye, plus I have my own personal lap warmer. So I can't complain." He reached down to rub Jake's ears, then pushed to his feet. "Will you be okay here while I head to the gym? I'll pick us up some groceries on the way home. You want anything?"

He was leaving her alone? Despite herself she sent a skittish glance around.

"Hey, you'll be fine. Do you think I'd even consider leaving you here if I didn't think you'd be safe? But of course I'll stay, if you'd rather."

He was right and she was being clingy. He'd already explained to her how difficult it should be for her stalker to cross the border into the States, and she had to get used to being on her own sometime. "No, thanks. Think I'll try and take a nap."

"Okay. I've got my cell phone on me if you need anything. Won't be long." He kissed the top of her head and left her sitting there with Jake.

****

Energized from pumping so much iron, Rayne loaded the grocery bags into the rental car and was climbing into the driver's seat when his cell phone rang. *Please don't let Christa be in trouble.* He'd been so wary about leaving her on her own, had almost decided to skip the gym but figured she'd prefer him out of the way so she could concentrate on her journal. When his caller ID announced his mom he sagged, then winced.

"Hi, gorgeous," he answered. He hadn't called her in over a week and hoped she wouldn't give him a guilt trip about it.

"Hi handsome. I've left a few messages on your machine, but you never called back so I thought I'd try your cell."

"Yeah, sorry, I'm out of town right now. Everything all right?"

"Oh yes, fine. Where are you?"

He sighed, knowing what she'd say. "Down at the beach house."

A telltale pause ensued. "Oh, really? I didn't think you had holidays till August."

Uh-oh. Busted. He'd promised to fly home for a visit during his next vacation time.

"Well, this kind of came up at the last second. I have a friend ... she was attacked."

"Oh, the poor thing, how terrible. Is she all right?"

"She will be. But the guy who attacked her is still loose, so I've brought her down here with me until things cool off at home."

He could practically hear the gears turning in his mother's head.

"So you two are dating, I take it?"

"No, Mom, we're not dating." He fought the urge to roll his eyes, even though his mother was safely on the other side of the country and couldn't see him. Grown up as he was, he didn't want the sharp side of her tongue on the subject of being respectful to your parent.

"You're not dating?"

"No, we're just friends."

"I see." Her tone said she clearly didn't. "Has Bryn met her?"

This could not be good. Ever since he'd invited his mom to come and spend a few weeks at the beach house all those years ago, Bryn and his mom had been close. They still emailed each other and they'd be gossiping like old hens about this in no time. "Yeah, they met yesterday, and Bryn is coming over for dinner tonight. I'm picking up the groceries now."

"Oh, that's nice. Say hi to Bryn for me will you, sugar?"

The Scarlett O'Hara drawl didn't fool him one bit. He'd bet his last dime his mother would be speed-dialing Bryn the second he hung up. "I will."

"Listen, Rayne, about this girl—"

"What about her?" He couldn't help the note of irritation that crept into his voice. He was sick of everyone questioning his motives when it came to women.

"Don't be upset," she soothed. "I'm worried that you might be getting involved in a dangerous situation, that's all. I mean, you said her attacker is still on the loose—"

"Mom, I'm a cop, in case you'd forgotten. And I guess that's the difference between me and other people. I don't just up and leave someone I care about when they need me."

The gasp on the other end of the phone confirmed he'd hit way below the beltline with that one. He squeezed his eyes shut and let out a sigh. "Sorry, I shouldn't have said that."

"Your father had his reasons for leaving, Rayne."

All these years later she would dare defend his actions? "Whatever." As far as he was concerned, there could never be a good enough excuse for a man to desert his wife and young son. Period.

"Maybe it's finally time you talked to him about it, honey."

"You know what, Mom? I don't really want to talk about Dad at all, so why don't you tell me what's new in

Charleston?" That was as clear as he could make it.

She brought him up to speed with the goings on in his hometown and he laughed at her new jokes, relieved she'd let the matter of his dad drop. For the moment.

"You're going to call Bryn now, aren't you?"

"That's a wonderful idea," she gushed. "Maybe I will."

"Uh-huh. Don't think about pumping her for information, Mom, because there's nothing to tell about Christa and me."

"Why, darling," she managed to sound affronted, "your personal life is your business. I just wanted to say hello."

Oh, brother. Like he was born yesterday? "Okay then, take care and thanks for calling. Love you."

"Love you too."

Any moment now Bryn would be answering a barrage of questions.

Back at the cottage he set the groceries on the counter. "Christa?" *No answer.* Adrenaline pumping, he checked the living room, her bedroom, the whole house. Had something happened to her? God, if she wasn't here, then—Why had he been confident enough of her safety to leave her alone? He'd played down the chances of her attacker crossing the border but hell, it wouldn't be impossible.

He nearly collapsed with relief when he heard her footfalls on the porch steps. She pushed open the screen door and poked her head inside, the sight of her there, safe, hair tousled from the wind, weakening his knees.

"Kiddo, where have you been? I was worried."

"Sorry. I was sitting on the steps. Didn't go far."

He tamped down his irritation. He had no right to get mad at her for venturing as far as the porch steps when he was the one who'd opted to leave her at the cottage by herself. In a way it was a boost that she'd felt brave enough to go outside at all and besides, he didn't want to spook her by admitting he'd been afraid her attacker had followed them. "I bought you some flowers. You like tulips, right?"

Her lower lip trembled and he feared she might burst into tears. Then, for the first time in days, she smiled. Actually smiled.

"I love them." She came over to sniff the burst of pink, yellow, purple and red petals. "They're so beautiful, Rayne. Thank you."

The pleasure on her face from such a simple gift made his heart do a funny little something in his chest. "And this one," he said, withdrawing another bloom, "is the closest to the color of your eyes that I could find." A perfect, long-stemmed iris.

Wistfulness filled her features. "Irises are my favorite. I don't think I ever told you that, did I?"

"Lucky guess. Here, let's check to make sure I was right." He touched the edge of a petal against her cheek, as if by accident. "Yep. Almost exactly the right shade." Her eyes darkened as he brushed the delicate flower over her lips.

She held her breath, then let it out in a rush. "They're beautiful," she repeated. "I can't remember the last time anyone gave me flowers."

"Glad you like them."

She helped him put away the food and set about gathering ingredients for dinner. "By the way, Bryn called a few minutes ago to say she couldn't make it tonight."

Oh, come on. Could Bryn and his mom be any more transparent? This was their idea of letting them have a "little time alone together" hoping a romance would spring to life, and then Bryn could report the juicy details back to Charleston, and Emily Hutchinson could fantasize that her son had at long last found the mother of her unborn grandchildren.

"So I thought I'd cook us dinner instead," Christa was saying. "How does ham with pineapple and scalloped potatoes sound?"

"Delicious. Want some help? I'm not exactly a gourmet chef, but I'm young enough to learn."

"That's okay. Why don't you go and relax for a while and I'll have dinner ready in an hour or so? Maybe take a walk on the beach and work up your appetite."

He didn't need anything to work up the appetite bothering him most. She did that without even trying. "I don't know about the walk. I don't want to leave you—"

"I'll be fine."

"Besides, by the look of that sky there's a storm

coming. I'd better get some firewood instead."

"I love storms," she breathed and headed for the window, gazing across the water. Already the wind was picking up, gusting against the old windowpanes. "There's nothing better than watching a storm from inside a nice cozy house, listening to the rain pelt the roof and the wind rattle the windows while the waves crash on the beach."

Rayne could think of something much more wonderful than that. His hazel eyes scanned the horizon, wondering what she was seeing that could evoke such a nostalgic expression. "I'd say we've got another couple hours before it hits. We can curl up beside a nice warm fire."

Her eyes clouded and her posture stiffened. He could have kicked himself. "Only if you want to," he amended, trying to sound casual.

The smile she flashed him was so forced it made him feel like a sleaze ball. "Maybe."

He gave her shoulder a squeeze, leaving her to do what she would in the kitchen. By the time he'd cut and stacked the logs, set the fire ablaze and completed a few other chores around the place, she had whipped up the potatoes and ham and a chocolate mousse for dessert.

They ate at the kitchen table, Rayne telling her stories of his past vacations at the cottage with Nate and his family. "I met Bryn my second time down here. She was with a group of hot girls Nate's sons and I were hitting on, and we found out her father's some high-ranking politician in Beirut. So we took her home with us, so she could talk politics with Nate, since he and my dad both did a tour there. Small world, huh?" He popped another forkful of ham into his mouth. "She goes there to visit her dad every summer."

"What does she do for a living?"

"Social worker." He helped himself to more potatoes. "Depressing as hell if you ask me, but she likes it. Anyway, every year we'd come down and terrorize her boyfriends. We'd follow them around on dates, scare the guys off. We had so much fun."

In the firelight her eyes gleamed. "Poor Bryn."

He gave her a warm smile and held up his glass for a toast. "But so far this is my most enjoyable vacation here yet." Their glasses met with a muted clink.

She blushed and sipped her wine, then cleared the dishes into the sink. The wind was beating at the cottage now, the rain splashing against the windows in fat rivulets. She was staring past them, at the waves slamming into the sand, as though caught in a trance.

She came toward him, illuminated by the glow of the fire snapping in the hearth. God, how he itched to kiss her that instant. But she stopped and went back to face the window.

"I'm going for a walk."

"Out there? You'll get soaked."

"I know."

Her first laugh, her first sign of enthusiasm in days ... how could he stop her? But he wouldn't let her out of his sight.

She sailed past him and out the screen door, the blast of wind slamming it behind her. Rayne leaned against the jamb as she skipped down the stairs and into the storm. He stood there, spellbound, almost hypnotized by the sight of her there on the beach, the wind whipping through her unbound hair, her head tilted back, feeling the storm. At the smile lighting her face he felt a swell of pride, watching her lift her arms above her head and twirl like a little girl, the gale swirling around her, the cuffs of her jeans getting wet from the pounding waves. She was healing, the storm washing her soul clean.

****

Amidst the crashing surf, Christa breathed in the windswept air and laughed out loud, the sound swallowed by the elements. She had never felt so free, so exhilarated. The storm reinforced something wild within her spirit, something that could never be torn from her, something that had survived the threats, the fear and the attack. She felt so alive, the rhythm of the surf pulsing in her veins, the wind charging her soul. She let the rain drench her face, let it wash away the bruises and the scars like a warm, gentle hand. Tears mingled with the salty spray and the raindrops, a shiver coursing through her. He could never break her spirit, never take this part of her away.

A tentative, languorous peace stealing over her, she

turned to face the cottage, the glow of the fire dousing the windows, beckoning to her. Rayne was waiting there for her. She was wet and cold, but somehow soothed by the violence of the storm.

She made her way back up the beach, the warm light spilling from the cottage seeping into her like mulled wine. Up the steps she climbed, her wet jeans cold and weighted around her legs, her hair heavy and soaking down her back, her bare feet chilled.

Rayne stood there, and her heart tripped all over itself.

"You look like you drowned out there," he remarked, reaching down to pick up a towel he had gotten for her. Her blue eyes held a serenity that hadn't been there before. "Come here. You must be frozen."

Her eyes drank him in. When he held out his arms to her, towel in hand, she moved toward him without hesitation and let him dry her hair in sure, relaxing motions.

"You need to get out of those wet clothes," he murmured from behind her, hands working steadily. She seemed transfixed by his voice, eyes closed, unmoving. "Christa?"

"Hmm?"

"Did you hear me?"

"Mmm."

He chuckled. "I brought you some warm clothes to change into. Go ahead and put them on."

Without protest she began peeling away the wet layers, stopping to enjoy the heat of the fire on her bare skin. To give her more privacy he left the room and was rummaging in the fridge when the first piece of soaked clothing hit the floor. He stopped still, instantly forgetting what he was searching for, and closed his eyes. This was torture. Thwap. That sounded like a pair of wet jeans landing on the polished hardwood. He imagined her standing there with nothing on, bathed in firelight, the curve of her hips ... he almost groaned.

"I'm ready," she called.

Covered from neck to ankle in the sweats he had found for her, her sodden clothing drying near the grate, she was sitting on the couch toweling her hair.

His fantasy stalled. "I thought you might want some tea. Milk and sugar?"

"Great, thanks."

His eyes were riveted to her the movement of her outstretched arms, her breasts. *Milk and sugar. Milk and sugar.* With a mental shake he urged himself toward the kitchen for the creamer and sugar bowl. When he came back her almost sated expression and languorous posture made her look like a woman who'd spent the past hour having really, really good sex. It drove him crazy.

She took a sip and closed her eyes. "Mmm, perfect."

He wanted so badly to lean down and kiss those gently curving lips. He'd imagined that same sleepy, contented expression countless times, but always after he'd taken her to bed. Or in the shower. Or on the kitchen table. "Wow. That must have been some walk."

"Yeah. I needed that."

Apparently. He lifted her legs and sat beside her, laying her thighs over his lap and tucking the throw blanket around her.

She sighed and let her eyes close again. "I could stay like this forever."

Her face angled toward the glow of the fire; her breathing deepened. It wasn't fair. He was rock hard and in bad shape, and she was falling asleep on him. The rain pattered against the windows as he gazed down at her longingly. She was fast asleep now, her breasts rising and falling in a deep, steady rhythm. What would she do if he leaned over and kissed her awake? He almost gave in to the need, only managed to resist her at the last second. Forcing the tension to leave his muscles, he rose and carried her to her bedroom. She was so exhausted she didn't even wake up when he laid her down, but rolled to her side and curled into a fetal position, trapping his hand between the supple weight of her breast and the mattress. He swallowed a moan.

Oh, sweetheart, don't do this to me. I'm only human. Before he could stop himself his hand tightened around her, fingers stroking. She sighed and arched closer. It hurt to do it, but he eased his hand away, still feeling the warm softness of her on his palm. He stood there watching her for a moment until he could move and left her room, his whole body throbbing.

****

He was whispering, things he meant to do to her, terrible things. Laughing at her, an ugly laugh, icy. As glacial as the gray eyes boring into to her. His bald head lowered and his teeth sank into her shoulder ...

Christa bolted upright in bed, checking her wrists and ankles for bonds. *Okay, okay, it's just a dream.*

She sagged against the pillows, trembling, wiping the sweat from her face. This was getting out of hand: she had to start getting over it somehow. She would feel so much safer if Rayne were in the room with her. He was only next door, for crying out loud. That warm, strong body was lying in bed right there on the other side of the wall. And here she was, alone and too afraid to go to him.

After debating the issue she got up, grabbed a blanket and closed the bedroom door behind her, wincing at the squeak it made before padding down the hallway toward the front room. Jake's toenails clicked on the hardwood and she hoped they wouldn't wake Rayne as she tiptoed past his door.

"Christa?" he called from inside.

Damn. So much for that idea. After a moment's hesitation, she opened his door. Forcing her eyes to his face, she swallowed, feeling like a lost little girl.

"Uh ... hi." Jake wagged his tail feebly in support. "We were heading to the front room. Did we wake you?" She felt badly for disturbing him again. He clicked on his bedside lamp, illuminating his bare chest and tousled hair.

"Another nightmare? You can always come sleep in here, darlin'."

Her heart leapt and she hovered there. Did she dare go and join him in his bed? She'd fallen asleep on him so many times now, what was the difference?

There's a big difference, her conscience yelled. She edged into the room anyway and closed the door behind her, intending to make up a bed on the floor. It was enough to be in the same room as him: no need to put herself through the torture of crawling between the sheets with him.

She moved toward his bed, keeping an eye on him. God, he wasn't naked under that sheet, was he? Her heart picked up its rhythm. I won't look, she promised herself as she spread her blanket on the floor, Jake claiming his spot at her feet and curling up.

"That's not quite what I had in mind."

The blanket jerked as her fingers clamped together.

"Look, the way I see it, if you can work up the courage to come into my room in the middle of the night, you must really have had a scare." He held out a hand to her. "So, come here." His voice was husky as he patted the mattress beside him.

No way. "I'll be fine down here. Better for my back. My mattress must be too soft or something because it's been aching lately," she babbled, "but thanks anyway."

"C'mon. I promise to behave myself."

Her stomach clenched. Among other things, she was terrified he would sense her attraction for him. So, she just wouldn't touch him, that's all. Steeling herself, she slid in beside him, her back to him. Jake was staring at her, his head cocked to one side. When Rayne's arm snaked around the curve of her waist to pull her against him she nearly jumped out of the bed, instantly went rigid, her heart pounding so madly she was sure he must have felt it. With every nerve ending sending off shockwaves she couldn't afford any more contact than was necessary. She clenched her eyes shut and willed herself to think of him as Michael, cuddling her when she was a little girl. That image didn't last for more than a tenth of a second, and her eyes sprang open.

She must have flinched because his arm tightened. "Relax, kiddo."

Somehow she managed to withhold the bubble of laughter. With effort, she relaxed against him and he snuggled closer, tucking his thighs beneath her hips. She swallowed. How many times had she dreamt of this? Maybe enough to have finally plunged over the edge. Maybe she was hallucinating and Rayne was a manifestation of her dementia.

But oh, sweet God he felt good. Safe. Secure.

"Comfy?" came his dry voice. She nodded, her neck so stiff she practically heard the joints squeaking. His hand reached up to brush the hair away and he rested his forehead against her nape, inhaled deeply against her skin. "Night darlin'," he whispered, sending goose bumps the length of her spine.

Now she was so nervous she'd probably never sleep. She wriggled away from him, desperate to put as little as an inch between them.

No sooner had she moved when he his hand tightened on her waist, holding her still. He cuddled her close until she relaxed against him before easing the pressure of his arm, at least having the decency keep his hips away from her. She lay awake for a long time, staring up at the ceiling as if praying for guidance.

CHAPTER 13

He couldn't get his pulse under control. Where the hell *was* she? He'd already checked her house, her boyfriend's place, the old lady's apartment on the beach, even her mother's penthouse condo in West Vancouver. Nothing. He circled her blonde friend's house again, on the off chance he'd catch a glimpse of Christa or her black truck. Nothing. She hadn't been there last night. Must have stayed with her new boyfriend, that arrogant piece of shit cop.

Maybe her dog was here. He could go after it as punishment. The thought circled his brain, tantalizing him. No. No point in that. Besides, it was beneath him to kill an innocent animal.

He drove aimlessly down the street. He *had* to get to her, redeem his failure. If that nosy old man from next door hadn't interrupted him he could have finished what he'd started. Now she'd escaped, must be away somewhere with that goddamn cop. They hadn't flown anywhere, or he'd have found out about it by hacking into the airline databases. Maybe he could find the cop's cell phone records, track them down that way. How many Rayne Hutchinsons could there be?

Rayne, he scoffed. What a pansy-assed name.

Had he taken her out of town, thinking it would avoid the inevitable outcome? Delay it, that's all. The idea of her being comforted by the son-of-a-bitch made him want to smash his fist through something. He imagined her looking up at her lover with her big blue eyes, all fragile and helpless when nothing could be further from the truth. For a woman she was damned strong, had shocked and impressed him with her will to fight. Turning the corner, the steering wheel sliding beneath his slippery palms, he glanced into the rearview mirror at his swollen, broken nose, at both eyes, puffy and bruised, at the furrows she'd raked across his cheek.

He'd been so close to having her, so close. Everything had been perfect, as if they were following a script in his head, but then his body hadn't cooperated and it had all gone wrong. The memory of not being able to enter her needled him like a shard of glass burrowed under his skin. He'd never had a problem getting hard before, and the humiliation still crawled through him. What the hell had gone wrong? His lust for that strong, sleek, struggling feminine body beneath him should have sent him over the edge, as it had time and time again in his fantasies. Instead he'd wilted like a shriveled carrot.

And then, in the throes of rage, he'd bitten her creamy skin. The mark had to be deep, and they would have made sure to document and analyze the precise puncture wounds his teeth had made. He'd left a similar mark only once before, on his last target, and if the cops ever thought to cross reference the two bites ... Careless of him, to duplicate such an action. He was usually more careful.

No matter. Even if they did match the two cases they still had to catch him, and he wasn't going to let that happen. No way would he go back into the prison system, where every kind of repulsive deviant licked their lips at the thought of screwing him in the shower room. Never again. This time, he called the shots.

A wave of fury pulsed through his veins. Wherever she was, did she think she was safe? That it was finished between them? Oh, no, that little demonstration he'd given her would plant the seed in her head of what he'd do to her for the finale. What would she do when he caught up with her? Turn white and scream? Try to run? The fact that her boyfriend was an ERT officer didn't worry him. He'd simply have to make sure she was alone. Only the last one had been as exciting for him, but she hadn't given him this much trouble. Those terrified brown eyes pleading with him as he choked her, hands flailing against the rope...he could still smell the blood, taste the terror. She had been the best, but also the riskiest. Leaving one minute later would have had him arrested, but he'd trusted his instincts. They'd pulled him in for questioning, raising his blood pressure, but had no hard evidence to pin on him. This time the result would be the same, the payoff even bigger. He would have to be patient, wait for the right moment. He still had time to perfect his plan, get it right. He had to. His life depended on it.

Back in front of his glowing computer screen, he went straight to work. Almost a half-hour passed before he found the record of phone calls. Hmm. Interesting. Four calls made to the same number in Lincoln City, Oregon. Two received from the same number. Another received from Charleston, South Carolina. He checked further back, noted that same number coming up every week or so. Must be someone significant to the cop.

Satisfied he was close to finding Christa, his pulse began to slow. A sense of calm flowed over him. They had to be in the States, he reasoned. Lincoln City seemed the obvious location, but he'd check the Charleston number too, just to be thorough. He was nothing if not thorough.

He reached across his meticulously organized desk for a pad of paper and pen, wrote down the numbers. Now all he had to do was find out whom the numbers belonged to, so he could set the wheels in motion.

Christa was still out there somewhere; she couldn't stay away forever.

****

"So," Bryn chimed, pulling out of the driveway, "Where do you want to go first?"

When Bryn had stopped by for coffee and offered to take Christa shopping with her, fear had risen like a ghost to grab her by the throat. She glanced in the side mirror, spotted an old lady driving a Cadillac, her blue-rinsed head barely visible over the steering wheel. No threat there, except maybe a rear-ender looking for a place to happen. "I want to get something for Rayne. You know, something to thank him for everything he's done for me."

"Nice idea. Like what?"

"I don't know. What do you think? I mean, you obviously know him *much* better than I do. After all, you've been friends for years—"

Bryn laughed. "We've never slept together, Christa."

Her mouth hung open. "I never th—"

"Oh, yes you did. I knew from the first moment I met you that you thought Rayne and I were an item."

Embarrassment coursed through her. Damn, she hated being so transparent.

"Well, anyway, we haven't. Rayne's like a brother to me. If we were to have sex it would be tantamount to incest, y'know?"

Relief flooded her: she had no reason to be jealous of Bryn's dark beauty. "He told me he used to scare the crap out of your dates."

"Exactly what a good brother would do, right?" She grimaced. "He saved my butt once. This one guy wasn't taking no for an answer and I was shoving him off me in the backseat of his car when Rayne reaches through the window and drags the guy out. Talk about an adrenaline junkie with a hero complex"

"That's him, all right." She took another glance in the side mirror. The ocean gleamed silver-blue in the late morning sun, waves crashing on the golden sand. After a few blocks with no sign of a tail, she began to relax.

"You're safe with me, girl." Bryn patted her hand. "I've got a black belt in karate and I'm not afraid to use it."

Rayne would never have agreed to let her go with Bryn unless he felt confident of her safety, so she figured the woman must be quite something. Had he told Bryn she'd been attacked? Surely she'd been curious about the bruising. She shifted in her seat. "I guess you can tell from my face that … I'm not sure if Rayne told you, but—"

"I know the gist of it."

The crushing sense of shame vanished, maybe because Bryn didn't make a huge deal out of it. She was a social worker after all, must be used to working with battered women. "Do you—have you seen this kind of thing before? In your work?"

Bryn's expression hardened. "All too often, I'm afraid. Though usually it's their partner who attacks them."

… your boyfriend's even bigger than me. Imagine the damage a guy his size could do. The words came out of nowhere, the photo of her and Rayne witnessing the scene playing out in a disjointed series of snapshots. The glint

of the knife, the taunts. She closed her eyes.

"Unfortunately there's no shortage of sickos out there," Bryn continued.

"I wondered if the women you've dealt with ... if they recovered afterward. Had normal lives, got married, had kids. That sort of thing." As she processed the words they brought comfort, made her feel less alone, less like a freak of nature for being targeted.

"Most of them, with the right help." She cast her a skewed glance. "You *are* getting help, right?"

Christa shook her head. "Not until I go back home. For now I'm writing in a journal about it. The social worker at the hospital told me it would help."

"No counseling, no therapy, nothing?"

"Not yet. It seemed more important to ... get me away from there."

Bryn pulled over and killed the engine, slewing around in her seat. "So let me guess—you're not sleeping? Having nightmares? Jumping at shadows, having anxiety attacks?"

She swallowed the lump in her throat, prayed the tears wouldn't overflow. "The dreams are the worst thing. I wake up feeling like I'm choking to death."

Bryn's eyes filled with sympathy. "You must be really strong to function so well. If it weren't for the bruises I'd never know anything had happened to you."

Strong? She didn't feel strong. Not anymore. She had been strong, before the psycho ruined her life, but not now. Now, she feared one good crack in her emotional armor would shatter her into a thousand pieces. Having fallen apart once already, after Cameron, she couldn't afford to let it happen again. "Without Rayne, I wouldn't function at all right now." Bryn's steady, understanding gaze gave her the courage to say it aloud. "I'm trying so hard not to be clingy with him, but it's tough not to. He makes me feel so safe ... I can't put it into words. But I'm afraid of becoming dependent on him. If I do, he'll feel smothered, and when he walks away I—"

"What makes you think he'll walk away?"

Uh ... his reputation? His track record? The reality that he could have any woman on the earth, so why would he pick one that was freaked out and neurotic?

152

"Look, I can't read the man's mind, but I can tell you he's letting you lean on him because he wants you to. As for being clingy, I think you're entitled to be after what happened, and I can't think of anyone I'd want watching my back more than Rayne—except maybe his dad. You didn't seem clingy at all to me the first night when you left us at the bonfire. If anyone's being clingy, I'd say it's him. When you went back to the cottage that night he jumped up like someone had stabbed him with a cattle prod. I've never seen him like that with anyone else, and I told his mom that. Told her he's got it bad this time."

A thrill raced through her, the seed of hope she'd tucked in her heart taking root and blooming.

Bryn took hold of her cold hand, giving it a squeeze. "Rayne's being protective of you, and rightly so until this guy is caught. If Nate has anything to do with it, he'll find him. And if you want to talk about what happened, you can come to me anytime, okay?"

Her heart constricted, the words meant so much. "Thank you." She leaned over and gave her new friend a hug.

Bryn wiped away the tears gathered on Christa's lashes. "So whaddya say? You ready for some retail therapy?"

She let out a deep breath. "God, yes. By the time I'm done, my Visa card will be melted around the edges." They shared a laugh, then headed along the sidewalk.

"About this gift for Rayne ..." Bryn prompted.

"I want to get him something he'll really love."

"A watch?"

"Not sure. But I'll know it when I see it."

Bryn stopped to browse through a rack of purses. "So, how are things with you two, anyway? You slept with him yet?"

Christa's mouth fell open.

"Oh, don't be such a prude. Have you?"

Technically she had slept with him, hadn't she? But not the way Bryn meant. "Rayne and I are only friends— he hasn't even kissed me. He only invited me down here to stay with him to help take ... to get me away from everything."

Bryn rolled her eyes. "That's what he told me, but

there's nothing wrong with my eyesight for God's sake."

"Oh." Her heart leapt at the prospect that a guy she'd considered so far out of her league might actually be interested in her, but how could she be sure it wouldn't be physical and short-lived?

"Don't you go pale on me. I didn't mean he would try and jump your bones the first chance he got. If that was all he wanted he'd have done it by now." She gave a reassuring smile. "Take it from me, hon, he really cares about you."

Why couldn't she believe it? Until he said or did anything to advance their relationship past friendship, common sense and emotional survival dictated keeping her feelings to herself.

Within an hour she'd found the perfect gift, and when they pulled up into Bryn's driveway Jake was watching them out the window, his flapping tail swishing the curtains from side to side. "There's my guy," Christa gushed, stooping to play with his ears. Bryn bent to gather the newspaper and mail on the front step on their way in.

"Package for you," she said, handing over a flat white box tied with string. Christa frowned. At Bryn's place? It had her name on it. Had Rayne left her a surprise? She pulled the string away, opened the box.

And dropped it with a gasp, hands flying to her mouth.

"What?" Bryn demanded, pushing past her to see.

"It's from him," Christa quavered, stricken. Her heart thundered in her ears, panic raking its icy claws over her chilled skin. He'd found her. How had he found her? Was he watching her now? She stared down at the hideous thing, unable to look away.

A gingerbread man, its eyes missing, holes punched through the body by something sharp. A bite was missing from its left shoulder.

She could almost hear that raspy voice whispering in her ear: *You can't catch me, I'm the gingerbread man.*

Gagging, she stumbled into the bathroom and threw up.

****

As he left the gym, his cell phone vibrated against

his hip. Bryn.

"Hi," he answered. "You guys done—"

"You've got to come over right now."

The fear in her voice hit him like a fist. "What's the matter?" His pulse quickened.

"Someone left Christa a special delivery here while we were away. A gingerbread cookie with a bunch of holes in it, and she freaked out."

His muscles clenched, heart tripping. He knew what it signified—that note the stalker had left her with the nursery rhyme in it. *Run, run as fast as you can...*"Christ, I don't believe this." How the hell would he have found them? He ran the rest of the way to the car. "I'll be there in ten minutes. Is she okay?"

"Don't think so. She's still in the bathroom, won't come out. I heard her throwing up."

God. "Tell her I'm coming."

"Okay." She sounded scared spitless. "It was the guy who attacked her, right? Should I call the cops?"

"I'll do it. I'll call Nate right now, let him know." He tried to make his voice soothing. "I'll be there soon, 'kay?"

"'Kay."

"Want me to stay on the line with you?"

"No, you'd better make those calls. I'm going to see if I can calm her down."

"Thanks. See you in ten."

"Nine," she corrected, and hung up.

He dialed Nate on the road and filled him in.

"Son of a bitch," Nate snarled in disbelief. "All right. I'll do what I can on this end, keep you updated if I find anything."

That's all he could hope for at this point, Rayne admitted bitterly. Pulling up in front of Bryn's, he jumped out and checked the perimeter, looking for footprints, anything suspicious. Nothing. Bryn met him at the door with an anxious expression.

"How is she?" he asked, though he could guess.

"Better. Pretty shaken up, though." She handed him a plain white bakery box.

The grotesque cookie lay there, its gouged eye sockets staring sightlessly at him. "Yeah, I'll bet." He studied the puncture wounds, noted the mouthful missing from the shoulder. He thought it odd, that someone would go to the trouble of mutilating a partially eaten cookie. It had to be deliberate.

He told Bryn to put it away in case they needed it for evidence later on, then found Christa huddled on the sofa with Jake, wrapped in a blanket. Her eyes filled with relief when she saw him.

"Hi," she whispered. The shadows under her eyes seemed even darker in her pale face.

"Hi, darlin'." He sat next to her and pulled her close. "Feeling better?"

She gave a slight nod against his shoulder, fingers fretting with the edge of the blanket. "Do you think he followed us here? Maybe saw me leaving with Bryn this morning and thought I was staying here?"

He wanted to put her mind at ease, but he had no explanation for it and didn't want to lie to her. "I don't know, kiddo, but I highly doubt it. To get across the border he'd have to have a fake passport—"

"Which is possible."

"It's possible, but not likely. I think this was his way of reminding you he's still out there." He could have left the package himself, but that meant he'd have had to clear customs at the border and stay close enough to monitor their activities. No way. Too risky, and Rayne would have noticed someone watching them. However, the guy *could* have done it without risking capture. Maybe he'd somehow traced them through cell phone records. He could have found Bryn's address that way, then phoned down and had it delivered. But then, what sort of bakery would deliver a mutilated cookie, even if the customer tried to convince them it was a joke?

His phone rang. He sat up and checked the ID. "Hey, Nate." He met Christa's gaze, waited for the news.

"Customs confirmed Seth has not crossed the border. Not by foot, bicycle, plane, car, bus or ferry, so unless he found a way to beam himself to Lincoln City, he's still up here."

"He hasn't crossed the border," he relayed to Christa, and she sagged against the cushions. He squeezed her hand. "That's good news."

"Yeah," Nate agreed. "But if he didn't follow you, how

did he do it? Did he trace your phone calls?"

"Maybe. Could have hacked into my account, or intercepted my mail I guess. It's all I can think of."

"And then Fed-Exed the package down?"

"No, it wasn't couriered. He must have ordered it down here somewhere."

"I can't wait to nail this guy's ass."

Rayne grunted. "Take a number."

"I'll check out the bakeries in the area, see if I can find out anything more. How's Christa holding up?"

"As well as can be expected."

Nate grunted. "All right, that's all for now, but I'll keep in touch. Tell Christa we're on top of everything."

"Will do." He set his phone down and blew out a breath, glanced down at her. "That's a relief."

She opened her eyes. "No kidding." Sighing, she rolled her neck around, looked to Bryn standing in the doorway.

"Want some hot cider or something?"

"That would be great, thanks."

He studied Christa's profile, the warm imprint of her body burning through the layers of cloth separating them. So strong, to bear all this and not break into a million pieces. She continually impressed him with her courage. He kissed the top of her head. "You stay here and relax for a while and I'll help Bryn."

The warmth in her grateful smile wrapped around his heart like a fist.

****

When Rayne followed Bryn back into the living room carrying a tray of steaming mugs, he stopped dead at the sight of her, staring, and Christa realized the blanket had been hiding her hair. "You cut your hair," he blurted.

She pushed the blanket off her shoulders and fingered the chin-length bob. "I was having a moment," she confessed as he set the tray down.

He stroked where the sweep of hair touched the curve of her jaw, leaving tingles in his wake. "I like it."

"She's been thinking of doing it for forever," Bryn piped up, "So I encouraged her, and took her to a stylist friend of mine. A few snips and she's a new woman."

Christa spared him an uncomfortable glance. "My

long hair was so much trouble. And this way no one will ever be able to grab me by my braid."

He held out a hand to her. "Brave girl. You look gorgeous."

The compliment warmed her all the way to her toes, even more than the cider. After drinking it she felt much better. The icy terror was gone, replaced with confidence her attacker was still across the border, and that she was safe while in Rayne's care. The gingerbread man had been a hideous reminder of what he'd already done to her, what he'd like to do to her. But for now, anyway, she was safe.

Safe and on vacation with a gorgeous man, and she was damn well going to enjoy the rest of it. No way would she let today's gruesome incident set her back.

Rayne and Bryn were wonderful with her, letting her quietly gather her nerves and then drawing her into more lighthearted conversation to take her mind off the incident. A couple of hours later when Rayne asked if she felt up to walking home, she agreed. She could use some fresh air, and they'd pick up the rental car tomorrow.

They said goodbye to Bryn and started up the beach toward home, tossing sticks into the foaming surf for Jake, who plunged into the chilly water without a care and raced back to them sopping wet, prize clenched between his teeth. The tide was out, leaving bands of seaweed and driftwood washed up in tangles of green and gray ribbon. Gulls winged in the cerulean sky, gliding past wisp-soft clouds in the salty breeze. Children laughed and splashed in the waves, chasing rainbow colored kites carried on gusts of wind, parents sitting on blankets with picnic hampers as they supervised the construction of sandcastles. Rayne slid his arm around her shoulders, as if trying to accustom her to the contact without scaring her. She appreciated his concern, but he didn't need to treat her like spun glass. It wasn't his touch that frightened her, especially after spending the night in his bed with him wrapped around her like a living blanket. She was afraid being intimate with him would trigger the memories of the attack and provoke an anxiety episode.

Now she barely tensed, though she stayed acutely

aware of the warmth and strength of that hand on her bare flesh, her skin buzzing with sensation. She dug into her bag and took a bite of the caramel apple she'd treated herself to.

"So did y'all have a good time shopping?" he asked, gliding his hand down her arm to catch her hand, lacing their fingers. *Please* don't let her palm get sweaty.

"Mm-hmm," she replied around another mouthful of caramel. It stuck to the corner of her mouth and she licked it away, the cut in her lip stinging. She covered the wince and he watched her with something close to amused adoration.

"What?" she demanded.

"You missed a spot."

She went to wipe it with her hand but he caught her fingers in his.

"Let me." He brought both hands up to cup her face, bent his head and touched his lips to the side of her mouth, absorbing the jolt that went through her. Her hands flattened against his chest, the caramel apple falling to the sand at her feet.

"Rayne?" Her heart stuttered. Could she possibly be misinterpreting this?

"Hmm?" he murmured, nibbling at the caramel, a grin tugging at his lips.

"What are you doing?" Her face was burning up between his hands. If he was teasing her again, she'd die.

"Giving you a second to get used to how this feels," he whispered, "so you don't panic when I kiss you for real."

"Oh ..." Good God, he was going to kiss her for real? She might not survive it.

He skimmed his thumbs across her cheekbones and brushed his lips over hers, testing, asking, as if he could feel the nervousness warring inside her, her body tensed for flight.

This is Rayne, and he cares about you, keeps you safe. She held her ground as he lowered his head and kissed her slowly, adjusting the angle and pressure until she rewarded him with a gasp, her fingers digging into his shirt. Her heart beat so hard and fast she was afraid it might stop. His mouth coaxed hers, making her toes curl in her sandals. His tongue slid across her bottom lip, stroking inside to tease hers. The roar of heat rushed through her body to the pit of her stomach, stunning her, left her reeling for breath and balance. Her shaking hands gripped his shirt as though it was a lifeline. He released her mouth, pulled back just enough to give her room to breathe, and gazed down into her face.

His eyes blazed with hunger. "That wasn't so bad, was it?"

She nodded, then shook her head to correct herself. If he'd done that to distract her, he'd succeeded. Breathing was a supreme effort.

But oh, God. If he kissed her like that again she wouldn't be able to stop.

****

He let go of her hand at the back door while she toweled Jake off, couldn't think straight he was so starved for her. God. He wanted to back her up against the door and kiss her until she let out that little gasp and dug her fingers into him again, until her knees gave out and she slid to the floor. Beneath him.

Since that would scare the living hell out of her, he busied himself putting away the dishes, the mundane chore clearing his head. Had he pushed too hard, too soon? She hadn't panicked and shoved him away, but the fear in her eyes had almost stopped him. Like a deer in the headlights. Had he really taken her so off guard?

She came into the kitchen and washed her hands, flashing him a brief, sweet smile. That haircut was damned sexy on her. It made her eyes look even bigger, bluer somehow. He could drown in them.

Blushing under his hungry stare, she removed a box from her bag and held it out to him. "I got you something."

"What for?" The last thing he wanted was for her to feel indebted to him.

"Just because."

He opened the velvet box to reveal a medallion. Stunned, he lifted the gold chain from its satin bed, rubbing his thumb over the image.

"They didn't have any Saint Christophers," she explained, her heart in her eyes, "but this is Saint Michael, the patron saint of police officers, so I thought it would be even better. I had it engraved on the back."

He turned it over in his fingers.

To my knight in shining armor. May this always keep you safe from any dangers you face. Love Christa.

He stared at it in wonder. Imagine her remembering the story about his mom's gift to his father. He'd only mentioned it once.

"I wanted to give you this because, through everything—" her voice thickened, and she swallowed. "Through everything that's happened, you've been there for me every single time I needed you. Including today."

He gazed down into her earnest face, let himself tumble into the wide blue pools of her eyes.

She reached up to hug him, turning her face into his throat. "So that makes you *my* hero, Rayne. Thank you for everything you've done."

"Chris ..." he said into her hair. "Sweetheart, I'll always be there." He pulled back to meet her gaze, made sure she knew he meant it.

She blinked away the moisture, ventured a watery smile. "So, do you like it?"

He couldn't bear to say she shouldn't have bought him anything, not when she was looking up at him with such heartbreaking uncertainty. "I love it. Put it on for me." He stood still while she reached around his neck to clasp the chain, breathing in the freshness of her hair and tingling at the brush of her fingers against the nape of his neck. It was all he could do to stop himself from burying his face in the curve of her shoulder and kissing her breathless. Instead he smoothed the crown of her head and said, "Thank you."

He let his hand rest there, loath to stop touching her in even that small way, convinced his chest would explode. Eventually he gave in and leaned down to kiss her, just a slow taste of her, enough to make their breath shorten.

His cell phone buzzed on his belt. *Leave it.* Her lips were so warm and welcoming. *No, it might be important.* Tearing himself from her, he checked the caller ID.

He held her questioning gaze. "Hey, Nate. What's up?"

"Just wanted to give you an update."

"Okay." He kept his expression impassive. "Shoot."

"We've received a few solid leads, alleged sightings of him at the ballpark and Christa's place, cruising around her friend's neighborhood and so on, but so far none have panned out. And still no evidence to suggest he's crossed the border."

Damn. Why did he keep thinking it was going to be simple?

"There is something else ..."

"And what's that?" He stroked his thumb over her cheek to reassure her, then stared out the window so she couldn't see his face.

"That cold case homicide a couple years ago. A TV reporter, tied up in the back of a vehicle and raped. Identified Seth before she died within hours of surgery for multiple stab wounds. Turns out she tried to get a restraining order against a stalker weeks before the attack, but didn't have enough on him to obtain it. Sound familiar?"

"Yeah." Very. And now that goddamn cookie with its sightless eyes and puncture marks made him want to throw up. "It was him?"

"According to the profiler we've been working with, Seth matches the perp's profile. White male between twenty-five and thirty-five, seems normal, even friendly to his victims. A neat-freak, almost obsessive-compulsive, needs routine to feel in control. Motivated by power, like most rapists, not sex. Apparently our guy's a real genius with computers, electronic stuff, so he could have hacked into Christa's alarm service provider's database and gotten her entry code, and he could have found your cell phone records, which would explain today's little adventure. We figure he's into some kind of tech support, the sort of thing he could do over the phone to keep contact with people to a minimum. A smart bastard, holds two degrees, one in computer science and the other ... the other's a double major in criminology and psych."

So that's what was up with all the mind games. And why he was so hard for the cops to pin down.

"And that's not all. Turns out he had a fucked-up childhood. Abused, possibly sexually but certainly physically, probably by his father, mother does nothing to intervene."

"Sounds textbook."

"Pretty much, except in Seth's case his step-dad was an ex-cop."

Rayne's heart picked up speed, fingers tightening on the phone. "Really."

"His print pulled from that stolen SUV matches the one taken at the reporter's murder scene, and this morning forensics made a positive match between the ... uh ... the bite marks."

Bite marks? What bite marks? He whipped around to frown at Christa. Was that what had happened to her shoulder? His heart pounded, his stomach curled. "Wait a minute—"

"The punctures match the other victim's wound exactly."

And now he knew why the cookie had been missing a bite from its shoulder. Sick to his stomach, Rayne turned away again, trying to conceal the way his muscles cramped.

All this time he'd assumed it was a knife wound, but the bastard had taken a chunk out of her with his teeth.

He swallowed the bile in his throat.

"Thing is, Hutch, so far Christa's the only one we know of who's tangled with this guy and lived to tell us about it. He's a slick bastard, not the type to leave loose ends, so—"

"I got it." He didn't need to hear the words. His guts clenched.

"I've already assembled a task force. We're doing everything we can, but both of you be careful, you hear?"

"Sure will, Nate. I'll tell her. Thanks for calling." *Damn. And she was just starting to deal with the fallout.*

When he was sure his expression was composed, he turned to face her. She was watching him, face pale, gnawing on her lower lip.

So it hadn't only been rape she'd avoided that night. If her neighbor hadn't been so conscientious she'd be six feet underground right now. And now her attacker would do everything in his power to make sure she couldn't ID him.

"What?" she demanded, her eyes troubled. "What did

he say?"

He set the phone down and gathered her against him, her warmth chasing away the chill of fear inside him. He wanted to know about the bite mark but couldn't bring himself to ask. As calmly as he could he broke the news about the investigation, holding her close while she absorbed the shock of it.

She pulled back and gazed up into his eyes, the fear there eating at him like acid. "But if it's true he killed that other woman, and I'm the only one who's survived, then ..." The horror dawned, her pupils constricting.

She shook her head and he stroked her hair, helpless to protect her from the truth. St. Michael pressed against his chest like lead. Some knight in shining armor he was.

He hated to say it, but she needed to hear the truth. He passed a hand down the side of her ashen face. "Then chances are, he wants to finish what he started."

CHAPTER 14

The last speck of blood red sun dipped into the ocean, enveloping the world in shades of lavender and sapphire. The breeze brought the tang of salt water with it, the dampness enough to form swirls of mist along the shore. Christa came in from the back porch and found Rayne building a fire in the hearth.

"This will warm you up," he said with a smile, tossing the match into the firewood.

After Nate's phone call on top of the cookie incident, she doubted she'd ever be warm again.

He dusted his hands on his well worn jeans and urged her to sit on the floor with him, settling her in the vee of his legs and easing her against his chest. "Better?" he asked against her ear.

She barely suppressed the shiver that coursed through her, focused instead on absorbing the heat of the fire and his body.

He turned her sideways so he could see her face, kissed the tip of her nose, her cheek, the corner of her mouth before covering her lips with his own. "I could kiss you all night," he whispered. "But I'm not going to because I don't want to scare you, and I don't want you to feel pressured."

She gave him a grateful smile. Nothing like mortal fear to stave off physical intimacy.

She cuddled into him, craving the sanctuary he offered. The flames licked over the logs piled in the grate, their crackle soothing along with the muted roar of the ocean and Rayne's heartbeat steady under her ear. Part of her wished he would try and seduce her, if only to shut her brain off for a while. All she could think about was being hunted, that a predator was out there somewhere, after her right now. "I don't know if I can handle this," she admitted.

His hand paused in its motion over her hair. "Do you mean us, or—"

"No." She doubted she could handle that either, but that was a worry for later on, when she wasn't terrified of being murdered. "That he wants to kill me."

"Don't, kiddo." He wrapped his arms around her, held on tight. "Don't think about it."

"How can I not think about it?" she demanded, part of her aware he was only trying to help. "I can't *stop* thinking about it." She was so tense she thought she might scream, her shoulder muscles in knots and an intense headache drumming at her temples.

"He's not going to get anywhere near you again because we're going to be that much more careful until he's caught."

Everyone kept saying he'd get caught, reassuring her he'd be in jail soon. But when each day passed with no positive updates, no promising news, it was harder and harder for her to believe. At the very least the psycho had turned her life upside down. She'd lost her chance at making the national team, been chased from her home and forced to quit working, then attacked. Apparently she would have been killed if not for Patrick, and it still wasn't over.

How could she go on like this? Aside from the stress and trauma she'd already suffered, she had a business to run and couldn't do it from Rayne's living room back in White Rock. Her employees were handling the current jobs fine, but what about future projects? She needed to be out there doing assessments, giving quotes, designing and pitching her plans for each prospective new client. Without recruiting fresh clientele, her business would wither and die as surely as a plant left to bake in the summer sun. And without money coming in, how could she pay her mortgage? How would she and Jake eat?

A charred log crumbled into the embers, showering red sparks up the chimney. She envied their freedom.

"What can I do to take your mind off it?" Rayne asked, rubbing her arms. His palms against her skin made her all shivery, jerking her mind from its morose track for the moment.

She arched a brow at him over her shoulder. "Knock

me unconscious?"

He sifted his fingers through her hair, igniting that spark of awareness between them, even stronger since he'd first kissed her. Of course that was *before* she'd known she was a marked woman, and this was *after*. Big difference. She yanked her attention back to the present.

"Let's go for a run."

She must not have heard him right. "You think I feel like exercising?"

"Got a better idea?"

Yes. She wanted to go outside, stick her head in the sand like an ostrich, and hide until it was all over. But a run? "All right, I guess it can't hurt." If nothing else, it might tire her out enough to let her sleep through the night for a change. She went and threw on some sweats and pulled on her running shoes. Already at the back door with Jake, he loped down the steps with her dog at his heels.

She fell into step beside him, breathing in the clean, brisk salt air, the crash of the waves and the softness of the sand muffling their footfalls. It didn't take her long to feel the benefits to her cardiovascular system, her legs pumping to stabilize her on the uneven surface. Her abraded ankles burned where they rubbed against her socks, but she understood now why he'd suggested the run. Her nervous system had been suspended in fight-or-flight mode, especially since the phone call this afternoon. Giving her body something to do with the restless, nervous energy was exactly what she'd needed to vent it from her system.

"You're in great shape," he complimented her after about twenty minutes.

He still had enough oxygen to talk? That was plain wrong. She wheezed a thanks, Jake's tongue hanging out of his mouth as he panted beside her. At least someone else was feeling it.

Thankfully Rayne soon slowed and came to a stop. "Let's walk back to cool down."

Bent over at the waist, sucking in oxygen, she gave him a weary thumbs-up. After a few minutes her breathing was under control, her mind alert and her body energized. "I needed that. How did you know?" Jake trotted over to have his ears scratched.

Rayne took hold of her other hand and laced their fingers together. "Because that's how I deal with my adrenaline overloads when I'm all keyed up and an operation gets canned."

He'd talked about being prepped for a stakeout or sting op, then having the plug pulled at the last minute. All those guys with their weapons locked and loaded, ready to roll, the air reeking of testosterone, then oops—sorry fellas, no action today. Go on back to the station and wait for the next call, play tiddlywinks or something. She squeezed his hand. "Well, it sure worked for me."

"Good. Running's one of the best things to help you unwind."

She tipped her head back to the sky, taking a deep breath of fresh, cool air. The stars were coming out, pinpoints in a sea of blackness. All the way back to the cottage he kept hold of her hand, the contact helping her to forget that Seth was still out there somewhere, wanting her dead.

After they had both showered she prepared dinner with the mellow notes of Tony Bennett's voice filling the room. Rayne came toward her with a smile that made her heart accelerate. "Dance with me."

Her mouth went dry. She craved being close to him, but what if led to something more and she couldn't handle it? "I'm not really a good dancer."

"It's easy." His warm hand wrapped around her right one, fingers enfolding hers in a confident grip. "I'll lead, you follow." His other hand slid down her spine to splay across her lower back, bringing her close against his body and making her grasp his shoulder for balance while the breath backed up in her lungs. The heat radiating from him filled her senses with his clean, soapy scent.

Her knees sagged. Putty, that's what she was, and the gleam in his eyes said he knew it.

"Let's see if this will take your mind off everything for a while."

The hand resting on her back seemed to burn through her shirt as it guided her, her belly jumping as her breasts made contact with the wall of his chest. He led her smoothly while she stared at the hollow near the base of his throat, too unsure of herself to look him in the eye. The anxiety remained, but now it was focused on the feel of that long, lean body against hers. Something dark and needy unfurled low in her abdomen.

"Close your eyes."

Christa obeyed the low murmur. Taking a deep breath to steady herself, she found it natural to lay her cheek against the muscular curve of his shoulder. Unable to resist, she nuzzled him, inhaling his scent deeply. Hints of soap and tangy cologne.

"You feel so good," he whispered against her temple.

Lord, so did he. Her whole body tingled. She was so exhausted, hadn't had a good night's sleep since the attack. Rayne was so solid and warm, the fire crackling behind her as the music crooned. They were barely moving now, swaying to the music. Her mind drifted.

"Hey. Here I am trying to impress you with my smoothness, and you're falling asleep on your feet."

"Was I? Sorry." She gave him a wry smile. "Bet that's never happened to you before, huh?"

He caressed her lips with his thumb. "A lot of things never happened to me before I met you. I'm in unfamiliar territory."

"Yeah? That makes two of us." She was utterly lost in him. When he bent his head she tilted her face, sliding her hands to tangle in his hair. He settled his mouth over hers and kissed her as though he wanted to draw the soul right out of her body, bent her backward just enough so she had to hold on tight to keep her balance. Digging her fingers into the muscles in his shoulders, she battled for control.

The ache in her chest intensified, her body raging a war between old fears of commitment, of abandonment, and this new insatiable need she was afraid to unleash. To separate the trauma of the attack from the security and emotional intimacy he represented.

Rayne took her deeper, stroking her tongue with his, sensation zinging down into the pit of her belly. His hands caressed her neck and shoulders, eased the length of her spine, then traced over her taut stomach and up to brush the curve of her left breast. She moaned and leaned into him, shocked at how good it felt. He brushed a thumb over her nipple, making her arch and gasp. Slow and sure, he kept moving his thumb while he licked into her mouth, leaving her trembling. She broke the kiss with a gasp and buried her face against his neck, shaking, battling the intense throbbing in her lower body.

Take me to bed. The crazy plea formed, crowded her throat. She wanted to forget all the crazy melodrama, even if for one night.

"You all right?" His voice was low and rough.

"Yeah." Her legs wobbled as he cradled her there in the firelight. Finally he broke the contact and stepped back.

He scrubbed a hand over his face and blew out a breath. "Ready to sleep yet?"

"I think that's probably the smartest thing for me to do."

"I think you're right." He straightened, dragged his fingers through his hair.

At least she wasn't the only one dying of need. "Rayne—"

"Don't, Chris. We'll take this as slow as you need to. Nothing's going to happen until you're ready."

If she hadn't been in love with him already, that would have done the trick.

****

As was already his habit, Rayne checked in on her before he went to bed, noting the spiral notebook clenched in one hand though she was fast asleep. He crossed the room to watch her for a moment.

She was breathing hard, her body twitching...another nightmare. He put his hand on her shoulder and she bolted upright with a strangled gasp, eyes wild and disoriented in her pale face. He stood still beside her, made no sudden moves as her eyes focused on him. "Easy, Chris," he said soothingly, not daring to touch her. "It was just a dream." Her face was glazed with perspiration and the mattress vibrated with her trembling.

She fought for air as if her throat was closed off, as if someone was strangling her.

"Jesus." His heart thundered, panic bubbling inside him. He forced it down, willing himself to appear calm for her.

The choking gasps lessened and her body shook even more wildly, as if she were going into shock. She reached out blindly and clung to his arm like a lifeline, tears streaming through her clenched lids. She gulped lungfuls of air and fell back onto her pillow, clamping her arms around her belly and moaning, curling onto her side.

"I'm gonna to be sick," she blurted, shoving at him and leaping out of bed to careen into the bathroom, the door slamming behind her.

Rayne went to stand there, wincing at the retching coming from inside. Should he go in and hold her hair back? The toilet flushed and then the basin tap was running. A minute later the shower came on, and he leaned his forehead against the doorframe.

After a while longer he knocked on the door. "Chris, are you all right in there?"

No answer. Only the sound of her grief muffled by the spray of water.

He swung the door open. "Chris?" he said again, barely making out her silhouette behind the shower curtain. She huddled with her arms wrapped around herself, choking back the sobs ripping from her chest. Trying to shut the pain away where he couldn't see it. He wished she'd just let go.

He hunkered next to the tub, letting the shower run for another few minutes before he reached in to shut it off. The dripping of water and her hitching breaths filled the humid bathroom.

She opened glassy, shadowed eyes to peer through the gap between the shower curtain and the wall, then flung herself into his arms and hung on.

He held her, trying to stop the trembling that shook her. Her fingers dug into his back, her wet torso soaking his t-shirt. "When will they stop?" she demanded in an agonized whisper.

He stroked her dripping hair, pressed a kiss on the top of her head. "I don't know, sweetheart." She let out a defeated sigh and sagged against him, silently conveying her trust.

He grabbed a towel from the rack and wrapped her in it, hauling her out of the tub and onto his lap. "You scared the hell out of me back there. I thought you were going to stop breathing."

"Sorry," she whispered unsteadily. "They're not usually this bad." She seemed to curl into herself.

Given all that had happened that day, he wasn't surprised she'd had another nightmare. He just hadn't known it would be like this. "Want to tell me about it?"

Her body went rigid in his arms. When she didn't say a word, he pulled back and searched her face.

"You know what happened." The heat in her tone revealed her vulnerability.

"That's the whole problem. I don't."

"Rayne, I'm sorry, but I don't want to talk about it."

He sighed and gave her a level look. "I know it's tough, but how can I help you with this if I don't know what you're going through, what you've been through?"

"Don't you understand? I don't want you to know what he did, what he said..." She battled more tears. "P-pass me my robe, please."

He grabbed it from behind the door and wrapped the thick terrycloth folds around her, held her close. She pushed away, swaying upright and moving to sit on the closed toilet seat. Her spine straightened and her shoulders went back.

"If you don't mind, I need a minute to myself."

In other words, *get out and leave me alone.* Her body language shouted it at him. Christ, he hated it when she shut him out. "Take your time." Her physical and mental retreat filled him with something close to panic. She was slipping away from him, and he was helpless to stop it.

****

Despite the robe covering her she couldn't stop shivering. He'd been more than patient with her, and he did deserve to know more than she'd told him. It wasn't just the attack, although God knew that was enough to make her panic all by itself. This new threat had scraped her raw.

Surging with helpless anger, she made her way into the sitting room, the fire still snapping in the hearth. Rayne was sitting on the sofa.

"I made you some tea," he said, his relaxed posture belying the tension between them. She felt as though she was about to face a firing squad.

She gratefully accepted the hot mug, glad she would have something to do with her hands, and paced about the room, avoiding his gaze.

No point in dancing around the subject. "I'm not ready to talk about the attack yet," she blurted. "So exactly what else do you want to know? The sordid details of my last relationship? Why I've turned into a nutcase?" He didn't react to her aggression, merely sat there with that maddeningly calm expression on his face.

"Hush, honey. Whatever you can tell me. I'm listening."

She continued pacing, desperate to burn off the nervous energy. "Okay, how about I give you the Coles Notes version." She prayed for strength. "Five years ago I was living in Tucson with my boyfriend of two years, and when I came home a day early from a softball road trip, I found him in bed with a friend of ours." Hannah, the blonde engineering student with the double-D implants. "Well, as you can imagine, I'd had no idea he was cheating on me. After she left we got into a huge fight, and the long and the short of it was that he was sleeping with her and a bunch of other women because—how did he put it? I wasn't 'putting out' enough," she used her fingers as quotation marks, "and I was frigid. He had needs, you know, and I wasn't taking care of them properly." The anger pulsed through her all over again. "I told him I might not be so 'frigid' if he'd tried thawing me out from time to time, and things went downhill from there."

"Truth is, I dreaded sex with him because I didn't enjoy it, but according to him there was something wrong with me, because it couldn't be his fault. Lots of other women wanted sex with him, so I must be the one with the problem. And he still expected me to 'put out' whenever he felt like it." There, she'd said it. Lightning hadn't struck her down where she stood. "So you do the math, Rayne. I hated sex for the two years I was having it, therefore I haven't had any since."

He opened his mouth to say something, but she held up a hand. "Bottom line, the first and only sexual relationship I've ever had was over five years ago, and it didn't do a damn thing for me." She gathered her courage and glanced at him, then into the flickering fire. "How can this ever work between us? I'm all closed up, and I don't know if I can open that part of myself again. Compare my history to your infamous sexual exploits and you can see why I'm a walking cautionary tale. Even before what just happened with the...the..." She buried her face in her hands.

"Chris, *stop*." He came over to put an arm around her. "Honey, I don't care how inexperienced you are, and as for your ex, he didn't deserve you. He was a selfish asshole who did a number on your self esteem, and I can't believe you put up with him as long as you did."

Sometimes she had trouble believing it herself.

"There's nothing wrong with you, trust me. You just about burned me alive when I kissed you, and we still had all our clothes on. And as for my past exploits as you call them, well, I'm a hell of a lot more grown up than I used to be."

She disengaged herself and gave him a pointed look. "Oh, come on, Rayne, an escort paid you—"

He threw his hands in the air, eyes burning with frustration. "She meant it as a *joke*. I never touched her. You don't know how *sick* I am of everyone throwing my past in my face when they don't have the facts straight."

She blinked at him while he hauled in a breath.

"Look, there's no need to be intimidated by my so-called 'reputation'. Trust is earned, I know that, but I feel like I'm walking on eggshells all the time with you. Have I ever given you reason not to trust me?"

No, not personally. But she'd heard plenty to make her wary of him.

"I'm half afraid to touch you in case it triggers a bad memory. You said you cut your hair so no one could grab you by it again. So if I put my hands in your hair when I kiss you, will that scare you half to death?"

"No—"

"Or what about your shoulder?"

She went white.

"Yeah, I know what happened. Does it still hurt, or is it the memory of what he did that makes you flinch when I get too close?"

The mention of it sucked the air out of her lungs.

"See? You're white as a sheet of paper because I even brought it up. I can't read your mind, even though I wish the hell I could. If you'd just tell me what happened, I'd have a better idea of what you need from me. Help me out here, Chris." He laid a hand on her shoulder, his hazel eyes earnest. "I care about you. I want this to work."

Man, how she wanted to believe it. But her emotions were in upheaval, the scars too deep. She was the proverbial basket-case, and what man would have the patience for that, especially one who could have any woman he wanted? She was ruined, a bundle of neuroses. And all because of a psychopath who wanted her dead.

She turned away. "It's no good. I can't talk about it yet, Rayne. It's too soon, and I'm still trying to sort through it all in my head. I'm not shutting you out on purpose, really I'm not. I don't have a clue how to deal with it all myself. I've been trying to write it down in my journal, and that's been hard but I think it's helping a bit."

She retrieved the bound notebook she'd brought from her bed, clutched it to her as if afraid he'd try to take it from her, revealing her burden of shame and fear.

His gaze never wavered. "Chris, I'm a cop. I saw you in the hospital, and I saw your bedroom afterward, so I've got a pretty good idea what he did to you."

More blood drained from her face, her heart knocking against her ribs. He might have an idea of what she'd suffered, but he didn't know the details. And he didn't know the reason behind the attack. "Trust me, some of the things in here would totally upset you. In this case, ignorance really is bliss."

His expression tightened and he held out a hand. "Chris—"

She jerked her arm away, tension in every rigid line of her body. "Don't. Please, Rayne. It was so awful, and I'm not ready to tell you about it yet. Okay?" She couldn't stem the sheen of tears flooding her eyes.

He stared at her for long moments, then relented with another exhalation. "Okay." He pulled her into his arms to hold her against his heart. "Okay. I guess it can wait a little longer."

She slumped against him, feeling like she'd been given the stay of execution at the eleventh hour.

CHAPTER 15

Next morning Rayne came through the front door into the cottage, still damp from the shower he'd taken at the gym. Christa was spending a few hours with Bryn, God help him, so he and Jake were fending for themselves. He peeled off his sweatshirt and shoes, headed into the kitchen for a glass of water, then stretched out on the living room floor, pulling one knee to the opposite shoulder and holding it, repeating the other side before sitting to work out the stiffness in his hamstrings.

Holding the position to let his muscles lengthen, he noticed Christa had left her bag on the couch, her journal peeking out of it. If only she could find the courage to share what had happened to her, he'd have a better idea of how to go about helping her heal.

Which was why he'd dearly love to read what was in that journal.

No, he couldn't betray her trust like that. She'd told him flat out she didn't want him to know some of what she'd written, and he had to respect that, but that only worried him more. What did the journal contain that was too horrible for him to know about? Words triggered by her darkest nightmares, the hell she had endured. His imagination had been too good at conjuring up the sort of terrible realities he'd faced as a cop. How long could he wait for her to be ready for him to find out what had actually happened to her?

On the other hand, no matter what had happened he would still want to be with her, so was it that big a deal if he were to find out? It wasn't as if he couldn't handle it. He'd been a cop for long enough, and after watching her being examined in the hospital and vomiting in the aftermath of a nightmare, he could deal with the rest of it.

His gaze went unerringly to the purple binding of the journal. It was like an elephant in the room with him. Christa would be gone awhile yet, the devil's advocate in him whispered. He could read the damn thing and put it away without her ever knowing, and then at least he'd have some idea how to handle things.

He moved onto his quads, wincing at the soreness there. He knew he should wait for her to tell him, but what if she never did? Some victims never talked about their attack. Ever. Those questions, those imagined scenarios would always be lurking in his mind, and then what?

It would eventually drive him freaking crazy, that's what.

****

Christa struggled with the key for a moment before pushing the door open. The house was quiet, and she wondered if Rayne had gone out for a run. "Rayne, are you here?" she called, heading for the front room. "I was going to make some cook—"

The bag of chocolate chips fell from her suddenly nerveless fingers and hit the floor with a thud.

Rayne was sitting on the couch waiting for her. Her journal was lying on the coffee table in front of him.

Silence hovered.

"What's that doing there?" Her voice shook. "Why is my journal on the table?"

He met her glare of accusation evenly. "I was hoping we could talk about it."

He wouldn't have read it, she told herself in panic. He wouldn't have done that to her. She turned away, gasping in shallow breaths. "I told you I *can't*." God, didn't he get it?

"I know, and I understand that. But we do need to discuss it. If we don't, it'll ruin whatever's between us."

He's right, but it's already too late. It's already ruined. How could she have been stupid enough to think this could work? Stifling a sob, she spun around.

"Don't!"

His command brought her up short, freezing her like a doe in the headlights. The raw pain in his voice burned through her like acid.

"Don't you walk out on me now, Chris," he challenged her hoarsely.

She stared back at him, a shaky hand covering her mouth, battling back flashes of the attack. *He started to cut off my clothes and I turned away, so he forced my head around to look at the photo.* Rayne must have sensed how fragile a hold she had on herself, because he whispered her name and started toward her.

"No. *Don't. Touch. Me.*" She held out a hand to ward him off and sank to the ground, wrapping her arms around herself. He reached for her again and she shrank from him, huddling in a trembling ball. Like a cornered animal with nowhere to go.

"Okay," he said, backing up a step. "It's all right, I won't."

It must have killed him to say those words to her, but he stayed where he was.

"I just want to help you."

"You *can't.*" Didn't he understand that she wanted to die? That he could never fathom how she felt? She was contaminated, her skin crawling with shame. She couldn't stand the pity on his face, couldn't stand the thought of Rayne touching her when she felt so dirty. Inside her head she was screaming, a hair's breadth away from losing it and fracturing into a million pieces. No way did she want him to witness that final humiliation.

In the expanding silence his steadying breath sounded loud. "I'm sorry," he rasped.

Sorry about what? She wanted to yell it at him. Sorry because he'd triggered this fallout, the volatility she'd been so determined to keep buried? Sorry she'd been attacked in the first place? Sorry because he pitied her? The one thing she couldn't stomach was his pity.

Or was he sorry because...

God, *had* he read her journal? Her eyes narrowed, the blood pounding in her ears. No. No way would he betray her like that. She could barely form the words to ask him.

"Tell me you didn't..."

His gaze bored into hers. "What do you think?"

What *did* she think? Did she trust him enough to believe he hadn't read a single word? She'd been out of the house and her journal had been right there. Would she have had the decency to resist such a temptation? That should be a straightforward answer, shouldn't it? Throughout all of this he'd been her protector, her hero. So why did it feel easier to believe that he had read it? Why couldn't she give him the benefit of the doubt?

He dragged a hand through his hair. "I can't believe you're even asking yourself whether I'm capable of that."

"What am I supposed to think? I come in and find you on the couch with my journal on the coffee table in front of you. It wasn't much of a leap."

"If you had any faith in me at all, you wouldn't jump to that conclusion." His voice vibrated with suppressed anger.

She wanted so much to believe him, but she couldn't. It was as simple as that. And where did that leave them?

Nowhere.

Pushing to her feet, she took an unsteady step away from him that brought her up hard against the stove, trapped between unyielding metal and the roiling emotions of the man before her.

Rayne had to have seen the pallor of her skin, the stark fear in her eyes, but still he moved toward her, as if he couldn't help it. He stopped a few steps away from her as she shrank into herself.

"I warned you," she accused, all the hurt bubbling inside her.

He stared at her, his jaw clenched, his eyes bright. He took a deep, shuddering breath. "Christa—" It didn't even sound like his voice.

"God, I didn't want you to find out this way." Her voice shook.

A spasm of pain crossed his face. "God *damn* it, Chris! Find out what? It's driving me out of my frigging mind wondering what the hell he did to you."

Did he really not know? Had he really not read her journal, her most private terrors in stark black and white?

Letting out a fragile breath, she shook her head slowly, feeling old and brittle. "It wasn't your fault. You were just the excuse he was looking for."

****

"The excuse he was looking for?" His stomach dropped. "Wait a minute—you think he did that to you because of *me*?"

She simply stared at him, unmoving. He didn't need her to confirm it, he saw the answer in her eyes.

"Why?" He battled the need to either put his fist through the wall or haul her into his arms and never let go. He would have reached for her if she hadn't looked so terrified of him, like he was a man on the edge. He certainly felt like one. He couldn't comprehend what she'd gone through, why she thought he was the reason for it, but the images from his imagination burned into his brain, leaving him sick and helpless. "Oh, Jesus." Guilt swamped him, closing over his head like quicksand.

"I'm sorry. I assumed you'd read my journal," she whispered, wrapping her arms around her waist. "But you're right. It'll only come between us if you don't. I can't tell you everything myself yet, but I'll let you read it if you want."

"No, Chris." He could barely speak. "I'll wait until you're ready."

She went to the coffee table and picked up the notebook, staring down at her hands before coming back and holding it out to him. Her throat worked as she swallowed, the journal wobbling. "Here. Go ahead."

He took it from her but didn't open it. Her courage humbled him, along with her readiness to forgive him, to believe he hadn't read the journal behind her back.

"Please, read it. It's better this way."

He held her gaze, in case she changed her mind. Did he have the guts to find out why she thought he was responsible for provoking some psycho's attack on her? "Are you sure? I mean totally sure? It might feel like the right thing to do now, but will you resent me for it? Regret it later?"

"More than if I let you blame yourself for this for the rest of your life? No way."

He went with her into the front room and they settled on the sofa, Jake jumping onto the cushion beside him. Could he do this? Should he let her do this? To hell with it. She wanted him to read it so he'd better go ahead and get it over with.

He opened the cover, his heart beating faster. *My Assault*, she'd entitled it, and he flinched. *Better toughen up.* He took a breath. Jake laid his head on his knee and looked up at him with worried brown eyes.

He rubbed the furry ears and turned the page. He'd already seen the crime scene, but experiencing the events through her eyes brought them to life. The images ran together as if he were watching a movie. Her attacker grabbing the end of her braid, hauling her to the floor, tying her hands and dragging her kicking and screaming upstairs to her room, tying her facedown on her own bed. He could almost feel the rope cutting into his own wrists and ankles.

He had to swallow hard to force the lump down his throat. If she'd endured this, he told himself, then he could damn well read it without chickening out. He turned to the next page. The words seemed to jump out at him, slamming into him like fists. His stomach twisted.

He put the picture of Rayne and me beside the bed and made me look at it. When I tried to tell him Rayne wasn't my boyfriend he called me a liar and almost choked me, then pulled out his knife and told me every time I closed my eyes or looked away from the picture, he would hurt me. He started to cut off my clothes and I turned away, so he forced my head around to look at the photo. I tried so hard not to show I was scared, but he knew I was. I screamed, I couldn't help it. I thought he was going to kill me.

Oh, Chris. He ached for her. The sentences of neat handwriting flowed into each other, one after the other as he compelled himself to continue, to stay calm.

He tried to force himself into me, but he couldn't, and then he lost it. He kept screaming and swearing, hitting me. I turned away again because it hurt so much, and that's when he sank his teeth into my shoulder... blood dripping down my back...

Goddamn bastard. His vision blurred and he gripped the edge of the couch. *Breathe, breathe.* His hands trembled in impotent fury, but he made himself read further.

... I was looking at Rayne in the picture because he'd threatened to take another chunk out of me if I didn't. He

said, "I can hurt you in so many ways, and your boyfriend's even bigger than me. Look at how helpless you are right now, and he's twice my size. Imagine the damage a guy his size could do. Worse than this, sweetheart. And once he had you he'd throw you away like all the others." That's when I realized he'd come after me because he was jealous of Rayne...

"Fuck!" he exploded, surging to his feet, his hands raking through his hair. He wanted to break something. He panted, a red haze swimming in his eyes. She'd been looking into his smiling face in the picture frame while she'd been tortured and almost raped. He'd never felt so volatile in his whole life, a dozen conflicting emotions pounding at him, a chaotic mixture of rage and anguish so powerful it made him dizzy. His body screamed in primal rage for him to *do* something, to track the bastard down and rip him apart until this pain went away.

He swallowed hard, found her frozen in place, eyes full of trepidation. Dammit, she *should* be afraid. The rage was building, pulsing and boiling under the surface of his skin. He couldn't afford to lose control, to scare her even more. He loped around the room like a caged animal, unable to look at her, sucking in deep, shuddering breaths, trying to clear his mind. Water flowing from a fountain. Snowflakes drifting. Rain falling on the roof.

He focused on the images until he'd calmed down enough to process it all, then sank onto the couch. He glanced up with hollow eyes and found Jake cowering behind the armchair, watching him skittishly.

Rayne made himself finish the journal. When he read the psycho's parting words to her, nausea churned.

Now every time you look at your cop boyfriend you'll think of me.

****

He looked like a shellshock victim. The anguish, guilt, rage and pity, all swirling in an awful maelstrom in his hazel eyes made her want to bolt past him and run outside, onto the beach, into the ocean. But the pain radiating from him held her immobile. No way would she leave him like this. Needing to ease him, she reached deep inside for the strength to face him.

The silence stretched out between them like an

invisible barrier.

His gaze bored into hers. "You weren't ever going to tell me, were you?"

Pain lurked behind the accusation, but she kept her eyes on his. "I don't know."

"And all this time you've been carrying that around in your head? God, you should have hated me, been scared of me. Terrified—"

"No. You've never done anything but protect me. How could I be afraid of you, blame you?"

He gave a snort and turned away, but she shot out her hand and grabbed his forearm, the muscles under her fingers tensed like steel, so taut they were trembling.

"It wasn't your fault," she repeated in a whisper.

He aimed his tortured gaze at her. "Really?" Rage and self-disgust made him lash out. "Because I just read what he did to you, and he seemed to think it was."

Unable to reassure him with words, she slid her hand down his arm and twined her fingers around his.

He didn't budge. "God, I'm so sorry." He gave a bitter laugh. "Sorry...how pathetic is that?"

"I'm sorry too, because I knew it would hurt you to find out." She squeezed his fingers.

"Chris, I..." His voice was low, shaken. "Come here." He held his arms out to her. "Just...please come here." Hesitantly, she took a step toward him.

His arms came around her, tightening as they locked her to him. Quiet tears spilled down her cheeks as she burrowed into his body, his strength surrounding her, protecting and comforting her. She wound her arms around his back and held on, answering his unspoken need for solace, pressed her hot cheek into the curve of his shoulder. He pulled at the neckline of her shirt and traced his fingers over the crescent scarring her shoulder where another man's teeth had marred her delicate skin. "Oh, God," he whispered against her hair, shaking, turning his face into the curve of her neck.

She took his face in her hands, eased his head toward her. "Look at me." He raised his reddened eyes to hers, making her heart clench. "I'm not afraid of you, just the opposite. You make me feel safe. I trust you, Rayne. I wouldn't be here with you if I didn't." Brave words, but they were the truth and needed saying. To prove she meant them, she lifted her face and touched her lips to his, reaching out with every ounce of yearning and hope inside her.

He shuddered and an answering tremor ran through her at the anguish writhing in him, straining for an exit, for some kind of release, as if every male instinct were raging at him to lose himself in her, to burn away every ugly memory with his body. Her quickening heart answered him, urging her to offer herself to him and provide the outlet to heal them both. But not like this. First she had to help him transform the energy from desperate passion to tenderness.

She stroked her fingers through his hair and over his face, gentling him, and stood on tiptoe to press her mouth to his, letting the newfound calm inside flow through her into him. Heartbeat by heartbeat, breath by breath. His breathing eased, his hands cupping her face.

Her gaze roved from his eyes to his lips and he bent his head and kissed her quivering mouth, fueling a hunger she thought would never burn in her again. She kissed him back, hesitantly at first, then with desperate craving, her fingers tightening on his shoulders while she opened her mouth under his. He made a low sound in his throat as she struggled to get closer to him, responding almost without realizing it to the erotic glide of his tongue. All hesitation was gone, burned away by the uncontrollable wave of hunger that gripped her. When he finally pulled back she clung to him for balance, found him staring down at her in wordless awe.

Her body trembled as she struggled to contain the need pulsing inside her. God. What had she unleashed? The answering heat in his eyes made her knees tremble. A charged silence crackled between them.

As though afraid she would pull away, he wound his hands in her hair. "Do that again," he whispered against her mouth, his heartbeat thundering against her chest.

When he kissed her again, she complied and his hands traveled over her face, her neck, her upper arms with reverence. A soft growl escaped him, making her dizzy. When his fingertips grazed the underside of her breasts, an almost accidental touch, she bit her lip and he stilled.

"It's...it's okay. I think." What was wrong with her? They'd done this before and she'd loved it.

"You sure?" His words belied the naked longing on his face. "The worst thing we could do right now is take this too fast."

It was all moving too fast, so what difference did it make? And in all honesty, part of her didn't want him to stop. The torment, the heat in his eyes made her heart pound. If she wanted to do this, if she wanted him, she was going to have to make the first move. Could she? What if she failed him as a woman? What if she had some awful flashback that prevented her from following through?

But this was Rayne, the only man she trusted enough to try and heal her sexual wounds. If they wound up being no more than a fling, the world wouldn't end. Life was too short, too precious to waste in fear, and she needed to find the courage to take what she wanted. And, oh, she'd never known she could want like this.

She lifted nervous fingers to the top button of his shirt and he took her hands in his. "Chris, you don't have to—"

Yes, she did. She needed this part of her back again.

She slid the first button through its hole and moved to the next one, eyes devouring the line of skin she exposed. When they were all undone he shrugged off the shirt and raised her hands to his mouth to kiss them, sliding his tongue into the sensitive space where her fingers joined.

"Touch me," he begged.

The starved note in his voice made something twist inside her and she splayed her hands against his chest, over his rapidly beating heart, awed by the strength of him. Taking on a life of their own, her fingers trailed over him as she'd wanted to do forever, reveling in the heat of his skin, the muscles shifting and bunching under her touch. He let her stroke him, swallowing a groan when her palms moved over his taut abdomen, grabbing them as they made their way to the waistband of his jeans.

"No," he whispered, bending to kiss her, brushing his fingers down the nape of her neck, making her shiver.

"This is going to be about you, Chris."

She quelled the nerves leaping in her belly. It would have been easier for her if he'd let her strip all his clothes off, explore every inch of him and give him as much pleasure as she could, without the added pressure of worrying whether her body would respond to him.

Willing the apprehension to drain from her, she closed her eyes. His knuckles slipped under her shirt and grazed her spine to the small of her back, then stopped. In answer to his hesitation she grasped the lace hem of her blouse, lifting it over her head. His eyes fastened on her face while she undid her flounced skirt and let it drop to the floor. She swallowed, fought the urge to cover herself. She'd heard that men didn't notice the imperfections on a woman's naked body—they were just happy to see it naked. She hoped it was true.

"God, look at you," he breathed, his eyes devouring her, his admiration making her feel like the most desirable woman alive.

With a groan he slid his fingers into her hair and kissed her as if he never wanted to stop. He took control smoothly, changing the rhythm of the kiss to an erotic slide and retreat of his tongue, making her strain against him with a pleading whimper.

Breaking the kiss, he moved to her jaw, licking the tender spot beneath it where her blood raced just beneath the skin. A million goose bumps broke out all over her. She gasped, neck tipping back to offer more and his hand curved around her skull to steady her as he zeroed in on the exact spot that lit her up like a Christmas tree. Head spinning, she surrendered to it, sucking a sharp breath between her teeth.

He hummed his approval against her throat, licking against the sensitive spot once more before claiming her mouth again. Then he knelt and lifted one of her feet, unbuckling the sandal and letting it drop before smoothing his hands over the arch of her foot and her ankle, up her calf to the sensitive spot at the back of her knee and along her thigh. Tiny points of fire burned where he touched. By the time he'd done the same to her other leg, she was shaking. Her body had come alive.

He grabbed a pillow for her head and guided her onto

her back on the thick rug to kneel beside her, then lifted her foot again and kissed the instep. His thumbs pressed deep into the arch as his lips smoothed over the tender skin. A small gasp escaped her at the warm, ticklish sensation. Their eyes locked.

His mouth slid up her leg to her hip, pressing a kiss low on her abdomen before trailing up between her breasts to linger on the front clasp of her bra. When her eyes urged him to continue, he undid the clasp and slid the lace off her, making a murmur of need.

The first touch of his mouth made her gasp and she arched toward him, moaning at every motion of his tongue, her body taut beneath him. He took his time, caressing and laving her until she trembled again. Urgency clawed at her. Gasping for air, she reared up to grab his shoulders and drag him down on top of her, desperate to feel his weight. Rayne complied, rolling to press a muscular thigh between hers, mouth still licking and nibbling with a torturous lack of haste.

She almost sobbed at the feel of him pressed between her legs, bucking helplessly to try and relieve the terrible pressure. All too soon he pulled back, mouth swallowing her incoherent words of protest and replacing his thigh with his hips, rocking his rigid body against her. Mindless, she cried out and wrapped her legs around him, the ache intensifying to an unbearable pitch. He did it again, that slow drag of his hips against her until she thought she'd die. His lips moving over her face, she barely heard his murmur of reassurance as he lifted his weight off her.

She wanted to weep. "No—"

"Shhh. I'm not going anywhere."

His hands moved downward, brushing over the scrap of lace between her thighs. Her hips lifted toward him in a silent plea. She looked at him kneeling there in front of her, still in his jeans, the muscles in his arms and chest flexing as he touched her. He was so erotic and gorgeous part of her thought she must be dreaming. And she wanted him naked and inside of her, now. But when she reached for him, he pulled away.

"No."

"I want—"

"Shh. I know. Just let me take care of you." At her tacit consent he hooked his thumbs into the waistband of her panties and tugged them down. She jerked at the touch of cool air between her thighs.

Icy gray eyes speared her mind. Her skin shrank away from the cold scrape of the knife as it sliced through her underwear. She went rigid, commanding herself to breathe, erasing the image, refusing to let the nightmarish specter take this precious moment from her. Rayne had gone still, watching her face.

"Want me to stop?" His hands framed her face, his shadowed eyes searching hers. "Tell me, darlin', I don't want to scare you."

The sweet concern in his voice helped ground her. Her body throbbed painfully. "I want this. I want you to help me do this." Maybe after this first time it would be easier.

She held her breath, reached out her arms when he stretched out beside her, heat sizzling through her veins at the skin-on-skin contact. She let him roll her onto her back and glide his hands over her breasts and quivering stomach, down the inner edge of her thighs, burying her head into his shoulder and biting her lip at the throbbing ache between her legs. His warm, gentle hands built the heat high enough to melt her fears.

"You're so beautiful," he murmured, nuzzling the curve of one breast as his fingers circled the skin of her thigh. Her fingers tightened on his shoulders and ever so slowly he moved inward, back and forth in a tantalizing motion until she parted her legs. He brushed against her, absorbing the jolt that went through her.

Burying his face in her hair, a growl reverberated through him. "God...you're drenched." The last word sounded strangled.

She felt so slick and soft beneath his touch that she whimpered, and he eased one finger into her, her body arcing of its own accord. The bubble of panic rose; she forced it down. What if she took too long? Would he become bored and frustrated, like Cameron had?

"Nice and slow," he coaxed, soothing and reassuring her even as he pushed her toward the edge. "Don't think, just feel."

She concentrated on the dark velvet of his voice, the tingling sensation elusive at first, then stronger. The tension built with every motion of his hand and she stiffened, fearing it would surge and then leave her stranded, half crazy. He swirled his fingertips over her most sensitive spot and she cried out, nestling her face against him. "Rayne—"

"Shhh, trust me."

She continued to hide and he allowed her the privacy, kissing the side of her face as he stroked her. He cuddled her close while the bursting pressure grew, drinking in each broken moan with his mouth as her breathing became shallow. Watching her face, he slid two fingers back in and rubbed a highly sensitized spot inside her.

It felt so good—so incredibly good. She arched into him and squeezed her eyes shut. "Oh, God." She was going to explode.

"There?" he asked as he repeated the mind-blowing movement, his thumb gliding over her swollen flesh.

She moaned and clutched at him, trembling and straining into his touch.

"Oh, yeah. That's it. That is *so* it."

Pleasure swelled to an unbearable tension until she wanted to sob. Instinctively, she fought it, afraid of losing control.

He bent his head and licked her nipple, swirling and suckling until she cried out and convulsed beneath him, a wail keening from her throat. "Shhh. I won't stop."

The soft vow pierced her, made the pleasure bloom so hugely that she couldn't hold back and the orgasm swept through her, bowing her up against his strength as he anchored her.

He made a growl of satisfaction deep in his chest and held her while the last tremors subsided, then cradled her head on his shoulder. She lay there for a while, her mind wiped clean. When she was able to move again, she leaned up to kiss him, sated and dreamy.

"I guess my body still works after all," she mused, her fingers outlining his face. Before he could reply she kissed him again, sliding her hand down to his jeans. The next move had never felt so instinctive. "My turn."

He swallowed as her fingers slid under his waistband, making his stomach muscles contract. "Only if you want to." His voice was rough.

"I want to." Not only had he given her more pleasure than she'd thought possible, he'd also made her feel secure and resurrected her self-esteem. Now she wanted to express herself by loving him the way he'd loved her. If she remembered how to do it right, she thought with a hard swallow.

She popped the button and tugged his jeans down his legs, then knelt and slid her palm over him. He hissed in a breath but remained still, and she reveled in her feminine power. She might be inexperienced, but she knew at least one way to please him. She drew his boxers down and held him between her hands, savoring his heat, the softness of the skin overlying his hard length.

He tensed. "God."

She rose on her knees and watched his face as she stroked him, tension creeping into his jaw and shoulder muscles. His hand wrapped around her fist, squeezing tighter, then slid up over her thigh to grip her hip as she continued the movement. She loved how he laid there so quietly, stretched out and utterly at ease with giving her control of his body, his eyes glittering up at her with unsuppressed need. She explored him, following every cue he gave her with his responses and his molten gaze. She wanted to draw the pleasure out, make him writhe.

With a growl he grabbed her hands but she ignored him, bending over him to press her breasts to his naked chest while nibbling her way up his throat to his jaw, licking her way into his mouth. "Wait," he gasped between kisses and closed his eyes, jaw rigid. "Slow down, honey." She did, wanting to make it last, kept on stroking him until he was shaking. Rearing up with a gasped curse, he gripped handfuls of her hair and kissed her until he collapsed with a shudder of ecstasy. "Chris..."

She smiled against his lips, kissed his flat tummy and scooted to curl up beside him. Maybe lovemaking was as natural as breathing with the right partner.

He opened his eyes. "Pretty proud of yourself, huh?" he asked, one corner of his mouth curving up. "You should be."

She felt incandescent, invincible.

"Don't move," he whispered, kissing her as he got up. "Be back in a second."

He came out of the bathroom a few moments later, still stark naked. A little thrill rushed through her at the sight of him, still astonished that she was free to touch and kiss that gorgeous body at will. Rayne bent and scooped her up, carried her to the couch and lay down, pulling her on top of his chest. Cuddling into him, she rested her head over the steady throb of his heart, stemming the tears that came out of nowhere. He hugged her tight, stroking her hair while the quiet torrent rushed through her. With a sigh she fell asleep, his heart beating beneath her cheek.

CHAPTER 16

Rayne woke alone, knew instantly something was wrong. He sat up in his empty bed, where he'd carried her sometime last night and tucked her securely against him. The bedside clock said five-thirty freaking a.m. He strained to hear the shower running, Christa moving about in the kitchen, but only silence came. Throwing on his jeans he made a quick tour of the cottage, finding it empty. Disappointment filled him. Then fear.

Stay calm, don't panic. Where could she have gone? Maybe Jake been desperate for a walk. But she wouldn't have ventured outside on her own, especially not after Nate's update. Christ, what if the psycho had somehow crossed the border, come after her? Or maybe ...

Maybe she'd jumped in the car and left for good.

God, had last night scared her that badly? He scrubbed a hand over his face.

On the heels of these awful thoughts, he ran and threw open the front door, practically sagging with relief when he saw the rental vehicle parked in the driveway. So she hadn't gone far, but where was she? He went back to the living room and peered out at the beach, seeing nothing but banks of fog and churning gray waves past the eaves dripping water. Maybe Bryn had seen her.

He grabbed the phone. She answered on the third ring.

"Hey, Bryn, I was wondering if—"

"Yeah, she's here. She was out walking her dog. At dawn."

Rayne exhaled and leaned his head against the wall and closed his eyes. "Shit." She'd scared ten years off his life. When he hung up, he flopped onto the couch and raked his hands through his hair. Should he go after her, or would that frighten her away even more? It bugged the hell out of him that he couldn't do anything but sit here with his thumb up his ass and wait for her. He was a man of action, accustomed to taking charge and solving problems. Well, he sure had a problem here. Last night he'd finally realized he was in love with her, and this morning she'd taken off.

That's right—God help him, but there it was. He loved her. Staring down into her trusting aquamarine eyes, his heart had teetered on the brink and free-fallen into the unknown. It hadn't scared him then, but this morning he didn't have a clue what the hell he was supposed to do next.

He was frustrated by her sudden withdrawal, hurt even. Life was about to take a one-hundred-and-eighty-degree turn. No more women for him, but he was fine with that. From now on, though, whenever he made a decision he had someone else's thoughts and feelings to consider. If things progressed between them they might even move in together, in his condo or her house, if she could face living there again after the attack. It would be weird giving up his place with the ocean view, his independence, but he'd been a bachelor for so long, it would be kinda nice to make room for someone else in his life. Someone he cherished, who made him a better person.

Was he capable of making this kind of commitment to her? Christa wanted the security of a committed life partner and someday, marriage and kids. If they got that far, what kind of husband and father would he be? Would he be able to meet his own expectations regarding those roles? Or would he self-destruct the way his father had and devastate the ones who depended on him?

The rational part of his brain knew it was a stupid thing to think. It's not like it was genetic or anything. Yet the fear loomed.

His cell phone shrilled from the bedroom and he ran to answer it, frowning when he saw it was work calling. "Hutch here."

"Lieutenant Morrow, Hutch. Sorry to interrupt your vacation but we've got a situation going down and I need you. Got an armed barricaded suspect holding his young son hostage. Military vet, high on meth and heavily armed. Negotiator's trying to talk him out, but nothing so far. We've got zero visibility into the house, and the way things are looking we're going to have to go tactical on this one."

"Has my team come in?"

"Yeah, they're being briefed right now."

He promised to be there, then hung up, frustration gnawing at him. He and Christa had come a long way in the past few days, and the few more he'd planned for them would have helped her heal even more. Now that they knew for sure the stalker was gunning for her she'd have to stay at his place under lock and key, but would she be safe enough there, even with the additional security his condo offered? The perp had been smart enough to get Christa's alarm code at home, so breaking into a secure building wasn't much of a stretch.

He rolled his head to ease the tension in his neck. Wonderful. Now he had to break it to her that she had to leave this place she'd grown to love, only to be locked up in his condo alone.

****

"Was that him?" Christa asked after Bryn had hung up.

"Yep. I think he was worried you'd left town without him."

She dropped her head into her hands. "God, I feel so stupid. What do I do now?" When she'd woken up beside him this morning, that little voice in her head had been screaming at her to get up and out of there. With his warmth curled around her she'd felt too fragile to face him. So she'd slid out of bed and taken Jake out on the beach, giving herself time to check her emotions and come to grips with the fact that despite his reassurances, this was probably going to be a fling. Bursting with the need to vent, she'd used her cell phone to call Teryl, her friend's lack of surprise about her and Rayne coupled with her caution to be careful only adding to her blend of elation and anxiety.

She'd kept Nate's news about Seth to herself, not wanting to stress Teryl out in the delicate weeks of the first trimester. Considering this increased threat to her life, she never should have left the cottage alone. She'd walked all the way to Bryn's, intending to turn around and start back, but had seen the kitchen light on and was dying for her advice.

Bryn pinned her with her intense stare. "Care to tell me what happened last night?"

Christa glanced down at her lap, toying with the frayed cuffs of her sweater. "Well nothing really, he...we..." She gave an eloquent shrug. "You know."

"You slept together?"

Oh, why was this so hard to talk about? "Sort of."

"And?"

Christa gripped her mug tighter and stared into its murky contents. "And I don't know what to do now."

"What do you mean?"

She shook her head, trying to find the right words. "He...he *overwhelmed* me. Not physically—"

"Well then, that sounds pretty damn good to me."

"You don't understand, I *lost* it, Bryn. I totally lost control and ended up crying all over him afterward." She whispered it, like she'd admitted to some sort of mortal sin.

"And this is the end of the world because...? I'm sure he understands you would be emotional after what happened to you. You probably needed a good cry, you keep everything bottled up so tight. What's the real problem here?"

She pushed up from her chair and began pacing. "It was like he had absolute control over every part of me— my body, even my heart." Her voice thickened. "I had no control and he wouldn't let me hold anything back, even though I tried. I felt so vulnerable, and then I lost it."

"Wow," Bryn breathed, fanning herself.

"I didn't know I could feel like that," she admitted.

"So you had amazing, mind-blowing sex, cried all over him, and then what?"

"I fell asleep on the couch and woke up beside him in his bed."

"So basically you took off in a panic because you're scared of...?"

Christa took a sip of cocoa, let the mouthful of hot liquid warm her. "I'm afraid of getting my heart broken again." It sounded so stupid, but hey, that was how she felt.

"And what makes you think he'll break it?"

She met her gaze, all the torment in her soul surely mirrored in her eyes. "Because he's not into long-term relationships, everyone knows that. And because I'm in love with him."

Bryn's brown eyes softened. "Christa, you must know you're more to him than just a casual fling."

"I hope so. But do I mean enough to him that I won't get my heart smashed all to pieces?"

"Maybe you should ask him that."

She snorted. "Yeah, right. He'd run so fast he'd leave skid marks."

Bryn patted her hand. "Look, sweetie, love is risky. That's how it works. But I told you before, I've known Rayne for a long time and I've never seen or heard of him acting like this with another woman. Whatever happens, at least you know he really cares about you. Look at it this way, a man had nuclear meltdown sex with you, then held you when you cried your heart out, and carried you to *his* bed, and you woke up *next* to him. Wouldn't you say it's a good sign that he wasn't the one up at five o'clock in the morning walking your dog?"

Christa couldn't help laughing. "That *is* a good sign."

"And I also should point out that you're not the only one feeling a little freaked out. He probably thought he'd scared you off for good."

"I feel like such an idiot. What am I going to tell him? Sorry about my psychotic behavior, Rayne, I'm sure it will pass?"

"Tell him whatever you want, but tell him soon. He's probably wearing out the carpet as we speak."

****

Bryn walked with her and Jake as far as the last few yards, the path climbing the dunes dotted with clumps of sea grass waving in the ceaseless wind. The air was cool and damp, promising more rain. Nerves jumped in her stomach. She would waltz in and say hello, smile at him, and put this whole awkward scene behind her. She would enjoy the moment while it lasted, take her cues from him. If he broke things off before she was ready, well, that was the risk she was taking. She'd just have to deal with it when the time came.

Realizing she'd stopped at the foot of the weathered porch stairs, she bolstered her courage and led Jake up to the back door. She let him in ahead of her, absorbing the jolt to her heart when she found Rayne standing in the kitchen doorway. Would the sight of him always take her breath away?

She forced the nerves down, smiled at him as if nothing out of the ordinary had happened. "Hi. We got all our exercise for the day, so we can spend the rest of it relaxing. I brought you back a cinnamon bun." Did that sound as ridiculous to him as it did to her?

"Thanks." He accepted the brown paper bag from her. "Do you want some?"

"No, thanks. I had some toast at Bryn's." She went past him to hang up her coat, saddened she'd caused this rift. She'd been intimate with him last night, and now look at the distance between them. All her fault, too. "Did you sleep well?"

He put the bun on a plate and set it on the table along with a cup of stale coffee. "Yeah, not bad."

Until you woke up alone and wondered what the hell had happened to me. Blood rushed to her face and she busied herself doing dishes at the sink. Better to get it over with and put her out of her misery. "I'm sorry about this morning. I didn't mean to make you worry."

"Are you okay?"

"I guess. Just kind of embarrassed about how I reacted last night. You know...after." *And now you probably think I should be on medication.*

He rubbed the back of his neck. "I'm sorry, Chris. I never meant to scare you."

"I wasn't scared. It was a little intense, that's all, but I'm fine now, really." To prove it she smiled at him over her shoulder. "I probably scared you to death, though, huh?"

"Only when you took off this morning without a word. I was afraid that you'd...that he'd..." He stopped, seemed to be picking his words carefully. "And I wondered if you were thinking, last night, about what you wrote in the journal, what he said to you about me."

I can hurt you in so many ways, and your boyfriend's

even bigger than me. Look at how helpless you are right now, and he's twice my size. Imagine the damage a guy his size could do. Worse than this, sweetheart. And once he had you he'd throw you away like all the others.

Oh, God, is that what he'd thought? "I would *never* think you were like him." Her voice rang with conviction.

He shifted his stance. "You have to know I would never—"

She came over to stop the words with her hand, the first time she'd touched him since last night, and she could barely keep from wrapping herself around him. "Don't," she whispered, "don't even say it. I know you would never hurt me."

He kissed the fingers covering his mouth, reached up to take her hand in his. "Never." He drew her into a tight hug, letting the rest of the tension drain out of him. "I wanted our first time to be so good."

"It was. That's partly why I panicked."

"How come?"

She buried her face closer. "Because, all right? I'm dying of humiliation here. Give me a break."

He tilted her flushed face up to his. "Tell me, Chris. If you can."

She pulled her chin from his grasp and steeled herself. If she was going to get her heart broken, it might as well happen sooner rather than later, before she'd spun all her hopes and dreams around a life with him. "I wasn't sure where you were at," she admitted, staring at the Nike logo printed across the chest of his T-shirt. "In terms of us." When he remained silent, she gazed up at him with her heart in her throat. "You know, if it was only a fling, or..." The disbelief in his stare made her afraid she'd really offended him.

"Oh, Christ, not you, too." He ran a hand through his hair, gave a humorless chuckle. "I really made a mess of everything, didn't I? I realize last night wasn't exactly perfect, but I figured at least you knew how I feel about you." His hazel eyes held hers fast. "You're not a fling. I care about you more than anything."

The smile began in her heart and spread upward to light her face as the relief filtered through her. "I care about you more than anything, too." No, more than that.

She was totally ga-ga, head over heels in love with him. But she was going to keep that to herself a little longer.

"Well, I'm glad that's out in the open." He chuckled and lowered his lips to hers.

"Me too."

The man was positively lethal with his mouth, both in the things he said and in the way he used it. She gave up thinking and kissed him the way she'd been dying to, sliding her arms around his neck and lifting on tiptoes to press against him, her tongue grazing his lower lip, but he made a sound of protest and pulled away.

"What?" The regret in his eyes worried her.

"I...we have to leave now. And if I keep kissing you like that I'm not going to stop and then there's no way we'd make it back by tonight."

She glanced toward the front door. He'd already packed their bags and set them in the entryway. "Why do we have to go?"

"Work called. There's an emergency, and I told them I'd come in."

It must be pretty bad if they'd interrupted his vacation. "Do they know you're hours from home?"

"It's an ongoing situation. I'll either be on sniper detail or with the entry team if we have to go in."

Go in? Fear flashed through her, the dangers of his job kicking her in the diaphragm, more vivid now that they were involved. She'd always worried about him on some level, but the risks had never been this real, this visceral. He could be killed.

"Don't look so worried, darlin'," he soothed as he headed to the door. "I'll be with my team, and we're the best."

"But—" She trailed after him. She'd gone into this knowing he was a cop, and she had no right to heap her fear for him onto his shoulders. But how was she going to cope with his life being at risk every time he went to work? Would she be glued to the TV? Listening for any news of a police officer being injured in the line of duty, like Teryl obsessively listened for news about fires? Rayne putting himself in harm's way tied her stomach in knots. And while he was out there saving other lives, where was she supposed to go? "But what about...him?" She still couldn't say his name aloud.

"You'll stay in my condo."

Panic grabbed her. "But he disarmed my security system, and—"

"Shhh. I know." He rubbed her back. "But my building has much better security. And I'll spend as much time at home as I can."

Did he not realize what had already been done to her in less than an hour? It would take a second for him to slit her throat.

He assessed her with a frown. "Maybe you should stay here with Bryn."

"No, I'd feel way safer with you."

"Okay. Me too, until this is over."

Jake nudged her thigh and she led him by his collar behind Rayne to the car. She had the next six hours or so to worry about being alone in proximity to her stalker, and then God knew how many more worrying about Rayne.

Warm fingers closed about the nape of her neck and she glanced up into his clear eyes.

"It'll be okay, Chris."

"You'll be careful, right?"

He opened her door for her. "I'm always careful, but even more so now because I've got you to come home to."

Buckling her seatbelt as he slid behind the wheel, Christa couldn't shake the dread closing in on her.

CHAPTER 17

Rayne crept along, yards separating him from the door of the suspect's house, camouflaged by waist-high weeds and rusted truck parts littering the yard. The shack drooped in disrepair, its frame sagging beneath tarps and plastic bags. Your typical rundown north Surrey residence, complete with a barking pit bull chained to the tangled mass of wire that once served as a fence. But what made Rayne most uneasy were the children's toys strewn across the yard.

The ERT was responding at the scene of a known crystal meth house where a man had taken his son hostage and demanded his wife be brought to him. The suspect had refused to communicate with anyone, even via a telephone link with the police negotiator. With every window blacked out and no one on the sniper team able to see into the building, Rayne was leading the main entry team in to take the suspect out.

The commanding officer had given them the green light to do a full breach if necessary, and lethal force had been authorized. Apparently the suspect was a former Special Forces soldier, well versed in weapons, tactics and explosives, like Rayne's father, so he knew firsthand how paranoid a Special Forces veteran could be. This guy was capable of anything, including rigging the whole place to explode. He would be well armed, stocked with enough provisions to see him through a nuclear holocaust, and highly motivated to achieve his goal—whatever that was.

With a motion of his hand, Rayne signaled his colleagues to ready for the ascent to the second-floor entry. His team was elite and he trusted every man with his life. After checking his weapon one last time he started up the stairs behind his shield man, slinking onto the raised deck, his teammates stacked behind him. Unable to detect any impending surprises, Rayne gave the okay and one of his guys smashed through the door, tossing a distraction device. Rayne ducked his shoulder inside, scanning the empty room, rifle extended. "Clear."

As point man he led his team inside, on the lookout for tripwires or anything else the crazy bastard might have set up. They stepped cautiously over the rotten floorboards, the neglected planks creaking in the silence. Praying they would hold their weight, he took another hesitant pace, carefully placing his boot. At a faint crack he froze, holding up his fist to signal a stop. His teammates went still, awaiting his instructions, and he shifted gingerly, seeking a better position. His foot sank.

"Shit," he breathed, trying to pull up. One of his men grabbed his fatigues to haul him out but the floor opened beneath him. Behind him, his teammate cursed and dropped his weapon, straining to hold onto Rayne with both hands, and then they were tumbling between the joists with nothing to break their fall. He slammed into the concrete floor on his side, knocking the wind out of his lungs, his helmet smashing against the ground. Pinholes of light danced in front of his eyes.

Before he could move, hands reached down and snatched his weapon from his grasp, kneed him onto his stomach, ripped open his thigh holster and pressed the barrel of his own automatic pistol to the back of his head.

Rayne lay there, hands on his head, pressed flat to the dirty floor until he was hauled into a kneeling position. The man was as thin as a stick with bruises and needle tracks marking the insides of both forearms. His eyes were bloodshot, his skin sallow and sunken over the bones of his skull. Held in front of him like a shield and crying softly was his son, who couldn't have been more than five or six-years-old, stark terror in the brown eyes staring down at Rayne. A sob found its way out of his chest.

"Shut up," his father barked, still training both guns on Rayne. The whimpers stopped. "Here, take this," he ordered, tossing one of the guns to another man, ragged and somewhere around middle age. "Seems we've got you covered, eh boy?"

Rayne glared. Where the hell was the second entry team?

"You wanna know how I caught you, pig? I'll tell you how, you goddamned sonofabitch. I'm ex-Airborne. A trained killer like you, only smarter. You better remember that." His fingers yanked off Rayne's earpiece then checked him for wires, ripping open a pocket and revealing the military insignia hidden there. "Our hostage has a Navy SEAL trident on him, for Chrissake. Can you believe that?" He whooped. "You expect me to believe this is yours? No SEAL I ever met would be dumb enough to fall through the goddamn ceiling."

Laugh while you can, you smug bastard. But he was right. How the hell had he let this happen? He had made the fatal mistake of underestimating his enemy, who threw his dad's trident onto the floor. He barely resisted the urge to grab for it.

Cold sweat gathered under his armpits. Why hadn't the other team come in yet? With two members down they should have performed the breach immediately. Something was wrong.

The boy started to cry again and his father shook him so hard Rayne feared the little neck might snap.

"Goddamn you, I told you to shut up."

"Hey, the kid's just scared—" the accomplice protested.

"Shut the hell up."

Rayne's eyes followed the gunmen. The father of the boy was obviously high on something, probably meth. *Stay calm, stay put or you'll wind up with a bullet through your head.*

The father dumped his son on the floor, the boy shrinking into the corner, drawing his knees up to his chest, wiping his runny nose with a filthy sleeve as he watched his dad with fearful eyes.

The terror Rayne saw there made his heart pound harder. If the kid didn't stay still and quiet, he dreaded to think what the father would do. He gave the boy a reassuring smile and was met with the same wide-eyed gaze. The sniper team outside still had no visibility so all he could do was wait until the entry team regrouped. His teammate beside him still hadn't moved. Was he dead?

His captors prowled around the shack, loading weapons, eyes darting in anticipation of the tactical team at any moment. His muscles began to ache, but still he didn't move, throughout all the taunting about how he would never leave alive, how they would all die if those pigs out there tried anything. He ignored the threats screamed at the police trying to contact the suspects from outside. Cold sweat dripped down his sides under his Kevlar vest, Christa's St. Michael medallion warm against his chest. *May this always keep you safe from any dangers you face …*

How much time had passed? The boy shifted against the wall, drawing his father's attention. Rayne held his breath as the eyes snapped to the son.

"You want those pigs out there to shoot me?"

The boy's eyes widened. "No, Daddy. No, I—"

"Anybody's going to get shot, it's you, little fucker." He stalked over to tower above the boy. "Your ma'd be real sorry then, wouldn't she? Her poor little son bleeding all over the place. Dead." The young face crumpled. "Be better off that way. Things were fine until you came along." He shoved him with his boot, sprawling him face down. The weeping cut into Rayne.

"Shut up," the father barked, but the boy only cried harder, cowering, gazing at Rayne with such anguish. The kid couldn't seem to get hold of himself after that. Every time he tried to stop crying a sob would tear free from him, each one making Rayne wince.

"I said shut the fuck up, boy. Goddamn you." He lunged with Rayne's pistol, aiming it at his son.

Rayne nearly stopped breathing. The boy screamed and covered his head with his arms. "Jesus, put that thing down," the accomplice wheezed. "Kid's scared to death."

"Shut him up. Make him shut up or I'll kill him." He hadn't moved his finger from the trigger.

The other man sent the boy a desperate glance. "Be quiet, Danny. Just be quiet, okay? Everything's going to be all right." He looked at Rayne then, and Rayne recognized the stark fear in the other man's eyes, felt even colder inside. The father was a ticking time bomb, holding a loaded pistol at his own child.

When Daniel cast a pleading glance at him, Rayne saw the idea to run forming in the boy's eyes. *Don't*, he prayed silently. *Don't move. Please God, don't let him move.*

But Daniel did move. With all the strength he could muster from his little legs he pushed to his feet.

It all happened in slow motion. Rayne saw Daniel get up, heard the father's warning. Intending to cover the boy's body with his own, praying his Kevlar vest would protect them both, he dove across the room and caught Daniel in a flying tackle just as the pistol shot cracked. He saw the spasm of pain that crossed Daniel's face an instant before they hit the floor, felt the thud of a second bullet in his side as he shielded Daniel's body beneath his. The third bullet hit almost instantaneously, then a fourth. Pain exploded in bright red pulses, blinding him as the entry team finally executed the breach. He dimly heard more shouting, the scramble of feet, the explosion of the flash bangs and more shots before his strength gave out and he collapsed on top of the boy. He smelled the blood, felt the warm stickiness as it pooled around them. He couldn't breathe, couldn't think of anything but Christa.

Suddenly everything was so clear. Everything important seemed to crystallize—his family, Christa. Christa standing over his grave, grieving. The coldness of it seeped into his soul. Why the hell hadn't he told her he loved her?

CHAPTER 18

Christa stood by the picture window in Rayne's apartment, gazing down at Patrick helping Jake into his battered Chevy pickup. He was going to stay with the Flannerys until this situation was resolved one way or another. As they drove away, the loneliness hit her.

The sky was leaden, the bay restless with choppy gray waves under a light drizzle. The weather matched her mood perfectly. Now even her beloved pet had been stripped from her life. Cut off from the outside world while a monster plotted her murder, she was trapped in Rayne's condo alone while he went after some bad guys. So far she'd refrained from watching the news.

She would have cried, but tears wouldn't help the situation so she refused to allow herself to give in. All she had to do was hang in there a few more hours and Rayne would be home, and then she would be okay again.

The phone rang, revealing Nate's number on the call display. "Nate?"

"Hi, Chris. How are you holding up?"

"Pretty well, thanks. It was sweet of you to call and check on—"

"It's Rayne."

The blood drained from her face. She'd known. Dammit, she'd known... "What about him?"

"He was on a call this afternoon when things went a little haywire, and well...he was shot."

Her knees buckled. "What?" She sank onto the couch, her hand snatching up the remote. The screen came to life, showing flashing lights and people running around shouting instructions, police and medical personnel rushing past the camera bearing victims on stretchers.

Nate's voice seemed to float somewhere in the distance. Rayne, shot. Bleeding through the bandages. His still body being lifted into an ambulance. She made a sound in the back of her throat, every drop of blood in her body freezing.

"Oh, God." Panic welled inside her and she hardly heard Nate's attempts to calm her. Rayne had been shot. She needed to get to him right away.

"Christa, can you hear me? Are you listening? He's being treated right now. He's *okay*, honey."

She gulped air, trying to stop shaking, her teeth chattering. He wasn't dead or dying. He was okay.

"I'm sending a uniformed officer over to get you. Stay inside with the door locked and make sure you check his ID before you let him into the building."

"Okay." The fear was almost paralyzing. "Hurry."

"Hang in there."

What choice did she have? She grabbed her purse and waited at the door, heart pounding as the seconds ticked by.

****

Rayne heard her calling his name and took a painful, bracing breath before pushing into a sitting position. He was still in shock, but the fear was starting to creep in at the edge of his mind and he wanted to make sure he held it together in front of her. She rushed in, eyes wide at the sight of the sling securing his wounded left arm across his chest. "Hey, kiddo."

He held out his good arm and she clung tight, fingers clenched on the fabric stretched across his shoulder blades, trembling. "Rayne, I—"

"Shh." She felt like heaven in his arms. He squeezed her closer as she covered his face in sweet, desperate kisses, wincing at the pain in his chest but not caring. He never wanted to let go of her again. "Just hold me." She obeyed, slipping her arms around his waist, being careful of his arm and cracked ribs. For a few minutes she stayed that way, cheek pressed against his heart, as if absorbing the feel of him.

He pulled back and cupped her neck with his good hand. "I need tell you something, but I want you to look at me when I do." She raised her blue eyes to his, held his gaze. "I love you, Chris. More than anything." It felt damned good to have the chance to tell her so. "Wish I'd told you before."

She gave him a watery smile, her face alight. "I love you too."

He leaned down and kissed her, his hand buried in her hair. He almost hadn't made it home today, had been reminded how fragile life was, and he didn't like how it felt one damn bit.

"I haven't been that scared since...you know," she told him hoarsely.

"Me either. I still can't believe it happened at all."

She sniffed and wiped her eyes, scanned his injuries.

"Only one bullet actually got me," He gestured at his bandaged arm where one had passed through his triceps and been blocked by the Kevlar vest, protecting his lung and heart. "The docs told me it missed anything real important, so it's just soft tissue damage. The vest saved me from the other two. Lucky me, huh?"

"Poor baby. Do you need anything?"

"Just you," he said quietly, bringing her gaze sharply to his. He knew she was feeling scared and helpless and wanted to take care of him, but he only wanted to hold on to her until he felt stable again. As though she sensed it, she laid her head against him and closed her eyes, offering her love and reassurance without hesitation.

They sat in silence for a long time, savoring each other's presence with a new appreciation. Life was so precious, so fleeting. He intended to relish every day from now on, and cherish the things that were important to him. Especially Christa.

****

"So," she said against his shirt when they were back home on his couch, "what happened today?"

He shifted to try and ease the aching in his ribs, but it lessened only slightly. The mere act of breathing was painful. "Murphy's Law happened," he answered and told her everything, grateful for her warmth pressed against him, chasing away the chill that gripped him inside. "My teammate's still in the ICU with a fractured skull but at least he's conscious, and the little boy was taken into surgery before I was, so I haven't heard anything," he finished, staring ahead at nothing. "I want him to be okay, Chris. I'll never forget the expression his face when he tried to run to me." His jaw clenched and his eyes

209

stung. "He was looking at me as if I was going to save the day, like I was some kind of goddamn superhero."

She murmured and rubbed his arm, but the lead weight didn't go away. The guilt felt like an anvil pressed on his solar plexus. If he hadn't fallen through the ceiling, Daniel would most likely be home with his mother, but instead she was sitting next to his intensive care bed, keeping vigil over the tenuous grip he had on life.

He pushed the image away and tightened his hold on her while she ran her fingers over his bandages as if her touch could heal him. And maybe it did, he thought, kissing her temple. Thank God she was being so brave about everything. He couldn't take it if she cried right now. "I could use a shower," he coaxed. "I can still smell the hospital on me."

"You shouldn't be getting that sling wet," she told him, all business as she stood and assessed him. "I'll draw you a bath instead."

He let her help him into the master bathroom and sat on the edge of the tub as she filled it. How beautiful she was, inside and out. "How did you do today?"

She gathered towels and soap. "Fine. I laid low here, like you said."

She eased off his shirt, careful not to hurt him but the pain still made beads of sweat pop out on his brow. He stood and let her pull his pants and boxers off, too sore to even think about making love to her, and since he'd thought about little else the past few weeks, it said a lot for how serious his injuries were. When she helped him into the tub he winced at the hot water stinging the abrasions on his knees and arms from where he'd fallen through and hit the floor. "I'm going to be one sore puppy in the morning."

She ran a hand through his hair, then washed him down carefully, eyes tracking every bruise and welt on his chest and arm. "God, look at you."

Truthfully, he wasn't feeling much pain at the moment. Her hands on his skin were prompting a reaction he hadn't expected, as if his body knew how close it had come to dying and was doing everything it could to remind itself he was still alive. He made himself lie back and let her take care of him, comforted by her gentle touch and her calmness. She brought him such a sense of peace.

All too soon she rinsed him off and toweled him dry, then moved him into his bedroom where she undid the towel at his waist, letting it puddle on the floor.

"Lie down," she told him, watching him with hungry blue eyes. Leaning over him, she grabbed a bottle of lotion she'd placed on the bedside table. "I want you to lie still while I do this," she was saying, but the blood had rushed out of his brain to pool in a more important organ, so he missed whatever else she told him under the roaring in his ears.

This was straight out of his fantasies—him lying helpless while Christa rubbed him all over with her oiled hands...Except he hadn't been shot up and bruised to hell in his fantasies. The look in her eyes was exactly right, though. Hungry and focused, staring at him as if he was the most magnificent thing she'd ever seen. At odds with the incredibly soothing touch she was using. The woman looked like she wanted to eat him alive. He squirmed. As he shifted on the mattress her cool hands stroked over his shoulders and chest, her gaze trailing down to devour his erection.

God. He sank onto the sheets and lay back against the pillow, body throbbing. Closing his eyes, he absorbed the tingle of her hands wandering down his chest and stomach, her lips trailing wet kisses in their wake, moving lower. He sucked in a breath as she gripped him in her slippery hands, wincing at the pain in his ribs. He didn't know if he could take the feel of her mouth on him right now without thrashing around. "Chris—"

She teased his navel with her warm tongue. "Are you too sore for this?"

"It might kill me," he admitted hoarsely, "but it's a hell of a way to die."

Only an idiot would stop her, so he lay there trembling in anticipation of the moment when she closed her mouth around him. He nearly came up off the bed, grabbing a fistful of the sheets in his good hand. Maybe it was because he'd almost died, maybe it was because he was wounded and at her mercy...whatever it was, he'd never felt anything so intense.

His fingers released the bedding to slide into her hair and hold her close, moaned and dug his head into the pillows, his body going up in flames. "Chris—" he warned again in a rough whisper, but she kept going, slowly, as if she was enjoying his pleasure as much as he was and was in no rush to finish. He stood it for as long as he could, letting it build and build until he was fighting to contain it. "I'm going to come," he whispered hoarsely, giving her a last chance to release him. But she only sucked him deeper and made a purring sound that destroyed him. He threw his head back with a deep groan, and exploded.

He collapsed onto the bed, as weak as a newborn foal, his heart thundering in his chest. His ribs were killing him and his arm throbbed, but it had been worth it. When he summoned the strength to open his eyes he found Christa lying with her cheek pillowed on his thigh, looking up at him with a satisfied glow in her eyes.

"Come here," he murmured, holding out a hand to draw her up beside him. Her presence soothed him. "I love you." Each time it felt easier to say the words out loud.

****

Early the next morning Christa was already busy in the kitchen when the phone rang. She set the steaming cinnamon buns on the stovetop to cool and wiped her hands on a tea towel.

"Hi, Nate."

"Morning. How's our boy doing?"

"Still sleeping."

He grunted. "Good. Sleep's the best thing for him right now. The ribs giving him much trouble?"

"His chest looks like a tie-dyed t-shirt." Every time she imagined the bullets hitting his Kevlar vest she felt sick.

"Listen, I've dug up some more info on our perp."

She stilled. "Okay."

"Turns out he has a sealed juvenile record, so we eventually got a warrant to look at it. Seems when Seth was fourteen he offed his stepfather. Sliced him up like a ripe tomato, then strangled him."

Her spine went rigid. She placed a hand on the counter to steady herself, thinking of that silver blade as

212

it slashed toward her. *Sliced up like a ripe tomato...*

He let out a weary breath. "We're following a tip that might lead to where he's been holed up, so I'll keep you posted. Tell Rayne to call me if I can do anything, okay?"

She hoped he could feel the net tightening around him. "Thanks, Nate."

She set the phone back in its cradle. So her stalker was a double murderer. Gee, nice to know. What might he be able to do with his technological expertise? Track her through her cell phone records? The national team website where her name was listed? It detailed the program's itinerary, down to travel days, camp locations. If she somehow made the final cut, he'd know where she was on those dates.

The phone rang again and she jumped. The number on call display was unfamiliar, so she let the machine pick up and a woman's unsteady voice came on, seeking "Lieutenant Hutchinson."

"Hello? Yes, he's here, but he's still sleeping. Can I take a message?" She reached for a pen but froze in mid motion. "Oh, no... no, I'm so sorry... yes, I'll tell him. Thank you for letting us know." She hung up, tears pricking at her eyelids. How should she break this news to him?

"Smells good in here."

She whirled around and found him coming into the kitchen, his hair sticking out all over the place, the sling awry, bruises spreading in violent purples all over his chest. "Morning. How are you feeling?"

"Sore." He smiled at her sleepily, leaned down to press a kiss on the top of her head, then reached for the coffee mug she'd filled. "Is that cinnamon I detect?" he mumbled. "Did you make me cinnamon buns?"

"Yes, but they're from Pilsbury. I found them in your pantry. Any idea how old they are?" Her tone told him how gross she thought that was.

He took a sip, sighed. "Mmm. Good coffee. You're spoiling me."

"Well, I think a little spoiling's in order, don't you? But let me know if I start driving you crazy with my fussing."

"I love you fussing over me."

"Yeah?" She groped for something to say to lighten the load and stall for time. "We'll see if you still love it when you've gained ten pounds from my cooking and put a lock on your bedroom door to escape me."

He stared at her over the rim of his cup, poised halfway to his mouth. "You're scaring me."

"I'm kidding. Here, come sit down." She followed him to the table with a plate piled with scrambled eggs and a gooey, frosted cinnamon roll. He looked tired, but otherwise surprisingly good considering he'd been shot the previous day. While he dug in with an appreciative sigh, she carefully slipped her arms around him and kissed the side of his neck. "You want your meds?"

He shook his head. "Who was that on the phone?" He glanced up from his plate. "Nate?"

She squirmed in her chair. She would tell him about her earlier conversation with Nate but this latest call was more important. What would it do to him? "No, it was a lady." She maintained eye contact with him. "She said she was Daniel's mother, that you'd seen her at the hospital and asked her to call."

He swallowed the mouthful of cinnamon bun, his body rigid. "And? How is he?"

She dropped her eyes, couldn't bear to see the hurt when she told him. "He didn't make it, Rayne." As the silence stretched she glanced up, saw the guilt and anger there and took his hand, frozen around his fork. "He passed away early this morning. Never regained consciousness. She wanted to thank you for all you did."

He sat very still. "Yeah, I sure did a helluva lot for him, didn't I?" He shoved his plate away and stood, his fist clenching at his side. "Goddamn it." His good hand raked through his hair. "Goddamn, it, Chris, he was just a little kid. Six-years-old and his father blew him away like it was nothing at all."

She bit her lip, those words forming images in her head she'd rather not see.

"He was looking at me with these wide brown eyes, scared shitless, like he was saying 'save me'." The torment in his voice speared her. "I threw myself over him as the guy started shooting, and the whole time I'm thinking 'I can't believe this is happening. No fucking way would a father shoot his helpless little kid'…but he did. Everything happened so fast. I knew I'd been hit, but I thought maybe I'd gotten to him in time, and when they did the breach and came in after us I lifted off him and he was staring at me. Staring right at me with those terrified eyes, but he wasn't breathing."

Her stomach clenched, the nausea making her throat spasm.

"I couldn't find a pulse, so I gave him a breath and was doing chest compressions when the paramedics showed up, and his eyes were still wide open." He shook his head, as if trying to make it all disappear. "I thought I saw his little chest move." A frown creased his forehead as he stood there on the other side of the kitchen, a million miles away from her.

She understood his need to pull away, knew exactly what that kind of deep shock felt like, how it numbed everything in an instant.

The phone jangled and she debated before going over to answer it.

The slightest pause. "Hello," a woman's voice said in a southern accent. "Who am I speaking with?"

"This is Christa."

"This is Rayne's mother, Emily."

"Hi, Mrs. Hutchinson." She met his gaze, raised her eyebrows. "One second, I'll put him on." She crossed the room, giving him a few more seconds to compose himself. As she washed the breakfast dishes she caught the gist of the conversation, him filling his mom in on his latest escapade, trying to reassure her he was okay and would be fine. "Everything all right?" she asked when he'd hung up.

"Yeah. I told her you were taking real good care of me."

"Oh, good. She sounded surprised when I answered."

"She *was* surprised. She wants to meet you. I guess Bryn's been telling her about us."

She set a sudsy mixing bowl on the counter. "Do you want her to meet me?"

"Yeah, I do," he said, surprising her into silence.

She stared at him over her shoulder, prevented from answering when the phone shrilled once more. "Hello."

"Chris, it's me," Teryl said. "How's Rayne doing?" She'd called Teryl and Drew last night, so they wouldn't learn the news from the TV.

"Pretty well, really, considering what happened." She didn't want to chat with her pal right now; she wanted to make sure Rayne was okay. She'd seen the awful grief in his eyes when she'd told him about Daniel, so no matter how hard he tried to shove it away, it was there, eating at him.

"That's great. Do you guys need anything at all?"

"Not that I can think of, but thanks. Everything good with you guys? Baby okay?"

"Yeah, it's still making me puke my guts out, which my doctor says means it's fine. Anyway, the national team head coach wants you to call her when you can."

Christa's heart rate picked up. That was all she needed right now, a call confirming she'd been cut from the program. She wrote down the number, her stomach in knots. When, oh when, was she going to catch a break? She felt like she had a black cloud following her around, like Eeyore. "Thanks, Ter. I'll call you if there's any news, okay?" She hung up, trying to put everything in perspective. In the grand scheme of things did a softball team really matter? The man she loved had nearly died yesterday, and a little boy had been killed by his own father. Being cut from the squad suddenly didn't seem so bad.

"What'd she say?" Rayne asked, coming up behind her to put his hand against her skittering tummy.

"The national coach called, I guess to find out what's going on with me."

"You'd better get back to her right away, keep her posted." He laid his fingers over her lips. "I'm okay, kiddo, really. I'm going to go lie down for a while."

She searched his eyes. "Are you really okay?"

"Yeah. I'm just...I don't know. Numb."

She squeezed his hand and followed him with her eyes until he disappeared into the bedroom. He was retreating to his cave to lick his wounds, and much as her instinct was to nurture him, he was entitled to some time alone. When he was ready to come out, he would find her waiting.

****

Rayne heard the beep of the numbers as she dialed, sensing her trepidation even though she was trying not to show it. His arm and ribs aching, he gingerly lay on the bed, listening to her muffled voice. One thing he was absolutely sure of, Christa wasn't up to playing ball, wouldn't be for a while, and no way would he let her go anyway near another park while that psycho rapist was still on the loose.

He sighed and closed his eyes, rubbing his hand over his face. Daniel was dead. He'd never been religious but he'd sure as hell prayed yesterday, spent a good chunk of the night praying the boy would pull through. He'd known the wounds were serious, had hoped Daniel felt no pain in his unconsciousness, had begged for a miracle.

And then there was his own mother, striving to keep her composure at the news of his injuries, trying to guilt-trip him into calling his father. "Your dad would understand," she'd cajoled him. "He's gone through the same thing."

Even if he had, Rayne still didn't feel like calling him. *Hey dad, it's me, your estranged son. So tell me, how did you cope with your post-traumatic stress disorder?*

Well, I'll tell you, son. I took off and left my wife and kid behind.

He pulled his mind from that train of thought and focused on taking slow, even breaths. He wasn't his father, never would be, because he wouldn't allow it.

A minute later he heard a sniffling sound. Oh, Jesus, he thought, swinging his legs over the side of the mattress. They'd cut her from the team, and it was that insane whacko's fault. "Chris?"

She came into the room, one hand clapped over her mouth as if determined not to cry, those blue eyes swimming with tears, her pain intensifying his own.

Her hand lowered, revealing a tremulous smile. "I did it," she whispered. "I made the team."

He blinked. "You *made* the team?" She nodded and he laughed despite the spasms in his ribs, held out his good arm and she flew across the room to him. "Chris, I'm so proud of you."

She laughed too, vibrating. "I'm in shock. I need a

217

good cry. My head's going to explode. I can't take it all in."
She looked up at him, wonder and confusion in her eyes.
"The coach said they'd already decided on me, so missing
the last camp didn't matter, especially under the
circumstances. The nationals aren't until August, and I
told her with all the pressure the police are putting
on...him, we hope this whole thing will be over by the
next camp. I know I shouldn't be able to smile right now,
with my stalker out there planning to kill me and the
little boy dying, and you recovering from a bullet wound,
but...it's crazy, right?"

"You're not crazy, and don't feel guilty. It's about
time we had some good news, and I love seeing you so
excited." She shone so bright she almost hurt his eyes.

"I can't wait until I can get out on the field again."
She snuggled next to him, the smile still on her lips. "Now
you can tell your mom you're dating a future Olympian."

"I think you should tell her yourself, kiddo." He gave
her a grin. "What do you say? You want to come with me
to Charleston and meet my mom?"

****

So she'd made the team after all. Good for her.

He leaned back in his chair, stared at the computer
screen that laid out the national team's schedule. The
next camp wasn't until the end of June, and he doubted
Christa would miss it, even if she was afraid of him. No
way would she would work so hard to make the team and
then not show up.

Never a dull moment in her life, Seth mused. Her
boyfriend had been wounded yesterday—he didn't know
the details, but from the news footage it didn't seem life
threatening. Which was too bad. Since Christa was still
holed up with that cop in his condo, and he wasn't about
to risk going after her there. That would be suicide. No,
he'd have to stay as close to her as he could without
getting caught, wait for an unguarded moment. Then he'd
spring.

His eyes strayed to the digital photo he'd printed and
framed, sitting next to his laptop. The kid he'd wired the
money to had captured the exact moment when she
realized what his last gift meant. Her face held that blank
look of terror he remembered so well. If he used a

magnifying glass, he could see the lines of strain around her mouth and across her forehead. The photo was so clear he could even tell how much her pupils had constricted when she'd looked up from that bakery box. Her beautiful eyes looked haunted, deep shadows smudged under them as if she hadn't been sleeping well.

Good. At least he wasn't suffering alone.

He shut off the computer, glanced around the cheap but clean apartment. Time to leave again. He'd been here far too long already, needed to change his appearance and move on, complete the next move in this chess game he'd initiated. He'd even leave the hard drive intact for the police to examine, simply to up the stakes. Most of the criminals he'd studied were idiots. They wound up in jail because they followed some pattern that made them predictable. Not him. Outsmarting the cops had become almost as big a thrill as hunting his prey.

His planning was almost complete, and this time nothing would stop him. He would finally get it right. His hands trembled as he wiped down the keyboard to remove the oil from his fingertips and folded the cloth into a neat square before tossing it in the garbage.

Did she know he was still coming after her? Probably. She was a smart girl. Beautiful, too.

Shame he had to kill her.

CHAPTER 19

Luke Hutchinson was wedged under the hood of his vintage Mustang when he heard the kid he hired to cut his lawn calling him from the garage doorway. "What now?" he barked, trying to muscle a badly rusted bolt out of the engine block. The Louisiana air was so thick and heavy he could have wrung his shirt out.

"Phone call for you—again."

"Can't you take a message?" Goddamn bolt wasn't budging.

"It's long distance. And it's a woman."

Luke growled and tossed the wrench on the driveway with a clang, then reached into his back pocket for the rag to wipe his hands. Didn't it figure that when a guy got a day all to himself to putter on his car, everyone he knew suddenly wanted to talk to him on the phone?

He stalked over and grabbed the cordless from the kid, who turned and disappeared back into the house, presumably to finish watching the baseball game. Lazy bugger still had edging to do.

"Hello," he said gruffly, wondering who in the hell it was that needed to talk to him so badly.

"Hi, Luke. I'm sorry to bother you..."

He sucked in as much breath as if someone had punched him in the stomach. He hadn't heard that voice in four years, but it still made him ache inside, probably always would.

"You're never a bother, Em. You all right?" Something bad had to have happened to make her call him. The last time was to tell him his uncle had died. Her sigh made him brace himself.

"I'm fine, Luke. It's Rayne."

Oh, Jesus. "What about him?" God knows he and his son didn't have a perfect relationship, but wasn't Rayne old enough and capable enough to call himself?

"He responded to a hostage situation yesterday, and things didn't go well." That cultured Southern voice paused, presumably as she gathered her nerve. "He was trying to shield the hostage. A little boy. Got himself shot."

Luke gripped the phone until his knuckles turned white. "Is he all right?"

"The bullet went through his upper arm, and they had to do surgery to stop the bleeding, but apparently there's no permanent damage. He cracked some ribs too, but his vest saved him from anything worse. Though they just found out the little boy he tried to save died ..." She choked back a sob.

"Oh, Em. Jesus, I'm sorry." He scrubbed a hand over his eyes. His son hadn't bothered to call and tell him himself. *Hey, Dad. Got shot at work. How are things in Louisiana?* "Is he still in the hospital?"

"No, they discharged him pretty much right away. I was going to fly out there to stay with him, but apparently he's got a girlfriend looking after him."

He made a noise in his throat to let her know he was still listening, wondering why she was telling him all this. Their son always had a girlfriend. Sometimes more than one.

"Well, anyway," she continued when he didn't pick up the thread of conversation, "apparently he's coming out here awhile. Don't be surprised if he drives down to see you. With his girlfriend." She let the significance of that speak for itself.

"Uh-huh. Was he planning also to maybe call me himself, or are you now officially designated as his messenger?" He couldn't keep the acid out of his tone.

"Don't be like that. I wanted to prepare you, so you could maybe think of how to help him. I figured if anybody knew what to do after what he's gone through, it would be you."

That much was true. Having your entire platoon blown to pieces right in front of you sort of made you a kindred spirit when it came to trauma. "I'll talk to him, Em."

"Thanks. Figured you'd know how to handle this better than me. I had a good cry of course. Always helps."

"I'm sure you did everything right. He obviously knew you would, so he called you first." Of course, he wasn't included in that cozy little circle of trust, not that he could expect to be. Not after what he'd done all those years ago.

"Well, I appreciate you talking to me, anyway. How are things down there? Y'all working too hard and sleeping too little as usual?"

Luke smiled wryly. She knew him too well. "Some things never change, I guess."

"I guess they don't."

Again she waited for him to fill the silence, but he dared not say any more. If her talking to him was one tenth as hard as it was for him to talk to her, then he wanted as little of it as possible. He wouldn't hurt her more than he already had, and God knew he'd hurt her plenty. And so he steeled himself against the aching pressure in his chest, and ended the call as gently as he could.

"Take care of yourself, Em."

"You too, Luke."

He heard the tears she tried to hide in her voice, then waited until she hung up before turning off his own phone, hating himself all over again.

****

Emily put down the phone and slumped into the sofa with a sigh. Nearly four years since she'd last spoken to him, over twenty since they'd lived under the same roof, but it hadn't lessened her love for him.

She wished it had.

She wished she barely gave him a second thought. Wished she didn't fall asleep every night aching to reach for his muscular frame, or wake up listening for his voice singing in the shower. Apparently more than two decades of being apart wasn't enough to make her forget him. Worse, their living separate lives had been his decision, not hers. He knew she'd take him back in a heartbeat, which was why he kept in contact with her as little as possible, but they'd almost lost their son yesterday. Luke knew exactly what it was like to stare death in the face, so she figured he could help Rayne through his trauma.

The day he'd come home with the first of his many

222

demons she'd been heavily pregnant with Rayne. The grandfather clock in the foyer had been striking two and frustration had surged because she couldn't sleep when she was so exhausted. Her back was aching too badly to let her stay in bed any longer and the baby, well into its eighth month, was kicking an insistent tattoo against her ribs. Amid the rhythm of rain on the roof she rose and drew on her robe, then padded downstairs into the kitchen to make herself some herbal tea. She had just set the kettle on the stove when a knock rapped on the front door. Glancing toward the porch, she saw the outline of someone standing there.

Hesitantly she made her way to the door and peered outside, unable to discern who was out there. Pulling her robe around her, she flipped on the porch light and undid the deadbolt, opening the door a crack. She let out a gasp and threw the door wide. Her husband stood on the doorstep, soaked with rain, face covered in bruises, jagged stitches bisecting his chin and left eyebrow.

"Luke," she breathed, launching herself at him, throwing her arms around his neck. "Oh, thank God. Are you all right?" She ran her hands over his shoulders and back, worried by his stillness. He didn't reply, only wrapped his arms around her and buried his wet face in her neck, holding her as tightly as he could.

Dread coiled in her stomach. "What happened?" He pressed closer, conveying his desperation and anguish without saying a word. He shook in her arms, and she held him hard against her for a time. "Sweetheart, come inside," she urged finally, tugging him into the house.

"Emily, is everything all right?" her mother called from the landing.

"It's Luke, Mama, and he's been hurt." She led him into the kitchen, pressing him into a chair, and hunkered down beside him, frightened by the stitches, by the haunted wildness in his eyes.

Her parents came downstairs. "Mama, will you please fetch me some towels, and Daddy, could you make a pot of coffee?" Her mother rushed to fetch the towels and Emily immediately began drying his hair. "Sweetheart, look at me," she said, taking his face in her hands. He raised dark, bloodshot eyes to hers.

223

"What's wrong?" she whispered, fingers stroking his cheeks, apprehension filling her.

He swallowed, gripped her hands. "They're dead," he said hoarsely. "They're all dead."

Emily put a hand to her mouth, feeling sick. "Oh, God, Luke ... who? Your team?" His anguish was more than she could bear.

"They just left us there, Em ... left us all to die ..." He shook his head as if he still couldn't comprehend, struggled to take a shaky breath. "I carried one of them out across my back, but he lost both legs from the knee down." He raised tear-filled eyes to hers. "Said he wished I'd left him to die."

She didn't know what to say, so she kissed him and held him close against her heart. Her father set a mug of steaming coffee on the table in front of Luke, then placed a firm hand on his shoulder.

"Good to have you home, son," he said quietly, then took his hovering wife upstairs to give them some privacy.

Emily handed Luke the mug and waited until he'd taken a few bracing sips, then pulled him from the chair. "Come upstairs, honey. Let's get you out of those wet clothes and into a hot shower." Soon he stood naked in the bathroom, Clumps of stitches dotted his body, along with plenty of deep, ugly bruises.

She ran the shower and handed him the towel when he came out. Never taking his eyes from her, he dried himself then followed her into the bedroom. It had been months since she'd seen him and he seemed fascinated by her new shape, placing his hand on the firm mound of her belly. She froze in the act of folding the bed sheets down and faced him, fighting the pang of self-consciousness.

"I'd almost forgotten how beautiful you are," he whispered, wrapping his arms around her.

Before she could say anything he pressed his lips to the swell under her nightgown, then drew her down beside him. He undid her robe and slid it off her shoulders, began unbuttoning her nightgown.

She knew she was blushing, and had to stop her arms from snatching the nightgown over herself. She felt so huge and clumsy. Just then, under his worshipful gaze, the baby did what felt like a somersault, her belly rippling.

Luke actually smiled, and reverently ran his hands over where his baby lay. He studied the changes in her body with a smile of male satisfaction, smoothing his hands over her and making her sigh with longing. He gathered her to him and kissed her, murmuring soft things against her skin. He was so warm and strong, and she'd prayed every night for him to come back to her ...

Emily clung to him, each moan and arch of her body begging for his touch, desperate for him to be inside her. Finally, he grasped her hips and lifted her onto him. Immobile for a moment, awkward and ungainly with her bulk, she relaxed when her husband gazed up at her with all the longing of his heart in his eyes.

"Make me forget, Em," he whispered, and her heart broke. And so she'd loved him with everything in her soul and body, crying out with him at the end and rolling to cradle him in her arms. She curled himself around him and he burrowed in close, their baby moving energetically between them.

CHAPTER 20

Christa could hardly believe how beautiful Charleston's historic district was. All the old homes in this part of town were maintained in wonderful condition, their gardens nestled in courtyards enclosed by wrought iron gates and sturdy brick walls. Rayne turned the rental car into a lane and pulled into a driveway.

"This is it."

"You grew up in this house?" She stared at the wraparound porch supported by white fluted columns, a fragrant evergreen Confederate jasmine winding its way along the trellis on the south-facing wall. Even though the building must have been over a hundred years old, it looked as though it belonged on the front cover of a *Southern Living* magazine.

"Yeah, it's not too bad for an old shack," he teased, and climbed out of the car. He went around the other side and waited for her, but she sat there.

"Are you coming?"

She pressed a hand over her abdomen. "I'm nervous," she admitted with a grin.

He rolled his eyes and took her by the arm. "You can stare down Olympic-caliber pitchers and survive people twice your size mowing you down at the plate, but you're scared to meet my *mom?*"

"Hey, this is really important to me, you know. The first impression is always the most important, and I don't want anything to go wrong."

"Nothing will go wrong," he assured her, grabbing the suitcases from the trunk and steering her to the back doorway. "For crying out loud, cut it out before you make me nervous too. I've never brought a woman home to meet my mother before, so don't make this any harder on me." He leaned down to the peacock-shaped euonymus topiary potted in an urn beside the door and fished around for the spare key.

"Mom, we're here," he called, and brought Christa with him into the bright kitchen. She picked out the antique furniture instantly, admiring the way everything was put together and recognizing the lemony scent of Murphy's Oil Soap.

"You're early," a feminine voice laughed, and then Rayne's mother swept around the corner. Christa caught an impression of medium-length brown hair and a pretty, oval face with vivid green eyes before the woman launched herself at her son.

He caught her and lifted her off the floor in a one-armed bear hug. "Hey, gorgeous."

She squeezed him back and pulled away, her eyes moist. "I'm so glad you're here." They say you can tell how a man will treat you by how he treats his mother, and so far Christa liked what she was seeing.

"And this sweet thing must be Christa." Emily held out a hand.

"Nice to meet you, Mrs. Hutchinson," she replied, shaking firmly. "I've heard so much about you."

"Not as much as I've heard about you, honey." Emily winked.

"Thanks to Bryn," Rayne muttered.

His mother ignored him. "I can't tell you how wonderful it is for a mother to know her son has finally found a woman who—"

"Mom," Rayne warned her with his eyes. "You're going to embarrass me."

"Well, of course I am! That's my maternal right. Christa and I are going to spend lots of time together, looking through all your naked baby pictures, and then I'll tell her every story I can think of about you."

"Really?" Christa beamed. "When are you going out, honey?"

"I'm not leaving the two of you alone together."

"Oh, he can be such a big baby sometimes." Emily pouted and drew Christa's arm into hers. "Let's give you a tour, shall we? Then we'll get you set up in your room...you *are* staying in your own room, aren't you?"

The blood rushed to her face. "Of course." Which earned her a pout from Rayne.

Emily patted her hand. "Just ignore him, dear. He'll get over it."

"Mom—"

"Don't you 'mom' me, sweetheart. I'm going to help Christa settle, and then we'll have tea in the garden. I hope you'll approve of my efforts, Christa. I understand you've got the greenest thumb going."

"Oh, I wouldn't say that. I've killed lots of things." She trailed after her hostess down the carpeted hallway past a gallery of portraits, whom she assumed were Rayne's ancestors.

"Well, I don't feel quite as badly, then." After checking out the formal downstairs rooms they climbed a mahogany staircase to a bedroom decorated in cream and pastel blue. "You'll stay in here, and Rayne will be down the hall in the next room. It's old-fashioned of me I know, but that's the way I am."

"It's beautiful," she gushed, smoothing a hand over the toile coverlet. "Is this bed an antique?"

"It is. My grandmother was born in it. And you have a lovely view of the boardwalk from up here." She went to the window and opened the sash, letting in a breeze that billowed the gauzy curtains. "Come and see Rayne's room."

A big sign on the door read "Enter at your own risk" above a skull and crossbones.

"I was going through a privacy phase," he explained.

Christa took in all the mementos, envisioning Rayne as a teenager with too much attitude. Military posters covered the walls, along with bookshelves crammed with volumes about the Navy SEALs. Could anybody say hero worship?

On the desk where he must have done his homework sat a framed picture of a man hunkered on his haunches cradling a deadly looking rifle, his face smeared in camouflage paint. She peered more closely. "When did you have this taken?"

"That's not me, sweetheart; it's my dad."

She flashed him a disbelieving glance and picked up the photo, staring intently at the man's face. "I know he's all covered in greasepaint, but I'd have sworn it was you."

He came up behind her. "Yeah, we look a lot alike."

"Like twins, except for their eyes," Emily said. "Look at this one." A smaller picture of Rayne and his dad, both in their dress uniforms, looking so similar and so gorgeous it was hard to believe they were real.

"Wow. Was this your graduation day? The one you told me about when your dad gave you his trident?" Rayne's dad had brown eyes, but something else about his gaze was unlike his son's, something she couldn't put a name to.

"Yeah." He massaged her shoulder with one hand. "It's my favorite picture of us."

No kidding. Even as a cocky teenager Rayne had a few inches in height over his father and appeared wider through the shoulders, but no one in their right mind would take on Luke Hutchinson. He looked like a lethal, finely honed weapon, exactly what the military had trained him to become.

"Here's one you'll like." Him as a boy, probably around nine or ten, grinning under the shadowed bill of his ball cap while brandishing his bat. "I won MVP in our league championship. Don't I look awesome?"

He looked like he would have burst his buttons, if his jersey had any. "A force to be reckoned with, all right." In the last ten minutes she'd learned so many personal details of his life. This was going to be an enlightening trip.

"Well, if you're finished walking down memory lane, let's go have some tea," Emily invited. "I've made some low country cooking for Christa, to make sure she gets a proper taste of Charleston."

Rayne's expression lit. "Crab cakes?"

His mom rolled her pretty green eyes. "Yes, I made crab cakes. And biscuits, and peach cobbler."

He grabbed Christa's hand and all but towed her down the stairs.

She laughed. "Oh Rayne, you're too easy sometimes."

After cobbler and sweet tea in the shade of the verandah they whiled away another hour or so chatting, Christa and Emily giggling like schoolgirls while Rayne went inside to call some friends. When he returned he announced he'd arranged to meet with a group of them at a local bar. "You *sure* you don't want to come with me?" he asked for the third time.

They were both still uneasy about leaving her alone, but he seemed especially scared about leaving her with his mother. "I'm sure. Your mom and I are getting along great. Just imagine the dirt I'm going to have on you when you come back."

"I can hardly wait." He stooped to kiss her. "Won't be too late."

Christa went into the kitchen and put on the kettle, then served up two helpings of the leftover peach cobbler, pouring cream over the top. She made a pot of Earl Grey tea and took it into the living room, where Emily was finishing up a phone call.

She patted the sofa beside her and hung up with a sigh. "My friend, Alex. He tends to worry about me when he's not here."

"Where is he now?" She set everything on the coffee table.

"In Portugal, on business. Truth be told, I kind of like it when he's away. He smothers me sometimes." She flashed a guilty grimace and reached for a teacup bearing delicate violets. "These were my great grandmother's. I've always thought tea tasted best in these cups. There's something about the history of them."

"A teaset like this would have cost a fortune, even in those days." She sipped and savored. "That's how I always imagined Charleston would be. Like these teacups. History and tradition everywhere. Wide verandahs with rocking chairs and courtyards filled with gorgeous gardens. People sitting on porch swings sipping afternoon tea."

Emily smiled. "You have a bit of a poetic nature, don't you?"

"A bit. My mother always despaired of the fact that I wasn't the most practical kid in the world."

"Well, I for one think the world could use a few more poetic souls. And I have to tell you I couldn't be more thrilled that my son has picked a girl like you." She shifted on the sofa, tucking her feet beneath her. "I was starting to think he'd never fall in love, that I'd done something wrong when I'd raised him. God knows his daddy never carried on like he did."

"Rayne doesn't really talk much about him, even though it's obvious he still admires him."

Emily set her teacup in its saucer. "It's been hard for him. He spent a few weeks each summer with his dad while he was growing up, when Luke was Stateside, but that's really all they've seen of each other since Rayne was eight."

"Rayne told me he just up and left one day." She chewed her lip. Had she been too bold?

"Pretty much," Emily admitted, reaching up to touch the skin below her ear, fingers moving unconsciously.

"I'm sorry," Christa said sincerely. "I didn't mean to make you sad. I just want to know everything about Rayne's life before I met him."

Emily patted her knee. "Don't apologize. It was a long time ago, and most of my memories of Luke are good ones. He was the absolute love of my life."

Christa sensed he was still the love of her life, but kept that opinion to herself.

"He was a wonderful father. You should have seen him in the delivery room. The man was a rock, never left my side for the whole twenty-two hours. And when we brought Rayne home I thought I'd die from sleep deprivation, so Luke took over at night. He never complained, not once, even though he was getting less sleep than I was." Her eyes looked faraway.

"Was he home much?" She imagined Rayne as a boy in his bedroom playing G.I. Joe, pretending they were his dad's SEAL team. The thought made her a little sad.

"Not as often as we'd have liked, but I knew what I was getting myself into when I married him."

"So how did you deal with him going away on missions when you knew he might not..."

Emily raised her brows. "Might not come back alive?"

"Exactly. I got my first—and hopefully last—taste of that the other day, and I'm not sure I can watch him go off to work every shift without losing my mind."

"Honey, I know how you feel. For some reason the men in this family can't be happy sitting behind a desk all day. So when they put themselves in harm's way for a living, we don't really have a choice but to support them and hope for the best." Emily took her hand, squeezed it tight. "You're very strong. From what my son's told me, you've handled everything life has thrown at you and made the best of it."

"Only because of Rayne." The pang hit her so hard her eyes stung. "He's been so wonderful with me through this whole thing."

"I'm glad. I can't imagine how it feels, having a stranger following you around."

She shuddered. "It's turned my whole life upside down. But the worst part is not knowing...when he'll come after me again. I don't feel safe anywhere."

"Just as well Rayne brought you down here then, away from it."

She blew out a breath and gave a weak laugh, the urge to cry subsiding. "Got any of those naked baby pictures you were telling me about?"

"Albums and albums of them," Emily said happily, and went to dig them out.

Christa enjoyed getting to know Rayne and his family through the visual history captured on the pages. One picture of Luke with Rayne perched on his broad shoulders, fishing rods in hand, reminded her of what Rayne had told her about the last fishing trip they were supposed to have taken. She tried to flip the page and distract Emily, but it was too late.

"This was the day before he left." Her face was pale, her eyes haunted. "I'd forgotten I even took it." She stared at it as if trying to make sense of it all.

Christa waited. She was ready for tears, yelling, whatever. Anything would be better than the lost expression on the older woman's face.

"Anyway," Emily continued, turning the page, "this is Rayne and me with Luke's mom in Montreal. He was born up there while we were at his grandpa's funeral, you know."

Luke was conspicuously absent, and she didn't think it was because he was away on a mission. Obviously, Emily had packed up her son and taken him to be with Luke's family. Empathy welled inside her. How could anyone pick themselves up and carry on when the love of their life walked away? She bit her lip, refusing to get teary again, although her eyes were blurring.

Emily's expression melted. "Oh, sweetheart, it's okay. Really." She pulled Christa into an embrace, patting her back. "I appreciate the sympathy, I do, but don't you dare cry. If you cry, then I'll cry too and Rayne will come home to a flood."

She forced a watery smile. "Sorry. I think I'm overtired."

"Well then, that's enough nostalgia for one evening. Why don't you go up and tuck yourself in? There's nothing like sleeping in an antique bed for curing jetlag."

"I'll take your word for it." She rose and cleared the coffee table. "Would you tell Rayne I said to give him a kiss goodnight?"

"'Course. Sleep well, dear."

"I'm sure I will." She rinsed the dishes before heading upstairs, brushed her teeth and washed her face in the guest bathroom that featured a claw-footed tub and a pedestal sink, then climbed into the old four-poster and pulled the down comforter over her with a sigh. The rustle of palmetto branches breezed through the open window, interspersed by the occasional swish of traffic along the street below. Even at this hour the air was muggy, the cotton sheets sticking to her skin, the unfamiliar music of cicadas drifting in from the garden. As she stared up at the silk canopy it was easy to imagine the house ringing with laughter at Christmastime, Rayne's boyhood eyes lit with the magic. Easy to imagine Luke and Emily on the porch swing together after they'd put their son to bed, basking in the simple pleasure of each other's presence. She lay there in the darkness, aching for Rayne's parents and wondering what the future had in store. Weren't there ever any happy endings?

****

Emily sat curled in the chair next to the fireplace, the photo album on her lap. She stared down at the last picture she'd taken of Luke, bleeding inside. All these years she'd wondered what she could have done to convince him to stay. The awful day he'd left had changed her life forever, would always be burned into her memory. Her fingers trailed over the faint scar under the angle of her jaw below her earlobe.

She lifted a hand to her face, realized she was crying and berating herself for opening old wounds, wiped away the tears. Part of her still felt broken inside, even after twenty-three years without him. To this day she'd kept her dark secret, having told Rayne only that she and his dad couldn't live together anymore. She hadn't wanted to further damage Rayne's image of his father, plus she'd known it would kill Luke if their son were ever to be afraid of him. So for all these years she'd kept silent, but now she questioned the wisdom of it.

"Mom?" Rayne's voice snapped her back to the present and she found him standing in the doorway, concern furrowing his handsome face. He looked so much like his daddy it hurt.

"Hi, sweetheart." She tried her best to put on a happy face. "How was your night?"

He sat on the couch beside her chair. "It was great to see the guys again. You okay?" He glanced down at the photo album. "Took a walk down memory lane, did we?"

Emily set it on the table, once again closing the door on the past. "Christa was disappointed there were only a few naked baby pictures."

He sank into the cushions. "What do you think of her?"

"I'm already in love with her." She took his hand in hers. "She seems like an absolute sweetheart, and I'm so happy for you."

He grinned and squeezed her chilled fingers. "I knew you'd like her."

"She's strong and independent, and she's kind. Exactly what you need." Exactly what she'd always wished her son would choose. Maybe she'd done a decent job with him after all.

He rubbed a hand on his jean-clad thighs before standing. "Is she asleep already?" His eyes tracked to the staircase.

"About an hour ago now. She was exhausted, so I sent her up to bed. She said to give you a kiss goodnight."

He scratched his neck.

"You look like something's on your mind. Is it about the little boy?"

"That's on my mind, but no." He paused in front of

the fireplace.

"Did your father call you?"

He tensed. "No, and before you ask, I didn't call him either."

Her stomach knotted, as it always did whenever they skirted this subject. "I did. To tell him what happened." She ignored the spark of resentment in his eyes. "He had a right to know, Rayne. No matter what happened he's still your father, and if anyone knows what you're going through, he does."

"Mom, I don't want to—"

"I told him you might be going down to visit him."

"You what?" Anger tightened his face. "That's about the last thing I want to do."

She ached at his suffering, much as he tried to hide it. "Honey, I was only trying to help. He's been where you are, so I thought if you could talk to him..." That they might be able to finally clear things up between them. Bond a bit.

The silence stretched taut, muscles working in his jaw. "All right," he said at length, "I'll call him. But I'm not making any promises."

Relief surged through her. "I understand."

"Anyway, there's something I've wanted to talk to you about and I don't want to put it off anymore. It's kind of important."

A flutter of nerves started in her belly. "Right now?"

"Yeah, if that's all right. In the library?"

Her eyebrows disappeared beneath her bangs. The last time she'd had a discussion in the library it had been right before Luke had hauled Rayne away to join the Marines. "Sure," she forced out, and followed him. He closed the mahogany pocket door, then stood there.

Emily watched him with growing trepidation. "You've got a terminal disease and you only have six months to live," she guessed.

He rubbed his eyes with his fingers. "Nothing that dramatic," he assured her, then dropped his hands to his sides with a sigh. "I think you'd better sit down, Mom."

Time to pay the piper. She'd known this conversation would happen one day, but it didn't make the sick feeling any easier to bear.

Emily dropped into a ladder-backed chair like a sack of cement and cocked an eyebrow at her son, drumming her fingers on the wooden arm. This had better be good.

****

Twenty awkward minutes later his mother shut the door behind her, leaving him alone in the mahogany paneled library. He'd always loved this room, with its mustiness of leather furniture and old books reminding him of his father. When he'd come home between missions and training ops he'd spent hours in here, Rayne lying on the floor coloring or playing with his action figures. He'd keep looking over at his dad seated in the tufted armchair behind the antique desk with a book and a cup of coffee steaming at his elbow, content to be in the same room with him.

Now he sat in that same chair across the room from the fireplace, its mantel crowded with photos of him and his parents. A carriage clock ticked next to them.

It wasn't quite midnight, an hour earlier than that in Baton Rouge. His dad would still be awake, a nighthawk who often stayed up until two in the morning. If he went to bed at all, that is. Because of years dealing with sleep deprivation in covert ops, or because of nightmares, Rayne couldn't say.

He stared at the phone, contemplating what to say, wondering whether this would be yet another exercise in futility. The hell with it. He dialed the number.

His dad answered on the second ring. "Em?"

"No, it's...me."

Silence filled the line. "Son, your mother told me you nearly bought it the other day. How you feeling?"

He rubbed his hand over his cramping stomach. Talking to his old man always did this to him. "Not bad. My arm still hurts like a bitch."

"Yeah, bullets will do that to you. You going for physical therapy yet?"

"Not until I get back. They wanted me to heal up a bit before I started."

"They get you help after the debriefing at least?"

He shifted in his chair. "Yeah, they made me talk to a shrink about it."

His dad grunted. "I bet that did a hell of a lot."

236

"Whatever. It's protocol." He was balancing on an emotional tightrope, this whole conversation had been a bad idea.

"You got your girl down there with you?"

Relieved at the change of subject, his shoulders loosened a bit. "She's a real keeper. Mom's crazy about her already."

"Now there's a surprise." He gave a dry chuckle. "I'd like to meet the lady who brought my son to his knees."

There it was, the proverbial olive branch, tentatively offered. He knew how difficult it must have been for his father to reach out, and he wasn't such a jerk that he'd throw it back in his face. Besides, if he planned to make a life with Christa, he owed it to her to put the demons of his childhood abandonment to rest.

"Yeah, she'd like that, I've told her all about you."

His dad let out a bark of laughter. "Yeah, I'll bet you have."

Later, when he climbed the stairs and peeked in on her, she was fast asleep, curled on her side, breathing slow and steady. The sight of her so peaceful squeezed his chest. The mattress dipped as he sat on its edge and she awoke in a rush.

"Hey," she whispered, wrapping her arms around him. In ten lifetimes he'd never get tired of the warm, sleek feel of her. "Have a good time with your pals?"

"Not as much as I used to. I missed you."

"Liar." A smile tinged her voice.

"It's true. I spent the whole night telling the guys about you." He lay down beside her. "Shhh," he said when she stiffened. "I just want to hold you for a while."

"But your mom—"

"Is downstairs." Imagine him as a grown man having to sneak in to his girlfriend's room like a horny teenager. He wrapped himself around her, sighing his contentment. "I talked to my dad tonight."

"You did? How'd it go?" Her whisper was a little strained as he nuzzled the tender spot under her earlobe, pulse hammering under his lips. After a moment more, she tipped her head back with a sigh to allow him better access.

He smiled against her smooth skin, loving the way

her breath shortened when he nuzzled her. "Better than I expected. I told him we'd drive down there for a few days. Okay with you?" His hand moved to give his arm a more comfortable position, deliberately brushing over her breast. She gasped and gave him a narrow-eyed look, wiggling away to put a few inches between them.

"Sure. I'd love to meet him." Careful of his arm and ribs, she rolled on top of him and pressed a kiss against his lips. He pulled back and frowned at her.

"You been crying?"

"What?"

"Your eyelashes are wet."

She rolled beside him to prop her head on one hand. "All these years later your mom still misses your dad. It makes me sad."

"Yeah, it's a pretty screwed-up situation, huh?"

"Sad," she corrected.

His fingers trailed over her cheek. "I would never do that to you, kiddo."

He sensed, rather than saw, her brows rise.

"If we ever got married," he clarified, part of him still cringing at the vulnerability. For him, the mere mention of marriage was a huge step, and saying it aloud made him feel horribly exposed. "Once I made that commitment, I'd be in it for the long haul."

The frown creasing her forehead made him fidget. His damn face was getting hot.

"I'm just saying I'd never walk out on you like he did her."

Her smile was so full of love he ached inside. She made him want to be a better man. "I already knew that, but I love you more for telling me. And I'm proud of you for calling him. I'm sure it wasn't easy."

"Hell of a lot easier than keeping my hands off you right now."

Between the debriefings, doctors appointments and flight to Charleston, they'd barely had time to breathe let alone make love. Even when they'd finally crawled into bed together, he'd been too damn sore to do anything more than hold her. But he was feeling more than up to it now. The thought tied his guts in knots. He wouldn't push her though, since she was nervous enough already about their first time. Having her lie there with one ear cocked for his mother wasn't real conducive to the mood he wanted for them. Maybe he should put her in the car and drive to the nearest hotel...

She snickered, easing the pressure in his chest. "You know what they say, good things come to those who wait." Lying pressed against him, her body seemed to hum with unfulfilled need. The air around them crackled with it.

He swallowed, forcing himself to stop imagining pulling the nightgown off her and sliding deep inside while she moaned and squeezed around him. God. It made him crazy to know how much she wanted him and not be able to have her. "Yeah. Good thing you're worth it." Truth was, he hated sleeping without her beside him. At least with her there, it was a little easier to forget the look in Daniel's eyes as he'd stared at him from across that filthy shack.

Pushing it all away with a deep sigh, he tucked her close and held her until she fell asleep, savoring the sense of completion.

CHAPTER 21

"I'm only saying that if the Confederates took the first shot, then technically it can't be called the war of northern aggression," Christa argued.

Rayne feigned horror and pulled her close, clapping a hand over her mouth and glancing around. "Shhh! That's blasphemy down here."

She yanked his hand away and gave him a mock glare. They stood in Battery Park, where in April, 1861, the cannons had opened up on Fort Sumter. Michael would be proud of her. "Can you believe people went up to the rooftops and watched the firing back and forth across the harbor?" With a sweep of her arm she indicated the row of stately antebellum houses lining the street opposite the boardwalk. "Can you imagine standing up there watching your city firing on a federal garrison?"

The late afternoon sun angled overhead, bathing everything in brushstrokes of molten gold. They strolled around the historic district, past the Rainbow Row pastel houses and the palmettos ruffling in the salty breeze rising off Charleston harbor, sparkles scattered across the water. Passing a wrought iron gate, she peeked into a courtyard where the trickling of a weathered marble fountain seemed to cool her by degrees. The sweetness of roses filled the humid air, almost dizzying in their fragrance. Paradise.

"The gardens down here are so amazing," she said, admiring the old-fashioned rose winding over the porch. "I should have brought my camera with me, so I could use some of this in my next project. People are big on old-fashioned landscaping, you know. I wish I could—ulp—"

He jerked her backward with one hand on her upper arm, pressing her against the cotton shirt pulled taut between his shoulder blades, shielding her there, his eyes riveted across the street.

Her heart stuttered as she tried peer past him. "What?"

He remained immobile, his muscles tensed. "Stay behind me."

She gulped, fingers curling into his shirt.

Several agonizing moments later he steered her from behind him. "Sorry. False alarm."

She gaped at him. "You thought you saw him, didn't you?" He scanned the street again. "You think he could have followed me here?" Chasing her to the other side of the continent wasn't totally beyond feasible for an obsessed stalker.

"I didn't say that."

Her heart thumped. He hadn't said *anything*, which spoke for itself.

"Don't worry, okay? It wasn't him and I overreacted. But just to play it safe, I'll call it in to Nate."

She opened her mouth to argue but he leaned down and kissed her. She pushed at his heavy shoulders, wrenched her head away. "Don't you dare try to distract me—"

"Shhh. It wasn't him, I swear." He cupped her face in his hand. "I wouldn't lie to you, kiddo."

Wouldn't he? Not even to protect her? She searched his green-gold eyes for any flicker of guilt. Seeing none, she didn't object when he settled his mouth over hers. As he kissed her the fear ebbed.

He pulled back, gave her a lighthearted smile. "Want to continue the tour?"

She narrowed her eyes, her heart taking its time returning to a normal rhythm. "If I say no are you gonna keep trying to distract me?"

"Yep."

She laughed, wanting to salvage the rest of the day. "Lead on, then."

He took her up King Street, past the fancy antique shops and boutiques. The layers of history overlapped, pavement meeting cobblestones, plaster and concrete concealing damage by artillery fire over a hundred and forty years ago. In the cemeteries marble headstones crumbled and tilted like rows of crooked teeth, their inscriptions barely legible.

"I'm so jealous you grew up in a place like this." Vancouver's setting might be mind-blowing, but it seemed brand new compared to Charleston.

"I still get homesick so I try to come back at least once a year."

She loved that he appreciated his hometown and enjoyed seeing his mother. Not everyone was lucky enough to have such a relationship.

"You hungry yet?"

She'd lost track of time. "I could eat."

"There's a great place up here that serves Low Country food."

That translated loosely to 'food cooked in grease' but she fell in love with the fried green tomatoes and okra, buttermilk fried chicken and biscuits with gravy, she-crab soup and fried catfish, followed by cornbread and cake made from Coca-Cola for dessert. He ordered a bottle of red wine and filled her glass three times.

"A fancy dinner and alcohol. You're not planning on seducing me, are you?" She raised an eyebrow at him, enjoying the buzz from the wine and the flirtation she hadn't engaged in since she couldn't remember when.

With a slow smile he set down his glass and reached across the table, gliding his thumb over her lower lip before raising his gaze to hers. "Would you like me to?"

Her toes curled before her abdomen fluttered. She couldn't look away from him. His hazel eyes glowed with a promise that made her mouth go dry.

The man was lethal. Teasingly, she smacked his good shoulder. "I am not having sex with you in your mother's house."

"That wasn't what I meant, but since you brought it up..." A gleam entered his eyes. "You sure about that?"

"And what are you going to do? Climb up the side of the house like a one-armed Spiderman and leap through my window?"

"Sweetheart, you'd be surprised what lengths I'd go to for you." His eyes smoldered like banked coals.

The hunger washed through her, making her body throb. She'd never felt anything like it and thought she'd die if she couldn't hold him deep inside her within the next five minutes. Her breath caught. "Rayne—"

He dropped his cutlery with a clatter, flagged down their waiter. "Check please."

But instead of sweeping her off to some dark corner he took her back to Battery Park. By then the buzz of arousal had worn off, leaving her wondering if she'd imagined the blaze of desire in his eyes.

In the center of the park they sat in the white gazebo as twilight settled with its hush of purple mystery. Scented with roses and honeysuckle, the night air caressed her skin, the stars twinkling to life with the promise of a full moon in the blue velvet sky. He was awfully quiet and she suspected he'd overdone it today. His arm was probably driving him nuts but he was too macho to say so.

He slid his good hand under her hair, kneading the muscles there because it made her purr. "I love you," he said, watching her in the half-light.

At the intensity behind the words she met his gaze. "I love you too," she told him with all her heart, resting her head on his shoulder and closing her eyes, savoring the peace of the evening and the warmth of his fingers on her neck. Lowering her guard like this should have made her feel vulnerable, but he would always watch out for her, keep her safe from any threat.

When she opened her lids his posture was rigid, his eyes moving over her face as if he was memorizing her.

"Your arm's bothering you, right?" She made a tutting sound at his swollen fingers.

He leaned down to kiss her, sliding his hand to the back of her head. When he pulled away he rose from the bench and tried to take off his sling, fiddling with the strap, so she helped him undo the buckle, accidentally banging his injured arm. He froze, hissing a breath through his teeth.

"Oh, I'm so sorry."

He forced a stiff smile. "It's all right, I'm fine." He finally got the stupid thing off and took a deep breath. "I need you to sit down for a minute, okay?"

"I am sitting down. What's with you tonight?"

He stood there, opened his mouth to say something, closed it again.

Then he sank onto one knee.

"Oh, God," she whispered, one hand flying up to her mouth. Was she having an out of body experience?

His head jerked up. "I dropped the padding from the brace," he explained, holding it up for her inspection.

"Oh. Right." God, what a moron she was. Here she'd thought he was going to propose. Her throat tightened until it nearly strangled her. *Way to go, Bailey, freak the guy out why don't you?*

When she risked peeking at him through her lashes, he was smiling at her.

"Well, there *was* something I wanted to ask you."

She swallowed the lump. "Okay."

"I wanted to know how you felt about us living together."

"We kind of are living together already."

He shook his head. "I meant after this is all over, that maybe one of us should move in with the other." His fingers caressed the sensitive spot beneath her hairline at the base of her skull. "All I know is I want to go to bed with you every night and wake up beside you every morning."

Her heart jittered. Cameron's infidelity had taught her a painful lesson. Was she ready to take such a huge step, especially after everything else she'd been through? She wanted Rayne, felt safe with him, loved him so much it hurt.

Despite her recent attack, part of her was dying to make love with him completely, to give him all of herself. But could she really trust a man with his reputation? Did she dare risk abandonment again? Once the initial blaze of passion and excitement wore off, could she stand wondering if he would look elsewhere to fill the void?

The old fears rose from the shadows of her mind, then Bryn's words came back to her. Love was risky. There were no guarantees, and both she and Rayne knew how precious and fleeting life was. She could either live holding back in fear of rejection, or reach out and grab her chance at happiness with both hands.

He must have taken her silence as reluctance. "I can move into your place if you want, put mine up for sale."

"You'd sell your luxury condo with the million-dollar view?"

"In a heartbeat, if it meant being with you."

The joy swelled from the secret depths of her heart. "You're sure?"

He lifted a brow. "What do I have to say to convince you?"

She rubbed her suddenly damp palms on her jeans. "It's just…if things worked out between us, I'd want…I'd want to get married and have a family someday." Was that clear enough? She couldn't take the next step in this relationship if she had no hope of those things.

"I know." He twined his fingers around hers. "A lot's happened in the past couple weeks and I don't want to rush you, so if you're not ready for this I'll understand. I just think it'd be smart to move in together for starters and see where things go. Take it one day at a time."

The pit of her stomach fluttered. He was saying all the things she wanted to hear, yet…

"I'd never do anything to hurt you, Chris."

She put her hand on his cheek, smiled when he kissed her palm. "I know."

"So? You gonna put me out of my misery or what?"

She laughed, her heart lighter than it had been in years, the leap of elation frightening. Committing herself to him should be the most difficult decision she had ever made, but in truth her instincts had already made it. She had never been more certain about anything. "I think we should go for it."

"That's great, kiddo. I'll do everything I can to take care of you, make you happy." He sealed the pledge with a soul-wrenching kiss and nuzzled her neck, shivering delight down her spine. "Now that we're officially shacking up together, you sure you don't want to have sex with me in my mother's house?"

****

A thump came from outside her window. Her eyes flew open, her heart pounding as she lay staring at the sheers billowing in the night breeze. A scrape, something sliding.

It can't be him…it can't…

All she had to do was scream and Rayne would be there before she could draw another breath.

A muffled curse drifted in, followed by a groan. If it

was him, why was she lying here waiting for him to attack her again? Throwing back the covers, she caught sight of Rayne's silhouette in the moonlight.

"What the hell are you doing?" She slid the sash open.

He was hanging onto the windowsill with a one-handed death grip, glaring up at her with bits of leaves from the climbing rose stuck in his hair. "Well, don't help me or anything," he muttered, and she came out of her stupor to grab him. He shuffled up and threw a leg over the windowsill, rubbing his sore arm. "I just crawled up the side of the house like Spiderman," he panted as he struggled to fit his body through the frame. "Didn't think I'd do it, did you?"

She smothered a laugh. "You could have really hurt yourself. More than you already have, I mean. You're crazy."

"Yeah. Crazy about you." He came toward her, eyes full of sensual promise. "I want to make love with the woman I'm going to be living with," he whispered, kissing her, deepening it until she was clinging to him for balance. "That okay with you?"

Would it be okay or would she panic? Doubt crowded her mind. Had she really agreed to let him move in?

"I want to lay you down on that antique bed and love you until you're too weak to move," he murmured against the sensitive hollow under her ear. "Only thing is, you need to be real quiet. I wouldn't want my mom to know I was in here having my wicked way with you." He smiled and nuzzled her throat. "Mmm, you smell like oranges."

"My bubble bath." Was that breathy voice hers? She was already trembling under his touch. He slid the satin nightgown off her shoulders to pool at her feet, leaving her naked. Automatically her arms came up to cover herself.

"Don't hide. You're beautiful." He lifted each hand to his lips, pressed a kiss to each palm, nibbling his way up her wrists to the sensitive inside of her elbows. "Come lie down with me." He stripped off his shirt and led her to the bed.

Heart racing, she climbed onto the four-poster with him, absorbing the shock of his weight as he landed on top of her, wrapping around him as her whole body sighed. She lifted her head to kiss him, the glide of his tongue making her gasp. Her skin burned as though she had a fever. Need pulsed deep in her belly. "Hurry," she urged, tugging at his jeans.

He shucked them off as fast as his injured arm would allow and resumed kissing her, licking urgently into her mouth and taking her breath away. She moaned while his lips traced a burning path down her throat, pausing to tease the fragile skin over her pulse point, his fingers brushing the curve of her breasts.

When he bent his head and swirled his tongue over her, the tingle was almost painful. "Rayne..." Her fingers locked in his hair, to hold him close or push him away, she wasn't sure which. She withstood the exquisite torture as long as she could, then reached down to take him in her hand, making him shudder. "Come inside me now."

"Uh-uh."

"Yes," she insisted, pulling his shoulders upward as he moved down to her stomach. She couldn't take much more, part of her wanting this first time over in case she freaked out on him. He kissed the inside of her hipbone, slid lower, and with a flare of panic she grabbed his head to stop its descent. "Don't," she whispered, quaking inside. No way could she stay quiet if he did what she feared he was going to do.

He tightened his hands on her hips and nuzzled her abdomen, the muscles contracting under his cheek. "Your skin's so soft," he murmured. "Let me do this, Chris. I've fantasized about it for forever."

He had?

He stroked his fingers between her legs, making her suck in a breath. "Don't you trust me?"

"Yes, but—"

"Then let me."

"But I—"

"I won't disappoint you," he coaxed, untangling her fingers from his hair and edging lower.

But what if she disappointed him? She shook her head, almost beyond speech with frustration and nerves. "I just want you inside me."

"Later," he promised. "When you're more relaxed." His tongue dipped into her navel, making her lower body clench.

More relaxed? Not likely.

Rigid with tension, dreading that first touch as much as she yearned for it, she jerked under his mouth and dragged a pillow over her face to stifle a wail as sensation careened inside her. He crooned reassurance, comforting her with slow sweeps of his hand even as he made her mindless. Devastating, his tongue laved soft and slow until she felt like melting ice cream, leaving her straining and trembling. His hands held her hips in a firm grip, holding her still while he pleasured her. When he slid a finger inside to stroke that mysterious spot, the pleasure magnified tenfold. Writhing against the sheet, she felt him tug the pillow away from her.

"Look at me," he said.

She shook her head, eyes squeezed shut, biting down hard on her lower lip to keep from moaning aloud. His thrust his finger deeper and she dug her head into the bedding, clapping a hand over her mouth to muffle her cry of need.

"Christa. Look at me." Patient fingers wrapped around the hand covering her mouth and dragged it away. He brought it to his hair and she tangled her fingers into its luxurious softness. When he did nothing more, she cracked open one eye and risked a peek.

He was wedged between her thighs, watching her, lips hovering a few inches above where she needed him so badly, and wet from...from what he'd been doing to her. Her eyes squeezed shut again. God, if he kept this up she was going to faint.

He pressed a gentle kiss against her center, and she trembled, biting back a moan, lifting toward him.

"Chris."

She shook her head.

"I can feel how close you are," he murmured, the heat of his breath making the ache between her legs unbearable. As if to prove his point, he licked at her gently.

She whimpered when he stopped, moving against that finger buried inside her.

"Look at me."

"No."

"Come on," he coaxed. "Just look at me."

God, she couldn't take it anymore. Unable to resist, she lifted her head and gazed down at him, panting, waiting.

He was the sexiest thing she'd ever seen. "Hold me," he whispered, tugging downward on the hand she had wound in his hair. "Guide me." She let go of the bedding with her free hand and slid it into the thick waves, shaking, and managed to hold his gaze as she pulled him toward her. With a purr of enjoyment he lowered his head and opened his mouth—

The instant his tongue found her she cried out and threw her head back, dragging the pillow back over her face. Her body opened to him even more, begging him as he licked, stroked and hurtled her over the edge. She fell back against the downy comforter, too weak to move.

He kissed his way up her body and pulled the pillow away. I told you so, his eyes said. She gazed up into his face, gilded in the moonlight streaming though the window, and fell in love with him all over again.

****

So this was what making love felt like.

He'd had sex plenty of times, but he'd never made love to anyone. Now he understood the difference.

He'd never been so focused on his partner before, so attuned to each sound and movement, every expression on her face. He'd never used his body to underscore the staggering emotion he felt for the woman beneath him. His heart pounded at the intensity of it.

He laced his fingers through hers on either side of her head, content to stare down at her while she recovered from her orgasm. She lay beneath him utterly relaxed, eyes sleepy and sated. The hunger inside him was almost unbearable but he fought it back, wanting to give her more, so he aroused her all over again, taking his time as he used his hands and mouth, ignoring the ache of protest in his healing triceps. He watched the need building in her, heard it in every broken moan, felt it in the beat of the pulse in her throat as he licked it.

"Rayne, stop—" She arched into him, her body

dissolving into shivers as the arousal began to build again. "No more. I can't."

"Sure you can." Her skin was like warm velvet. "Just be patient."

Savoring each gasp, every breathless cry she gave, he explored her body, his mouth pleasuring her breasts, all of her, learning exactly where to linger, exactly how much pressure to exert to make her mindless. The feel and taste of her drove him out of his head.

When he was satisfied she was as starved for him as he was for her, he let go of her hands and came up on his knees while his fingers trailed along the center of her body. She caught her breath when he caressed her, teasing her with whisper-light caresses until she opened and bowed up off the bed, begging for deeper contact.

With a guttural sound, she pulled him down, hands moving over his hips to the engorged length of him. He grabbed the condom from his jeans pocket beside him, sheathed himself and settled his weight over her, balancing on his good arm.

He stilled above her, the enormity of what they were about to do registering in his numbed brain. Until now he'd never thought about how vulnerable a woman was at this moment, how much trust she had to place in her partner. Especially this woman. Her guileless blue eyes gazed up at him, body and soul wide open, trusting him to be gentle and cherish her with his much stronger body. In reassurance he kissed her tenderly, fighting back his own need.

Holding her gaze, he shifted his weight and eased his throbbing length into her, just deep enough to tease the glow he'd ignited inside her, careful not to rush her. She wrapped her legs around him, straining against him, seeking more of the pressure she wanted, but he stayed there like that, not letting her move, making her body focus on the sensation of him inside her until the knowledge of what he was doing registered on her face. He held her gaze, letting everything he felt for her show in his eyes. "I love you, darlin'."

She rewarded him with a tremulous smile and reached up to touch his face. "Show me."

Hell yes he would.

Needing to witness her expression, he gathered her tightly against him and sank all the way in, fighting to hold back as her body shuddered beneath him, legs tightening around his hips. When she wrapped her arms around his shoulders with a blissful sigh, he started to move. Not in a thrusting motion, but a slow, subtle caress that made her cry out and arch helplessly. Smiling at her shocked expression, he angled himself to please her, giving her that specific friction to trigger the charge deep inside. She cried out and dug her fingernails into his back, fighting to get closer.

He subdued her sensual struggles, gentling her with butterfly kisses and murmurs of reassurance, waiting for her to relax before rebuilding that throbbing pressure inside her. "Shhh, trust me." He pressed a kiss to each tightly closed eyelid. "So close, Chris," he promised, willing her to believe him, loving her desperation, the way her eyes went hazy with the pleasure he was inflicting.

He moved slowly, steadily, patiently as he taught her all he knew about giving. But God, the sight of her, eyes squeezed closed, head tilted back as she moaned. The urgency in her made his blood pound as he neared the edge of his limit. He groaned, closing his eyes a moment to get control.

"Let go," he coaxed, hoping she wasn't fearing the intensity, reaching down to stroke the slick, ultra-sensitive place between her legs. No way was he going to let her pull back now. "Let go and come for me."

Relentless, he held the rhythm, built the pleasure until she made a mew of distress and came apart beneath him, clutching him, adrift.

Still he moved, wringing the last cry from her until she lay limp beneath him. With a hoarse groan he buried himself as deep as he could inside her and allowed himself to let go, dropping his head to her shoulder in surrender as release wrenched through him.

As he pinned her there with his weight she held him close, stroking her hands over his hair tracing the ridges of muscle either side of his spine down to the rise of his hip. He snagged her hand in his.

"Give me a minute before you start again," he muttered against her temple, sighing as he snuggled into her. "As soon as I can move, you're going to be in big trouble." Like maybe next Tuesday.

She squirmed beneath him, unbelievably making his body stir inside her. "Is that right?"

He rose on one forearm to kiss her smiling mouth, stunned at the hunger roaring up. "Don't say I didn't warn you."

She pulled him down into a hungry kiss.

CHAPTER 22

Waking in his own bed next morning, Rayne regretted giving into Christa's pleas and going back to his room. His mom would never have embarrassed them by saying anything, but he'd gone anyhow to put Christa at ease. He would have loved to wake up with her curled against him though, pick up where they left off a few hours ago.

He stretched his stiff, sore arm over his head, imagining her sleepy sigh as he woke her with a trail of kisses up the length of her spine. Her back would arch, and she'd make that little hum of pleasure that set his pulse racing. The fantasy raced onward until she was on top of him with her head flung back, eyes closed as she moved faster and faster...until his cell phone rudely interrupted.

Sighing, Rayne flopped over and grabbed the phone from the nightstand. Yup. It was Nate, and as usual his timing sucked.

"Morning, sunshine," Nate greeted his gruff hello.

"It's three in the morning your time. This must be important."

"Got some interesting news for you."

"Fire away." Maybe it was best Christa wasn't there after all, because she always worried when Nate called. With good reason.

"Our perp left a laptop in the apartment he'd rented. When we retrieved the stuff from the hard drive we found the airline ticket confirmations in your names. He left it there purposely. Wanted us to know he's found you."

He sat up. "Persistent, isn't he?"

"Yeah. After you called yesterday and told me you thought you saw him, we checked out the airports and a security camera showed a man resembling him waiting to board a flight to Atlanta. None of the names on the

253

passenger list matched, but we're checking them all out in case he's got other aliases we don't know about yet."

Oh, man, this was bad. Tension crept up his shoulders. "I already told you it wasn't him yesterday."

"You sure?"

"Yeah. His description was close. But when he looked back at us the second time, I knew it wasn't him." He'd never forget what the son of a bitch looked like.

Nate hesitated. "I dunno, Hutch..."

"Unless he's had cosmetic surgery, then I'm sure."

Nate grunted. "Well, keep your head up, just in case. We're checking passenger lists now, so I'll get back to you when I know something more. In the meantime, maybe you should plan on taking a road trip."

"We're going down to see my dad for a few days." Let's hear what Nate had to say about *that.*

"No kidding? It's about damn time. Say hi to the old fart for me."

"Will do." Getting out of town seemed like a hell of a good idea.

Pulling on some clothes, he made his way down the hall to Christa's room, when he heard her moving around in the kitchen. He didn't want to start the day by telling her about the phone call. Her self-confidence had grown so much last night, and he wouldn't let anything ruin that.

He came up behind her at the sink where she was slicing strawberries, nuzzled the back of her neck. "Morning," he murmured, enjoying her indrawn breath as he teased her nape.

"Morning," she answered brightly. A little too loudly. "Sleep well?"

"Darlin', best sleep I've had in years."

Her cheeks went pink, eyes darting to the staircase. "I'm glad to hear it."

"You gonna look at me?"

She pressed her lips together, eyes on the fruit in the sink. "Not unless you put a shirt on," she whispered tensely.

Feeling shy, was she? He grinned. "My mom's in the shower, sweetheart," he laughed. "She can't hear us."

"Oh." Her aquamarine gaze swung up to his. He

snagged one of her hands and brought it to his mouth to nip a ripe berry from her fingers. She whirled around and he hauled her tight against him. Her blush deepened.

"Missed you this morning."

In answer she leaned up on tiptoe and kissed the breath out of him. When she pulled back, her eyes were sparkling. His body was rock hard, a fact that didn't escape her attention. She smiled in satisfaction, laughing when he growled and hauled her closer.

The sound made his heart squeeze. He wished she had more to laugh about so he could hear it more often. Instead, he was about to tell her something that would take all the laughter out of her again. He drew a breath and took the bowl of berries from her. "I'll get this. Come sit down and eat something."

He waited until they had finished their breakfast and were sipping coffee before he broke the news. "Nate called this morning."

Her eyes met his, held. "Oh? What did he have to say?" She got up to take the dishes to the sink.

Nothing good as usual, he thought grimly, and told her.

She swayed, the air squeezing out of her lungs in a wheeze. "I need to sit down." She dropped into the kitchen chair and leaned her head into her hands. "So that could have been him you thought you saw yesterday."

"The build and height were right," he admitted, "but like I said it was a false alarm. You weren't in any danger."

"Rayne, you were shielding me with your body."

"That's my job, sweetheart, so I won't apologize for that. I'm supposed to be protective of you. And I will be." He kissed her forehead. "What do you think about a drive to Baton Rouge?"

"Sure, but I can't run from him forever."

"I know kiddo, but right now it seems like our best option. Besides, maybe this is the kick I need to go see my dad."

****

By the time they hit the outskirts of Baton Rouge, Christa was exhausted. She hated having to be constantly on guard, her heart tripping every time she thought she saw someone resembling *him*, wondering where he was and what he'd planned for her. She tried her best to shove it to the back of her mind and enjoy her time away with Rayne.

Last night, though she'd worried it was too risky he took her to a Braves game in Atlanta, meaning it to distract her from the stalker's threat, but being at the ballpark only reminded her of Seth sitting behind home plate, vision pinned on her. She'd spent most of the innings scanning the crowd for those frigid gray eyes, comforted only by Rayne's presence and her confidence in his ability to guard her.

This morning they'd flown into New Orleans and picked up another rental car. No sooner had they driven out of the airport than Nate had called, Rayne squeezing her hand the whole time he talked to him.

"They've followed up the airport security camera sightings," he reported afterward, "but no one's traveling under his name. So they're checking out aliases and forged passports, all that stuff."

She tossed the magazine she hadn't been able to focus on down to the floor, staring out at the subdivisions and strip malls. He was out there, tracking her across the country. She suppressed a shudder.

Soon the properties they were passing were on larger lots, separated by tracts of forest. Finally they turned down a road bordered by woodland and slowed at a mailbox that read: Hutchinson.

Nerves jumped in her belly. "So, what should I be expecting here? Booby traps? Pet alligators?"

Rayne laughed and ruffled her hair. "He got rid of all those years ago."

The house that came into view at the end of the driveway was a modest two-story colonial surrounded by a well-manicured lawn. The trimmed shrubbery met her approval, as did the way the yard set off the symmetrical aspect of the house. When the door opened and Luke Hutchinson stood there in the late afternoon light, she might have been looking at a slightly shorter version of Rayne twenty years from now.

The two men greeted each other with a stiff handshake and to smooth things over she nudged Rayne to prompt an introduction.

He finally remembered his manners. "Dad, this is—"

"Christa, I'm Luke." He held out his hand, seeming to take up all the space on the porch, even though Rayne had him by three or four inches in height and twenty pounds in muscle. The force of his personality blazed out of the melted bittersweet chocolate of his eyes.

"I can see why my son wants you all to himself," he continued in that honeyed drawl.

"And I can see where he got his looks and charm from," Christa countered, earning a grin. No wonder Emily was still in love with this guy. How could any woman get over someone with that face and charisma?

"If you're finished gawking at my old man," Rayne remarked dryly, "maybe we could go inside."

Christa blushed. "Sorry, I couldn't help myself."

"I like her already," he told Rayne, leading them into the kitchen. "Guest room's upstairs so take your stuff up, Rayne." He regarded her with those hypnotic eyes. "You hungry? I'm making gumbo."

"You can cook?"

"Hey, a man's gotta do what a man's gotta do. You can only eat so much mac and cheese without gagging on it." He went to the stove and stirred the simmering stew.

She sat on a stool next to the counter, breathing in the aroma of onion and garlic and chilies. "I've never eaten gumbo before." Was it going to be as hot as she'd heard?

"About time you did then. I tried to keep it on the mild side, but you might find it a little spicy."

A thump sounded above and she glanced up at the ceiling.

"Guess he can't made up the hide-a-bed with one arm, can he?" Luke wiped his hands on a kitchen towel. "I'll go up and give him a hand—" he gave an ironic grin, "—no pun intended."

"Can I help with anything in the meantime?"

"You can drain the rice in a minute, if you like."

She hopped off the stool and removed the lid from the second pot, switched off the element and lugged the rice over to the double sink to drain it.

"Here, let me help—"

She shrieked, whirling around and sloshing rice and hot water all over herself and the kitchen floor. Luke froze. She pressed a scalded hand to her chest, the room going hazy around the edges of her vision.

He dragged a chair over and placed her in it, pushing her head between her knees. "Just breathe, honey," he instructed, not touching her but staying close while she struggled to control her gasping, her hands and face clammy.

She inhaled a few choppy wheezes and once she could breathe normally again, she slumped.

"Sorry," she choked, willing her heart to slow down. "You surprised me."

Luke took hold of her hands, checking for burns where the water had splashed. "I'm the one who's sorry. P.T.S.D., right?"

"It's that obvious, huh?"

He studied her face while dabbing at her with a tea towel. "I've been there myself, chère. You feeling sick to your stomach?"

"Yes," she moaned, hiding her face between her hands. "Oh, God, what a horrible first impression."

"C'mon." He bent to scoop her up, despite her weak protest. "Let's get you outside for some air." He set her down on a deck chair on the back porch. "You okay on your own for a minute? I'm gonna give the floor a quick wipe."

"Sure." He went inside and reappeared with a glass of amber liquid.

"Ginger ale. It'll help settle your stomach."

She took it gratefully and swallowed a few sips. "I'm so embarrassed."

"Hey, nothing to be embarrassed about. I know how it is." He perched beside her, putting a fatherly arm around her shoulders. "What a hell of a family we're gonna make, huh? And to think we all seem so *normal*."

His teasing brought a laugh from her.

"What happened?"

They swiveled to see Rayne standing in the doorway, his forehead creased in concern. Under his scrutiny her cheeks grew hot.

"She's all right," Luke assured him. "Just scalded

herself draining the rice." She smiled her gratitude and he winked. "So, who's hungry?"

He'd managed to salvage most of the rice and served it into big bowls, ladling the stew on top. Most of the nausea had faded, though she wasn't sure she was up to spicy food. She swallowed the first bite and tried her damndest not to cough, but her eyes watered.

Luke grinned. "Want some milk?"

"Please," she rasped, the gumbo burning all the way down to her gut.

"Five alarm gumbo?" Rayne guessed.

"Nah. Two alarm, max." Luke handed her the glass of milk and Rayne a bottle of beer.

To let her taste buds recover from their scalding she set her spoon aside. "I'm so glad I'm finally meeting you," she told Luke. "I've heard so much about you I feel like I'm sitting here with a legend."

One dark eyebrows shot up. "And all the stories you've heard are good ones, right?"

She hoped he would interpret her grin as a "yes".

Rayne wolfed down a mouthful. "So how's business going? Any more trips planned to Iraq?"

"Maybe in another few months. The crew I've got over there now is doing a good job, so I can stay here awhile yet." He gestured to Rayne's arm. "How are you healing up?"

"Pretty good. Only bothers me when I've overused it."

During the silence that settled over them, Christa dipped her spoon into her dinner, casting a sidelong glance at Rayne. Both men seemed intent on finishing their food, the clink of silverware scraping their bowls magnified by the tense quiet.

"You guys want to watch the rest of the ballgame?" Luke offered, ending the awkward breach.

"Sure," Christa said, maybe a little over-enthusiastically. She slid her bowl away, half-full.

"Too hot for you, huh, tenderfoot?"

"I think I have second-degree burns all the way down my esophagus," she teased. "Would you mind if I used your shower to freshen up? It's a little sticky down in this part of the country."

"Help yourself."

In the guest bathroom, she froze. "Ah...Rayne? Could you come up here for a minute, please? I think there's something hiding in the drain of the tub..."

Luke roared. "I think she saw her first Louisiana cockroach. I called the exterminators but those little suckers are as hard to kill as Osama bin Laden."

"You'd better stand on the toilet seat, darlin'," Rayne called up the stairs. "He might be hungry."

****

Later Rayne and Luke went onto the screen porch and stretched out in the Adirondack chairs, crickets chirruping as the stars punctured the evening sky.

His dad handed him a beer. "So, how are things with Christa? Your mother said she's had a rough go of it lately. Called me again probably the second you pulled out of her driveway to tell me you're planning to shack up together, and mentioned Christa had been through a lot of trouble."

Rayne huffed out a breath and settled back. "Yeah, it was bad. This guy had been following her around, leaving threatening notes, you know the drill. Nate and I were hoping he might go away, but she wasn't that lucky. He almost raped her, put her in the hospital."

A spark ignited in the depths of his eyes. "The guy in jail?"

"That's the worst part. Nate's got a team on it, but he's still out there somewhere."

"Nate's on the case now, then?" That seemed to satisfy him. "How's she handling it?"

"She's a trooper." Rayne fidgeted with his beer bottle.

"And you? How are you handling it?"

His fist clenched. "Sometimes I think it would be worth the jail time just to get my hands on the son of a bitch."

"I'd feel the same way."

"Just so long as he's nowhere near Christa when it happens, they can blow him to kingdom come with an RPG for all I care."

"Nah. Shotgun. Hurts more."

"Even better, I could send my old man after him. You could make him shit his pants first."

His mouth quirked. "You getting bloodthirsty in your

260

old age?"

"Whatever works." Rayne scratched his chin. "They'll get him eventually, I know that. But it won't be soon enough for either of us."

"She's something else."

"No kidding. Good thing I've brainwashed her into thinking I'm awesome."

He cleared his throat. "I hear you asked for Grandma Boo's ring."

Rayne whipped his head around. "Mom told you?"

Amusement twinkled in his dad's eyes.

Rayne sighed, smothered a chagrined laugh. "Yeah. I told Mom I figured I'd be needing it for Christa some day, asked her if it would be all right."

"Actually, Christa kinda reminds me of your mother."

"Yeah?" He was sure Freud would have something disgusting to say about that and he didn't want to go there.

"How is she, anyway?"

"Fine."

"She still dating that Andy guy?"

Rayne shot him a glare. "It's Alex, Dad, and she's been dating him for almost eight years."

"Yeah, right."

Rayne barely refrained from rolling his eyes. As if the guy's name wasn't burned into his father's memory for all time. Wasn't it too late to be jealous?

"He still treating her right?"

Rayne set his beer on the arm of the chair, tamping down his irritation. The way he saw it, it was none of his dad's damn business. If he cared about her so much, he wouldn't have up and left her all those years ago, wouldn't have stayed away. "Yeah, she seems happy. From what I know of him, he's a good guy."

His old man grunted. "She called me the day after you were shot, you know. She was really torn up about it."

"It was a close call all right."

"For what it's worth, son, from someone who's been there and done that, don't play the 'what if' game. I figure you're beating yourself up about it, but the bottom line is that little boy died because his old man was a messed-up piece of shit. Period. Not because you screwed up—"

"But that's exactly it. I did screw up," he insisted. "I fell through the goddamn floor. Bam, hit the ground and then the guy was holding my own weapon on me." His palms dampened and he felt again the chill of his pistol pressed against his head. He didn't mention the guy sneering at the trident, didn't want his dear old dad to know he carried it around in his fatigues like some pathetic kid with a hero-worship complex. One of his teammates had given it back to him in the hospital.

"Accidents happen. You're better trained than anyone else on that squad, so if it happened to you it coulda happened to anyone. You did everything you could to save that little boy, and that's something you can be proud of. You can't always save the day. Believe me, I know."

The guilt, the grief, seared him. "It's his eyes, dad," he said finally. "I can still see his eyes staring up at me." That was the image he had to banish, more than the bullets slamming into him. Those wide, scared eyes begging him for a miracle.

"The nightmares will fade. I'm more worried about what's going on in your head."

"There's a lot going on, that's for sure." He gathered his courage. "With me getting shot, everything became real clear all of a sudden." Ah, the hell with it. Why not just say it? "I'm moving in with Christa," he began, "and maybe someday we'll get married and have a family. Before all that happens, I need to know—" he paused to meet the dark eyes, "—why did you ditch us like that?"

His father stiffened, eyes closing. Here was a man who'd known he would eventually have to answer for his sins, and now the day of reckoning was here. He let out a deep breath. "I had to, Rayne. It was the only thing I could do."

Uh-uh. Not good enough. Rayne leaned toward him. "Why, for God's sake? That's all I want to know. Why did you do it?"

"You know what happened that day—"

"No, I *don't* know. That's the whole damn point. For twenty-three years I've wondered what happened, and nobody would tell me anything except that you two couldn't live together anymore."

His father stared back at him. "Your mother didn't ever tell you about the day I left?"

"Not a thing. So did you screw around on her and she found out?"

His dad sat ramrod straight, eyes flashing. "I would never have done that to your mother."

"Then what?" He rubbed his eyes. All this time his dad had assumed he had known, but his mother had kept the truth from him. Why? She must have had her reasons, but what could they be? His father's chiseled face, the sad and weary eyes, stirred dread in his gut.

"You've seen the scar on her neck, right?"

"Yeah, what about it?"

He swallowed. "How do you think it got there?"

Rayne couldn't believe it. Didn't want to believe it. *No* way. "You *cut* her?" He'd never even seen his parents fight, so for his dad to take a knife to her...

His dad's head dropped back, his fists clenched. "She came up behind me while I was sharpening my hunting knife to take on our fishing trip, and by sheer reflex I slammed her up against the fridge with the point of the blade against her jugular. I came this close to taking her head off." He held his thumb and forefinger a hair's breadth apart.

Rayne's skin chilled as he imagined it. The shock and fear in his mom's green eyes staring up at the man she'd married, the man she loved. Like a rabbit caught in the jaws of a wolf. His father frozen there, then dropping his hand and stepping back from her, full of horror at his own deed.

"She started shaking, the aftereffect of adrenaline, and slid down the fridge to the floor. She never took her eyes off me. And the look on her face...something inside me crumpled and died. I'd almost slit her throat before I realized what I was doing."

Anguish crashed over him.

"I threw the knife across the room, buried the blade into the wall. She'd pressed her hand to the wound, blood dripping through her fingers. I can still smell it."

Rayne scrubbed his hands over his face.

"So I peeled off my shirt and pressed it against her throat, held her as if she might disappear on me. I'd told her to never, ever surprise me like that, and she said it was her fault, that she forgot. But the next time, she might be dead."

All this time, he hadn't known, would never have guessed what had triggered the abandonment.

"I yanked the knife out of the wall and she went real still, as if I might march over and finish the job. I'd finally done it. Snapped, exactly like I'd always been afraid of, and your mother was huddled there on the floor, looking as if she'd run screaming into the street if I so much as flinched."

"And then you just left?"

"Hell yes, I left. I had to. I went upstairs and packed my bags. It was too damn dangerous for me to stay. If there'd been something I coulda done about it I would have, but..."

He didn't need to explain the terrible reality of a Special Forces soldier, fresh from a deadly covert operation where a second's hesitation would cost you your life, thrown back into suburbia to be a husband and a father. He simply hadn't been able to make the adjustment.

"You know the score. During my training and missions I'd been transformed into a killing machine, and no amount of counseling was going to change that. I was so afraid I'd do something worse than nick her throat the next time. What if it had been you that day instead of your mother? You'd never have come near me again." His eyes brimmed with self-hatred. "I knew you both deserved better than pussyfooting around me, having to treat me like a ticking time bomb. But I'll never forget the sight of your mother crumpled on the driveway, sobbing. Ripped my fucking guts out."

Pain twisted deep in Rayne's chest. "All this time I assumed you left because you didn't want us."

His father set a firm hand on his shoulder. "I left you because I loved you both so much. I wanted you to have a better life than I could give you. Would you have wanted an old man who lost it on the fourth of July when the fireworks popped? Who hit the deck like a mortar attack was going down every time a car backfired? I refused to do that to you. I was like a high-voltage line with the insulation stripped off. Believe me, you were better off without me around."

"I'm sorry," he said simply.

"No, son, I'm the one who's sorry. I'm sorry you thought I walked out on you, and I'm sorry I wasn't there for you as much as I should have been."

Rayne opened his mouth to say something, closed it again just as fast. He swallowed tightly and stared up at the night sky, blinking hard to rid the moisture from his eyes. "You were still my hero, you goddamned idiot," he said, meeting his father's too-bright gaze. "All those years you were gone, blaming yourself, I still worshipped the ground you walked on."

"You trying to make me cry like a girl, or what?"

Rayne grinned, the band around his chest loosening as he took the first deep breath he'd drawn since the conversation started. "Do you? Cry like a girl?"

"Only when the Braves win the World Series." His old man gave him a mock glare. "And that information is classified. You tell anyone and I'll cut your heart out."

CHAPTER 23

The frustration was driving him crazy, making him desperate and careless. Careless would get him killed.

Following Christa down south had been too risky. He'd been at the airport, ready to go, then talked himself out of it. The odds of getting caught had been too great, even with his false passport and appearance. He'd dyed his short hair black and grown a goatee, tucked rolls of cotton into his cheeks to alter the shape of his jaw. Sunglasses concealed the unusual gray of his eyes. He didn't want to wear colored contacts—he had them of course, but he wanted her to know it was him the second she saw him.

The craving was an insatiable hunger, gnawing at him. He desired her, despised her, ached for her. He wanted to be inside her before he killed her, might even be kind in his method of ending her life, if she treated him right. Unlike Henry. He'd deserved an agonizing, lingering death and Seth had been sure to give it to him, pressing the point of a knife against his flabby throat, Henry's eyes bulging, mouth opening and closing like a gasping fish.

She was coming home tonight, due in at seven p.m. They'd head straight for the cop's place. He could go after her there, if he chose. Simple enough to access the condo building and bypass the alarm. He didn't care for taking on her lover, however. He might be desperate, but he wasn't stupid.

Sooner or later he'd have his chance. If nothing else, Christa had taught him a lesson in patience. Something that didn't come easily to him, and he was grateful to her for that.

One slip, that's all he needed. He'd wait for that one mistake, that one instant of bad judgment, then wham. It would be over.

****

Christa awoke early in Rayne's bed, to his hands moving over her skin. So this was how it was going to be from now on, waking up next to him, enveloped in his love. Although she didn't care where she was as long as she was with him, she missed her house and hated that the stalker was keeping her away from it. The time away with Rayne had kick-started her long process of healing, but she still balked at the prospect of sleeping in her own bedroom, in her own bed. The room was tainted, her whole life had been tainted.

Realizing her body had tensed beneath his loving hands, she shut off her mind. Pale gray light streamed through the wooden slats, the squawk of gulls muted by the double-glazing. She sighed and snuggled deeper into her cocoon. Rayne pressed against her back, his warmth and strength surrounding her. Though his arm still bothered him he'd been pronounced fit enough to return to work, and today would be her first day without him.

"Don't wake up," he whispered against the curve of her shoulder, granting her the gift of lying there while he traced her sensitized skin as though he couldn't get enough of her, lingering over the places that raised goose bumps on her flesh. She purred and stretched, letting his fingers skim her back and waist and hips, sliding lower between her thighs until she murmured dreamily, opening to his touch. Rayne stroked her, his lips brushing the hair at the nape of her neck. He was hard against her and she pressed toward him, languorous.

He kissed her neck, fingertips sliding over her aroused flesh. She moaned as the pleasure bloomed brightly, squirming against his erection. He pushed against her without trying to slide inside, content to drive her half crazy with frustration, bringing her close to the peak before slowing. His murmurs faded beneath the thump of her heart, her trust in him the only thing keeping her from screaming at the excruciating pleasure.

Beyond the ability to beg, she whimpered when he moved her upper leg forward, easing into her from behind and adjusting the angle to give her maximum friction. Instantly her mind shrieked, breaking the spell they'd woven.

His knee pressing into her spine, splaying her against her mattress while he tied her wrist to the brass headboard. The feel of him trying to push into her from behind. She went rigid.

"Stay with me," Rayne murmured, trying to guide her back into the moment with patient, tender hands. He held her, awaiting her assent, a solid presence filling her. She wriggled away.

The bed shifted as he sat up. "Chris?" He was careful not to touch her, always mindful of not doing anything that might scare her, always holding back, tempering his strength and the raw passion buried beneath all the tenderness.

She took a steadying breath, bringing herself back to the present as the horrible images faded. Steely resolve formed in their wake. No more. She would not let the past steal another damned second from her. It was high time she took back control of her life, of her sexuality. And she'd start right now.

In answer, she rolled over and pushed him onto his back, soothing the concern in his eyes with a deep kiss. Her hands tangled in his hair as her lips moved over his face. Coming down on top of him, she reveled in his growl of approval, using her entire body to caress him, then followed with slow movements of her hands and mouth. Each gasp and moan she wrung from him added to her confidence, her own pleasure. By the time she straddled his hips, she was trembling with need. Poised above him, she moved back and forth in a tantalizing motion, mesmerized by the desperate hunger burning in his gaze.

Control. She'd needed it, and he'd given it to her. Her body quivered as she teased them both.

His jaw clenched. "Chris..."

"Not yet," she whispered, enjoying the delicious torture too much. His hands wandered over her heightened flesh until she whimpered, and when he reared up to close his mouth on her breast she cried out and finally sank down to take him inside her body with a shudder.

His eyes closed, neck arching as he groaned, a picture of male ecstasy. The sense of power thrilled her, the control making her feel like a benevolent conqueror, lavishing pleasure on her lover. She moaned at the feel of him filling her, stretching her to bursting, loving the way his hands gripped her hips so urgently while she moved. He reached down to caress between her legs with devastating skill as his mouth pulled at her breast. Her head fall back with a shuddering gasp. She arched and moved in her own rhythm, craving the orgasm he was building for her, working herself up and down the length of him, mewling, his sleep-roughened voice coaxing her toward the edge, more intense than she'd ever known. She let go with a cry of triumph and collapsed to lie against him in a state of grace. Rayne locked his arms around her and surged faster until he stiffened and groaned with his own release, his muscles relaxing as he held her against him.

His sleepy chuckle ruffled her hair. "God, I love you."

Christa smiled contentedly against his chest.

****

By mid-morning she'd almost worn a hole in Rayne's carpet. He'd gone in to work for a briefing and training exercise, leaving her with her lucky bat and strict instructions not to set foot outside the door, nor to let anyone beyond the security phone in the foyer. A few more days like this and she'd be climbing the walls.

The phone rang, saving her sanity. Teryl's cell phone. She snatched up the receiver. "Thank God you called, I was starting to go out of my mind."

"Ch-Chris..." Her voice hitched.

Alarm swept through her. "What? Teryl, what's wrong?"

A heart-wrenching sob. "I think—I think I lost the baby."

She sucked in a breath. "What? Where are you?"

"In the hospital. I g-got out of bed this morning and started b-bleeding."

Oh, God. Without thinking she grabbed her purse from the table. "Is Drew with you?"

Teryl sniffed. "He's at the fire hall...has to w-wait for someone to relieve him." She gulped down more sobs. "They s-said there's nothing they can do, that if I'm going to mi-miscarry then it's going to happen. I have to come back in one w-week to have another blood test, to see if..."

To see if the baby was still alive or not. "Oh, Ter, I'm so sorry." The pain in her friend's voice clenched her stomach. She had to get to the hospital somehow. No matter what the circumstances, Teryl would have done the same for her.

"I'm so scared." Her friend fell apart then, choking on noisy sobs.

"Hang in there, hon. I'll be there as soon as I can." Even though leaving the condo put her at risk, she had to be there for Teryl. But how, with Rayne at work?

Ending the call, she considered her options. She could call a cab, but she'd have to go outside the security gate to meet it. Her truck was parked in the underground garage, secure behind the electric gate that could only be opened with a computerized access card. She'd be safe enough down there, wouldn't leave the vehicle and at the hospital she could park at the curb and run inside. With plenty of people around, no one in their right mind could try and abduct her.

But then, Seth clearly wasn't in his right mind.

The way she saw it, she didn't have a choice. She was going to have to drive herself to that hospital alone, and that was all there was to it. She left a message on Rayne's cell, knowing she'd probably catch hell later on but hoping he would understand why she had to do this for her childhood friend.

Hurrying out the door, she took the elevator down to the well-lit garage and headed for her truck, maintaining her vigilance. Checking under it and in the back seat to make sure it was empty, she climbed in, locked the doors and started the engine. In spite of all her precautions, her palms were clammy as she pulled out of the building and onto the street, employing all the anti-surveillance techniques Rayne had taught her. Clouds swollen with rain hung low, the Gulf Islands blanketed by mist, the sea pewter-gray. Fat raindrops splattered on the windshield, then unleashed in a torrent, blinding her despite the rapid swish of her wipers.

For God's sake, what else could go wrong?

Her fuel gauge beeped, the dashboard warning light alerting her that she was almost out of gas. She blew out a breath, mentally kicking herself.

For crying out loud, Bailey. Why'd you have to ask?
****

Sitting in a car across the street from the cop's condo, raindrops sliding down his windshield, he stared through scratchy eyes at the third-story window. Christa was all alone up there, would be for some time yet. His blood heated. This might be his only opportunity. Should he risk going in now?

Hovering there, he was startled when the security gate squealed open and her black Chevy pulled out of the underground garage. Was she really leaving the building? Alone?

Surely it couldn't be that easy.

Yes, that was her, behind the wheel. He started his own engine, tamping down the geyser of excitement gushing through his veins. His breathing came in rapid, shallow pants and his hands dampened the steering wheel as he pulled out some distance behind her.

Where was she going? What could make her be so rash?

Silly question. Fate—it was crossing their paths one final time, as he'd always known it would. Anticipation hummed. This was his chance to get it right. All he had to do was wait for her to stop, and she would be his. At last.
****

Making sure she kept practicing Rayne's anti-surveillance techniques, she drove along Marine Drive. Her fuel gauge was buried in empty, making even the short trip to the hospital questionable. She could chance it, but did she want to risk running out of gas and being stranded? Damn.

Now she would have to either head straight back to Rayne's place, or stop for gas. How close was the nearest full-service station? She didn't know. She'd always been capable of filling her own car. Frustration coursed through her. Was this what her life had become? To hell with it, she'd stop for gas like any normal person. If she had to step out of the truck at all it would only be for a minute, and other people would be around.

She passed the first gas station because it looked too empty. At the next one she pulled in behind an elderly gentleman filling his Lincoln, checking one last time in her mirrors to make sure no one had followed her. After hopping out to insert her credit card into the pump and filling her tank, she ducked back into her vehicle. Out of habit she pulled out her wallet out and tucked the receipt inside, replaced her credit card while starting the engine.

Next thing she knew a hand was on her shoulder. Her breath snagged.

"Hello again."

That voice. That god-awful voice.

Her blood turned to ice, her fingers frozen.

She scrambled to open her door but he grabbed her hands and wrenched her around, pressing something hard and metallic against her ribs. Instantly she stilled. Her gaze traveled down to the black barrel of a pistol.

"You make one move toward that door and I'll pull the trigger." Glacial gray eyes pinned her from beneath black brows, his mouth twisting below a goatee as he motioned her to shift into drive and step on the gas.

Those cold, flat eyes...how they had haunted her nightmares.

Should she scream? He surely would kill her. She risked a glance out the window. He slammed his elbow into the side of her head, thudding it against the window. *Not again. I'd rather die.*

As they pulled onto the road with a squeal of rubber he grabbed the steering wheel. "Now we're going to finish this properly." His eyes lit with cruelty. "You already had two strikes against you. First, screwing that cop, and second, getting away from me. You know what that means? This is strike three, Christa."

Her heart pounded against her ribs.

He settled back with the gun jammed into her side, flicked a chilling glance at her. "You're out."

****

Once they left the gas station he made her trade places with him, and she sat in the passenger seat like a marble statue, cringing from the muzzle shoved under her galloping heart. Would a shot there kill her outright, or only tear through her flesh and bone and organs and make her bleed to death?

Even if he has a weapon, chances are he won't use it because it would draw attention to him, and if he did, the odds are he would only wound you. Nate's words flooded through her terrified brain.

Better than being raped and tortured.

They merged onto the freeway toward Vancouver, him glancing at her every so often to taunt her with victory in his eyes. Her phone was in her purse, which had fallen under the driver's seat, out of reach. Most likely he'd shoot her before she even dialed the first digit of 911. She pressed herself as far away from him as possible, frozen against the door like a mouse caught in the gaze of a snake, waiting for it to strike.

As she stared at him, all the fear and hatred bubbled up inside her, coalescing into a molten ball of rage in her gut. If he was going to take her out, she damn well wasn't going to sit there and let him—she'd see to it he suffered first. How? Think, think...what had Rayne taught her? If you jab someone hard enough at the temple, you can cause internal hemorrhaging.

She had both hands free and he was driving, so his attention was diverted, but if she missed the right spot would it disable him enough? And if it did, then what? She couldn't jump out at this speed or she'd kill herself. She couldn't even flag down help because he kept the gun trained on her. Her mind screamed in panicked denial. What could she do?

Nate's advice for kidnapping victims came back to her. Once you were in a car with a kidnapper, your chances of survival were slim. So what did you do?

You crashed the car.

Her heart rate stabilized as her escape crystallized in her mind. She had to disable him long enough to wrench the steering wheel from him. She would only get one shot at this, so she had to get it right first time. She felt detached, almost calm as she planned her move, the speedometer reading one hundred twenty kilometers per hour. It was going to be one hell of an accident, but she'd rather die in a car wreck than at his hands. Her breath hitched.

She waited until he had to slow behind another vehicle, just over ninety now. Another car was boxing them in, and when he made a shoulder check her hand shot out to jab at his eye.

His foot came off the gas pedal as he jerked his head away at the last instant, her stiffened fingers glancing off his nose. He yelled, lashing out with his gun hand to strike her face. The force of it sent her slamming into the door but she recovered fast, adrenaline surging, and when he lifted his hand to his nose in reflex, she lunged over and yanked the steering wheel toward her with all her might.

He shouted and pulled the trigger.

The truck careened sideways and hit the gravel shoulder, its speed and momentum hurling it onto its side. It flipped in mid air, her scream echoing in her head. The roof smacked the ground with a crunch, and then she was only aware of the shattering of glass and the screeching of metal before everything went black.

CHAPTER 24

The call to action interrupted the briefing. Female victim abducted by white male at gunpoint from a gas station. Black Chevy Avalanche, partial plate number...

A bottomless hole yawned beneath his feet. Rayne's heart stopped beating, the words coming at him from the end of a long tunnel, paralyzing him. He didn't need to hear the license plate. *Sweet Jesus, he's gotten her. Somehow he's finally gotten to her.* Without realizing it he was on his feet.

"...the truck rolled off the freeway...emergency personnel dispatched..."

Holy Christ, they'd gone off the freeway? Grief clawed its way up his throat, came out as a strangled cry.

"Hutch? What's wrong, man?"

"Christa..." He could barely get her name out of his dry throat.

"It's her?"

Everyone stared at him, churning up his stomach. Why weren't they heading to the gun locker? They had to move. *Now.* Christa was out there, her life was in danger. If she was still alive.

The room spun and he almost checked out.

Breathe, you have to breathe. You can't help her by panicking. Get the team organized and into the trucks. Focus...

He sucked in a breath as everyone scrambled for equipment. Somehow he forced his legs to work, only to run into his commander. The man put a hand square against his chest, looked him in the eye. "You know the rules, Hutch."

They weren't going to let him go.

Screw. That.

"Take a minute. You're in shock."

"I'm not in shock," he growled. But his body sure

thought he was.

His commander studied him, lips thinned. "Truck leaves in four minutes."

****

Sirens wailed somewhere in the distance and Christa fought to open her eyes. She was alive, caught in her seatbelt, hanging upside down in her truck, an awful pain in her stomach. One image after another, it all came back to her. The truck hitting the shoulder, the world upside down as they spun through the air. Before that, the crack of a gunshot.

She lifted her hand...something warm and sticky trickled down her face and neck, coating her fingers. Her blood. Had he shot her? Beside her, her abductor struggled to escape the twisted mass of metal, bleeding from his nose and forehead. The gun lay within inches of his groping hand.

Groaning, she fumbled with the buckle of her seatbelt, released it and thudded against the roof. Pain burst inside her. Nauseated and lightheaded, she dragged herself over shards of glass lining the crumpled window frame. She had to escape him.

She inched out, pain stabbing her skull, her shoulder aching. Her abdomen hurt so bad she almost blacked out again. Hideous, searing agony. She couldn't breathe properly. Had she broken a rib, punctured a lung? *Hurry. Hurry, you're almost there.*

A hand snared her ankle and she screamed, kicking at it. He shoved his way out beside her and hauled her to the ground, his bloody face a mask of blinding rage.

"You fucking crazy bitch!" He slammed her shoulders onto the ground.

Stars exploded in her head, the fight draining out of her.

He was panting, grabbing her arm, trying to yank her to her feet, but she collapsed in a heap. Police cars skidded to a stop behind them, and she was now the only thing between him and a bullet to the head. If they took a shot at him, it would be to kill.

"Move!" He grabbed her under the armpits, shoved the gun under her chin and hefted her in front of him. She cried out in agony. "Get up and move." The icy muzzle of the pistol dug into her tender skin. Her pulse throbbed against it in terror.

****

Rayne ran up to the police barricade, flashing his badge at the officer posted there. "Hutchinson, ERT." He hurried over to the cruisers blocking the accident site.

"Is she all right?" he demanded, craning his neck to see beyond the crush of emergency vehicles, the breath whooshing out of him when he spotted the mangled wreckage of her truck lying on its roof beside the shoulder of the freeway, a tangle of metal and broken glass.

And there she was, the woman he loved with all his heart, sagging in front of the bastard who'd wrecked her life, his gun pressed to her, a human shield.

Christ, not again. Pleading brown eyes flashed in his memory, a little boy silently begging him to save his life. He couldn't get his heartbeat to slow down. He was so scared for her he could barely breathe.

His lieutenant approached. "The perp won't talk to the negotiator, and we're running out of time. This guy's way too unstable. I want the guy most qualified with a rifle to take up a sniper position to the east of them." He pointed at the field flanking the freeway.

They all looked at him—former U.S. Marine, son of a Navy SEAL. The weight of their stares bore down on him and he fought the gnawing fear in his gut.

The older man's eyes delved into Rayne's. "Tell me straight, Hutch. Can you handle this?"

He nodded mechanically. "Yeah."

"You shouldn't be here. I know it and you know it. Your objectivity is compromised. Right now though, we don't have time to piss around with protocol. I'd volunteer if I thought I could make that shot, but even with one decent arm you're a helluva lot better with a rifle than I am. Right now, there's no other viable option to protect the hostage."

"Understood, sir." He moved toward the flashing blue and red strobes of the cruisers, his feet like lead, panic spurting with each step. Could he take a shot while the guy was using the woman he loved as a shield? He would damn well have to pull the trigger. He couldn't afford to fail her.

He trained his binoculars at the grassy plain, took a deep breath. The bastard was dragging Christa further from the road, his head turning to assess the police positions.

He swallowed hard. Her face was ashen, her body limp. How badly had she been hurt in the crash? Did she have the strength to get herself out of this?

Time to put his training into action, to call upon everything he'd ever learned. He studied the topography, noted the gusty wind and drizzle steadily soaking his shirt. He would have to aim a little higher to make up for the impact of the moisture on the bullet.

His colleague gave a nod. "We've got you covered from up here. Good luck."

Rayne dug deep for courage and set out with his game face on. He circled to the left, advancing in a crouch. Just like deer hunting, he told himself, trying to distract his brain.

Again, Daniel's eyes pleaded. Daniel pushing to his feet...his father's warning...him diving to catch Daniel in a tackle...the crack of the pistol shot...the spasm of pain on Daniel's face. He gritted his teeth, didn't dare think about the mortal danger Christa was in.

He worked hard to keep his breathing steady, using every trick he knew to slow his racing heart as he drew nearer to his target. Once in position, he sank onto one knee and raised his weapon, adjusting the sight until the crosshairs met between his quarry's eyes.

If the bastard so much as flinched, he'd put a bullet through his skull.

****

"Drop your weapon! Let the hostage go."

Seth froze, his mind churning. He could *not* be trapped. There had to be a way to lose them. He glanced behind him, found nothing but the open field, no cover in sight. Pain sliced through his skull, blinding him. His right leg wouldn't cooperate, blood staining his pants and seeping over his boot, each step a separate agony. He couldn't drag her much further and keep hold of his gun.

Christa was bleeding, her beautiful eyes glazed, maybe dying. Sweet, sweet Christa. If only she had been his. That was all he'd wanted. Was it too much to ask?

And now look at the price they were paying. If she died, he had no chance. Without her life to use as a bargaining chip, he would wind up dying in jail as an old man.

Screw that. He'd rather die here and now than rot in prison for the rest of his life.

He stumbled back another few steps, shaking with fatigue and adrenaline. "I'll kill her," he yelled, keeping the cops in front where he could see them. "Stay right there or I'll kill her, I swear to God." Tears stung his eyes.

"D-don't," Christa mumbled, squirming from him.

She was trying to escape again. His soul howled in protest. He'd been so close to having her...

He tightened his grip around her, his hand twitching on his gun. His heart drummed in his ears. Blood pumped heavy and thick. Thump-thump...thump-thump...thump...thump...

"Drop your weapon."

The command came from his left. A fucking cop, less than a hundred feet from them, was sighting him down the barrel of a rifle.

His gaze moved from the black hole at the end of the muzzle to the officer's face. Deadly hazel eyes. The eyes of Christa's lover.

His bowels churned.

Christa gasped, tried to support her weight on her trembling legs, but he held her immobile. Panic suffocated him. Would her boyfriend risk taking a shot while she was in front of him?

He backed away but the man's gaze never wavered from his face, his hands steady on the weapon. Fear freezing his spine, he met the unflinching hazel stare.

He was staring into the eyes of his executioner.

Swallowing, he released the pistol's safety, the click as loud as a gunshot. It echoed through his hollow brain.

"Drop it," came the next warning. The voice was low and calm. Lethal.

If he raised the gun he would be killed.

Too late now. No choice. No going back.

His trembling hand lifted upward. His eyes closed, imprinting on his lids the memory of Christa smiling as she tended the flowers on the old lady's balcony. She wore a lacy white blouse and a ball cap, her long ponytail falling down her back as she tipped the watering can. Crystal rivulets of water spilled out of the spout. The breeze tugged at her blouse, a tendril of hair swept across her face. Her head tipped back as she pushed it away, laughing, cheeks flushed pink, exposing the delicate line of ivory throat. She looked so happy. So beautiful...

His last breath entered his body.

Hand still creeping upward, he held that image of Christa in his mind.

****

The pain was unbearable. Like someone had stabbed her in the gut and poured battery acid in the wound. Pinned in Seth's sweaty, panicked embrace, her vision kept wavering. Her heartbeat echoed in her head, her uneven breaths sounding like a hacksaw cutting through a metal pipe.

Blackness closed in.

No. She couldn't close her eyes. Had to keep looking at Rayne. If she let go and closed her eyes she would never open them again.

She forced her heavy lids open and focused on Rayne, wanting to break free and run to him. But that was impossible. Seth was not going to let her go. Ever.

Grief welling in her chest, she stared at the man she loved. Crouched down on one knee in the long, tangled weeds, he held his rifle steady, his eye to the scope. He had to be freaking out inside, but he looked so calm, every inch the trained soldier he was. She tried not to show how terrified she was, but she was mindless with it. The pain blew through her belly like a blowtorch, and she doubled over, tears leaking over her lashes.

Rayne, she thought, sending out a prayer for him. She didn't want this for him. Didn't want him to have to take a life after what he'd been through with Daniel. But she didn't want to die, so if shooting Seth was the only way to save her, then...

Please God, don't let him miss.

Behind her, Seth's breath quivered in and out like a cornered animal, his forearm digging convulsively into her diaphragm. His gun hand twitched, and she choked back a sob.

The sharp click of the safety releasing slid a fresh

wave of terror down her spine. She tried to shake her head, couldn't.

I don't want to die...I don't want to die...

"Drop it."

Rayne's clipped command made her eyes snap open. She stared at him across the abyss as Seth's gun hand inched upward.

So, this was it. This was how she was going to die.

A spurt of adrenaline lashed through her body, a desperate will to live beating at her with panicked wings, but she was powerless to do anything. The gun continued to move upward.

One last time she drank in the sight of Rayne poised just across the field, hoping to take it with her, wherever she was going. There had to be something more after this life. Something good and peaceful to make up for the suffering.

I love you, she mouthed, hoping he saw it, and shut her eyes. Panic and despair swamped her, her eyes flying open. She couldn't let go, didn't know how.

A sharp crack rent the air.

The bullet hit with a hollow thud.

Falling, body weightless. Numb.

Blackness. Peace.

CHAPTER 25

Rayne stood back while the paramedics carried Christa to the ambulance, his whole body shaking in the aftermath of the adrenaline crash. When he'd fired, she'd hit the ground like a rock and for a paralyzing instant he'd thought he'd missed and shot her. But the neat, dime-sized hole in the victim's forehead proved Rayne had hit the bastard straight between the eyes, and still he'd held on to her, even in death.

It freaked him out to think about it. If he'd missed by a few inches Christa would be the one sprawled in the wet grass with the back of her head blown off.

Nate ran up to him but he shoved him aside. "Get the fuck out of my way," he snarled, half crazy with fear.

"Give them a minute, Hutch. You know they're trying to stabilize her, and the best way you can help her is to stay out of their way."

Every cell in his body was screaming at him to go to her, but somehow he stood there as they lifted her inert form into the ambulance. After what seemed like eternity, one of the paramedics stuck his head out. "Anybody here named Rayne?"

He hopped in beside her and took her chilled hand in his. "I'm here, kiddo, I'm right here. You're going to be okay." Her eyes opened a fraction.

"Keep her awake," the paramedic reminded him as he reported her status to the hospital. "Pulse 110; B.P. 95 over 60 and dropping. Pain in left shoulder and left upper quadrant. Internal bleeding likely."

Rayne's stomach plummeted.

"Pupils dilated and slow to respond. Probable concussion."

He leaned over her and cupped her pale, blood-streaked face in his hands. "Stay with me, Chris. Come on darlin', open your eyes and look at me." He stroked her cheek, watched her fight to open disoriented blue eyes and blink up at him, frowning. "I'm here, sweetheart," he repeated, his eyes wet as he gazed back at her. "You're going to be okay, Chris. Just keep looking at me, all right?"

If he lived to be a hundred, he'd never forget the way she'd looked at him and told him she loved him right before she'd crumpled next to the dead body of her nemesis. He'd never been so fucking scared in his entire life, and the nightmare wasn't over yet.

"Pulse 100, B.P. eighty over sixty, unstable," the paramedic radioed and glanced at Rayne. "The trauma team's standing by for us in the O.R."

Fear jolted Rayne's heart as he continued murmuring to her, maintaining eye contact and willing her to fight. He couldn't lose her, he just couldn't. She would be okay, and then they could get on with their life together. He refused to accept any alternative.

The few minutes it took to speed to the hospital were the longest of his life, and by the time they arrived Christa's eyes were closed. "Don't you leave me, Chris," he croaked, clinging to her hand as the medical team loaded her out of the ambulance. He squeezed her hard, needing to get through to her. Maybe she could still hear him, still feel him. "I love you, don't leave me. *Please.*" The last word tore from his raw throat in a strangled sob.

"Sir, you'll have to go to the waiting area now." A nurse elbowed him away from the stretcher. "We need to get her into surgery right away."

Releasing her hand was the hardest thing he'd ever done. He bent and kissed her blood-smeared lips before they whisked her away from him.

Seconds after the doors shut behind her, Rayne bent over at the waist, gulping air into his lungs. His knees buckled, sending him to the floor like a puppet with its strings cut. Fatigue and fear crashed over him and he gagged, stumbled into the men's room and threw up until he was dry heaving. How could he bear it if he lost her?

When the spasms passed he slid down and dropped his spinning head to his hands. A moment later a hand touched his shoulder. He lifted haunted eyes to find Drew standing over him, his face drawn.

"You okay?"

No, he wasn't okay. He was terrified Christa was going to die. "Fine."

"Let's get you cleaned up and go sit in the waiting room."

Nate and Teryl were already there, and all four of them sat like shipwreck victims, tracking the minute hand as it crept around the clock.

****

Christa awoke in a strange room with a dry throat and a dull pain in her abdomen. With supreme effort she opened her eyes and glanced around...a hospital room. The accident...crawling out of her crashed truck, her captor dragging her with him at gunpoint. Looking up into Rayne's eyes behind the crosshairs of a rifle. The release of the safety catch on the pistol at her ribs, the crack of Rayne's rifle. The blackness and the hideous pain clawing in her belly when she came to.

But she was alive. By some miracle, she was still here.

Her throat worked as she swallowed. If Rayne had missed by inches, she would be dead.

Rayne. He'd been beside her in the ambulance, talking to her the whole time. He wouldn't be far away, right? She turned her head, wincing as a hot, bright pain split her skull. When she opened her eyes again he was looking out the window, his back to her.

"Rayne," she managed in a croak. His head whipped around and as he came over to gather her up in his arms his eyes were suspiciously wet.

"Sweetheart," he whispered, his face pressed into her hair. His broad shoulders shook. Those arms around her felt like heaven.

She patted his back, swallowed a cluster of tears. "What's wrong?" The words hurt her raspy throat. "Am I going to die?"

He buried his wet face into her neck a moment longer, just holding on. "No. You're not going to die. I'm just an emotional wreck right now." He kissed her chapped lips and eased her down. "How are you feeling?"

"Sore. What did they do to me?"

"They had to take out your spleen because you were

284

bleeding internally," he explained, squeezing next to her hip on the narrow bed. "And you've got a concussion and some broken ribs. Your doc said you'll be going home in a couple of days."

"It hurts when I take a deep breath. I wondered if I'd broken my ribs because the pain was so bad when I tried to get out of the truck." Metal screaming apart around her...

"Oh, God, don't talk about that yet." He tightened his hold, as if to reassure himself she was okay.

Her mind flashed images at her like clips of a movie reel, and she saw herself staring down at the gun in her ribcage as they raced down the highway. "I crashed the truck, like Nate told me."

He laced his fingers through hers. "I figured you did, kiddo. If you hadn't done it, you probably wouldn't be alive right now. You're so goddamn brave you terrify me."

That hit home, and she started to tremble. "But it's all over now, right?"

He broke eye contact, looked down at their intertwined hands. "He won't ever bother you again."

The constriction in her throat nearly choked her. "So he's...dead?"

He met her gaze. Nodded.

A barrage of emotions hit her. Elation that it was over, that she could get on with her life without fear of being raped or murdered; sadness that it had to end in another death; guilt that Rayne had been the one forced to take the shot. He'd been through so much with her already, and it must have been hell for him to aim the rifle, to have to kill to save her, as he'd been unable to for little Daniel.

"You okay?" She lifted a hand his haggard face.

He leaned into her touch, gave a brave attempt at a smile. "Now that I know you're okay, yeah."

They both had so much to work through, so many scars to heal. But she could do it. With him beside her, she could do anything.

And Teryl of course...Oh, how could she have forgotten? "What about the baby?"

He jerked upright so fast he almost fell over. "Huh? What baby?" His eyes traveled down to the sheet covering her abdomen.

"Not me, Teryl. Is she okay?"

A mixture of relief and regret crossed his expression. "She's doing all right, what with this on top of everything else. She feels responsible for making you try and drive yourself to the hospital."

She let out a breath, careful of her stitches. "It's not her fault. I should have checked the interior before I got back in the truck." She clung to him and he drew her close, careful of her ribs and incision, chasing away the chill with his warmth. "Do you think you could just hold onto me and not let go for about a week?"

"God, yes."

She tried blink the moisture away from her eyes, but they filled too fast. Tears spilled down her cheeks. "I guess I've got a ton of emotional baggage to deal with. Are you sure you still want to move in with me?"

He set her away from him and took her face between his hands, brushing away her tears with his thumbs. "I'm sure, kiddo. You're stuck with me."

She sniffled. "Promise?"

He rested his forehead against hers. "Cross my heart."

EPILOGUE

He'd brought her home. The bedroom had been completely redone, and he'd bought them a new king-sized bed. At first he'd been set against moving in with her here, but she'd worn him down. Coming home was a major step for her in the healing process, and it was time she got on with the rest of her life. Her precious, bright-futured life with him.

"Are you sure I'm not hurting you?"

She smiled against his throat and rubbed his back in reassurance. "For the hundredth time, I'm sure. Where are you taking me anyway?"

Rayne made his way through the living room, ordering Jake out of the way when he danced too close to them. "You'll see."

He carried her out the French doors to the patio, through the garden to a pocket of lawn tucked amongst the flowerbeds while Jake ran circles around them. The scent of roses and honeysuckle made her smile, reminding her of Charleston, and she closed her eyes to breathe in the sweet summer air. Sunlight streamed through the leafy branches, dappling them in shadow and light, the warmth bathing her upturned face, feeding her starved senses. A bee hummed past, the drone of a distant lawn mower melding with Rayne's footsteps, hushed by the grass.

"Here we are."

She opened her eyes. He'd spread a blanket on the mowed lawn, covered it with her favorite foods. A platter of watermelon, grapes and raspberries sat alongside a pasta salad and an oversized chocolate cake. Champagne chilled in one of her gardening buckets.

"Oh …"

He laid her carefully on the blanket and propped pillows around her, then settled behind to brace her. "Like it?"

Tears blurred her vision. "I love it."

Dropping a kiss to her shoulder he tucked the plush robe he'd bought for her around her legs and reached past her to grab the bottle. "Champagne, to celebrate us moving in together."

Her throat closed up, it was too much.

He wrapped an arm around her. "Sweetheart, please don't cry. I can't stand it when you cry."

"I can't help it. I'm just so h-happy."

"Good." He kissed her neck and placed a flute of bubbly in her hand, then poured one for himself and raised it. "To us."

"To us," she echoed, loving the sound of that. She tipped the flute and took a mouthful of the sweet liquid, was about to swallow when something hit her lip. Frowning, she held the glass up to the light.

And found a ring.

She cried out, dumped the champagne through her fingers and caught the ring in her hand. Diamonds and aquamarines, and it looked old. "Oh!"

Rayne was beaming. "My great-grandmother's. She was married to my great-grandfather for over sixty years, so I know it works." He took it from her numbed fingers and sank onto one knee in front of her, the timeless, courtly gesture bringing more tears to her eyes.

"I know we were going to take it one day at a time, but we've already been through so much together, I figure anything else life can dish at us will be nothing by comparison." His smile made her catch her breath, probably always would. "I love you more than anything, kiddo, and I want to spend the rest of my life with you. Will you marry me?"

Muffled sobs stole the power of speech, so she held out her arms to him and nodded.

He grinned. "That's a yes?"

She nodded again, cried harder, wiggled her hand until he slid the ring onto her finger. Then she was hugging him, kissing his face. Jake bounded over and joined in, licking Rayne's ear. Holding her close, he tumbled her into the pillows, took her face in his hands and smoothed her hair, that smile spearing her soul.

No matter what the future held for them, all she had to do was look into those hazel eyes to know she was already batting a thousand.

A word about the author...

Kaylea Cross has dreamed of being an author since she was a child. A Registered Massage Therapist, this mother of two is an avid gardener, artist, Civil War buff, bellydancer and former nationally carded softball pitcher. She lives near Vancouver, B.C. with her husband and energetic little boys.

Visit Kaylea at www.kayleacross.com

Printed in the United States
134910LV00004B/1/P

9 781601 543103